For nothing is hidden that will not be made manifest, nor is anything secret that will not be known and come to light.

Luke 18 v 17

Books by Alex Willis

Non-Fiction

Step by Step Guitar Making 1st and 2nd editions

Standalone fiction

The Penitent Heart

The Falcon, The Search for Horus.

The Road Home

Buchanan Series

Book 1   The Bodies in the Marina

Book 2   The Laminated man

Book 3   The Mystery of Cabin 312

Book 4   The Reluctant Jockey

Book 5   The Missing Heiress

Book 6   The Jockey's Wife

Book 7   Death on the Cart

BUCHANAN

The
Laminated Man

Alex Willis

First published in Great Britain by Mount Pleasant Press 2017
This edition published by Mount Pleasant Publishing 2020

ISBN 978-1-913471-10-1

Text set in Garamond 12 point.

Cover photo © Nancy Willis 2017
Cover Layout © Alex & Nancy Willis 2017/2020

Acknowledgement

I would like to extend my gratitude to, Insp. Giuseppe Mariano of the Italian police, and Senior Special Agent Dan Haggerty of the FBI for their insights into the workings of the Mafia.

This book is dedicated to my lovely wife Nancy.

1

Hello, and good morning. This is BBC Sussex Breakfast with Olli Stephens. The time is six o'clock, it's Saturday the seventeenth of June and here to read the news this morning is Fred Walker – Fred.'

Thanks, Olli. When asked about the government's response to the Grenfell fire, the Prime Minister said in an interview …

'Jack, you can't wear that shirt to the wedding.'

'Good morning, my dear. Wasn't planning to, I'll change it later. You wanted me to take the bags of clothes down to St Wilfred's and cut the grass, remember?'

'Ok. Since you are so organised this morning, maybe I should have asked you to sweep the driveway as well.'

'It's on my list, I've plenty of time.'

Southern Railway said in a statement that the upcoming drivers' protest is completely unwarranted …

'Jack, after thirty-five years, you never cease to amaze me,' Karen said, wrapping her arms round her husband. 'If that's the case, can you stop in at Morrisons on the way back? I've made up a list. We're short of vegetables and fruit and make sure you get the sourdough bread, we're going to have a ploughman's lunch tomorrow afternoon.'

Brighton and Hove Albion have broken the transfer record by …

'Sure, how about milk?'

'Better get four pints.'

The much-anticipated reopening of the Saltdean Lido is set for ten …

'Beer?'

'We have plenty.'

'And wine?'

'Sorted – Artisvin, delivered yesterday, the beer and wine are in the garage.'

And today's weather is set to be fair and warm. The expected highs inland will be twenty-seven Centigrade, or eighty-one Fahrenheit in old money. There will be light breezes along the coast. Fantastic weather for the much-anticipated outdoor wedding of the year between local businessman Sir Nathan Greyspear and Susan ...

'What would I ever do without you?'

'You'd do just fine – as long as you had your job and your beer.'

'You know me too well.'

In other news, a body found this morning in a burnt-out van in an industrial area of Hampden Park ...

'Don't be long, Jack,' said Karen, as Buchanan went out the kitchen door for the garage and the clothes for St Wilfred's.

♦

'Cutting it a bit fine, Jack.'

'I stopped in at Starbucks for a coffee.'

Karen shook her head, and looked into the shopping bag. 'Good, you managed to get everything.'

'Even managed to find the sourdough bread.'

'You are a clever boy,' she said, hugging him and kissing him affectionately on the lips. 'Jack – there's no time for that. Now I think it's time you scuttled off upstairs and got ready. We can't be late for Nathan and Susan's wedding.'

Buchanan looked at the kitchen clock, then back at his wife.

'Don't you worry about me. I had my shower when you were out. All I need to do is get dressed and do my hair,' said Karen.

♦

'What time did we say to Jill and Stephen for tomorrow?' said Buchanan, as he stepped out of the shower.

'Knowing how you and Stephen will be celebrating this evening, I suggested they be here by one o'clock.'

'Good, I could do with a lie-in.'

'Why don't you come to church with me? It'll do you good.'

'An extra hour in bed will do me more good.'

'Oh, Jack.'

'Oh Jack – what?'

'Oh, never mind, one day you'll understand.'

'The only standing I need to do right now is to be at Nathan's right hand at his wedding. I'm best man, remember?'

'Well do I! Pity you weren't at the rehearsal.'

'You know duty comes first.'

'You finish your best-man's speech?'

'Did it at Starbucks. See, it's not just women who can multi-task.'

'Go get dressed you – you muckle saftie.'

♦

Buchanan drove slowly up the Castlewood driveway, taking care not to spin the tyres in the gravel. He glanced sideways at the trees lining the driveway; they stood like soldiers on parade.

'Look at that, Jack,' said Karen. 'Someone's tied large pink bows to the trunks of the trees, how lovely.'

Buchanan stopped under the canopy in front of the entrance and got out. He waited for Karen to get out before he handed his keys to the valet, who carefully drove off to park the car.

They walked, hand in hand, up the magnificent stairs to the huge polished mahogany doors, which were opened as they approached.

'Jack, you go see Nathan, I'll wait in the bar with the other guests,' said Karen.

'Ok, see you later.'

Buchanan walked across to the reception desk. 'Excuse me, Jack Buchanan – I'm the best man. Can you let Sir Nathan know I'm here, please?'

'Certainly, sir, one moment.'

As he waited, Buchanan thought back a year to the first time he'd visited Castlewood. The painting of Moonbeam, Greyspear's latest horse, still hung on the wall behind the reception desk. Then, he was trying to find the killer of two people whose bodies had been found in the Eastbourne marina.

He smiled inwardly to himself when he thought he once considered Nathan Greyspear could have been capable of those murders.

The receptionist put down the phone and said, 'Sir Nathan says to go right up, he's waiting in the morning room. It's the second on the right at the top of the stairs.'

'Thank you.'

Buchanan walked across the marble-floored reception hall and up the curved staircase to the first floor. Hanging on the stairway wall were several portraits of Sir Nathan's worthy ancestors. Though on closer examination Buchanan thought they all bore more than a slight resemblance to Sir Nathan himself. Then, why not? Sir Nathan Greyspear was a self-made man, why not a self-made history, represented here on the wall by these portraits of six generations of Greyspears?

Buchanan walked down the first-floor hallway to the morning room and entered. Greyspear was standing in the bay window surveying the final preparations for the wedding.

'Perfect weather for your wedding, Nathan.'

'Ah, Jack, you're early. I heard about the body in the van – said to myself, bet Jack's in there sorting it out.'

'You know me well, but not today. It'll just be some traveller who forgot to turn off the stove when he went to sleep.'

'Glad to hear that, can't have my best-man run off at the altar. Something to drink?'

'Ah, what is there?'

'Come on, Jack, my wedding day, what do you think?'

'Whiskey?'

'There is that if you'd like it. I'm drinking an award-winning sparkling wine.'

'Champagne?'

'No. Not quite, it's the English equivalent, Ridgeview. It's beaten many of the classic champagnes. We're having it at the wedding today. For my taste, I'd drink it any day over champagne.'

'Well, if you're drinking it, I suppose I'll have to have a glass as well.'

'Your speech?' asked Greyspear, handing Buchanan a sizable glass filled with Ridgeview.

'In here,' he replied, patting his jacket breast-pocket.

'Hope it's not too embarrassing?'

'Oh, it is, it is – just you wait.'

'Just as I thought. Come, let me introduce you to my groomsmen. Not sure if you will know any of them, but I'm sure you will by the end of the day. They're a good bunch of chaps.'

Buchanan followed Greyspear down the hall to a room on the end.

There was a buzz of male voices emanating from the room. It went quiet as Greyspear entered.

'Gentlemen, I'd like to introduce you to my best man, Detective Chief Inspector Jack Buchanan.'

Buchanan followed Greyspear round the room, being introduced to those assembled one at a time. The only name he recognised was that of Jack Nevis, a harbour live-aboard. The focus of Jill's recent first murder case as the senior investigating officer.

'How are you. Jack?'

'Fine, thanks to your sergeant.'

'Ah, yes. Jill's first time as a SIO. Tell me, whatever happened to the falcon statue? Did that rat Kaufmann get away with it?'

'Unfortunately, no-one knows where it is. Maybe it just lived in the imagination of Dashiell Hammett and never really existed.'

'Good one, Jack, let's keep it that way. So, how are your wife and children?'

'Nancy's fine, and, if you listen you can hear the children

running wild out on the lawn with the other kids.'

The chit-chat was interrupted by a knock on the door by one of Greyspear's servants.

'Ah, Dennis, time to go?'

'Yes, sir, the bride has just arrived.'

'You hear that, men? My bride has arrived. Let's go.'

♦

'Susan looked so beautiful, didn't she, Jack?' said Karen, as they wandered through the Castlewood gardens.

'Yes, she was a picture. Made me think about –'

'Retiring, perhaps?'

'No. I was going to say before I was interrupted – the next wedding we are going to.'

'Stephen and Jill's? No rude jokes at that one for you. Remember you're going to be father of the bride.'

'Funny, I'm more nervous about that speech than any court case I've ever had to give evidence at. Even when I gave the testimonial for Jock MacTaggart when he retired – and he was the Lord Provost.'

'Oh Jack, stop putting yourself down, you were brilliant, especially the bit about the rugby ball in the shower.'

'Yes, that was a hoot, his friend Charles told me that little titbit. It's just – I always feel a bit drained after one of those talks.'

'Talking about drains, who was that little Italian chap you were talking to?'

'He introduced himself as Toni Palmari, made out he was a friend of Nathan, and I think he's an American, not an Italian.'

'He didn't look like he was discussing the weather. What did he want?'

'Not quite sure. He went on about how, with Nathan's help, he was about to revolutionise policing, then went on to talk about transportation.'

'Isn't that the job Nathan offered you?'

'Not sure.'

'You think Nathan has given up waiting for you to decide if you are going to take the job?'

'I don't know, I'm sure he would have said something about it if he has.'

'Why don't we go ask him? He's just come out of the marquee.'

'Nah, I'll do it later. This is his wedding day, he won't want to talk business.'

'Nonsense, Jack. He's your friend, c'mon — Nathan, do you have a minute? Jack wants to ask you something.'

'Oh, hello Karen, just looking for my bride, have you seen her?'

'I saw her go in the house a few minutes ago with Nancy and her children.'

'Ah, of course, they want to see the horses. Now Jack, what is it you want to ask? A start date maybe?'

'Not quite. I was talking with one of your guests, a Toni Palmari, he made out you were going to be working with him in a scheme to revolutionise policing?'

'Where on earth did he get that idea? No, of course I'm not. He suggested I use his company for transporting our boats to and from the Mediterranean, that's all. Said he could provide full security and save us a fortune in transport costs.'

'Sounds a bit dodgy to me. What did you tell him?'

'I told him to send in his proposal and we would look it over at the next board meeting.'

♦

'See, Karen, nothing to worry about,' said Buchanan, as they wandered through the Castlewood gardens. 'Nathan isn't going to abandon me.'

'I'm glad of that.'

'Me too.'

'Jack. Look at the clematis, it's all over the hollyhock.'

'The hollyhock grows straight up into the sunshine and allows the clematis to wrap around it and grow as well – a symbiotic relationship.'

'Isn't nature just wonderful?'

'Yes. It's just like the wrasse and shark. As long as the wrasse continues to provide a teeth-cleaning service to the shark, the wrasse is permitted to exist. Unfortunately for the hollyhock, the clematis will end up killing it.'

'You've had too much champagne.'

'Not champagne, my dear, Ridgeview. Nathan swears by it as being far superior to champagne.'

'Nonetheless, it's time we were off. I'll drive, you've celebrated a bit too much.'

'Thanks,' he said, passing Karen the car keys.

'Even if you don't, I've got to be at church for eight o'clock. I'm serving coffees and teas at the nine o-clock service.'

2

Still hungover from the Saturday wedding celebrations, on Monday morning Buchanan wandered into his office and sat down at his desk. He ignored the urgent message stuck on his computer screen to call the crime commissioner – time enough for that later. He took the blueberry muffin out of the bag, the top off the coffee cup and sniffed the aroma.

He glanced at the weekend incident board: a mugging on Seaside Road; a sizable drug bust on Cavendish Place; an incident at the Arndale shopping centre expansion, where an old safe with outdated bank-notes had been found in a building basement; tools stolen from a building site; a body found in a burnt-out van in Hampden Park; and a missing eighty-year-old grandfather in Meads. Just another happy weekend in Eastbourne. At least the new plans for the pier had been well received. A threatened demonstration had turned into an impromptu party on the pier, complete with a petting zoo and topped off by the appearance of two docile, cuddly, lion cubs.

So much had happened since he'd left Glasgow. In the space of a few months he and his team had solved three murders, one disappearance, and had saved the Crown Prosecution Service a substantial amount of expense when a murderer had died while attempting to avoid arrest. At least Buchanan's partner, Jill, had come out of the affair with a great deal to celebrate. Not only had she acted as the SIO investigating yet another murder in the marina; but she'd become engaged to one of the PC's in the case and, much to Karen's delight, Jill had asked Buchanan to walk her down the aisle. Jill had gone from being just a partner to one of the family, almost the daughter that Buchanan and his wife never had.

In spite of this good news and the excellent outcome of the

case he'd worked on, he still couldn't shake his feeling that something was wrong – something was very wrong. Since when did the crime commissioner want to talk to him first thing on a Monday morning?

Historically, Mondays were always the worst, especially with all the weekend paperwork that had to be processed. He smiled, and reached for the first item in his in-basket. You never saw Morse sort paperwork, he'd be off down the pub with Lewis.

He shook his head, tossed the file back into the in-basket, swivelled round in his chair and stared out the window. He reached for the muffin and coffee, leaned back in his chair and put his feet up on the desk. Here he was, a senior detective with the rank of detective chief inspector, and no cases to inspect. At fifty-two years-old and a career that spanned thirty-four years, he realised he was at the zenith. So why, on Friday afternoon, when he was about to go home early for the first time in – he couldn't remember the last time – had the recently promoted ACC wandered into his office and said quite casually – *Do you realise you qualify for a full and immediate pension? Why not retire and leave it to the younger ones?* Leave it to the younger ones! What a load of tosh. When he'd said he was good for another twenty years, she'd told him he needed to come visit her in her office and they would discuss his future.

Most of his working life, except for the last few months, had been involved in fighting crime in Glasgow. Now, living in Eastbourne, he was, for the first time in his life, beginning to relax. He shook his head at the idea of retirement.

Buchanan turned his attention back to what was the issue of his continuing employment as a policeman, albeit in a senior capacity. When he'd started with the police, a career path to inspector was long and arduous, but he'd persevered and had risen to where he was today. For some time, he'd realised he was surplus to requirements and had suspected, over the last weeks whilst in Eastbourne, senior management hoped that he'd just drift off into the sunset and retire.

Sadly, he had to accept the fact that, as a senior crime investigator, his day had come and gone. Sergeants were now doing the work of inspectors, constables were doing the work of sergeants, PCSO's were doing the work of constables.

Now inspectors were spending their time in offices checking the paperwork of the sergeants, constables, and PCSO's. His previous boss, Assistant Chief Constable Atkins, had missed her promotion to chief and had announced her departure to a senior management position working for G4s.

Karen had declared she was happy living in Eastbourne, and said she would love to settle somewhere in the area. Especially now, with the expansion of the Arndale shopping centre being well underway with its new and exciting places to eat and shop.

Buchanan did have to admit it was a very nice place to live, and after Sir Nathan had invited him and Karen for a meal at Castlewood, Sir Nathan's country club, he was looking forward to getting out on the cross-country course on Mercury again. If only he could get time.

Of course, there was the offer from Sir Nathan to come and work for him. Not building boats but heading up his fledgling security firm. The offer was a good one: higher salary, proper expense account, and free first-class travel, usually in the company turbo-props. The only downside was he'd have to behave when driving, no more blue-lights and sirens.

He would of course, for once, be his own boss, no ACC to answer to, no bloody politics, or press hounding him. No one involved in his current job would miss him. Jill, his partner, though she was getting married, would always be part of the family, but had her own career path to travel.

His mind was made up, he'd retire and take Sir Nathan's offer to come run his security firm. He reached for his phone, but, before he could pick it up, it rang.

'Buchanan. Who's this?'

'Inspector, it's control, I'm looking for the duty SIO.'

Buchanan looked up at the duty roster. 'You want DI Hanbury.'

'Sorry, sir, he's working on the body in the burnt-out van.'

'Have you tried Street?'

'Yes, sir. She's currently on route from Brighton.'

'Hunter?'

'He's with Street.'

'How about Dexter? Tried his phone?'

'He's assisting DI Hanbury.'

Buchanan looked back at the duty roster and shrugged. It was his name next on the list.

'Then it's me. What have you got?'

'Thanks, sir. We've just had a report phoned in about a dead body.'

'Not the one in the burnt-out van? Thought you said Hanbury was working on that?'

'No, it's another one.'

'Details?'

'Body was discovered this morning at eight forty-five by a John Enright. He's an alarm engineer, called out to an unoccupied factory on Edison Road.'

'How do I find it?'

'Turn in to the industrial estate by Gardners Books. You go under a bridge and take the first on the right. The factory is at the end of the road.'

'I know the area; my wife's church is down there somewhere. Should be there in five minutes.'

Buchanan hung up and wondered what Street was doing. He reached for his mobile on the charging stand and realised the battery was almost flat, but at least there was enough to call Street.

'Jill, it's Buchanan. Where are you?'

'On the train. We went to a concert in Brighton after leaving you and Karen yesterday. On the way home Stephen's car died. Took the breakdown service ages to get to us, by then we'd missed the last train.'

'How long will you be?'

'Should be in the office in thirty minutes.'

'No, don't come to the office. We have a body.'

'Where?'

'A factory unit on Edison Road'

'What's the address?'

♦

Buchanan drove in through the factory gates and stopped beside the alarm engineer's van. He got out of his car and introduced himself.

'DCI Buchanan. You called in the report?'

'John Enright, yes,' he replied, his hands visibly trembling. 'How could anyone do such a thing?'

'Do what, Mr Enright?'

He shook his head and replied, 'You'll see, follow me. Just don't know what the world's coming to.'

'How did they get in?'

'Front door.'

'Was the lock forced? I don't see any damage,' said Buchanan, as he glanced at the doorframe and lock.

'All we get is an alarm at the response centre.'

'It doesn't tell you which door or window?'

'No, just that a sensor has detected either a door or window being opened. Sometimes a gust of wind inside the building, or movement, will set the alarm off.'

'Bit basic for an alarm system?'

'Does the job. You'd be surprised what can happen to an empty building when it's without tenants. The owner had the alarm fitted, didn't want the building stripped.'

'Copper?'

'Yes. Happens quite often when a building sits vacant for a

while.'

'So, when the alarm came into your response centre, what happened?'

'It was logged.'

'When was that?'

'Friday evening.'

'And you're just responding now?'

'They don't have weekend coverage.'

'Just that, and no one felt it was important enough to send someone out to investigate?'

'Well, I'm here now.'

'How did you come to find the body?'

'I got into the building –'

'How?'

'I have a key.'

'Go on.'

'I opened the door and thought that was funny.'

'What was funny, Mr Enright?'

'The alarm didn't go off, it was never reset.'

'So, the alarm didn't go off when you entered?'

'That's correct.'

'Ok, continue.'

'I looked at the alarm code and saw it indicated a door having been opened. The main power was off in the building so I used my torch to look for any open doors or windows.'

'You have to look at every door and window?'

'No, not quite. The alarm panel indicates which zone of the building the alarm was triggered from.'

'Which zone was it?'

'Back of the building, the fire door out on to Lottbridge Drove.'

'How did you find the body?'

Enright shook his head as he replayed the memory. 'By accident. After I'd checked the fire door was closed, I thought I might as well do a complete sweep of the building just to make sure there weren't any other doors open. I'd got almost all the way round the building when I saw the – shit, how can people be so fucked up they'd do something like that to another human being?'

'Would you show me what you found, please?'

Buchanan followed Enright as he continued with his story. 'Since the building is unoccupied the landlord would only pay for a Monday to Friday eight am to eight pm response service.'

'Not sure I understand?'

'He figured since the building was unoccupied and empty, who'd be so foolish as to try stripping out a building at night and in the dark? You'd be surprised how often we get called out in the night to a break-in, only to find out that a pigeon flew in during the day for a nap, then woke in the night and tried to get out and, in the process, set off the alarm.'

'And was that what happened Friday night?'

'Not quite.'

'What do you mean?'

'We got an alarm indication about ten-fifteen, then it cleared twenty minutes later at ten-thirty-five.'

'So, your response centre thought it was a pigeon?'

'Or a rat.'

'Rats!'

'They sometimes chew through the cabling.'

'What do you do if it's a pigeon that set off the alarm?'

Enright turned to Buchanan and made a gesture of holding up a rifle and pulling a trigger. 'Unfortunately, it's the only way, Inspector. Want to see the body?'

'Just a minute, I need to put on my overshoes.'

Buchanan followed Enright as he opened the fire-door from the reception area and walked into the factory.

'What did they do here before it closed?'

'Fibreglass moulding. Lots of prototype works for the

automotive, aviation and marine industries.'

'Where's the body?'

'Over there, behind that pile of steel drums,' he said, indicating with a nod. 'It's in the oven, on the rear wall. Hang on a minute, I'll turn the lights on for you, bit dark at the back.'

Buchanan walked round the pile of drums and accidentally bumped into one of them. He looked in the gloom and saw that several were rusting, a black ooze leaking from splits. Annoyed, he looked at his jacket and saw that the one he'd bumped into had left a wet sticky smear on the cuff. He took out his handkerchief and tried to wipe off the mess. It smelled like – it reminded him of the time he attended the recovery of the body of the notorious gambler, Jimmy Grant, from the bilges of an old steamer being broken up in Troon.

He stood in front of the industrial oven and waited for Enright to turn on the lights. There was no door on the front, instead above the opening hung a large, rusty, steel roller shutter. Buchanan waited. The lights came on and he saw what had spooked the engineer.

Fastened to a sheet of plywood, leaning against the back wall, was the body of a man. His arms were outstretched, and the body completely encased in fibreglass. Buchanan looked closer and saw a dartboard behind the body's head and a dart with bright red feathers sticking out of the forehead.

'Are you sure it's not just a mannequin, Mr Enright?'

'Look for yourself, Inspector. No human hand could craft that face.'

Buchanan walked further into the oven and stood in front of what had spooked Enright so badly. He shook his head and stared. The body had been nailed through the clothes, pinning the body to the plywood.

'The poor bastard, what did he do to deserve this?'

'Awful, isn't it? What he was thinking as they held him and nailed him to the plywood is anyone's guess. Using his face as a dartboard, then spraying the fibreglass on him is too gross to contemplate.'

'We'll need a statement from you, Mr Enright. Maybe best if you wait outside.'

'Yes, you're right, I'm feeling a bit faint with all the fumes. I'll be in my car if you need me.'

Buchanan followed Enright out into the car park to wait for Street. She arrived a few minutes later and parked beside Buchanan's car.

'Morning, Jill.'

'Sorry I'm late.'

'Where's Stephen?'

'He's got the day off, gone to the car dealers to look at a car. I hope he's going to trade in his old one, keeps breaking down.'

'Must be nice to get a day off.'

'What about Saturday, the wedding? Doesn't that count as a day off?'

Buchanan shrugged. 'I suppose you're right there. What I'm talking about is just a day where you can – *aw*, let's forget it.'

'You could have many of them if you wanted. It's your decision.'

'Not you as well. The whole police force thinks I should retire.'

'Sorry, not what I meant.'

'Doesn't matter. The body's inside. You'll need your overshoes, there's stuff all over the floor.'

'What does it look like?'

'Wait and see for yourself. Don't worry, it's not messy.'

'No blood?'

'If only.'

Street followed Buchanan into the factory, keeping to his tracks to the oven.

'Was he dead when they did that to him?' she asked.

'Look at his face. You tell me.'

'Oh shit, he was alive! What must he have thought?'

'Notice anything, other than our friend here?'

'What do you mean?'

'Look around, what do you see?'

Street walked out of the oven and looked around.

'Lots of footprints in the dust on the floor, be difficult to sort them out. Looks like it was a busy place once, at least it must have been with all these empty workbenches. But – I don't understand what that trailer is doing inside the factory, looks so out of place.'

'Maybe it failed its roadworthy test. Or –'

'Or what?'

'Remember I told you the story about my neighbour borrowing my lawnmower?'

Street shook her head.

'Oh – thought I'd mentioned it once. Well, anyway, he borrowed it and kept it locked up so I couldn't just nip round and get it back.'

'Why did he keep it locked up?'

'He'd broken it and was too tight to get it fixed, hoped I'd just forget it.'

'Some neighbour. What did you do?'

'Left it behind when we came south.'

'So, you think this trailer was borrowed and not returned?'

'Or something worse.'

'You're losing me again.'

'Just thinking out loud, I'll let you know when I've figured it out.'

'Good, don't like being left behind – why are you smiling, what did I say?'

'*Left Behind* – a book a friend of Karen's once wanted me to read.'

'And did you?'

'Tried to, got a bit weird, never finished it.'

'So, back to the business at hand,' said Street, as she walked further out into the workshop. 'Other than the empty benches, the place looks quite deserted.'

'Precisely, what does that say to you?'

Street walked over to one of the abandoned workbenches. 'Empty factory, no machinery, rubbish scattered on the floor. I'd say they went bust, liquidators sold off all the machinery and what couldn't be sold was just left.'

'You think so?'

'Yes, especially if the scribbled poem on this workbench has any truth in it.'

'What does it say?'

Friday came, as Friday will, to find the workshop quiet and still
They called out, 'Come here quickly, John, we think something has gone wrong
Yesterday we had oak, beech and wenge, now all we've got, is an empty bench
We were sure we were doing right, working late into the night.'

Now today, at the crack of dawn, we arrive at work but are now forlorn
We worked hard and followed the plan, sparing no effort, to a man
We don't know how we've got to here, all we know is something's queer.
We've sharpened our chisels, gouges and plane, won't you now please explain?'

'Shush,' said John, and was about to say,
'I'm sorry men there'll be no pay.'
When up spoke Jake, 'Don't be so sad,
The boss will just get more money from his dad.'

'How about this one?' said Buchanan.

'Go on.'

Here I stand, broken hearted
Came to work, but never started.'

'I suppose those describe what was going on here before they went broke.'

'Just what I thought,' said Buchanan. Walking over to one of the other empty benches, he laughed.

'What's funny?'

'Listen to this one:

> *'He floats through life with the greatest of ease*
> *The daring young man and his powder disease*
> *His actions are clumsy, his intentions unclear*
> *Without change he'll end in the mortuary'*

'But why was the fibreglass spray stuff left behind?'

Buchanan waked over to the drum of resin and stared at the label. 'The resin is out of date.'

'Thought that product dating only applied to food?'

'Good point, I'll follow that up.'

'Want me to check with the real estate people?'

Buchanan nodded. 'See if you can find out who used to be here, and while you're at it find out the names of the company directors.'

'Do you have any ideas as to what this is about?'

'Not your normal kind of killing where two people have an argument. This is a ritual slaying.'

'Like some sort of offering to the gods, that what you mean?'

'No, lass, this is someone sending a message.'

'To who?'

'That's what we have to find out before the killer needs to send any more messages.'

'Why, do you think there might be others?'

'As I just said, this is not one of your normal murders; this was premeditated, and carried out by more than one person.'

'How many?'

'Let me see,' he said, looking at the corpse. 'Two strong men to hustle our victim in to the building and hold his arms outstretched while a third nailed him to the plywood. One of them operated the fibreglass chopper gun and of course, there's the mastermind.'

'That's at least six, you'd struggle to get all of them in a car.'

'Just what I was thinking. We're probably looking for some sort of people carrier.'

'Or a van, that would be less conspicuous, especially round here with all the businesses on this estate. Gardners work 24/7, no one would notice a white van.'

'Good point, let's see if there are any CCTV cameras in the area.'

'But when did he die? Encased in the fibreglass, he could have been hanging there for days.'

'The alarm was received in the response centre at ten-twenty Friday night; our Mr Enright discovered the body at eight-fifteen this morning. Thankfully that gives us a window of hours, not weeks. Hopefully forensics will give us a better idea.'

'Wonder how they'll do that?'

'We'll have to ask the doctor.'

'Has he been called?'

'I believe he has been informed.'

'Can we get out of here? It's too creepy looking at him hanging there,' said Street.

'Indeed. Let's go, we'll wait outside for the CSI team. I'll call control and tell them at this point it's just an isolated case. No need to declare the murder a major incident.'

Buchanan followed Street out into the fresh air of the first really warm day of summer.

'Feel better, lass?'

'Thanks, the smell of resin was making me light-headed.'

'Brought back memories of our visit to Greenock?'

'That's where I smelled it before – I was trying to remember.'

'I wonder if they did any work for Greyspear?'

'Who knows?'

'Might be worth asking.'

'I will, but first we need to find out more about the business. Of course, it is possible it has nothing to do with the killing.'

'Good point, Jill.'

'So why does the crime commissioner want to have a word with you?'

'How did you find that out?'

'It was me who put the message on your computer screen. He called Friday afternoon and wanted to talk with you, that's all I know.'

'I went home early. Karen's found a house and we went to meet the real estate agent.'

'Where is it?'

'In the village of Westham, not far from where Nichols used to live.'

'And I suppose there's a pub nearby?'

'There is. The Heron is just a short walk up the road, and just the other side of the castle is Priory Court hotel, the Royal Oak and Castle, and a few yards further down the road is the Smugglers Inn. It's also a short drive to the marina and Karen's sister's house.'

'Beer to your liking?'

Buchanan smiled. 'It's Harvey's.'

'Good, I'm glad you've found somewhere to live close by.'

'Why?'

'Because it means you're not going back to Glasgow.'

'I suppose it does.'

'Will you miss it?'

'I'll tell you next year.'

'When do Karen's sister and her husband return from Paris?'

'At least another couple of months. We should be fine staying in their house till our purchase goes through.'

'What about the house in Glasgow? Will you keep it?'

'We haven't made up our minds yet. We'd like to keep it and continue renting it out, there's no mortgage.'

'Sounds a good idea.'

'Be a pity to have a mortgage again, especially since we worked so hard to pay the other one off. But, in the meantime, I see the good Doctor Mansell approaching with the Crime Scene Investigation Team, and *three* squad cars.'

Mansell parked his car and walked over to Buchanan. 'Well, I see you're continuing where you left off.'

'I find them, Doctor, not do them in.'

'That's not what I hear. Where is he?' said Mansell.

'Follow me, I'll introduce you. Oh, Jill, can you organise a cordon? We don't want anyone wandering in to see what's going on.'

Mansell donned his overalls then followed Street and Buchanan into the factory and over to the oven.

'I suppose you want to know when he died?'

'And what he had for his last meal, Doctor.'

Mansell shook his head and put down his bag 'You do find them, Buchanan,' he said, looking at the face of the deceased. 'Can't tell much from here, I'll tell you about his last meal when I get him back to the office.'

'How long, Doctor?'

Mansell stood and thought about the task ahead. 'I suppose it shouldn't be too difficult to trim down the plywood to fit on my table. Cutting the fibreglass from the clothes while retaining suitable uncontaminated pieces shouldn't pose a problem,' he said, looking carefully at the body. 'It's getting the face and hands out while not leaving the skin behind that will take a bit of research.'

'I have complete faith in your abilities, Doctor. Give me a call when you're done.'

'Thanks. Oh, what did the crime commissioner want?'

'Not you as well. Who told you about it?'

Mansell shrugged. '*He* did, he was in the office, asked if I knew where you were.'

'Is nothing private anymore?'

'I suppose it's ok to remove the body?'

'If you've done all you need to here.'

'Good day, Buchanan. I'll let you know as soon as I have the results of the post-mortem.'

'What next?' asked Street, who'd just re-joined them.

'Let's have a look around inside the factory while we're here.'

'Shouldn't we talk to Mr Enright first?'

'He's having a cigarette to calm his nerves, plenty of time later.'

'Still miss them?'

'What – oh, cigarettes? I suppose I do. Last night I had a dream that I was smoking again and woke feeling guilty.'

'Your first?'

'What?'

'The bit about feeling guilty.'

'It was the feeling I'd let Karen down.'

'I'm sure you'll win through. After all, how many years did you smoke?'

'Too many. Look, talking about my smoking habits is not getting the job done, let's get to work.'

'Where shall we start?'

'We need to find out how they got in.'

'The front door, isn't that what set off the alarm?'

'Apparently not, the alarm just tells them one of the sensors has detected a door or window being opened, or a pigeon has been trapped in the building. Enright said he thought it was the rear fire door.'

'What about the windows?'

'Good idea. Let's have a look at them – none have bars or grills.'

They walked around the inside perimeter of the factory looking for tell-tale signs of entry through the windows till they got to one of the emergency doors.

'Do you see what I see, lass?'

'Where?'

'Over there,' he said, pointing into the gloom and to the wall beyond a stack of large square plastic containers. 'The fire door.'

'Is it open?'

'One way to find out,' said Buchanan, as he carefully made his way over to the fire exit, then stopped. 'Footprints in the dust, lass, watch your step.'

Street avoided the footprints and walked over to Buchanan. She looked at the partially-open door then down at the footprints. 'Difficult to tell how many of them were here. Though I would bet that those prints are what we're after,' she said, pointing to the freshest set that led off back into the factory.

'You're right, they're the freshest and appear to be on top of the others, and,' he said, peering at the door lock, 'I'd say this is where they entered the building.' He pushed at the door with his fingertips. 'The lock's seen better days and, if this is where they entered the building, over there is where the intruder was headed.'

'They?'

'Figure of speech, Jill. I'd say there was only one who came in this way, the other footprints are probably from the people who used to work here, or those who emptied the building when the company went bust,' he replied, looking out through the open door and onto the concrete path almost hidden behind a wall of brambles, nettles and unkempt bushes.

'That's one thing about our job that'll never happen.'

'What will never happen, Jill?' he said, looking down the path in both directions.

'Going bust, there will always be criminals for us to chase.'

'You've got a point there,' he said, then thought about the different ways a modern policeman could find his job gone bust. From department cutbacks, stress-related impairment, medical disability, to involuntary retirement, they were all waiting to run the unwary career-minded copper out the door.

'Are you all right? You've gone quiet.'

'What? Oh, yes, I'm fine. Just thinking about something.'

'Shall we follow the footprints, see where our intruder went?'

'Good idea, you lead.'

Street took out her flashlight scanned the area. 'Looks like they go into that room under the mezzanine floor, he must have known where to look. Those aren't the prints of someone fumbling in the dark, they go straight to that door.'

They walked either side of the footprints and stopped at the door to the room.

'Better get the SCI's to take copies of these prints,' said Buchanan.

'Looks like our intruder was joined by someone, see, several sets of prints,' said Street, shining her flashlight across the floor.

'Or he came back afterwards to shut off the power.'

'What about Enright? Didn't he say something about having to go and turn on the lights for you?'

'That makes sense. Let's see what's behind this door first,' said Buchanan, reaching up with his hand to touch the top of the door. He pulled it open and peered inside. 'Got that flashlight of yours?'

'Here.'

Buchanan shone the light into the room and found it was a small room with power panels and control boxes covering three of the walls.

'What is it? What's in there?' asked Street.

'Looks like where all the power is controlled from.'

'Alarm panel?'

'Not that I can see – but what I can see is the footprints go in and come back out again, someone probably had to turn on the power to the lights and power points in the oven. If that's the case, then these steps that lead away must end up back at the front door.'

'Wouldn't they go to the alarm panel first?'

Buchanan thought for a minute. 'That makes sense. He – assuming it was a he, came in through the fire door, walked over to this room, turned on the lights and outlets then, as you say, went to the alarm panel. After it was all over he came back and turned off the power. Shall we see if that's what happened?'

They continued following the footprints and ended up standing in front of an open, hinged cupboard door on the wall in the main entrance. Buchanan took his car key and used it to pull the door open.

'Looks fine to me,' he said, looking at the digital display on the alarm panel. 'Let's go have a word with Mr Enright, see if he can shed any light on how the alarm unit reset itself.'

'Maybe the alarm response centre did it?'

Buchanan shook his head. 'The alarm people said the alarm only rang for about twenty minutes, then shut off.'

'So, someone must have reset it Friday night – our intruder?'

'Probably, and they had to know their way around the building as it was dark. Let's see what Mr Enright has to say.'

They walked outside the factory and over to Enright's car.

He was sitting in the driver's seat, smoking and talking on his mobile. 'Yes, Joyce, they want me to stay around. No, you'll have to get Geoff to cover that – hang on. Do you want me, Inspector?'

'Yes, Mr Enright.'

'Joyce, I'll call you back.'

Buchanan waited for Enright to hang up from his call and climb out of his car.

'How can I help, Inspector?'

'I'd like to go over the timing of the alarm.'

Enright looked down at his dispatch note. 'It says here that the alarm came in at ten twenty-three and cleared at ten forty-five.'

'Did your response centre reset the alarm?'

'No.'

'What about timing? Could it have reset itself, like a car alarm does?'

Enright shook his head. 'Not this one, has to be done at the panel.'

'So, someone had to be in the building to turn it off?'

'Yes.'

'How would they do that?'

'By punching in the code.'

'Just like most alarms, a four-digit code?'

'Yes.'

'How would someone get that code?'

'Usually someone is designated to oversee setting the alarm codes, usually the building manager, they then would assign codes to individuals.'

'So, as long as the manager hasn't changed or cancelled anyone's codes, they'd still be active?'

'I suppose so, Inspector.'

'Is there any way to get around the codes?'

'Some systems allow the engineer to bypass the codes, but that's a highly-guarded secret known only to the manufacturers' tech support people.'

'Have you ever had to call them for help?'

Enright shook his head. 'No, never had to go that far. We have a special program in our laptops that allows us to bypass the codes.'

'So, if someone stole your laptop, they could access the alarm system and override the code?'

'It's not quite that simple. Our laptops are all password protected. To log on to the alarm system we have to input our password.'

'Just like when you withdraw money from the cashpoint machine?' said Street.

'Yeah, just like that. Three tries and you're locked out, then it's over to tech support.'

'Did you look at the panel inside here?' asked Buchanan.

'Looked at the display when I got here, all looked normal.'

'Could you have another look while we're here?'

'Sure, don't know what you expect to find though.'

'Is that your phone?' asked Street.

'Not mine,' said Enright.

Buchanan reached into his jacket, but before he could answer the ringing phone, it died. He shrugged 'Flat battery' and returned it to his pocket. 'Jill, could you go check with the CSI's, see if they've checked the alarm panel for fingerprints? Also tell them I want the whole building gone over.'

'Will do, back in a minute.'

She returned a few minutes later. 'All clear. They said there were plenty of prints, all looked like they'd been there for months.'

'Hmm, I expected that. I suppose our intruder used gloves.'

Buchanan and Street followed Enright back into the building and watched as he pulled back the cupboard door and looked at the alarm panel.

'Well, Mr Enright, all look like it should?' asked Buchanan.

'As I said it would.'

'Does the system keep a record of when people log in and out?'

'Yes. Also, this system is connected to the electronic door lock. Every time someone comes in they must use their key fob. The system records the code number of the door fob, and time and date of entry.'

'And would there be a record of the codes entered, with the times of entry?'

'Yes.'

'Could you have a look and see what's in the memory?'

'I'll need my laptop to do that.'

'We'll wait.'

Enright shoved a block of wood in the door as he went out to his car.

'Amazing,' remarked Street, 'we have all this technology in our lives, but still rely on a block of wood to keep a door open.'

'What's wrong with that? He's just saving himself the bother of taking his key out of his pocket.'

Street shrugged, then said, 'We already know when, what good will knowing the code used be?'

'When you've checked with the real estate agent and found out the name of the owner of the previous business, we should be able to track down the facility manager and get a list of names of those who had door codes. Then it's a simple job of matching a door code to a name.'

'You reckon it'll be that simple?'

Buchanan looked at her, smiled and said, 'If only. But of course, that will only be of use if the door was opened from outside. Don't forget, someone was already in the building and had silenced the alarm with a legitimate code.'

Enright returned with his laptop. 'Could one of you hold the laptop for me, please?

'Sure,' said Street.

Enright placed his laptop on Street's outstretched hands and unscrewed two screws from the side of the alarm panel. Free of its retaining screws, the face of the panel swung open. Enright took a cable that was plugged into the laptop and inserted the loose end into a socket on the control panel circuit board.

'Looks like an interesting job,' said Street.

'Not so bad, a lot simpler than working on PBX's.' replied Enright, as he powered up the laptop.

'What do you mean?'

'PBX's – business telephone systems,' he said, shaking his head. 'Used to install, service, and programme them.'

'Why did you give up?' asked Street, as Enright keyed a code into the laptop.

'Response times. Used to cover the south east. Company guaranteed their customers a four-hour window for getting their systems back up and running.'

'Seems like plenty of time.'

'It's not when you're stuck in a traffic jam on the M25 by Heathrow and you have to get to Southend, diagnose and fix the fault, all within the four-hour window. Ah, here we go.'

'What have you got, Mr Enright?' asked Buchanan.

'How far back do you want me to go?'

Buchanan thought for a minute, then asked, 'How far back can you go?'

'There's about six months here, though not much during the last two months.'

'What about Friday night?'

'Oh, that's here all right.'

'Ok, we'll take the six months. Can you save it to a disk?'

'No problem, though it would be just as easy to email it to you.'

'I'll take the disk; emails can get lost in the system.'

'Fine, I'll just pop out to the car and get one.'

Coming back, Enright downloaded the info, ejected the disk and handed it to Buchanan, who passed it to Street.

'Thanks, Mr Enright. If we need to ask any further questions, we'll get in touch through your office.'

'Do you want a statement from me?'

'I'll have one of the constables take your statement before you go.'

'Ok.'

As Enright drove out of the gates, Street said, 'Back to the office, Buck?'

Buchanan looked at Street, '*Buck*? What's that all about?'

'Sounds better than, *boss* and *sir*, brings back too many memories of being in the MDP, and calling you "Jack" feels disrespectful.'

'But you yourself told me when we first met that everyone in the department goes by their first name.'

'The name Buck fits you like a shoe, describes you to a *T*.'

Buchanan smiled and thought for a minute, 'I suppose you've got a point. But,' he said, shaking his head slowly, 'just call me Jack, and if it makes you feel less awkward in front of the others, you can refer to me as chief, how's that?'

She smiled. 'Ok, Jack it will be,' though in her heart she wished someday she could just call him "dad".'

'Jill, you head back to the office, I'll wait here till the doctor and CSI's have completed their initial investigation.'

She gave him a quizzical look.

'I'm going to Starbucks. Want anything?'

'Well, if you're going to Starbucks, can you get me a caramel Frappuccino?'

'How you can drink that beats me.'

'It's great, you should try one someday.'

'No thanks, I'll just stick to straight coffee.'

Buchanan watched Street drive out of the gate, then returned to the factory investigation. He went inside and stood out of the way, watching as Mansell carefully cut around the outline of the body through the plywood. With the help of one of the CSI team, they placed the body, still encased in fibreglass, into the waiting body bag lying on the coroner's gurney.

'Permission to remove the body, Buchanan?' said Dr Mansell.

'If you're done.'

'Done? I'm yet to get started, Buchanan. What a bloody mess this is.'

'I'm sure you'll sort it out, Doctor,' said Buchanan as the doctor followed the gurney out of the factory.

'Excuse me, sir,' said a white-robed CSI investigator.

'Yes?'

'We're done, can we go as well?'

'Found anything significant?'

'Whoever did the spraying will have vestiges of resin and glass on their clothes. If you look at the footprints close to where the body was covered in fibreglass, you can see where they stood. The overspray not only went on the floor, but on their shoes and probably the lower ends of their trousers.'

'Will it wash off their trousers?'

'Unlikely. The diameter and lengths of the glass strands are so small they will probably never wash out and, for that fact, neither will the microscopic globules of resin.'

'How many intruders were there?'

'I'd say about six.'

Buchanan smiled. 'So, all I have to do is look for someone wearing the *right* trousers.'

As he was getting into his car, Buchanan was interrupted by an individual holding a small notepad. It was Anton Miasma, the crime reporter for the *Eastbourne Herald*.

'Inspector, another dead body in Eastbourne?'

'I've nothing to say, Mr Miasma. When I have anything to report, the office will let you know.'

'Just a short statement, Inspector. Please.'

'Ok, Sussex Police are responding to the discovery of an unidentified body in a factory in Hampden Park. Cause and circumstances surrounding the death have still to be determined.'

'That all, Inspector?'

'For the moment it will have to do, Mr Miasma.'

3

Buchanan drove down Seaside Road, turned right at the Tesco roundabout and left into Hammonds Drive. Street had already parked in the police compound and, to his annoyance, someone had parked a powder-blue Mercedes SLC with its top down in his space. A car he didn't recognise. He parked next to it and headed for his office.

Street was waiting for him. 'I've had a look at the disk, not sure what to do with the information.'

'Your coffee,' he said, handing her a large clear plastic cup.

'Thanks – straw?'

'Oh, here,' he said, taking one out of the bag.

He took a sip of his coffee, leaned over Street's shoulder and looked at the screen on her computer. 'What have you got?'

'I assume this is when the break-in is detected, and this column shows when the code is entered, and the alarm silenced,' said Street, 'and I suppose the third column is for when the alarm is reset, pity it's blank for Friday evening.'

'Looks that way.'

'Enright said the alarm didn't go off when he entered. I suppose whoever was last out just pulled the door closed as they left.'

'Probably, but it would have been nice to know when they left the building.'

'Did you see the crime commissioner?'

'No, why? Is he in the building?'

'His car's in the car park. He's here with the ACC.'

'Have you met him yet?'

'First time for him, I've met the ACC before, she's all right. They were both waiting in the office when I came in.'

'Here, in this office?'

'Yes, why?'

'My head is on the block.'

'Why, what have you done?'

He shrugged. 'Not sure.' The memory of the altercation last year in Porters Bar in Glasgow, and the subsequent deaths of the two protagonists still weighed heavily on his mind. Not that he was sorry for them, they deserved what they got. No, it was the furore the press had stirred up and what the senior management thought that was the problem. Had they finally decided it was time to get rid of him? Was that why the PCC and the ACC were both here in the station? But they couldn't do that to him, he hadn't even had time to present his side of the story. There would have to be a hearing at least. Now last Friday's comments made sense: they wanted him to jump before they had to push him. Well, he had news for them: this lad was not for jumping.

'Jill, did they say anything to you about me?'

'No, just asked where you were.'

'What did you tell them?'

'I said you'd gone to the garage.'

'And?'

'I think they assumed you'd gone for petrol, I forgot to mention that Starbucks is beside the garage.'

'Good thinking. Get anywhere with finding out who used to rent the building?'

'Estate agent said it was a company called CSM.'

'What does CSM stand for?'

'Crown Specialist Mouldings. I'm working on tracing the directors at the moment.'

Buchanan walked over to the window and looked down at the car park. Two people were getting into the Mercedes. 'Jill, what does the crime commissioner look like?'

'He's slim, about six-four, fair hair.'

'I think he's just leaving.'

Street got up from her chair and came over to the window. 'Yes, that's him with the new ACC. What do you think of him?'

'Same way I do about most politicians.'

'Is that what you think he is?'

'What can I say?' he said, holding out his hands, palms up, and shrugging. 'At forty-two he's got to be the youngest police and crime commissioner in the force.'

'Is that what bothers you?'

He thought for a moment. 'He's just a bureaucrat, what does he know about policing? When did he ever walk the beat at night, and in rain or snow? A college boy, that's what he is, bet he's never made an arrest in his life. Just think of the cost of the department. Do you know what his budget is for the coming year?'

'No, haven't a clue.'

'One and a quarter million pounds. Just think how many coppers we could get on the beat with that!'

'How many?'

Buchanan ruminated for a moment before replying, 'I'll tell you how many – fifty. Just think of it, Jill. Fifty new, talented and enthusiastic PC's on the beat.'

'I take it you don't like him?'

'That's not what I mean. How can you be a good copper unless you get out on the streets, mix with the public, feel a few collars, bang up the bad guys, get your hands dirty with the filth of life?'

'Is that what you'd think about me, if I got to be an ACC?'

'What? No of course not, you'd make a good assistant chief constable – crime commissioner even.'

Street smiled. 'You're biased.'

He shrugged. 'So, what's wrong with that?'

'Nothing at all. Shall we get to work? We've got a killer to catch.'

'Good, he's gone,' said Buchanan, turning away from the

window. 'CSM, you said?'

'Yes.'

Buchanan picked up his phone and dialled a number from memory. It rang four times before being answered.

'Susan, hello, it's Jack Buchanan. Is Nathan available? He is? Is he meeting with anyone? Ok, I'll head over there.'

Street looked up from her screen and asked, 'Going to see Sir Nathan?'

'Yes.'

'Aren't they going off on their honeymoon?'

'Not till the end of the month.'

'Is he at Castlewood?'

Buchanan nodded as he picked up his jacket from the back of his chair. 'Yes, Susan says he's gone to look at his horse. Call me on my mobile if you need me.'

'Did you charge it?'

'Damn, forgot,' he said, removing it from his jacket and sitting it on the charging stand.

'Here, borrow mine,' 'she said, handing Buchanan her mobile phone. 'What shall I tell the ACC if she asks for you?'

'Tell her I'm doing what I'm paid to do, out investigating a murder.'

◆

Buchanan drove into the Castlewood country club, parked in the shade and walked around to the stable block.

The stables were laid out in the shape of a quadrangle. The entrance was through a magnificent cut-stone arch in the middle of one of the walls. In the middle of the opposite wall were the tack and feed rooms and the head groom's office. The remainder of the quadrangle contained the horse boxes. Pride of place in the centre of the yard stood a weathered, marble, circular water trough topped off with an ornate bronze statue of a horse's head. The yard was a hive of activity, horses were being brushed, saddled and unsaddled, walked and ridden out.

Amongst all this activity stood a tall, bright-eyed, muscular horse, a farrier working on one of the shoes.

Buchanan headed for the man standing beside the horse. 'Nathan, nothing wrong with Moonbeam, I hope?'

'Jack, good to see you! And thanks again for Saturday, still don't know how you found out all that stuff about me.'

'Ah, a policeman's secret. Something wrong with Moonbeam?'

'No, just having the farrier replace one of his shoes.'

'Is he all right?'

'Yes, he's fine. Cast one of his rear shoes yesterday while out on a gallop.'

'Glad to hear it's nothing more.'

'So, Jack, what brings you out here? Fancy a ride on Mercury? Thought about my offer?'

'Still thinking, and sorry, too much on my plate to have time to go for a ride.'

'Don't wait too long.'

'No, I won't. Nathan, have you heard of a company called CSM?'

'Crown Specialist Mouldings?'

'That's the one.'

'They went bust a couple of months ago, did some work for us. Why?'

'Something I'm working on. How about directors, know anything about them?'

'Not much. I think the problem was with one of the managers.'

'Do you know his name?'

'Look, the farrier is about done with Moonbeam, let me get one of the lads to walk him for a bit, then you and I can go for lunch. You are hungry?'

'Yes, but I need to get back to the office, so I'm afraid it will have to be a quick coffee.'

'All right, hang on minute, and I'll be right with you.'

♦

'How's Karen?' asked Greyspear, as they walked across the stable yard towards the clubhouse.

'She's fine, especially now since we've found a house that she likes.'

'Where is it? Or should I just guess?'

'Not the Harbour.'

'Pity, would have been nice to be neighbours.'

'Our budget doesn't stretch to millionaires' row.'

'Who calls it that?'

'The estate agent.'

'Where are you buying?'

'Westham.'

'Ah, not quite close enough for us to walk over and ask for some sugar.'

'I suppose it's not. But there are at least four pubs within walking distance.'

Still chatting they walked into the clubhouse and through to the restaurant.

'Good morning, Sir Nathan. Your usual table?'

'Yes please, Andre. Just coffee for us though.'

They followed the waiter to the table.

'I'll be right over with your coffees.'

'So, Jack, why all the interest in a bankrupt company?'

'First, what did they do?'

'Mostly prototype work, a bit of finishing off, and short production runs.'

'With fibreglass?'

'Yes, why?'

'Did they do work for your company?'

Greyspear's reply was interrupted by the delivery of their coffees.

'Thanks, Andre,' said Greyspear. 'We gave them a couple of

prototype jobs to do,' he shook his head slowly. 'It took for ever to get the parts from them, and their quality control was pretty dire. A real pity, I always like to support local businesses. In the end, we had to go elsewhere for future work.'

'And the directors?'

'I seem to remember originally it was a family affair. Company by the name of Perfection Mouldings. Started by two brothers sometime in the early fifties. The elder brother died as a result of injuries sustained in the war. The younger brother took over, but drank himself to death.'

'Is that where CSM comes in to the picture?'

'Not yet. Ownership of Perfection Mouldings was passed to a distant cousin.'

'What happened to it?'

'A man called Julian Denman, that's what happened. He inherited the company, and a substantial inheritance, with strings.'

'What kind of strings?'

'Julian Denman had to be gainfully employed continuously for five years, otherwise his substantial inheritance would go to another distant relative.'

'Do you know the name of the relative?'

'Sorry, don't know that.'

'How do you happen to know all about Denman?'

'He used to be a member of the club. When he drank too much, which was quite often, he'd unburden himself and tell anyone who was within earshot all about his problem.'

'What happened to him?'

'Not sure, we only dealt with the current owners.'

'You personally?'

'No, it would have been someone in our production department, probably Matt Hall, he's our production manager.'

'Do you have his number?'

'Call Susan at the office. She's in our harbour office this

morning, need the number?'

'No thanks, already have it in my phone. Oh, hang on, my phone's in the office, I've borrowed Jill's.'

'I'll write down the office number for you. Susan will put you in touch.'

'Thanks.'

'So, Jack, given any thought to my offer?'

'As a matter of fact, this morning I was just a phone call away from saying yes.'

'What stopped you?'

'The case I'm working on now.'

'Surely the force must have other detectives who could handle that? What about Jill? She seems to be a very competent investigator.'

'She's already assisting me on this case.'

'Well, if you change your mind, the door's always open.'

'Thanks, I'll print that on the insides of my eyelids.'

'Are you sure you don't have time for lunch?'

Buchanan shook his head and stood up. 'I'll give you a call. But in the meantime, I'm on the hunt for a killer.'

◆

Buchanan returned to his car, started the engine and put on the air-conditioning. Before he drove off he called Greyspear's PA, and of course now his wife.

'Susan, it's Jack.'

'Good afternoon, Jack. If you're looking for Nathan, he's at Castlewood.'

'Thanks, I've just had coffee with him. He said to call you, I'm after a name and phone number.'

'Whose phone number do you want?'

'I need to talk with your production manager.'

'That's Matt Hall – hang on a minute, I'll see where he is. Be right back.'

Buchanan listened as a lark ascended into the cool summer

air.

'Jack, he's in a production meeting in our Eastbourne office this morning.'

'Can I have the phone number?'

'I'll transfer you, hold on.'

The phone rang twice before being answered. 'Greyspear Yachts, how may I help?'

'Yes, it's Detective Chief Inspector Buchanan. Could I have a quick word with your production manager, Matt Hall?'

'Is it urgent? He's in a meeting.'

'Er, yes, I'm investigating an incident in a factory in Hampden Park.'

'Let me see if he can come to the phone.'

No music on hold this time.

'Inspector, Matt asks can he call you call back in ten minutes?'

'Yes, that's fine.'

'Can I have your number?'

Buchanan thought for a moment then realised he'd forgotten Street's mobile number. 'Call our switchboard, they'll track me down. It's 01273 475432.'

'Thanks, I'll make sure he calls you when he gets out of the meeting.'

Buchanan put the phone in the docking station and headed for Hammonds Drive. He got as far as the beginning of the Polegate bypass when Street's phone rang. He punched the answer button on his steering wheel. 'Buchanan.'

'Inspector, it's Matt Hall. You wanted me to call you?'

'Ah, yes. Need to ask you about CSM, do you have time?'

'CSM?'

'Crown Specialist Mouldings.'

'All I know about them is they did some work for us. Why are you asking?'

'Mr Hall, do you have a few minutes? I have a couple of

questions I need answers to.'

'Not quite, I'm heading to Paris for a meeting, really short on time.'

'Are you flying from Gatwick?'

'No, ferry from Dover.'

'What time are you leaving?'

'I'm in the car at the moment, just passing through Pevensey Bay.'

'Fancy a coffee?'

'Sorry?'

'I'm on the Polegate bypass Why don't we meet at the Starbucks on Bexhill Road? It's on the roundabout by the garage. I won't keep you long.'

'Know it, be with you shortly.'

Buchanan sat on a stool by the till, watching and waiting. Ten minutes later, Hall arrived and walked over to him.

'Inspector? Matt Hall. How can I help?'

'Want a coffee?'

'Yes, thanks. I'll have a medium Americano.'

Buchanan took his place in the line while Matt Hall grabbed two seats at an empty table.

'Hi, Jack, you want a refill?' asked the barista.

'Hi, Jade. Yes, and can I have a medium Americano as well, please?'

'Well, Inspector, what was it you wanted to ask me?' said Hall.

'Sugar?'

'No thanks.'

'Mr Hall, I was given your name by Sir Nathan this morning. He said you, being the production manager for Greyspear's, could tell me about CSM.'

'They went bust.'

'I know that, but do you know who was in charge when they went out of business?'

'Julian Denman. Never could figure out how a bankrupt person could still be in charge of a company. Not sure what he's doing now, or where he is.'

'Do you know what caused CSM to close?'

'I think they tried to diversify too much, it would have worked, but –'

'But?'

'Some of the guys who worked there told me that when Denman inherited Perfection Mouldings he inherited more than just the company. Like his uncle, he not only liked the bottle, but he also had a delectation for powdering his nose, if you know what I mean.'

'Cocaine. The downfall for many. How do you come to know all this?'

'I used to play squash at David Lloyds with one of the guys who worked at CSM. We'd usually go for a beer afterwards. You know what it's like after a few beers: *loose lips sink ships*, I think was one of the sayings during the Second World War.'

'And did he sink any ships?'

'Nothing directly, just the usual scuttlebutt about who's doing what, and what they shouldn't be.'

'So, nothing specific?'

'There was one story he told me, this was after the company closed, blamed its closing on Denman. At first I thought he was just pissed off about losing his job.'

'At first?'

Hall looked at his watch.

'You ok for time?' asked Buchanan.

'Not really, I should be on the road, but listen. The story was that one of the directors was on the take, fiddled expenses in a massive way. Used to take girlfriends on holiday and pretend he was on a business trip, that sort of thing.'

'I doubt if he's the first to do that.'

Hall shook his head. 'You need to talk to Jake, he'll tell you all about what went on.'

'Thank you, Mr Hall. Do you have a phone number for Jake?'

'Hang on, got it in my contacts on my phone, I'll text it to you.'

'Thanks, I'll get in touch with Jake. Any other incidents come to mind?'

'One of the sales reps for Hansons tried to offload a huge order for resin and catalyst on us that Denman had ordered but not paid for. A couple of weeks after CSM closed, I had a phone call from the rep offering it at almost fifty percent off the price.'

'Sounds like a deal, did you accept?'

'We're BS5750 approved.'

Hall saw confusion grow in Buchanan's face. 'It's the UK quality control standard. In Europe they call it EN2500. Our QA statement requires us to have a full audit trail for all materials. All the way back to their production. Besides, the resin we'd been offered was orthophthalic, we use isophthalic, so we couldn't have used it even if we'd wanted to.'

Buchanan shook his head at the technical information. 'What was his response when you said no?'

'Quite odd really, he was really desperate for me to take the offer. When I refused, he took another five percent off. At any minute, I expected him to get down on his knees and plead for me to take the stuff off his hands for free.'

'Oh, since we're talking about resin,' said Buchanan, taking his handkerchief out of his pocket and passing it to Hall, 'don't suppose you could tell me what kind of resin this might be? It's all right, I haven't blown my nose on it.'

Matt Hall passed it by his nose then screwed up his face in disgust.

'What's the matter?'

'Inspector, I have an MA in chemistry. This evil-looking stuff on your handkerchief is certainly not any resin I have ever come across. It reminds me of transformer oil, but it's mixed with something else. Where did you come across it?'

'In a barrel in the factory where CSM used to be. It's one amongst many.'

'I'm not trying to tell you your job, Inspector, but I'd get that oil tested. Transformer oil contains polychlorinated biphenyls, or PCB's for short, they're a carcinogen.'

'Stuff that causes cancer?'

'Yep. Sounds like someone is fly-tipping toxic waste.'

'That's possible. Though it could be the barrels are there waiting to be collected. CSM moved out quite quickly as I remember.'

'You really believe that?'

Buchanan shook his head.

'Me neither. You would be wise to contact the Environment Agency, they'll know what to do if someone has been fly-tipping toxic waste.'

'I'll do just that. Now what about the resin you were offered? Sounds like the salesman's job was on the line.'

'Tried to tell me no-one would be any the wiser. Even offered to refund part of the cost in cash.'

'A kick-back,' said Buchanan, shaking his head slowly.

'Yes, something Sir Nathan would never tolerate.'

'Do you remember the rep's name?'

'Prince, Clive Prince, company name was Hansons.'

'And you've told me all you know about Denman?'

'Afraid so, Inspector. Give Jake a call, he'd be only too happy to fill you in on all the dirt.'

'Thank you, Mr Hall, we'll be in touch if we have further questions.'

Hall downed the last of his coffee. 'Why are you asking about Denman?' he said, returning his empty cup to the table.

'We found a body in his former factory this morning.'

'And you think it's Denman?'

Buchanan stood up and stretched. 'We're still waiting for the results of the post-mortem and positive identification of the deceased.'

'Is there anything else, Inspector?'

'No, thanks, I'll be in touch if I have any further questions.'

◆

Buchanan walked slowly up the stairs and along the corridor to his office pondering about the identity of the body in the factory and the big *if*. If it was Denman, then who was the mystery benefactor?

'Ah, there you are, Jill. Have a look on the computer and see if the name Julian Denman's lurking somewhere in there.'

'How did you do at Castlewood?'

'Nothing solid. Anything?'

'There are three Denmans listed. One is a Janine, the next is an Alexandra, and the third is a Julian.'

'Is he local?'

'An address in Eastbourne.'

'Why's he in there?'

'Reported his car being vandalised.'

'That all?'

'It was a Ferrari, someone poured paint stripper all over the body. Basically, wrote the car off.'

'Anyone prosecuted?'

'No, though we have a name of an Antonia Formisano being questioned as a possible suspect.'

'Anything else?'

'The report states he was visiting Castlewood country club for dinner, and when he went to get his car he found that someone had poured paint stripper all over it.'

'Castlewood? Now that's interesting. I'll call the club and ask Nathan if he has any further information on the incident.'

'While you do that I'm off to Tesco's for a sandwich, I forgot to eat lunch. Want anything?'

Buchanan just shook his head.

◆

'What did he say?' asked Street, when she returned from Tesco's.

'Mr Denman was asked to leave after an unfortunate incident with one of the staff.'

'What was that?'

'He got over-friendly with one of the female staff.'

'Antonia?'

'The very same.'

'There's not much recorded about the incident,' said Street, as she scrolled through the records on the computer. 'Apparently, Antonia refused to press charges.'

'Why? Did she give a reason?'

'Nothing recorded. Do you think there could be a Mafia connection with our friend at the factory?'

'Why do you say that?'

Street shook her head. 'He was a user of cocaine, a bit of a womaniser, tried it on with Antonia, and you said yourself the death of the man in the factory was a message to someone.'

'Just because she has an Italian-sounding name doesn't make her part of some Italian Mafia vendetta, but – it just might be an interesting lead to follow.'

'I'll add that to my list,' Street said, shrugging.

'What about the directors? How many were there?'

Street consulted her notes. 'There were three: Daniel Jackson, James Baker, and a Paula Morelli. Could there be some sort of connection between Formisano and Morelli?'

Buchanan thought for a moment, then shook his head. 'Too coincidental, but worth following up. Do you have addresses for all the directors?'

'Only what Companies House have on file.'

'And they are?'

'Jackson's address is in Birmingham, Baker's is in Poole, and Morelli lives in Eastbourne out by Saffrons.'

'No information on Denman?'

'He's a struck-off director, bankrupted a previous business and is now barred from holding a directorship in any company. There's an address in Langney for him, probably just used as a postal address.'

'Yet Matt Hall said Denman ran the company in the absence of the other directors.'

'It does happen, unfortunately.'

'Are any of the directors in the phone book?'

'Yes, Baker's number is not in service, Jackson's forwards to a number in Glasgow.'

'And nothing on Denman?'

Street shook her head.

'What about Morelli?'

'Morelli has a call blocker in operation. Unless your number has been registered, the call goes to an answering service.'

'Can I have the number?'

'They're back, by the way,' said Street, as she passed Buchanan the phone number written on a piece of paper

'Who's back?' he said, picking up his phone.

'The ACC and the crime commissioner.'

'Where are they?'

'They drove into the car park as I returned with my sandwich.'

Buchanan put down the phone and massaged his chin.

'Are you all right?'

'Hmm – yes, probably nothing. She'll be just showing him around the station.'

He picked up the phone again and dialled the number written on the slip of paper, letting it ring till the answering service responded. 'Yes, this is Detective Chief Inspector Buchanan of Sussex CID. I would like to talk to Paula Morelli – yes, I realise that, but this is police business – thank you.'

'Can they help?' asked Street, as Buchanan hung up.

'They'll contact her and let her know I wish to speak to her.'

'We could always go visit her. We have her address, and we'd be out of the way of you know who.'

'What? Ah yes, what a wonderful idea! Let's go.'

♦

'Where are we going?' asked Buchanan, as they drove along King Edwards Parade.

'The address on file with Companies House says she lives in a fifth floor flat on Blackwater Road.'

'Which flat?'

'Didn't give a number. Turn right up ahead, onto Carlisle Road.'

'That takes us past the Winter Garden and the Congress Theatre?'

'Yup. As you pass the Winter Garden take the first right past the tennis club. At the next junction turn left onto Blackwater. Morelli's flat is on the right at the end.'

'You ever been?'

'Been where?'

'The tennis tournament.'

'Once – managed to get tickets to the 2012 ladies' finals.'

'Enjoy it?'

Street let out her breath and said, while shaking her head slowly, 'These women are real athletes, how they manage to keep going beats me.'

'Who was playing?'

'Finals were between Tamira Paszek and Angelique Kerber.'

'Who won?'

'Tamira Paszek. Great contest.'

'You play?'

Street shook her head. 'A bit, but nothing like the professionals. This is Blackwater, turn here.'

'I used to play badminton,' said Buchanan, as they parked in front of a five-story block of flats.

'Ever try squash?'

Buchanan smiled. 'With this body? You must be kidding.'

'Do you good.'

'I'll think about that.'

♦

The entrance to the flats was secured by a magnetic door lock which could only be opened with a key code or by buzzing one of the tenants with a call button.

Street looked at the buzzer panel for Morelli.

'See her?' asked Buchanan.

Street shook her head. 'No Morellis live here.'

'Let me have a look,' said Buchanan, bending down to look at the list of names beside the call buttons.

'Fifth floor it said?'

'Yes.'

'Right, shouldn't be difficult to find the correct one. Let's start with Flat 1.'

Buchanan pushed the buzzer and waited. When he got no answer on the sixth ring, he pressed the button for Flat 2, with the same result.

Flat 3 answered after two rings. 'Max, is that you?'

'No, sorry, it's Detective Inspector Buchanan, Sussex CID. I'm looking for Mrs Morelli. Can you tell me which flat she lives in?'

'Flat 1. Not sure if they are in at the moment; they're very quiet neighbours.'

'And you are?'

'Angela Dickson.'

'Thanks, Angela. I'll try Flat 1 again.'

He pressed the button for Flat 1 again and waited. This time it answered.

'Hello.'

'Good afternoon, this is Inspector Buchanan of Sussex CID. I'm looking for a Paula Morelli.'

'Ah yes, Inspector, the answering service said you'd called. I was going to call you, you needn't have come all this way to ask your questions.'

'Since we're here, can we come up and ask you the couple of questions, please?'

'Just a minute.' The door lock buzzed. 'Take the lift to the fifth floor. My husband will let you in the front door, he will want to see your warrant card.'

'Careful ones, aren't they?' said Buchanan, as the lift creaked and wheezed its way up to the fifth floor.

'These flats require a healthy bank balance to purchase. They're just being careful to make sure we are who we say we are.'

'Wise, or could it be for another reason?'

'Now who's talking conspiracy theory?'

Buchanan shrugged. 'Just pondering.'

The lift jerked to a halt and he pushed the door open.

'Flat 1, there it is,' said Buchanan, walking over and pressing the doorbell.

The door opened and stopped, held by a strong security chain.

An aged and tanned male face peered between the door and the doorjamb. 'Inspector Buchanan?'

'Yes,' replied Buchanan, holding up his warrant card. 'And this is Detective Sergeant Street. Can we come in for a moment? We won't keep you long.'

The door closed, followed by the sound of the chain being taken off its latch. It then opened fully to reveal a tall, fit, wiry-looking man who looked to be in his early sixties.

'Come in, please.'

'Mr Morelli?' asked Buchanan.

'Yes. If you'll follow me I'll take you through to the sitting room, my wife's waiting in there.'

Buchanan and Street followed Mr Morelli down the corridor and into the sitting room.

'It's the policeman, dear.'

'You're not what I expected, Inspector.'

'I rarely am, Mrs Morelli.'

'You said you wanted to ask us some questions?'

'Were you a director of CSM?'

'I still am, till it's wound up.'

'So, the company still exists?'

'In name only.'

'Can you tell me anything about the other directors?'

'You said you're a policeman?'

'Yes.'

'And you are not with HM Revenue Department?'

'Mrs Morelli, we are investigating a death in the factory where CSM used to be situated, that's all.'

'There were three of us: myself, James Baker, and Daniel Jackson.'

'Julian Denman, where did he fit in?'

'He wasn't a director.'

'What was his position in the company?'

'Prior to CSM there was a company called Perfection Mouldings.'

'What happened to it?'

'Julian Denman ran it into the ground, took out more than the company could earn.'

'Why was he working for CSM?'

'He came with the leftovers of Perfection Mouldings when CSM purchased the company. We didn't know about his nefarious activities till it was too late and we couldn't get rid of him.'

'You owned CSM?'

'My husband and I did. It was a family business till we

purchased Perfection Mouldings.'

'You, Mrs Morelli, are listed as a director, but not you, Mr Morelli. Could you explain that, please?'

'Our family came to England in 1958,' said Mr Morelli. 'My grandfather had passed away and the family thought it would be a good idea to resettle in England and make a fresh start. No special reason for it being just my wife who is a director.'

'The family, Mr Morelli, how many of you were there?'

'As well as myself, there were my wife, my sister and my mother.'

'Is your mother still alive?'

'Oh yes, she's just celebrated her eightieth birthday.'

'And the company, did you start that when you arrived in England?'

Mr Morelli nodded. 'In Italy, we had a small family business. My grandfather had started a small delivery company which, with careful management and his keen eye for business opportunities, grew to where we employed a team of twenty drivers. As if paying protection to the Mafia wasn't enough, my grandfather also had to contend with the rise in Fascism, followed by the Nazis. When the Americans landed in Sicily he thought the struggle was over, peace was at hand, but it wasn't to be for him. As the US army was making its way west, my grandfather suffered a massive heart attack and died.'

'How awful,' said Street.

'Yes, my mother was devastated. After the war ended, she tried to keep the business going but after ten years of struggling she finally decided it was time for a new start.'

'Is that when you decided to come over to England?"

'I couldn't see my mother struggle any more with the memories. I thought a move to England would get us away from all the causes of the great sadness that had descended on us.'

'I understand. What were some of the nefarious activities of

Mr Denman, Mr Morelli?'

'Made out it was he, and he alone, who kept Perfection going. Said it was his contacts that brought in the work. Turned out it was loyalty to the former brothers who started the company that kept the remaining customers loyal.'

'That doesn't sound nefarious.'

'Let me tell you about a little scam Denman tried a couple of times. He would make out that an item that was supposed to be delivered by noon hadn't been sent, so he'd order a taxi to deliver it.'

'I suppose in these time-conscious days that sort of thing's bound to happen.'

'Inspector, there never was a delayed delivery. He'd make up a package filled with old crumpled newspapers, head to the accounts department and make out an expense claim for hundreds, then collect the cash to cover the long-distance taxi fare. He'd insist that he meet the driver by the front door and hand over the cash.

'That's bizarre,' said Street.

'In exchange,' continued Mr Morelli, 'he'd be given an envelope containing his weekly supply of cocaine. As soon as we realised what he was up to we made sure we called the customer to ascertain if the item was really required, or had even been ordered in the first place.'

'Surely that wouldn't bankrupt a company?' pondered Street.

'There was a new scam after the taxi one was stopped,' said Mrs Morelli. 'In this he employed one of his friends as a quality control inspector. Some expert he was. An out of work taxi driver. This person just happened to be one of the local dealers. Denman put him on a huge salary and said his work would be out of the office most of the time checking on product installation. Of course, he never actually went to any customers unless Denman went with him as an excuse to have a few days out of the office on expenses.'

'Was that all he got up to?'

'No, unfortunately. Last year he had one of the installation crews over at his house.'

'Being friendly?'

'They were redecorating it – with company materials. – and he told the office they were on-site working.'

'How did you find out?'

'The customer called the office and wanted to know when their job would be finished,' said Mr Morelli. 'As part of the takeover proceedings we had to take him on, and at his previous salary, and give him shares in the company.'

'Do you know where the other former directors are living, Mr Morelli?'

'The last I heard of James Baker was he'd gone off to run a salmon farm in Scotland. Daniel Jackson went back to nature and inherited his uncle's bespoke furniture company in Lancashire, it specialises in handmade oak interiors.'

'And Julian Denman?'

'Nothing, I've no idea where he went.'

'Company records show him living in Eastbourne.'

'It's a free country, I suppose he's entitled to live where he may,' said Mrs Morelli.

Buchanan turned back to Mr Morelli. 'Mr Morelli, do you happen to know the whereabouts of Mr Denman?'

He shook his head slowly. 'Inspector, except on occasional company functions, I know nothing of Mr Denman's whereabouts.'

'When was the last time you saw him, Mr Morelli?'

His eyes darted to his wife then back to Buchanan. 'I don't remember.'

'Mr Morelli, does the name Antonia Formisano mean anything to you – or your wife?'

Once again Morelli's eyes darted to his wife, except this time they remained on her.

'Inspector, Antonia is our daughter,' she said.

'Do you know where she is just now?'

'In Italy – she lives there with her husband and our grandchildren.'

'How long has she lived there, Mrs Morelli?'

'Two years.'

'About two years ago, there was an incident at Castlewood country club concerning your daughter and Julian Denman.'

'Antonia had nothing to do with that, Inspector,' said Mr Morelli.

'Nothing?'

'She was in Italy when the incident with his car happened.'

'It's not the incident with the car that I'm primarily interested in, Mr Morelli. Did your daughter and Julian Denman have a relationship?'

He laughed. 'You think she would have a relationship with that creep? On more than one occasion he made a nuisance of himself, but she always managed to fight him off.'

'Why wasn't it reported?'

'Antonia refused to make a fuss. She was going back to Italy to get married and didn't want to get involved.'

'Someone did report an incident though, said they heard a girl shouting and screaming obscenities. Was that Antonia?'

Morelli shrugged. 'It's a wicked world, Inspector.'

'The police report of that night said the grounds were searched but nothing was found. Did Denman attack Antonia?'

'Inspector, as far as we are concerned, nothing happened. It was all a misunderstanding.'

'And Antonia is still in Italy?'

'I spoke with her last night,' said Mrs Morelli.

'And neither of you know the whereabouts of Julian Denman?'

'No, Inspector, we have no idea where he is, nor do we care,' said Mr Morelli.

'Could you describe him for us, please?'

Mrs Morelli looked up at her husband. He nodded.

'Julian Denman is tall, just about 1.8 metres and overweight for his size. Caucasian, that's what you call them?'

'Go on, Mrs Morelli, please.'

'I'd say he would weigh about ninety kilos, face looked like he had high blood pressure and he has grey, curly hair.'

Street looked at Buchanan; he shook his head.

'Is he dead, Inspector? Is that why you're here?' asked Mrs Morelli, a smile growing on her face.

'Do you know if he had any relatives, Mrs Morelli?'

They both shook their heads.

'Thank you for your co-operation, Mr and Mrs Morelli. We'll be in touch if we have further questions.'

As the lift creaked its way down to the lobby, Street asked, 'Do you think the body is Denman?'

'Let's see what Dr Mansell has to say.'

♦

There was another note on Buchanan's desk when they returned. This time he had been summoned to a meeting with the crime commissioner, in his office.

'What does the note say?' asked Street.

'Was looking forward to meeting you, call my secretary and make an appointment for one-day next week.'

'Well, at least he sounds friendly.'

'Softly, softly, catchee monkey, more likely.'

'You're too suspicious, he just wants to get to know you.'

'More likely wants to explain the benefits of retirement.'

'Why would they want to get rid of you? You're too valuable, with all your experience.'

'Bottom line, it's all about money, and besides you do a damn good job at sergeant's rank. Why pay me when they can get someone like you for a lot less?'

'How can you compare my few years in the force to your

lifetime of investigating? I'm just a babe compared to you.'

'And that makes me a grandpa?'

'Now you're making fun of me.'

'Sorry, Jill, got a bit carried away.'

'Oh, your phone is charged, it's on your desk.'

'Thanks,' said Buchanan, passing her phone back.

'Seriously though, how can the police disregard the experiences of senior officers and just throw them out as though they were yesterday's rubbish?'

'It's not quite that bad, some are retained for training, others come back as consultants, and there was talk of setting up a team of retired senior officers to investigate cases that are outside the scope of regular policing.'

'How about consulting?'

Buchanan thought about Sir Nathan's offer to run his security firm.

'Or you could just go private, be a consulting detective.'

'You mean deerstalker and pipe stuff?' said Buchanan.

'No, not quite what I meant, besides, Sherlock Holmes wasn't married. What I mean is you could start your own investigating business, find crooks in the corporate world.'

Buchanan shook his head. 'It's not that simple. I had a friend in Glasgow who was coming up for thirty years' service. He quit his job as a DI and went to work for a private security company. He told me later it was the steepest learning curve he'd ever experienced.'

'Why?'

'Main reason he gave was that as a DI he had a boss and people working under him who he could delegate investigating and secretarial work to. Also, having someone senior to report to freed him from worrying about carrying the can if things went wrong. In private security, you do it all. No, Jill, a cop I stay, at least till this case is resolved.'

'So, what next with this case?'

'We could do with a name and a cause of death.'

'Thought asphyxia was the likely cause?'

'Yes, it probably is. We know the what, and can guess at the when, but we still need to know the how and – most importantly – the why.'

'I still wonder if there's a Mafia connection somewhere.'

'I'm listening.'

'What I'm getting at is, suppose Denman actually raped Antonia? In some families that's an attack on the family honour worthy of castration at the least. Papa then talks with some friends back home.

'How would they know about the factory and how to find their way around the interior?'

'You have a point there, but – suppose it is Denman, and suppose the family decided he needed to be taught a lesson?'

'Go on.'

'Papa makes a call back home to the family, discusses the situation, says enough time has passed and with the business going bust, Denman becomes *persona non-grata*. Then Friday night, probably just as he is getting ready to go to bed, Denman gets a knock at the door. He opens it to find two gentlemen suitably suited, wearing dark glasses and Frank Sinatra hats. They invite him to go for a quiet drink with them,' suggested Street.

'He wouldn't just go with two total strangers, would he?'

'He would if they persuaded him with some sort of get rich quick scheme. Then, when he wasn't watching, one of his visitors would put something in his drink.'

'As a script for a TV show it might work,' said Buchanan. 'Though a couple of years ago, I was at a conference about personal protection. One of the speakers told us about a case of a foreign diplomat being simply grabbed in a busy restaurant without anybody realising what was going on.'

'How was it done?'

'One of the kidnappers walked past the table where the victim was eating and engaged him in some trivial conversation, while the other kidnapper dropped Rohipnal in his drink. The rest was easy. They suggested a walk, and out the door they went, hand in hand.'

'But how would the kidnappers know there just happened to be a drum of usable resin available?'

'Do you have that print-out form with the ins and outs of the factory?'

'Yes, here,' said Street, handing the report to Buchanan.

'Hmm, not what I was looking for.'

'What were you looking for?'

'Signs of entry during the prior few days. Last entry was three weeks ago, and that was nine in the morning.'

'Hang on a minute,' said Street, shuffling through some papers on her desk. 'Ah, thought so. What was the date of the entry?'

'The twenty-first of May.'

'That was the day of the auction for all the workshop and office equipment.'

'So, the building would have been open to anyone who wanted to have a nose around?'

'Not quite, the auction was an invitation-only event, and it took place in the car park under a tent. From what I can determine, nobody went inside the building.'

'Have a look – there should be a list of those who attended?'

Street smiled. 'I'll add that to my list. Wait a minute – you said that Matt Hall told you the resin supplier had tried to offload a huge consignment of resin but was turned down?'

'Yes, something about it being the wrong kind of resin.'

'Suppose the sales rep had a hand in the killing? Revenge for being screwed out of a sale.'

'Unlikely, Jill, but worth following up. Too late now, but as part of your to-do list call Matt Hall at Greyspear Yachts and see if he has a phone number of the rep and or the company he worked for.'

'Won't there be something like a delivery note on the drum in the factory?'

'Hang on, I took some photos of the crime scene on my phone.'

'You mean my phone?'

'So I did.'

Street turned on her phone, swiped to the photo section and looked at the photos Buchanan had taken of the scene. 'Nothing helpful as far as the drum of resin goes. I'll get on to Matt Hall in the morning.'

'He may not be in the office; told me he was off to Paris for a meeting.'

'I'll still call, at least I can leave a message.'

'Do you realise what we're doing?'

'Yes. We're assuming the body found in the factory is that of Julian Denman.' Street looked at her watch. 'Is it really six-thirty? No wonder I'm hungry. You eating alone this evening?'

'Yeah, probably catch up on paperwork while I'm eating.'

'Where is Karen, or shouldn't I ask?'

'She's with her mother, again.'

'How long's the visit this time?'

'How long's a piece of string? One minute her mother is at death's door, yet as soon as Karen shows up, she's as right as rain.'

'Want company?'

'Won't you be having dinner with Stephen?'

'Not this evening. He phoned to say they've gone to look at a car in Brighton.'

'They?'

'Yes, he and Morris.'

'Thought Morris was a family man, home by teatime and the kids in bed by seven o'clock?'

'It's Morris's cousin that's selling the car.'

'Oh. What is it?'

'No idea, probably something with racing stripes and a noisy exhaust.'

'Stephen'll get over it, give him time.'

'Maybe. So, what do you fancy for dinner?'

Buchanan shrugged. 'You choose.'

'How about that Scottish takeaway we had when we started on the body in the marina case? I seem to remember we did some good thinking that night.'

'It will be like old times.'

'Old times? Seems like it was only a few months ago. Doesn't matter though, I'm still hungry.'

'Chicken tikka masala it will be, and I'm paying – at least I still have an expense account I can use.' Buchanan sat drumming his fingers on the desk while waiting for his call to Jasmine Gardens to be answered.

'Shall I pop over to Tesco's and get something for us to drink with dinner?'

Buchanan grinned. 'End of the aisle where the water is, you'll find little bottles of St Omer beer. Hang on, I've got a fiver somewhere.'

Street smiled and said, 'What, no whiskey chaser?'

Buchanan shook his head. 'Can you imagine what the top brass would say if they made a surprise visit and saw a glass of whiskey on my desk? No, I'll stick to a couple of small beers with my dinner.'

♦

While Street drove over to Tesco's, Buchanan called Mansell.

'You still working, Buchanan? Thought you lot went home at five for tea.'

'That'll be the day. How are you getting on with our plastic friend?'

'Trimming the plywood reminded me of the time I helped

my aunt cut out dressmaking patterns.'

'With a saw?'

'No, Buchanan, we used scissors for that. This time I borrowed an electric jig-saw. Removing the fibreglass from the clothed body wasn't the issue, took quite a bit of gentle prying and easing it off the bare skin though. Couldn't do much with the hair, he's now nearly bald, but did manage to get the resin of off his face and hands.'

'Prints?'

'Near perfect set, I've sent them off to see if they match any of our known friends. I asked for the results to be emailed to you. You are still on the system?'

'Cheeky.'

'I did a DNA swab, sent that off as well, but don't hold your breath for immediate results, they said everyone has to wait their turn.'

'What about the prints? You did tell them it's a murder inquiry?'

'You could try giving them a call; maybe you could be more persuasive than me, a mere doctor.'

'I might just do that. In the meantime – cause of death? In layman's terms, if you don't mind?'

'Asphyxiation, by polyester and glass embalming.'

'Bet you've never put that in a report before.'

'No, I certainly haven't. What's for dinner?'

'Chicken tikka, why?'

'Need company of breathing adults, been around too many cadavers today. I'll get myself a pizza – got anything to drink?'

'Jill's getting some beers.'

'Fine, be with you in about twenty.'

♦

'What did Doctor Mansell say about the cause of death?' asked Street, as she watched Buchanan guzzle down a beer, reach under his desk and put the drained bottle in the empty Tesco bag.

'You can ask him yourself, he's joining us for dinner.'

'Did you order enough to share?'

'He's bringing a pizza.'

'Really? Didn't think he'd be a fussy eater. Oh, did he say much about the corpse?'

'Just that he'd had a difficult time removing the fibreglass. I imagine he'll want to tell us how difficult it was and how clever he'd been at getting the stuff off.'

'What's the house like?'

Buchanan shook his head slowly. 'Oh, you mean the one Karen liked?'

'Is there more than one?'

Buchanan smiled. 'No, there's only one. She fell in love with it at first sight.'

'How many bedrooms?'

Three upstairs, two with en-suites. Downstairs there's a large family room, separate dining room that has an opening through into a very large kitchen, and off the dining room there is a conservatory.'

'Garden?'

'Yes, there's a very nice garden, and a double car garage.'

'Sounds expensive.'

'Hmm, it is. We're still hoping to keep the house in Glasgow and rent it out.'

'Makes sense, that should keep the monthly payments down.'

'We've a meeting with a financial advisor later this week to see if there's a way to rent the house in Glasgow and still afford a mortgage on the one in Eastbourne.'

The discussion on houses was interrupted by Buchanan's phone ringing. He picked up the receiver. 'Buchanan. It is? Great, I'll be right down for it.'

'Dinner?' said Street.

Buchanan nodded. 'Be right back.'

He returned a few minutes later with their dinner and accompanied by Doctor Mansell.

'Hello, Jill. You're eating that stuff too?'

Street smiled. 'It's really tasty, Doctor. Want to try some?'

'No thanks, I'll stick to my pizza.'

'Well, Doctor,' said Buchanan, downing the last of his fourth beer, 'how did you manage to get the fibreglass off the corpse?'

'I treated it as a cast.'

'Like when someone has broken an arm and the doctor wraps it in a lightweight fibreglass cast?' said Street.

'Very similar, though the fibreglass used in casts is a much thinner layer, and has bandages to keep the cast away from the skin.'

'So how did you get the fibreglass off?'

'I started with the clothes, used a vibrating cast-saw and shears.'

'Is that part of your regular mortuary kit?'

'No. I borrowed them from the fracture clinic. They weren't very happy with me; they complained I'd used up a year's supply of blades. They're a real bunch of pillocks.'

'Who are?'

'Hospital management, bitching over a few saw blades. Yet when it comes to their salaries and expenses, it's an open cheque book. I just wish the government would sort out NHS funding.'

'What would you do – if you were in charge?' said Street.

'What would I do?' said Mansell, taking in a deep breath and swallowing the remainder of his third beer, 'I'll tell you what I'd do. I'd split the funding stream. Healthcare provision would get one hundred percent, while healthcare management would be given what was left of the budget and told to just get on with it.'

'They wouldn't like that,' said Buchanan.

'They'd get over it. They'd have to if they wanted to keep their cushy jobs.'

'Didn't take you for a rebel.'

'I'm not, I'm just fed-up to the back teeth with the government trying to privatise the NHS by the back door.'

'Is that what you think?' said Street.

'Look, let's not get into the funding issue, I have to live with it every day.'

Buchanan smiled. 'Something we have in common, Doctor.'

Mansell frowned 'What do you mean?'

'You have budget restrictions; we have job position restrictions. Promotion is almost non-existent. In fact, the MET in London are doing away with my rank and that of commander by 2018. What does that say to new recruits about their chance of rising through the ranks?'

'Shall we change the subject? I'm getting indigestion.'

'I'm all for that, Doctor. What about the hands and head of the corpse?'

'Ah yes, now that was a challenge. For the back of the head, using the cast saw, I cut the fibreglass in strips about twenty-five millimetres wide. I then reached in with a pair of curved-bladed surgical scissors and cut the hair away from the fibreglass – probably the weirdest short back and sides ever given.'

'What about the skin?'

'That was a lot more difficult. This time I used a veterinary bone-saw to cut the fibreglass in twelve-millimetre-wide strips; it has a small fine blade and has a very short stroke. Finally, using a bamboo chopstick whittled down to a blunt chisel point, I gently pried the fibreglass away from the hands and face. Thankfully he'd instinctively closed his eyes, so I didn't need to remove resin from the eyeballs.'

'Yuck, that's not something I'd like to think about,' said Street.

'Nor I,' continued Mansell. 'He'd been sweating profusely, so by the time his face was covered, the sweat acted as a form of mould release. I think that was what caused the elevated level of styrene in his blood. Also the sweat helped to keep the skin relatively free from the fibreglass. Thankfully I didn't need to use any chemicals'

'Why was that?' asked Street.

'Polyester resin when cured is almost impossible to dissolve; the best that can be achieved is to soften it a bit. I took a photo of his face, so you could use it to identify him,' said Mansell handing Buchanan an A4 photo of the dead man.

'Looks like he tried to shave in the dark with a blunt razor,' said Street. 'Do you have a digital copy? I could load it into my computer and make him look a bit more alive, using photo software.'

'Sure, give me your email address and I'll send it over.'

'What about the blood test, anything of interest?' asked Buchanan.

'Just the usual suspects.'

'And they are?'

'He'd been drinking; his blood alcohol level was 75.'

'Not too drunk to drive then?'

'No, but the high level of cocaine would have precluded that. There was also a high level of styrene in the blood, probably from breathing in the fumes as the fibreglass was applied.'

'What a way to go.'

'It's possible he was partially aware.'

'Why do you say that?' said Street.

'I also tested a sample of his urine, and along with traces of alcohol and styrene, I found a trace of GHB.'

'The date rape drug?' said Buchanan.

'Yes. It's just one of a group of drugs favoured by young adult partygoers. It purports to create a feeling of euphoria and increase an individual's sex drive. But unfortunately, three of its side effects are that it causes severe sweating, a loss of awareness of one's surroundings, and sometimes it leads to unconsciousness.'

'So, the dead man would have been easy to get out of his

house, bar, or wherever he was at the time, into the van, and finally to the factory?' said Street.

'As I said, I believe he was at least partially aware of what was going on.'

'How can you tell?' asked Street.

'When our bodies have a fright, or get excited over some danger, our adrenal glands release adrenalin into the blood stream. This causes the heart rate to increase, with increased levels of oxygen in the blood. Your eyes dilate, and you sweat, somewhat profusely. It's all part of the body's flight or fight mechanism.'

'So, what are you telling us about our dead man?' asked Street.

'With the traces of GHB, elevated adrenalin levels, and styrene in his blood, I'd say he was quite aware of his surroundings as he gulped in his final breaths. At least enough to know what was about to happen to him. But probably not aware of how he got into his situation.'

'Find anything in his pockets, Doctor?' asked Buchanan.

'Nothing that could identify him directly, I've bagged and labelled them for you,' he said handing over an evidence bag.'

Buchanan took a pair of evidence gloves out of his desk drawer and opened the bag. 'No wallet, keys or phone. Just forty-five pounds in notes and some loose change and a receipt for two drinks at the Polygon Bar.'

'A bit expensive,' said Street, looking at the receipt.

'Do you know where the Polygon Bar is, Jill?' asked Buchanan.

'There's a lane that runs between Station Road and Mark Lane, actually it's more of a car park than a lane. The bar is somewhere in the middle, painted light green with a rainbow stretching from one end to the other. There's a garish neon sign over the door. I think it just opened a month ago.'

'Fancy going for a cocktail, Doc?' said Buchanan.

'No thanks, I'll stick to my Harvey's.'

'Suit yourself. Jill, how quickly can you get the photo of the dead man enhanced?'

'Just need the doctor to send it over, shouldn't take more than an hour.'

◆

At ten to nine in the evening there wasn't any difficulty in finding a place to park. Ignoring the private parking sign, Buchanan pulled into a spare slot across from the Polygon's front door Street followed Buchanan into the bar. They waited on the small landing as their eyes became accustomed to the dimly-lit interior.

The inside was decorated with a Polynesian theme. There were strings of plastic flowers hanging from the ceiling in great colourful loops and multi-coloured lampshades spread a dim, multi-coloured glow on the tables. Interspersed with the lamps, staring quizzically down at the patrons, were an assortment of stuffed parrots perched on plastic branches. The ambience of the bar was struggling with the bland dance music belting out over the ceiling speakers. A young woman, obviously enjoying the music, was busy behind the bar taking glasses out of the dishwasher and placing them on the overhead glass shelves.

Eyes accustomed to the gloom, Buchanan and Street walked down a short set of stairs and over to the bar. In the middle of the shelf on the rear wall was a huge stuffed parrot hanging upside down.

'What' do you think is the meaning of the parrot hanging upside down?' said Buchanan.

'It's a dead parrot, a *polly-gone*,' said Street. 'Get it?'

'Very funny. – Excuse me,' Buchanan said to the bartender.

The young girl stopped arranging the glasses and said, 'You're excused. We're not open till nine, come back then if you want a drink.'

'Detective Chief Inspector Buchanan and Detective Sergeant

Street, we're here on business,' said Buchanan, showing his warrant card. 'And your name is?'

'Carly, Carly Fiorina.'

'Were you working last Friday night, Carly?'

'Yes'.

'Do you recognise this person?' asked Street, showing Carly the photo of the dead man.

'We get lots of people in here.'

'How about this one?' asked Buchanan.

'Might have done, it was very busy.'

'Tell me how you ring up an order for drinks on the till?' said Buchanan.

Carly looked at him with a puzzled look.

'I order a drink, you pour it, what happens next?'

'I tap my fob on the till, enter the amount and the money tendered. The cash drawer opens and I give you your change.'

'And receipt?'

'Yes, but most times the customers just leave it laying on the bar.'

'Does the receipt show who served the drink?'

'Yes, that happens when we fob in.'

'Can you tell me who served these drinks last Friday night?' said Buchanan, showing Carly the receipt in the evidence bag.'

She looked at it and said, 'I don't know. The receipt doesn't have a name, it's our employee number that gets printed. You'll have to ask the manager.'

'And where is the manager?'

'She won't be in till about ten. It's Monday night, one of our quiet nights.'

Buchanan looked at his watch, then to Street. 'Heard from Stephen yet?'

'No, why?'

'Fancy a drink? I'm buying.'

'I said we don't open till nine,' said Carly.

'We'll wait,' said Buchanan.

'I'll give Stephen a call,' said Street, 'see how he's doing.'

She took out her phone, scrolled through the directory, then tapped the screen. The sound of the ringing could barely be heard over the music. 'Stephen, it's Jill – I'm with Jack. No, we're still working on a case. How are you getting on? Bought the car? Good, will you drive it home tonight? Be careful. You can use my driveway if you want, Natalie's away with her boyfriend so there's space. I'll park on the road –yes, bye, love you.'

'Well, what did he say?'

'He's bought the car and will drive it home tonight. I said he could park it in my driveway, his flat has no parking spaces. Morris will follow in his car and be available to help should anything go wrong.'

Buchanan turned to Carly, made a gesture of looking at his watch, and said, 'Goodness me, it's five-past nine. I think I'd like a drink, what about you, Jill?'

She smiled. 'Diet Coke, please, with ice.'

'Make that two, Carly, and I'll have the receipt, please.'

Carly pressed a button on the till, then passed the receipt to Buchanan.

'Now what do you think of that, Carly? This receipt for our drinks has the same employee code printed on it as the one I have here in the evidence bag.'

Carly shrugged. 'So, I served the drinks.'

'And you don't remember to whom you served them?'

'Like I said, we're a very busy bar. I can't be expected to remember every customer by sight.'

'Do you have door staff in the evening?'

'Yes, they start at ten.'

'Always the same people?'

'Most nights.'

'Will tonight's door staff be the same as last Friday night's?'

She shrugged. 'No idea. I've got other customers to serve.' She turned away from Buchanan and served the leggy bleached-blonde who'd just sidled up to the bar.

Buchanan and Street took their drinks and walked over to a table beside the far wall where they could keep an eye on the door.

'What do you think, Jill?' said Buchanan.

'She was being quite unhelpful, evasive even, and – she has an Italian surname.'

'You still think that is a link?'

'You remember the last case we worked on together?'

'Yes, the bodies in the marina, why?'

'One of us said that case had similarities to one of Agatha Christie's novels –'

'*The ABC Murders?*'

'That's the one. I got curious about that story and read it, and quite a few since.'

'That's nice; I prefer Chandler or Kellerman for late night reading.'

'Well, this case we are working on reminds me of the Agatha Christie story *Murder on the Orient Express.*'

'I've seen the movie, movies actually, thought Suchet's version the best. '

'Well, don't you see the similarities?'

'Not really. Explain.'

'Denman rapes Antonia, the family seeks revenge, a sort of restoration of the family honour.'

'Go on.'

'Well, the family decide to let time pass, put Denman off his guard. Then, out of the blue he's here in the bar and runs into Antonia, and yes, I realise her mother said Antonia is happily married and living in Italy. But for the sake of argument, let's assume Antonia was in the country last Friday night, in this bar even. She says something to Denman, like she's forgiven him, changed her mind about him. Would like to have a drink with him and put the past to rest.'

'You are still assuming the dead man was Denman.'

'I know, but keep with me on this. Denman offers to buy the drinks, and when he's not watching, Antonia slips the GHB into his drink.'

'And how does she get him to the factory?'

'The resin man, bet he's got a white van.'

'And why would he help?'

'Loss of business. Remember the story in the Orient Express – everyone in the carriage had an axe to grind and was related to each other in one way or another.'

'Quite a list of characters, far more than we have in our case.'

Street shrugged. 'That may be, but doesn't alter my thoughts.'

'Ok, go on with your theory.'

'Well, with Denman probably sexually fired up, he thinks he and Antonia are going to go a second round. He probably assumes that resin man is a taxi driver ordered by Antonia to take them to her flat.'

'That's plausible.'

'But instead of going to her flat, they drive to the factory and do Denman in.'

'And who let them in the factory, turned on the power and turned off the alarm system? Also, who nailed him to the wall? And let's not forget someone had to operate the chopper gun?'

'I don't know, maybe resin man helped alarm man and between them they got Denman into the building and nailed him to the wall. Maybe resin man operated the chopper gun.'

'As a thesis on a murder, it could work. But we still don't even know if it was Denman who was murdered.'

'We should tomorrow, that is if the fingerprint and DNA results are back.'

'True, but in the meantime, let's have a word with the door staff.'

Buchanan and Street climbed the stairs up to the landing beside the front door and waited while the two doormen checked the ID's of the incoming guests.

'Excuse me, Carlos, Oskar,' said Buchanan, looking at both doormen's ID's. 'DCI Buchanan and DS Street. We're wondering if either of you saw this person in here last Friday night?'

Oskar shook his head. 'Didn't see him last Friday night – Carlos?' He handed the photo to his partner.

'Yeah, he was here, came in when you were in the can, Oskar. Friday night is his regular night, Inspector.'

'Only Friday?' asked Street.

'He's banned from here on weekends,' said Oskar.

'Why?'

'Can't keep his hands off the young ladies, makes a right nuisance of himself. Has to settle for the older ones.'

'Was he with anyone last Friday night, Oskar?'

'Not when he came in.'

'How about one of the older ones, did he pick any of them up?'

'No, and that's the odd bit.'

'What do you mean?' said Street.

'Most of the Friday night ladies are older, usually single, looking for a bit of company, and are not too particular with who they go home.'

'And last Friday night?'

'He left with a looker.'

'Did you say hooker?'

'No, I said looker. What I mean is, he's a bit scruffy, she looked like one of those models you see on television advertising expensive Italian sports cars.'

'Can you describe her for us?'

'Tall, about your height, Sergeant, slim build and she had long dark hair. She looked European. I think her eyes were brown.'

'Did you ID her?'

'Everyone gets ID'd.'

'Do you remember her name?'

'Out of the hundreds we get every night, not a chance. But she did have a French driving licence.'

'Thanks, Oskar. If we can get a picture of her, we'll be back. Did you see them leave?'

'Yes, they left in a van'

'What kind?'

'Didn't see a name on the side, looked just like any white van does.'

'No company name, or phone number on the back?'

'Nope, just a typical white van.'

'No identifying marks?'

'It was quite well taken care of, except there was a splash of green paint just under the side door, like a tin of paint had spilled and run down the edge under the door.'

'Thanks guys, you've been a big help.'

♦

'What next?' asked Street, as they got back in Buchanan's car.

'A phone call,' he said, scrolling through his contacts. He tapped the screen and put the phone to his ear.

'Who are you calling?'

'Nathan Greyspear – shush. Yes, it's DCI Buchanan, I need to have a word with Sir Nathan, if he's there? It is police business and, no, you may not enquire what it's about. I'll hold.'

Street had a puzzled look on her face.

'Antonia used to work at the country club; they may have a photo of her.'

'That's smart of you, no need to bother the family.'

'Yes, I'm still here. Good, I'll hang on for him.'

'Couldn't we just drive out to the club and ask him?'

'We could, but if he has a photo, I'm going to ask him to

email it to me, and then we can pop back to the Polygon and ask Oskar and Carlos if they recognise her. Ah, Nathan, sorry to bother you on a Friday evening. No, I'm still following the case I mentioned earlier and was wondering if your office at the club would happen to have a photo of Antonia? No, she's fine, just need a photo of her for the file – and Nathan, if you do have one, could you email me a copy right away? No, my personal one will do fine. I'll wait.'

'Using technology?' said Street. 'You surprise me.'

'It's been a long day and I'd like to get home. You hear from Stephen since his last call?'

'Yes, he texted a few minutes ago and said they'd managed to make it home safely, said something about having to tow it back.'

'Ah, Nathan – you do? Great. I'll watch for it – not sure when I'll have time to come out to the club, just getting started with this case – ok, I'll give you a call when I get time, bye.'

'Success?'

'Yup, he didn't have a copy in the personal file, but has a photo taken at one of the functions which he will scan in and email, said I should have it in a few minutes.'

Buchanan's phone dinged. 'That was quick,' he said, opening the email.

'She's very attractive,' said Street, 'wish my hair looked that good.'

Buchanan looked over at Street. 'Your hair is fine. Let's go.'

They walked back over to the Polygon.

'Carlos, do you recognise this person, the one on the right?'

'What is it?' asked Oskar, who'd just opened the door to the club.

'The inspector wants to know if we recognise the lady in the photograph.'

'Yeah, she was in last Friday night. Left with that guy whose photo you showed us earlier.'

'Thank you again, guys. We'll be back if we have any more questions, and you don't remember anything about the van they left in?'

They both shook their heads.

'How about the driver?'

'A right tosser,' said Oskar. 'He parked right outside the door. I told him to move, said he was blocking the fire escape route.'

'What did he do, did he move on?'

''No. He wound down the passenger window and told me to get stuffed.'

'What happened next?' said Street.

'I said if he didn't move, I'd call the police. That shook him, I think he was on something and didn't want to get caught.'

'Would you recognise him if you saw him again?' said Buchanan.

'Probably.'

'What about CCTV?' said Street, pointing up to a camera above the door.

'Only shows people coming in and going out, doesn't cover the road,' said Oskar.

'Thanks guys, can we get you here if we need statements?'

Oskar and Carlos nodded.

'Can I drop you at home, Jill?'

'We done for the day?'

Buchanan nodded 'It'll be a busy day tomorrow, and I for one need a good night's sleep to prepare for it.'

'Is Stephen going to be working with us on this case?'

'He and Morris – as soon as they are done with what they are currently working on.'

4

'You're up early this morning,' said Karen, looking up from her tablet.

'Is that coffee I smell?'

'Just made a fresh pot.'

'You're up early yourself,' said Buchanan, as he poured his coffee. 'I've got a murderer to catch, besides couldn't sleep.'

'It's time you retired, Jack. You've done your bit for society.'

'Not while there's bad guys out there. Is there any toast?'

'There's raisin toast on the plate beside the butter dish.'

'Thanks.'

'Jack, you can't go on for ever. What about Jill, you said she's capable?'

'She certainly is that, but –'

'But – you just can't give it up, can you? You're like the old thespian who doesn't know when to bow out on the last curtain call.'

'Bit philosophic for six-thirty in the morning.'

Karen shook her head, looking back down at her tablet.

'What's caught your attention?'

'Curtains and bedding for our new house.'

Buchanan bent down and kissed her on the cheek. 'I hope you have a successful search. I hear what you're saying, just let me finish this case and then we'll see about a holiday, just the two of us.'

'And retirement?'

'Yes, I promise, we'll talk about me retiring.'

Karen looked up at him, smiled and said, 'You win, finish this case and we'll discuss when you retire.'

♦

Buchanan headed for the office via Starbucks and his morning coffee and muffin. He liked to be the first one into the office in the morning. He found the peace and quiet gave him time to contemplate, time to organise his thoughts and set targets for the day.

Street was next in. 'Have you arranged for Stephen and Morris to join us?'

'Morning, Jill. No, not yet.'

'Avoiding calling the chief?'

Buchanan looked at his watch and shook his head. 'Probably not in her office yet.'

'What will you do if she asks when are you coming in to meet with her?'

'Is this a conspiracy?'

'What do you mean?'

He shook his head. 'Doesn't matter, I'll give her a call in a minute. First, I want to know about the fingerprint results.'

'Shall I call?'

'No, I'll do that. There should be someone in by now.' He picked up his phone and dialled the number for the fingerprint department. 'Yes, it's DCI Buchanan. I'm looking for the results of prints taken from a corpse. Yes, they're the ones – ok, I'll hold. It is? Fantastic. Thanks.'

'Well, is it Denman?'

Buchanan smiled. 'Yep, positive ID.'

'What now?'

Buchanan thought for a moment, then said. 'What would you do – if it was your case?'

'I'd go back and have a word with Mrs Morelli. But first, I'd like to know if Antonia was in Eastbourne the night Denman died.'

'That's exactly what I'd do. How would you go about that?'

'First I'd call the chief and find out who I have as leg men.'

'Ok, hint taken – I'll call her.'

'I'll be right back, got to powder my nose,' said Street.

Buchanan picked up his phone and called the ACC.

'What did she say?' asked Street, when she returned.

'We'll have Stephen this afternoon and Morris as soon as he's finished in court.'

'Great, be good to have the team back together again. And the other matter?'

'She wants to see me, *now*.'

'Want me to come with you?'

'Thanks, that would be nice, but I think you'd be more valuable here. I shouldn't be long.'

'I'll give Stephen a call, find out where he is,' said Street.

'Thought you'd be pleased to get time away from him?'

She shook her head. 'No, we work well together.'

'You two still looking for somewhere to live?'

'Yes. Hope we find one by the wedding – can't imagine getting married then living separately.'

'You could use our estate agent; he's been very helpful finding us a house.'

'No thanks, ours is finding plenty of places to look at. It's just Stephen, he's so fussy, says there must be a garden and a garage.'

'Nothing wrong with that.'

'I suppose not.'

'Right, I'd better be going, see you when I get back.'

♦

Buchanan drove up Malling Hill from the Cuilfail tunnel, turned left onto Church Lane and on down to police headquarters. He stopped at the security gate and showed his warrant card, 'Detective Chief Inspector Buchanan to see Assistant Chief Constable Jane Atherton.'

'Thank you, sir,' said the uniformed constable. 'Visitor parking on the left.'

Buchanan climbed the familiar steps to the ACC's office and entered the outer office. The photos of the previous chief constables had now been replaced by watercolour paintings of the Cuckmere Valley.

'Detective Chief Inspector Buchanan to see the ACC,' said Buchanan, looking at the name tag, Hillary Bascom, pinned to the ample bosom of the ACC's secretary.

'Please sit and I'll inform her of your presence,' said Hillary.

Buchanan watched with fascination as Hillary pressed the speaker button on the phone and dexterously navigated the telephone keypad without damaging her beautifully manicured and decorated fingernails. The sound of electronic ringing emanated from the speaker. It rang three times. 'Ma'am, Detective Chief Inspector Buchanan has arrived.'

'Good, please show him in.'

'I heard,' said Buchanan, standing and walking to the ACC's office. He grabbed the door handle and went to open the door, but it didn't budge. He turned and looked at Hillary. She smiled and pressed a button on the desk, the lock released, and Buchanan opened the door. He looked back at Hillary, she was smiling enough to melt an iceberg.

'Come in, Buchanan, sit down. Coffee? Or would you prefer something stronger?'

Buchanan looked up at the office clock and back at the ACC and smiled. She also was smiling.'

'Coffee, black, no sugar, please.'

'I'll have coffee as well, Hillary.'

'Well, Buchanan, we finally get to time to chat. How are you?'

'I'm fine, Ma'am.'

'Still enjoying living down on the coast?'

Buchanan's reply was interrupted by a knock at the door and its immediately opening. Hillary entered with a small tray with two coffee mugs, a cafetiére and a plate of biscuits.

'You like yours black, Inspector,' she said.

'Thank you,' said Buchanan, accepting the mug of fresh coffee and wondering how many of his foibles were known this far from Eastbourne. He took a sip of coffee and put the cup back on the table.

'Well, Buchanan. Have you settled in to the genteel life on the south coast, or are you pining to get back to the hills and the glens of your homeland?'

'We're buying a house.'

'Where?'

'In Westham, three bedrooms, two with en-suites. My wife is currently looking for curtains and bedlinen.'

The ACC's face brightened noticeably. 'I'm so glad to hear that, Buchanan.'

'Oh, why?'

'I've been reading about you,' she said, holding up a thick folder. 'Thirty-four years in this folder, Buchanan. Thirty-four years of *toe-to-toe fighting against those who would subvert our way of life.*'

'I've heard that said before.'

'Ah, my predecessor. Yes, I took it from one of her speeches. I'm thinking of getting an extract framed and hung on my office wall. You're a bit of an old-fashioned policeman, aren't you?'

'I don't think I'm following you on that.'

'I've been told that you actually go out with your subordinates.'

'It's the best way to get the job done, never ask someone to do something you're not prepared to do yourself.'

'What are you working on at the moment?'

'A death in a factory in Hampden Park. My sergeant seems to think that there are Mafia connections.'

'Do you think it's self-contained, an isolated incident?'

'Too early to say, there is a possible revenge angle that we are following. A family honour issue.'

'Good, keep me informed, I don't want to have anything blow up in my face, especially since I have to deal with the crime commissioner.'

'Excuse for asking, Ma'am, but does he have any policing experience?'

'What do you think?'

Buchanan smirked. 'That bad?'

'I couldn't possibly comment,' she said, looking from side to side as if to make sure there was no one listening. 'Absolutely none, Buchanan. It is my belief that he is using this position as a stepping stone to one day being the home secretary. You realise that he will be treading on both our reputations to advance his own?'

'That's all right, I've been down that road before.

'All the same, Buchanan, watch your back. I can only protect you so much.'

◆

'How did your meeting go with the ACC?' said Street, upon Buchanan's return from Lewes.

'Absolutely fine. Got the impression she's actually on our side.'

'Glad to hear that. What's first?'

'I'd thought of calling on Mrs Morelli, but if she's involved I don't want to spook them into doing a runner,' said Buchanan, leaning back in his chair. He was still smiling from his meeting with the ACC.

'So, what will you do?'

'I'm going to contact immigration and see if they can get a match on Antonia's photo. If so we will know if, and when, she's come into the country recently.'

'Does that work?'

'Not always, but I'll give it a try anyway.'

'While you're doing that, I'll see if I can track down the resin salesman.'

'Was Matt Hall any help?'

'Some, he verified the salesman's name. I'll call the distributor and ask them where their Mr Prince is.'

'I could do with a coffee refill. Want one?'

'Thought you were going to call immigration?'

He shrugged. 'I sent them an email, included her photo.'

Street nodded as she dialled. 'White, with one.'

♦

'Your coffee,' he said, putting the cup on her desk. 'How did you do with the resin company?'

'Took a bit of doing. Their receptionist wanted to know which area we were located in; said that rep was on holiday and would be back next week and could I wait till then?'

'You did tell them it was a murder enquiry, didn't you?'

'Yes – they don't listen very well. I did get the information in the end though. They confirmed his name is Clive Prince. Want his mobile number?'

'Thanks.' Buchanan dialled the number then hung up.

'What's the matter? You don't look pleased.'

'This number is not taking incoming calls.'

'Very evasive man, Mr Prince. What will you do?'

'Can you call them back and get his home address? Make sure they understand it's a murder enquiry.'

'Will do.'

Street made the call and then hung up.

'Get an address?'

'Yes, last house on the end of Milfoil Drive in Langney.'

'Thanks,' said Buchanan, downing his coffee.'

'Going to see him?'

'If he's in, but –' Buchanan looked at the office clock, 'at this time of the day, he'll probably be in a pub somewhere. At least that's where I'd be if I were on holiday.'

♦

Buchanan parked at the end of the road beside a Yamaha

motorcycle, being careful not to run into the rider who was checking the fuel in the tank.'

'Excuse me, I'm looking for Clive Prince.'

'Sorry, mate. You've missed him. Saw him drive off about an hour ago.'

'Did he say where he was going?'

The motorcyclist shook his head. 'No, keeps to himself. Bit of a miserable old git, has a nice dog though.'

'Thanks.'

'No problem.'

'Nice bike, lose the licence plate?' said Buchanan, looking the bike over.

'It's a track bike, just waiting for a ride to Brands.'

'Brands?'

'Brands Hatch. Getting the bike ready for a race next week.'

'Yamaha?'

'Yeah, TZ750, goes like a bat out of hell – that's when it's running right.'

Buchanan shook his head. 'Rather you than me, best of luck.'

'Thanks.'

Buchanan walked up the path to Prince's house and rang the bell. No response. Then he knocked hard on the door. He saw movement behind the frosted glass panel. The door opened and an older lady circumspectly peeked through the gap. She held on to the door as she looked at Buchanan's warrant card.

'Good morning. I'm DCI Buchanan, I would like to talk to Mr Prince.'

'He's not here.'

'Then where might I find him, er – Mrs Prince?'

She looked at him, then up to the corner of the door frame. Buchanan followed her gaze expecting to see a miniature Clive Prince hiding in the corner. All he could see was a large spider's web with a huge spider struggling to entomb a wasp.

She shook her head, sniffed, and returned to staring at

Buchanan. 'What I mean is he's checking his samples.'

'Samples? What kind of samples?'

She shrugged. 'I don't know. It's his business, I never interfere.'

'And where might he be checking his samples?'

She shrugged again.

'You don't know?'

'I've never been to it.'

'You don't know where *it*, is?'

'All I know is it's a garage in Pevensey Bay. He rents it from a fisherman he met in the pub.'

'Do you have any idea where in Pevensey Bay?'

She started to close the door.

'One more question, Mrs Prince, then you can go back to your busy day. Does your husband have a phone?'

'He has one for business.'

'Do you have the number?'

'No.'

'What happens if you have to get in touch with him?'

She shrugged. 'He doesn't like me to call him during the day.'

'Suppose it's an emergency?'

'I'd call his office and they'd forward the message, but I don't like to call him. He is a very important man with his company. They rely on him to make the sales that keep everyone working. He'd be angry that I'd taken his time away from his customers. He always says, if he isn't selling, he isn't making any money.'

'Would he call you right back?'

'No, as I told you, he's always very busy with his customers.'

'Have you ever been to *it*, the garage?'

'No, all I know is it's near the beach.'

'How do you know that?'

'He called me once to tell me he wouldn't be home for dinner and I could hear seagulls and the sound of waves.'

'Thank you, Mrs Prince,' said Buchanan, passing her his

business card. 'Would you ask Mr Prince to call me when he gets home? It is very important.'

She nodded and her face relaxed; the ordeal was over.

♦

Buchanan pulled the car door closed, watched the Yamaha being loaded into a panel-van and then driven off to a day at the track. He called Street on his mobile.

'Jill, it's Jack. Know of any lock-ups that you can rent in Pevensey Bay?'

'There's a couple, why?'

'Trying to track down the elusive Mr Prince; according to his wife he's at his garage checking his samples.'

'There's two that I know of. First one's on the right as you drive into the Bay from the station. The other is on the left as you pass the lights.'

'Either of them near the beach?'

'The second one is. Go through the lights and take the first road on your left, that's Bay Terrace. The terrace is short, it turns to the right at the end. You should see the garages on your left.'

'Got it. Anything happening in the office?'

'The crime commissioner called again, wanted to know where you were?'

'What did you tell him?'

'Said you were out looking for the killer of the man in the factory.'

'Good lass, thanks.'

'You realise you can't avoid him forever?'

'There's time enough to meet him after we've caught Denman's killer.'

♦

Buchanan almost missed the garages and had to back up. The garage doors were all closed and there was no sign of the elusive Mr Prince. He paused for thought, then reversed into a driveway beside the garages and saw in his rear-view mirror what he'd been looking for. Directly behind him, down a weed-infested driveway, was a row of concrete garages, their roofs covered in weeds and grass with hungry-looking seagulls pacing back and forwards.

He reversed down the driveway and stopped. He got out, locked the door and took a moment to take in the scene. At the end of the driveway on the right was a row of ten garages. Their moss-covered doors faced the weathered brick wall of a car repair workshop. Spaced along the brick wall were steel-framed windows that hadn't seen a window cleaner this side of the new millennium. A large yellow skip, full to overflowing with dented car doors, crumpled bonnets and rusted silencers, sat outside the closed sliding garage door at the end of the workshop.

Buchanan reached for his cigarettes, then remembered he no longer smoked. He shook his head and pulled out a tube of fruit gums and shoved an orange-flavoured sweet into his mouth.

Buchanan sauntered slowly towards a pale blue Volvo estate parked outside the third garage. The garage door was up, and Buchanan could hear the noise of someone inside singing a tuneless song. The rear door of the estate was up, looking like a fighting cock getting ready to do battle. Several cardboard boxes lay scattered on the ground at the rear of the car.

The singing stopped as Buchanan's feet crunched on the gravel; a bald head poked out from the garage, followed by a wire-haired Scottish terrier. It ran out of the garage and stopped three feet from Buchanan, barking loudly while enthusiastically wagging its tail.

Buchanan bent forward and carefully offered his hand to the dog. It came close, sniffed the offered hand, saw there weren't any treats, then retreated and resumed barking.

'Dougal, shush, come here.'

The dog looked back at his master, looked back at Buchanan, gave one more bark then retreated into the garage.

'Clive Prince?'

'Er, yes,' he said, discarding a well-smoked cigarette onto the gravel.

'Your wife said you might be down here.'

'What – what do you want?'

'You sell boat paint and stuff?'

'Not quite. Sorry, I didn't catch your name?'

'Buchanan, Jack Buchanan.'

'Jack, I don't actually do any direct selling myself. I'm a rep for Hansons, they sell direct to businesses. I'm afraid if you want some of our products you'll need to call our office, they'll put you on to one of our resellers.'

'Oh, I'd hoped you could have helped.'

'What was it you wanted? I could give you a couple of names of companies who use our products. I'm sure their sales departments can get you what you require.'

'It wasn't paint actually, I was hoping to buy some laminating resin.'

Prince shook his head. 'I – we only sell paints, that sort of thing. What's your company?'

'Oh, it isn't for me, well, not directly. I'm making an enquiry for a friend as well. We're thinking about going into business together.'

Prince shook his head again. 'Not much I can do for you or your friend. I don't actually sell laminating resin. That's a different division, sales are handled from our Southampton office.'

'What does Hansons sell, Clive?'

'Hansons are the second largest supplier in the UK of marine and automotive paints, polishes, and protective waxes. Additionally, we can supply specialist paints and lacquers, not just for the marine and automotive industries. We also supply the necessary power and hand tools and miscellaneous materials to apply our products. And of course, we provide product training with all necessary safety equipment that is required when applying our products.'

'And you're sure you couldn't supply my friend with a few barrels of laminating resin?' Buchanan watched Prince's face and saw a nervous tick start on his right eye.

'What do you mean by laminating resin, Jack?'

'For making boats, that sort of resin.'

The tick became more pronounced. Prince shook his head. 'No, but I'm sure if you called the office they could put you on to our Southampton office, they'll have reps there that can help you.'

'Suppose I was only looking for a few barrels of resin? Just to start with, Clive. A private sale, just for my friend and me. We'd pay cash. You sure you couldn't you arrange that?'

'You didn't say what your friend does for a living?'

'He's a policeman, like me.'

A neck tremor joined Prince's nervous tick. 'Doing a bit of moonlighting, eh? I thought that was reserved for firemen.'

'Policeman's pay is not what you might imagine, Clive. These days with cutbacks one has to be prepared for all eventualities.'

'So, you want to get into boatbuilding, that it?'

Buchanan nodded. 'Just thinking at this stage, need to look at all the costs to see if we could make a profit at it.'

'Boatbuilding?' Prince said, shaking his head side to side slowly. 'These days you'd be lucky to cover your costs.'

'My boss keeps hinting I should retire.'

'Why? I thought you lot were always short-staffed.'

'Top heavy, that's what we are, at least that's what the MET in London are saying. My rank is to be done away with.'

'You don't sound so happy about it.'

'Why the hell should I be happy about it? Thirty-four years I've given them. Now look at me, fifty-four and surplus to requirements.'

'You should try being a sales rep, new targets every three

months, regardless of how well you did the previous quarter – you smoke?' Prince said, offering Buchanan a cigarette.

Buchanan reached out then withdrew his hand and shook his head. 'Trying to give up. These are my cigarettes these days,' he said, taking out his tube of fruit gums.

'Wish I could. I'm on twenty a day. Doctor says my lungs look like a treacle mine. I've tried all sorts of tricks to give up, even hypnotism.'

'Hypnotism?'

'Only been twice so far, hypnotist says it's early days. I think he's a quack. But since my company has paid for the first four sessions, what've I got to lose?'

'And you can't help with laminating resin?'

Prince shrugged, the tick stopped, the tremor remained. 'How much would you want? I do know someone in our Southampton office. He used to work for us in retail before he transferred to industrial sales a couple of months ago. I could give him a call. Oh, and you say it would be a cash sale? Would you want a receipt for it? My friend would want to know that – that is if he has any to sell.'

'We would pay cash, initially, Clive. Just till the business got up and running. And tell your friend not to bother with a receipt.'

'Give me your phone number, if I can help I'll call you. Er, where are you thinking about doing your building?'

Buchanan passed his card to Prince, their eyes met, Buchanan smiled.

'Detective Chief Inspector. Hmm, and you're surplus to requirements?'

'That's what my boss keeps intimating. As far as somewhere to build, we've been looking at some vacant factories, mostly too big for us. Though I've been told there's one just become available down by Gardners Books.'

Buchanan watched for a reaction on Prince's face, and got

what he wanted.

'What about Mountney Bridge estates? There are several small units there that might suit you better'

'Haven't tried there yet. The ones we've already had a look at in Eastbourne are a bit too pricy for us. These garages here would be perfect, if there was one available.'

Prince shook his head, 'I think they're all taken, and unless you got,' he said, gesturing with his arms, 'three in a row they would be too small – even if you're only making rowboats.'

Buchanan shrugged. 'Ah well, it's early days yet. Give me a call if you can help.'

'I will do that. Good to meet you, Jack,' Prince said, reaching out to shake Buchanan's hand.

'Good to meet you too, Clive.'

Buchanan had his car keys in his right hand and, in reaching out to take Prince's offered hand, he dropped them on the ground. He shook Prince's hand then bent down to pick up his car keys. Without him noticing, Buchanan also picked up Prince's recently discarded cigarette end.

♦

'Jill, can you get this off to forensics, please?' said Buchanan, as he walked into the office.

'Sure, what is it?' she said, looking at the cigarette stub. 'Oh, how did you do with Mr Prince?'

'He's afraid of something – or someone.'

'Why would you think that?'

'He has a nervous condition. As soon as I asked about laminating resin, a tick developed in his right eye. Then when I mentioned I was a policeman he started to shake, you know, like people who have Parkinson's do?'

'So, you hit a nerve,' she said, looking at the cigarette end in the evidence bag. 'This cigarette?'

'It's his. I want to see if it will put him at the scene of the crime. I seem to remember the CSI's picked up a couple of stubs at the scene.'

'Probably Enright's. He was smoking when I arrived.'

'The ones in the car park, yes, but the ones inside the factory, I doubt if they will be Enright's. The cigarette stubs found by the CSI's in the factory are the ones I'm interested in – there were several fresh ones found by the oven.'

'So, you think it's possible that Prince strung up Denman, then covered him in fibreglass?'

Buchanan shook his head. 'I doubt it. I don't think Mr Prince could hang up his wife's laundry.'

'Why do you say that?'

'You can tell a lot about a person by their handshake.'

'And Mr Prince's?'

'Weak and clammy, like holding a wet dishcloth. No, I don't think Mr Prince did in Denman. He probably was at the scene though, maybe left when he found out what was about to happen.'

'But why would he be there in the first place, especially if it was nothing to do with him selling resin?'

'Let's wait for the forensics on the cigarette, then we'll bring him in and make him sweat a bit.'

'Oh, you've had a response from immigration.'

'What did they say?'

'You'll like this. Photo matched, but –'

'But? I don't like buts.'

'It wasn't Antonia, it was her twin sister, Paula.'

'Didn't know she has a sister.'

'You wouldn't. This one lives in Paris with her husband and adopted children. Took a bit of tracing. Immigration and the internet were a big help. Turns out she's a model for a French clothing designer.'

'So why was she here?'

Street shrugged. 'Don't know. Probably here to see Mama.'

'I think it's time we went back to talk with Mrs Morelli,' said

Buchanan, standing. 'You drive, I need to think.'

♦

Buchanan pressed the bell for Flat 1, the Morellis, and waited. No answer. He tried Flat 3.

'Yes, who's there?'

'Mrs Dickson, it's DCI Buchanan. Sorry to trouble you again, we're looking for the Morellis.'

'I think they've gone out. Just a minute.'

The door buzzed and they entered the lobby. Buchanan and Street patiently waited as the ancient, arthritic lift creaked its way up the lift-shaft to the fifth floor. Buchanan opened the lift door and pulled the gate back. They exited the lift and pressed the Morellis' doorbell but as expected got no answer. Buchanan knocked. Still no answer. The door to Flat 3 opened.

'Ah, Mrs Dickson. You said you thought the Morellis had gone out. Do you know what time they went out?

'I heard noises very early this morning. Unlike them to make a noise, they're usually so quiet.'

'What kind of noise?'

'It was Mr Morelli, he kept shouting for Mrs Morelli to hurry up.'

'That was all, just hurry up?'

'Yes, why? Has something happened to them?'

'No. I'm sure they're fine. I understand their daughter came to see them recently?'

Mrs Dickson shook her head. 'I don't know, we've been away visiting George's mother, she lives in Crawley.'

'Do you know if there's a key holder for the flats?'

'I think Mrs Dreyfus in Flat 1 on the ground floor is one. She has keys to most of the apartments.'

'Street.'

'I'm on it, back in a minute.'

She returned five minutes later with Mrs Dreyfus.

'Can I see your warrant, please?'

'We don't have a search warrant, Mrs Dreyfus. We simply wish to ascertain all is well with the Morellis.'

'I meant your identification. I've seen your assistant's; can I see yours?'

Buchanan took out his warrant card. 'Here you are, this what you're looking for?'

She sniffed. 'Got to be sure who I let into the apartments. This way.'

Buchanan followed Street, who followed Mrs Dreyfus, into the Morellis' apartment.

'Hmm, what do you think?' said Street, looking at the chaos of clothes strewn on the floor and across the settee.

'I'll check the kitchen, you have a look in the bedroom,' said Buchanan. 'Well, first impressions?' he asked, as they met back in the living room.

'Looks like they've left in a hurry. Wonder what spooked them?'

'This is not good,' said Mrs Dreyfus. 'Mrs Morelli won't like this one bit, she's such a tidy person. *Everything in its place and a place for everything*, that's what she says.'

'Mrs Dreyfus, did Mrs Morelli say anything to you about going away?'

'No, Inspector, but I haven't spoken to her since last week.'

'Thank you, Mrs Dreyfus. And you're sure Mrs Morelli didn't say anything?'

'No, Inspector. As I said, I haven't spoken to her since last week.'

'Mrs Dickson, did you hear anything more than Mr Morelli urging his wife to hurry up? Please try to remember, it's quite important,' said Street.

'Oh, I think I heard Mr Morelli say something to someone in the hall, then the door shut.'

'What do you think you heard?'

'He said, *Just the two cases–* and *station*, yes that's it. They were going to the station, it was the taxi driver Mr Morelli was talking to.'

'Do you remember exactly what time that was?'

'Let me see, I don't sleep very well these days, quite often get up early and catch up on programmes with the BBC iPlayer. I'd been watching a programme on BBC4. Ah, that was it, a really, lovely piece about local East Sussex craftsmen, did you see it, Inspector?'

'No, sorry, Mrs Dickson, if I'm lucky I'm still asleep at that time. You were about to tell us when the Morellis left.'

'Oh, yes. It was just about four-thirty.'

'In the morning?'

'Yes, that's what I remember.'

'Is it normal for the Morellis to be up at half past four?'

She smiled and shook her head, 'No. Though Mr Morelli usually goes out for his morning paper about six. Regular as clockwork he is.'

'And you didn't hear them say anything else?'

She thought for a moment, and shook her head slowly. 'No. Sorry, Inspector, nothing else. Just the sound of the door shutting and the lift going down.'

'Thank you, Mrs Dickson, you've been very helpful.'

'Glad to be helpful, hope they're all right.'

'I'm sure they'll be fine, probably a last-minute holiday.' said Street.

'Mrs Dreyfus,' said Buchanan, 'when was the last time you were here in this flat?'

'Last Wednesday. Mr Morelli had said there was a problem with the dishwasher not draining properly, and did I know a reliable plumbing firm.'

'And you came up here and told him about a plumber?'

'No, not quite. I gave him the number of the firm I use. On Friday, Mr Morelli called to say they'd be away for the day and could I let the plumber in and wait while he fixed the dishwasher.'

'And did you?'

'Yes, I took the plumber up to the Morellis' flat and waited while he repaired the dishwasher.'

'Did he fix it?'

'Suppose so, I'm not a plumber. Yes, he must have done. He hasn't been back and Mrs Morelli didn't say anything.'

'Sorry, don't quite understand?'

'Mrs Morelli only says something when things aren't quite right, if you get my meaning, Inspector.'

'Was he quick?'

'Who, the plumber?'

'Yes, that's what I meant.'

'Yes, I suppose he was. At least he figured out the problem right away. He said something about the pump and would have to go down to the van for a new one.'

'How long was he gone for?'

'Just down to his van, he was back in less than ten minutes.'

'Did you stay in the flat all the time?'

'Of course I did.'

Street twigged where Buchanan was going with his line of questions.

'Mrs Dreyfus, would you mind having a look round the apartment with my sergeant and tell us if you see anything that doesn't look right?'

'Oh, I don't think that's quite right, it's their apartment. I wouldn't want anyone poking their nose round mine when I'm not home.'

'Just a cursory glance, Mrs Dreyfus,' said Buchanan. 'Is this them?' he asked, picking up a photo in a gilt frame on the coffee table.

'Yes, that's them, I think it was taken when they were on holiday in Italy last summer. Oh dear, you think something terrible has happened to them? Oh dear, oh dear.'

'Please relax, Mrs Dreyfus. I'm sure they're fine. As I said, they've probably just gone on a couple of days' holiday.'

'Oh, if you're sure.'

Buchanan nodded to Street who took her phone and photographed the photo of the Morellis.

'Just a cursory look round, Mrs Dreyfus, my sergeant will go with you.'

♦

'Just a family matter? And *my sergeant will go with you.* You do realise the implications of where this investigation is taking us?' said Street, as they drove back to Hammonds Drive.

Buchanan pursed his lips and nodded slowly. 'Yes, Jill, only too well do I understand where this investigation is going. The Morellis were creating an alibi for the Friday evening. What did you see when you looked with Mrs Dreyfus?'

'Other than the untidiness, nothing out of the ordinary.'

'What about the kitchen?'

'That was tidy, cup and plate in the drainer by the sink.'

'Cup and plate singular?'

'Yes.'

'What about the cupboards, fridge, freezer?'

'Looked well stocked. Just what you'd expect for a couple who shop occasionally. Nothing out of the ordinary.'

'Hmm.'

'What?'

Buchanan shook his head. 'Oh, nothing, just an idea.'

'What next, then?'

'Get a copy made of the photo of the Morellis, then I think it will be a good idea if you start a mugshot gallery. So far, we have Denman and the Morellis – there will probably be more by the time this investigation is over. Could you also get on to Southern Rail and find out which trains depart after four-thirty in the morning? Once you've done that get on to British Transport Police and have them see if they can track the

Morellis' movements.'

'And you?'

'I'm meeting Karen at the bank, we have an appointment about the mortgage for our new house. They want a sample of my signature. After that I've got an appointment with my doctor and a very important call to the Italian Embassy.'

♦

'How did it go, have you got your mortgage?'

'Everything signed, sealed and ready to deliver when the exchange happens.'

'Bet Karen's excited.'

'She is.'

'How did you get on at the doctor's?'

Buchanan shrugged. 'As well as expected, least that's what the doctor said.'

'And that's all he said?'

'Mumbled something about my weight and lack of exercise. Doesn't he realise I'm too busy for the gym? He wants to see me again in a month's time, says he wants to keep an eye on my progress. Said since I'd been such a heavy smoker he was keen to see how my body recovered.'

'Hmm, hope it does.'

'Have you the information on the trains I asked you to get?'

'Yes, there's a train to Brighton at 05:08 and one for Victoria. That's odd…'

'What is?'

'They show a train to Brighton leaving at 05:08 as well as a train to Victoria at the same time, and they both leave from the same platform, Ah, here's the answer: you get off the Victoria train in Lewes and join another train for Brighton.'

'And Hastings trains?'

'The first one in the morning is at 04:50, and I think that one goes on through to Ashford International.'

'And Ashford has connections to the Eurostar service.'

'You think the Morellis have done a runner to somewhere in Italy?'

'Have a look and see what time the Eastbourne to Ashford train gets in at. Then see when the next train to Paris is.'

'Got it. Eastbourne to Ashford service arrives at 06:07 and the next train to Paris is at 06:24. Plenty of time to make a connection.'

'What about BTP and the security videos?'

'They're working on it. They said it takes time for the computer to compare the sample with the actual video recording. They're short-staffed today.'

'But it was four-thirty in the morning. Can't be many people go through the station at that time of day.'

'There was a concert on at the Bandstand, a Jersey Boys tribute band. Lots of people missed the last train home so the station was full of revellers and passengers trying to get to work.'

'Just fine. Did they give you any indication how long they'd be?'

Street shrugged. 'Just said they'd be done when they were done.'

'Give them another call, tell them it's a matter of life and death.'

'You're joking, right?'

'No, we're up against something – something beyond anything we've had to deal with before.'

'Even our first case, the bodies in the marina?'

'Sadly, yes. The embalming in fibreglass of Denman wasn't just a simple murder. It has all the hallmarks of something or someone who –'

'Someone who? You're not making sense.'

'This someone, this evil genius – Jill, what I have to tell you goes beyond normal policing. The person we seek performs his evil deeds not just in Eastbourne but, if my hunch is correct, all over Europe and who knows how much further.'

'Really?'

'Remember when I responded to the call about the body in the factory?'

'Yes, I was with you.'

'Remember seeing a stack of steel barrels?'

'Yes, some were leaking, smelled awful.'

'Well, I got some of that stinking stuff on my jacket and used my handkerchief to wipe it off my cuff. Matt Hall had a sniff of it and he says it's a toxic concoction of transformer oil and something else. I've just sent it off for analysis.'

'And who is this mastermind you think dumped those barrels in the factory?'

'Ah, there's the genius of the whole situation, Jill. The man, and I believe it probably is a man, pervades the streets, towns, and cities of Europe and no one is the wiser. I'm positive that if you met him in the street, shared a taxi, or even a table in the finest of restaurants, you'd be none the wiser of the evil that courses through his veins.'

'Are you all right? Shall I get you a coffee?'

'Never better. Oh, what a challenge this is going to be, Jill. It will be my magnum opus, my swan song. I can finally give then all the two-fingered salute and say I told you so. Then walk out the door laughing.'

'I'll call BTP and tell them to get their skates on.'

'Good.' Buchanan sat on the edge of his desk, rubbing his chin and whistling tunelessly.

Street hung up the phone. 'Got them!'

'Got who?'

'The Morellis. They boarded the 04:50 to Ashford.'

'And that connects with?' said Buchanan, smiling.

'The Eurostar to Paris and the rest of the continent.'

'Well done, now I want –'

'You want me to find out which train they changed to in

Paris, right?'

'Got it in one,' said Buchanan, walking over to the door. 'Be right back. Want a coffee?'

'Please, vending machine will be fine.'

♦

'I have a surprise for you,' said Street, as Buchanan returned with their coffees.

'You know I don't like surprises. What is it?'

'You'll like this one. I pushed BTP on the CCTV at Ashford, and guess what?'

'By the look on your face, I'd guess the Morellis never got on to the Paris train.'

'Exactly.'

'But why not? Did they get on the Brussels train instead? No, that wouldn't make any sense.'

'Neither train.'

'Neither? Then just which train did they get on?'

'They walked all the way down to the front of the Paris train and got on. Then just before it left, they got off at the back and right back on the Brighton train they'd just arrived on.'

'They must be really scared of someone to go to all that trouble. Don't tell me they came back to Eastbourne?'

'All right, I won't tell you they came back to Eastbourne. But what I will tell you is they stayed on all the way to Brighton. Got a positive ID from the station CCTV cameras in Brighton.'

'How far can the cameras track people?'

'Right out to the taxi rank and, yes, they did get in a taxi. Morris has gone to Brighton to see if he can find the taxi driver who picked them up.'

'When did he get back?'

'Just a few minutes ago. The case he was on collapsed. The defendant changed his plea to guilty when the victim described what had happened. Pity the case had to go that far. Costs the taxpayer a fortune each time the lawyers get involved.'

'You sound sore. Trouble with buying your house?'

'No, it's not that. I just get annoyed when the press goes on about how expensive the police are. Do you know what those plonkers in Whitehall have done now?'

'No, what have the Whitehall plonkers done now?'

'They've only gone and hacked off four-point-two million from the central government grant to the National Police Air Service. Just hope they don't expect helicopter support when their cosy mansion gets burgled and their prize poodle is abducted.'

'What was the original amount?'

'Sixteen and a half million. But I bet you they haven't cut the MP's expenses, I bet they still get their train fares paid, chauffeured limos and subsidised beer at the Palace'

Buchanan was stopped short when the phone rang. 'Buchanan. Who's this? They did what? Ok, get back here, we've got work to do. We must find them. And stop at Starbucks and get us a coffee, this station muck isn't fit to pour down the drain. Yes, get one for Jill as well.'

'Who was that?'

'Morris. He talked to the taxi driver, who said he took the Morellis to Newhaven.'

'Newhaven! They must really be scared if they are going to this much trouble to hide their tracks like that.

◆

'Thanks for the coffees, Morris,' said Buchanan, taking a sip of his. 'What did you find out from the taxi driver?'

'The taxi driver confirmed he drove them to the ferry terminal, even helped carry their bags into the departure lounge.'

'Did he see them go through security?'

'I asked him, but he said he had another fare to go to.'

'You think they did the Ashford move again?' asked Street, smirking.

'Jill, may I remind you, we're not playing Mornington

Crescent.'

'Sorry, couldn't resist.'

'Jill, you remember what Mrs Dreyfus said when we were in the Morellis' apartment?'

'*Everything in its place,* or something like that. She said that Mrs Morelli was extremely tidy?'

Buchanan nodded. 'I have a thought, no more than a thought. Morris, I want you to go with Jill to the Morellis' apartment. Talk to Mrs Dreyfus and get the names of every tenant in the building. Also, ask her if anyone has been away on holiday, and if any of the tenants rent out their apartments. When you've done that, Jill, go have another word with Mrs Dickson, ask her who she's seen, or heard, on the landing during the last couple of weeks.'

'Will do. Come on, Morris, the game's afoot.'

While he waited, Buchanan called Hunter. 'Stephen, are you available yet? You are? Good, get to the office as soon as you can. As Jill says, the game's afoot.'

While he waited for Dexter and Street to return, he read on his phone the newspaper account of the death in the factory and smiled to himself, thinking if they only knew the whole story. But did *he*? And he was the senior investigating officer. Did he really understand what was going on behind the scenes?

The first to arrive was Hunter. They were joined a few minutes later by Street and Dexter.

'Right,' said Buchanan, 'first I think a recap of where we've got to. Stephen, you are finished with the other job you were working on?'

'Yes, all done. Shoplifter won't be doing any lifting for the next three years.'

'Good, then this is where I think we have got to so far. Monday morning, I was called to a report at the old factory on Edison Road. The body, one Julian Denman, was found nailed to a wall in an industrial oven; he'd been encapsulated in fibreglass. Jill joined me shortly after. The entry alarm had been triggered sometime just before ten on Friday evening, then extinguished shortly after. Due to the terms of the security contract, an alarm engineer wasn't dispatched till the Monday morning; it was he who initially found the body.

'It turns out that the deceased was a former employee of the last company that rented the factory, CSM. The company had gone bankrupt due to bad business practices, mostly attributed to the deceased. The deceased was also a frequent user of alcohol and cocaine, and had a reputation as a womaniser – a real sleazebag. As part of the equation, a Mr Clive Prince, a salesman for Hansons –'

'Hansons? Who are they?' asked Dexter.

'According to my conversation with Mr Prince, they supply all kinds of paints, waxes and finishes, plus an own-brand of power tools, to the marine, automotive and aviation industries.'

'What's he like, Prince?' said Hunter.

'About five-ten, overweight for his height, grey going bald and wears glasses, possibly varifocals. He tried to offload an order for laminating resin that had been ordered by the deceased, to a Matt Hall of Greyspear Yachts. The resin order had been placed prior to CSM ceasing to trade, but unfortunately for Hansons, and Prince in particular, the order was due for delivery after the closure of CSM.'

'Where do the Morellis come in to the story?' asked Dexter.

'A couple of years ago their daughter, Antonia, had a run-in with Denman. At the time, she was working as a waitress at Castlewood. Denman was a member and the story is that one evening Denman tried to go where she didn't want him to.'

'Was anything done at the time?' asked Hunter.

'No, Antonia refused to press any charges.'

'But why? we treat sexual violence with tact these days.'

'Two nights later someone poured paint stripper all over Denman's Ferrari, a complete write-off, and he wasn't insured for vandalism.'

'Serves him right,' said Hunter. 'Do you think there might be a Mafia angle to the story? You know, family honour being besmirched?'

'It's possible. The Morellis, at least Mrs Morelli, is, or was, a director for CSM, depending on where the insolvency lawyers have got to with winding up the company. Denman is attributed with being the main cause of the company's demise.'

'So where does Prince fit in, other than the resin issue?' asked Dexter.

'Not quite sure at this point,' replied Buchanan. 'I'm waiting for forensics to come back to me on some cigarette ends found at the scene. I collected a fresh discard of Prince's and hopefully we'll get a match with one of the ones found at the scene.'

'He doesn't sound like the type to me to string someone up, even if he got stiffed for a couple of thousand,' said Hunter.

'Maybe, maybe not, anyway I think we should keep an eye on Prince, see what he gets up to. Jill, Morris, what did you find out at the Morellis' apartment?'

'Mrs Dreyfus was only too keen to tell us who lived where, but I don't think you'll bother with them, at least all except for who owns Flat 2 on the fifth floor.'

Buchanan grinned. 'Let me guess. One Mrs Paula Morelli?'

'You're no fun,' said Street.

'Only half correct,' said Dexter, 'the flat is used as an Airbnb apartment. According to Mrs Dreyfus the Morellis originally owned Flat 2, but moved to Flat 1 when it became available. Apparently, the views south across Eastbourne were more to their liking. They tried to sell Flat 2 but when it wouldn't sell they kept it on, mostly so family could visit. During the rest of the time it's either rented out or sits empty.'

'Did you ask her if anyone was staying in it just now?'

'Yes,' said Dexter.

'She said she wasn't sure,' said Street. 'Where do we go now?'

'I think we'll put a surveillance team on Flat 2. See who goes in and out.'

'Who's going to do that?' said Street.

'You three,' said Buchanan. 'How's Mrs Dreyfus at making tea?'

'You suggesting we move in with Mrs Dreyfus?' said Street.

'Not all day. Jill, go see her before she gets her day started, make up a story that would have you on her doorstep early in the morning.'

'I know, I could say I need to know when the post is delivered.'

'I suppose that would work. Stephen and Morris, get one of the unmarked transits and park inconspicuously down the road at night. Shouldn't be too arduous for you.'

'How long are we to do this? The Eastbourne Women's Tennis Tournament will be starting soon.'

'Just a couple of days. Let's see – this is Wednesday – we'll give it till Saturday morning. We should have a picture of the comings and goings of Flats 1 and 2 by then.'

'1 and 2?' said Street.

'I don't think the Morellis have gone very far. I believe if you were to walk into Flat 2 right now, you'd find them playing happy families with their daughter Paula.'

'Really?' said Street.

'Yes, I do,' said Buchanan. 'It is my gut instinct that sometime just before Denman was killed, she arranged to come over and move into Flat 2. Then, when the Morellis needed to lay a trail, she was waiting at Newhaven to bring them home. Jill, when you've finished with Mrs Dickson, I need you back at the office, we've a mountain of paperwork to catch up on.'

'Will do. I've still got to check on the CCTV situation on Edison Road.'

'Are we working this weekend, Chief?' said Hunter

'Why?'

'I've promised to take Jill up to London on Saturday to a show.'

'What are you going to see?'

'I've got tickets for *Motown*.'

'Ok, you can have the weekend off, you as well, Morris. But I want you all back here first thing Monday morning early. I don't want this investigation to run away from us. Or the press to think we're sleeping on the job.'

5

'Morning, Chief.'

'Good morning, Stephen,' said Buchanan, looking at the office clock. 'Bit early for you?'

'Had to take the car in for repair; my friend said if I dropped it in at his house first thing he'd have a quick look at it.'

'What's wrong with it? You've only just bought it.'

Stephen shook his head. 'Don't remind me of that.'

'Thought you and Jill were going to drive to London on Saturday?'

'That's what we thought, ended up taking the train. We stopped at the garage in Hickstead for a coffee. When we went to leave, there was a grinding noise from the transmission. I called the AA to see if they could figure out what was wrong.'

'And did they?'

'The engineer said the clutch thrust-bearing had gone.'

'Were you still able to get to London?'

'She said we might be lucky and get there and back, but she didn't recommend it. We ended up being towed back home.'

'Why not the garage?'

'I have a friend work on my cars. Jim works for himself from home. He warns all his customers not to drop cars off without first letting him know. Apparently last year, when he was on holiday, one of his neighbours had a car towed away because they thought it had been abandoned.'

'The police wouldn't just have a car towed without good cause.'

'It wasn't taxed or insured. Jim was going to do some repairs to it prior to getting it MOT'd.'

'What happened to the car?'

'The owner had to pay to get it out of the pound, but when he found out how much, he just abandoned it and let them scrap it.'

Their automobile discussion was interrupted by Street's arrival.

'Good morning, Jill, Stephen's just telling me about your ill-fated trip to London.'

'Thanks for reminding me.' She looked at Stephen and shook her head. 'Why we couldn't just have a regular car, I don't know. And why didn't you listen to your friend? He told you the clutch needed work. I just can't see why we need an old sports car, especially one with a leaking roof.'

'It's just a small leak. I'll get it fixed.'

'I should hope so, remember we're supposed to have dinner with your parents this Sunday.'

'Don't worry, Jim said he'll get right on it this morning.'

'He'd better.'

'Excuse me,' interrupted Buchanan, 'would you two mind if we discuss what were here for?'

Before they could comment, Buchanan's phone rang. 'Buchanan. Who's this? Mrs Prince, how can I help? He didn't – has he done this before? He hasn't – when was the last time you heard from him? And he hasn't been home? Don't worry, Mrs Prince, I'm sure he'll turn up. I will, goodbye.'

'What's wrong?' said Dexter, wandering into the office, his hands full with a sandwich, bag of crisps and a bottle of 7UP.

'Mr Prince didn't come home last night.'

'Should we be concerned?' said Hunter.

Buchanan shook his head. 'I don't like this one bit, wouldn't be surprised if Mr Prince showed up in the morgue.'

'His wife doesn't know where he is?' said Hunter.

'She said he got a phone call last night, just after dinner. He didn't say who it was, just put his jacket on and walked out.'

'Want one of us to go interview her, Chief?'

'No – not at the moment, Stephen. First, I want to hear how the surveillance went on Flats 1 and 2. Stephen, you first.'

'Not much to report, Chief,' Hunter said, opening his notebook. 'No one came in or out who matched the Morellis' description, but there was a Tesco home delivery very early this morning. I talked to the driver and he confirmed the delivery was to Flat 2 on the fifth floor.'

'What was in the delivery?' asked Buchanan.

'Enough food for a family of four that would last a couple of weeks.'

'So, they've decided to lay low, but till when?' said Buchanan. 'Jill, what about you?'

'Mrs Dreyfus is such a lonely woman. She told me her life history and all about the people who live in the flats.'

'What about the Morellis? Did she say much about them?'

'First, you need to hear her story.'

'Why?'

'You'll see. Mrs Dreyfus has a friend at church who was married to one of the CSM managers.'

'Was?'

'Yes. They divorced about five years ago.'

'Get the name of the husband?'

'Julian Denman.'

'The same Denman?'

'The very same.'

'Did she say why they divorced, or do I need to guess?'

'Infidelity and his predilection for drugs.'

'Do you have a name for the friend?'

'Dorothy Armstrong.'

'How about an address?'

'Yes. It's a house on Belmont Road, Southampton. It's a couple of roads over from the station. She told Mrs Dreyfus she couldn't stand to live anywhere she might run into her ex.'

'Should we go talk to the Morellis?' asked Dexter.

'No. Not yet, let's make them think they've managed to evade whoever is after them.'

'So, what will we do?' asked Hunter.

'Stephen, Morris, Jill's a bit snowed under. I want you to go door to door and see if any of the companies on Edison Road have CCTV that cover their car parks, and the road. If they do, see if they caught sight of Prince's Volvo driving past at any time, but of course especially a white van on the night of Denman's killing. Also, when you are asking, find out if there has been any activity at the factory since it closed.'

'And me?'

'Jill, I want you to go see Mrs Prince, get a statement about her husband's movements, though I don't expect you'll get much from her, she hardly said a word to me. Then come back to the office, I want us to go see what we can find out in Southampton.'

'Where will you be? If what you say about Mrs Prince is correct, I don't expect I'll be very long.'

'I said she didn't have much to say to me – perhaps a womanly approach will get more out of her. I'll be in the office.'

'Ok, I'll see you later.'

Buchanan waited for the three of them to leave, then called forensics. 'DCI Buchanan. Do you have the results of the samples I sent in? Good, what was that evil-smelling stuff?'

◆

Buchanan was reviewing the forensics report on his oil sample when he was interrupted by his phone ringing. 'Buchanan, Who's this? Where? I'll be right there.'

He hung up and called Street. 'Jill, are you done with Mrs Prince? Ok, meet me in the old market car park by Pevensey Castle. I'm afraid I think I know where Mr Prince is.'

◆

Buchanan turned into the Pevensey market car park and

stopped in front of the blue and white police tape. He wound down his window. 'DCI Buchanan.'

'Your team is waiting down in the lower car park, sir,' said a police constable.

'Thanks,' said Buchanan, letting his car roll down the slope. He parked beside Street's car.

'How did you get here before me?'

'I was done with Mrs Prince and was on my way back to the office when you called. Do you think it's Prince?'

'Let's go see,' said Buchanan, as they walked over to another constable. 'Where's the body?'

'Best way is to follow that path round the base of the castle, sir. The body is at the bottom of the embankment. Be careful, sir, it's quite slippery.'

'Is the doctor here?'

'Not yet, he's on his way.'

Buchanan led the way, staying off the path and managing not to slip on the damp grass; Street followed.

'Look at that,' said Buchanan.

'Look at what?'

'The path, a lot of footprints to sort out, though the SCI's are good at that sort of thing,' said Buchanan, stopping to look at the ground. 'You see what I see, Jill?'

'The path is well used, but since it rained hard a few days ago, those footprints over there look quite fresh.'

'I wonder how tall the wearer was? Look at the size of the prints.'

They continued along the grass beside the path to where two uniformed officers were talking. They stood straight as soon as they saw Buchanan.

'The body?' said Buchanan.

'Over here, sir. It's behind the big oak tree, not a very pretty sight.'

'Murder never is, Constable.'

Buchanan made his way round the tree and stopped. 'Shit, I thought Denman's death was awful – but this takes the biscuit.'

'What does?' said Street, as she followed Buchanan round the tree. 'Oh, how gruesome! Are those nails in his hands?'

'Looks like someone's been practising crucifixion. The poor bugger's been nailed to the tree. Let's get out of here and leave this to the CSI's and the doctor,' said Buchanan. 'We're only making things worse for them by trampling all over the scene. There must have been several of them to do this, don't want our tracks destroying theirs.'

'Is that Mr Prince?'

Buchanan let out his breath. 'Yes, I'm afraid it is.'

Buchanan and Street retraced their steps to the car park to wait for the doctor and CSI team.

'What do you think, Jack?'

Buchanan shook his head. 'The work of a madman. Shit, what I'd do for a cigarette just now.'

'How long's it been?'

'Since the last one, my final cigarette? Six weeks, four days, and twenty-three hours.'

'Glad I never started.'

'Never tempted?'

'Oh,' said Street, nodding her head, 'a couple of times when at boarding school. Mostly after lights out in the dorm. Mavis Chalmers used to cadge them from the gardener in exchange for, well, I'll leave the what to your imagination.'

'With me it was the old air raid shelters behind the science block.'

'Ever get caught?'

'A few times, but mostly by Prentice G, the prefect. He used to confiscate all the cigarettes, then he'd go smoke them with his friends down by the river after school.'

'Typical, do as I say, not as I do.'

'About time,' said Buchanan, turning to see who had just

driven into the car park. The CSI team had arrived, with Dr Mansell following.

'Well, Buchanan, what do you have for me today?'

'A crucifixion, Doctor, not much blood though.'

'How did he die?'

'I'll leave that to those more qualified than me,' said Buchanan, as he and Street watched Dr Mansell suit up in his crime-scene overalls.

'Well, let's go then,' said Mansell, 'get dressed, can't have you wandering all over the scene muddying up the evidence.'

'If you don't mind, I think we'll wait here. Wouldn't want to get in your way,' said Buchanan.

'That messy, huh? Didn't think you were squeamish, Buchanan.'

'Go have a look, you'll see why. We'll be in the castle tea room. What do you know about the castle, Jill?' asked Buchanan, as they walked back to the car.

'Not much, but there's a tourist board information poster over there, shall I have a look at it?'

'Why not? We've got to wait for the doctor, anyway'

This castle is renowned for being a medieval castle and former Roman fort.

At the end of the Roman occupation the castle fell into disrepair but was reoccupied in 1066 by the Normans, becoming a strategic defence position.

It had a brief renaissance between 1940 and 1945 when it was a garrison for troops from the Home Guard, British and Canadian armies plus the United States Air Army. Machine gun pill-boxes can still be seen sitting on top of the crumbling external wall.

'Interesting, fancy a cup of tea?'

'Are you buying?'

'Come on.'

♦

'Buchanan, just for once, why can't you find a nice simple murder, like a stabbing, or how about a simple shooting?' said Mansell, as he walked into the tea room and sat down at the table. 'May have to take the damn tree with us to the morgue.'

'Would you like to order?' asked the waitress, who'd seen Mansell walk in.

'Er, no. Some of us have a job to do.'

'Why? Why do you need to take the tree to the morgue?' asked Street.

'Because it's not only the hands that are nailed to the tree, he's got four dirty great nails through the back of the mouth into the tree.'

'Really?' said Street. 'You think you'll have to take the tree with him?'

Mansell shook his head. 'On second thoughts, maybe not. Might just whip the head off below the scull instead.'

'You're joking, surely?'

'Yes, Buchanan, I am.'

'Glad to hear that. What will you do?'

'I've called for a tree surgeon. I'll get them to chainsaw the area directly behind the head, then remove the remainder of the tree when I get the body on the table.'

'You're becoming quite an authority on DIY, Doctor. What's next, pouring concrete, or a bit of bricklaying, perhaps? Tell you what, Karen and I have just bought a house – fancy doing some decorating?'

'See what I have to endure, Jill?' said Mansell, shaking his head. 'I'll let you know when I'm done. Now if you'll excuse me, I've a bit of tree trimming to do.'

'What next?'

Buchanan looked at his watch. 'A drive to Southampton and a talk with Hansons. It's time we found out what we can about

Prince, and of course we need to find out who his contact was at Hansons.'

'Mrs Armstrong – should we go see her while we're in Southampton?'

'An excellent idea. We won't say anything about Prince, though. I think we'll just say we're following up on the Denman killing. Be diplomatic, who knows, she may still have feelings for the jerk.'

'If we find out who Prince's contact was, what do you plan to do?'

'If he's on the fiddle, he may be reluctant to talk to us. I think we'll tell him we're worried about Prince, say he's been reported as missing by his wife, that should elicit something from him. But first, I think we should pay a visit to Mrs Prince and break the bad news.'

'It may not be such bad news as you think.'

'Why's that?'

'I got the impression when talking with her that she'd not miss him much.'

♦

Buchanan and Street waited for the late Mr Prince to be carted off to the morgue and Dr Mansell to return.

'Tea to your liking, Buchanan?'

'Yes, thank you, Doctor.'

'And the cake?'

'Yes, the cake was also to our liking. What about Prince?'

'Glad you've got time to sit around drinking tea. I'll call you as soon as I'm done with Mr Prince. Where are you off to next?'

'Mrs Prince.'

'I suggest you let Jill do the talking. Sounds better from a woman.'

Buchanan nodded. 'Yes, of course.'

'Where after?'

'Southampton.'

'Got your bucket and spade?'

'This is work, Doctor.'

'That's what you say. I'll call you,' said Mansell over his shoulder, as he walked off to his car

'We'll drive to the office and drop off your car, Jill,' said Buchanan. 'I'll radio for a female officer to join us. Dr Mansell is quite correct, bad news like this always comes better from a woman. When we're done, I'll drive us to Southampton.'

'And where will you be?'

'I'll wait in the car.'

'Fine by me.'

◆

'What did you think about your chat with Mrs Prince?' said Buchanan, as they passed Arundel Castle. 'How did she take the news of her husband being dead?'

'People accept bad news differently. When I was told that my parents had been killed in Iran, I was devastated.'

'And Mrs Prince, how did she take the news?'

'Weird. We were welcomed into her front room. When I told her about the death of her husband she just shrugged and said, *That's life*, then asked would we like a cup of tea?'

'Did she look agitated or worried? Any tears?'

'No, though I did watch her hands. She just sat there wringing them; something was definitely worrying her.'

'No tears?'

'Crocodile ones, and she did the old lady thing with her sleeve.'

'What do you mean?'

'My gran used to do it, always had a handkerchief stuffed under the sleeve of her jumper. Constantly took it out to blow her nose and wipe her eyes, even when she didn't have a cold.'

'You think Mrs Prince's crying into the hanky was put on?'

'Yep, but I still think there was something bothering her.'

'Wonder what it is? We'll give her a few days then go back

and see if she'll open up.'

'Maybe she was paid, or threatened, to keep her mouth shut.'

'Possibly – and, she wasn't grief-stricken at the news?'

'Not in the least.'

'Did she say much else?'

'I thought she was a bit reluctant to talk at first, but after the second cup of tea she became quite chatty.'

'About what?'

'Gardening mostly. She was on safer ground there. She showed us round the back garden and pointed out all the plants, and included their Latin names.'

'What about her husband?'

'Not much. Said they'd been married for eighteen years.'

'Children?'

'None. I got the impression she would have liked them, but hubby kept putting it off. In their early years of marriage, he kept saying they needed to make sure they could afford them. She eventually gave up pestering him.'

'Callous git, children are not something you purchase. Anything else?'

'She has a sister who has four children.'

'Bet they get spoiled by their aunty.'

'I believe they do. While I was there, Mrs Prince was sewing costumes for one of her niece's school plays.'

> *Oh, what a gift we have*
> *Children by the door*
> *Smiling faces, welcoming embraces*
> *Trust before they know.*

'Do you write down your poetry?' asked Street.

'No. Someday, maybe when I retire, then I'll have the time.'

♦

They stopped at the Roadchef services on the M27 to stretch their legs, and much-needed coffee.

'Why do you drink that stuff?' said Buchanan, as he watched

Street sip on her drink.

'Caffè Frapuccino? You shouldn't knock it if you haven't tried it. Here, would you like a sip.'

'No, thank you, I'll stick to my Americano.'

'Stick, that's the word for you.'

'Very funny. Where do we get off the motorway?'

Street took her phone out and looked at the display. 'We take the M271 to Redbridge Road, drive to the first roundabout then take the First Avenue exit. Before we get to the railway we turn right, that's still First Avenue. Hansons is on the left at the end.'

'Let's hope there are no dead bodies waiting for us.'

'Why does Dr Mansell give you such a hard time?'

'He's just trying to wind me up, says he's never had so many gruesome deaths to investigate.'

'How do you respond?'

'I tell him he's had it easy for too long, time to earn his keep.'

'He told me he likes working with you.'

'Oh, really?'

'Yes, says it's fun to work with an old-fashioned policeman.'

'I'll take that as a compliment. Right, let's go see what mischief we can cause at Hansons. Your turn to drive.'

Street turned off First Avenue, stopped at the security barrier, and wound down the window.

'Detective Sergeant Street and DCI Buchanan here to see the sales manager,' she said to the security guard.

'Do you have an appointment?'

'We don't need one,' said Buchanan, showing the guard his warrant card.

'Would you park over there?' The guard indicated an area beside the security cabin. 'You'll need to sign in, I'll let reception know you are coming over.'

'Why all the fuss about visitors?' asked Buchanan, as he signed the visitors' book.

'Have you ever seen the YouTube video of the PEMEX gas

plant explosion in Mexico?'

'No, why?'

'If you had, you'd understand why we check people in and out of this site. We hold thousands of tons of highly flammable chemicals on site. Should there be an emergency, we want to know everyone has been accounted for. Saves the fire department risking their own lives looking for people.'

'Thought that might be the case. Good to hear you people are serious about safety.'

'Reception is across the car park by the blue building. Please park in the visitors' car park.'

'Why did you have to wind the security guard up like that for?' asked Street, as they drove across to the visitors' car park.

'Didn't like the way he asked us why we were here.'

'It's his job. You heard why they need to know who's on site.'

'I suppose you're right, I'll think nice thoughts about him to make up for it.'

They parked in the visitor area and went in to reception.

'Good afternoon. Can I help?' asked the receptionist.

'Detective Chief Inspector Buchanan. Could I have a word with your sales manager, please?'

'I'll see if he's in.'

Buchanan and Street waited while the call was made.

'Hi Jean, is he in? Good. I've got a couple of police officers who want to have a word with him – a chief inspector and a sergeant. Ok, I will. Bye.'

'Dave Roberts will be right down, Inspector. Can I get you something to drink while you wait?'

'A coffee would be nice?'

'Ma'am?'

Street nodded. 'Coffee would be great, thanks.'

As they sat and drank their coffees Buchanan said, 'Bit bleak for a reception.'

'I think it fits its purpose. Reception desk with receptionist. What I assume is a lift door. Room decorated with cream and green wall paint. Cream painted ceilings with fluorescent lighting. Waxed linoleum flooring. What's wrong with that? It is a factory reception in an industrial area, not John Lewis in Oxford Street,' she said, looking at Buchanan's face.

'These industrial sites give me the creeps,' he said. 'My uncle Dan was killed in a coalmine gas explosion, he and the rest of his shift.'

'Oh, I didn't know that.'

'I don't talk about it.'

A bell dinged, the lift door opened and a tall red-headed man exited. 'Inspector, Sergeant – Dave Roberts. How can I help?'

'Is there somewhere we could talk in private?' said Buchanan.

'Sure, there's an interview room on the first floor, we won't be disturbed in there. Would you like something to drink?'

Buchanan shook his head. 'Any more coffee and we'll float.'

'Fine, follow me.'

Roberts showed them into a glass-walled room. 'Please sit Sergeant, Inspector.'

Buchanan sat with his back to the window, Street on his left, facing Roberts.

'What can I do for you, Inspector?'

'Do you have a salesman working for you who recently transferred from your retail division?'

Roberts shrugged. 'I'd have to check with personnel. Do you have anything more than that to go on?'

'His area would be somewhere in the south-east.'

'We have more than one representative in the south-east. Can you be a little more specific as to the area?'

'The person we are anxious to talk to would have just recently come to your industrial division from retail, possibly sometime in the last couple of months, and work in the Eastbourne area.'

Roberts took out his phone and dialled. 'Hello, who is this? Marcia – good. It's Dave Roberts. Have a look on our files for anyone who's transferred in to industrial sales from retail – try the last three months, probably had accounts in the Eastbourne area, I'll hold. Sure you don't want coffee, Inspector?'

Buchanan shook his head.

'Ah, what do you have Marcia? Frank Simms? Thanks – no, he's not in trouble, just someone needs to get in touch with him urgently, bye.'

'Mr Roberts, do you know the whereabouts of Frank Simms?' said Buchanan.

'Not without calling him.'

'Would you do that, please?'

Buchanan got up from his chair and walked over to the window. He fancied this panorama, it was much more interesting than the one from his office. There was an unobstructed view over the railway line and car parks to the Solent. He watched as the QM2 made her way up the channel. As Roberts chatted on the phone to Simms, Buchanan continued to watch as the QM2 moved slowly forward, now heading for the terminal.

'Inspector, Frank's in Dover. He'll be heading back this way first thing in the morning.'

'Ask him if he'd call in at my office on the way past in the morning. Hammonds Drive police station Eastbourne.'

'Frank, the inspector asks can you stop by his office tomorrow morning? Hang on, you speak to him. Frank Simms, Inspector,' said Roberts, passing his phone to Buchanan.

'Frank, it's Inspector Buchanan. I need to have a quick word with you – my office is on Hammonds Drive – that's in Eastbourne. Tell you what, you'll be coming along the A259, how about we meet at the Starbucks in Pevensey? It's just at the roundabout at the end of the A259 – yes, that's right, just behind the BP garage. Ten o'clock? Fine, see you there.'

'All sorted, Inspector?' said Roberts, as he took his phone back from Buchanan.

'Don't look so concerned, Mr Roberts. Your Frank Simms isn't an axe murderer, or anything like that.'

'Good. So why do you need to talk to him?'

'We're investigating a report of a missing person in the Eastbourne area. We need to talk with anybody who may have information on their whereabouts.'

'And you think Frank's somehow involved?'

'Just standard police procedure, Mr Roberts. We have to talk to everyone who may have had contact with the missing person.'

'And the missing person – was he one of Frank's customers?'

Buchanan thought for a moment. 'Would you remember if your company had any dealings with a company called CSM? They were based in Eastbourne?'

'I seem to remember they went into liquidation a couple of months ago. Not sure if they owed us anything. I could check with accounts, if that would help?'

'Everything helps, Mr Roberts.'

Buchanan turned back to the window as Roberts called his accounts department. The QM2 was now resting against the cruise terminal quayside.

Roberts hung up his phone. 'Inspector, not only did they not owe us anything but other than an initial order of resin, and a few sporadic orders since, they've hardly used their account since opening it. You could have a word with the rep who looked after that account, he'd probably be able to give you more information than I can.'

'And who would that be?'

'I'd need to call our retail division, hang on a minute.'

Once again Buchanan stood and turned to look out of the window and contemplated his future. He reverie was disturbed by Roberts.

'Inspector.'

'Ah, yes. You have a name?'

'Yes, it's a Clive Prince you need to talk to. I have his number here, but there might be a problem.'

'Oh, what's that?'

'His wife called the office this morning to say he didn't come home last night. His office hasn't been able to get in touch with him either.'

'I'm afraid they won't be hearing from him, Mr Roberts. Mr Prince was found dead this morning.'

'Oh! What happened? Was it an accident?'

'I'm sorry, we don't have all the details yet.'

'Oh, how sad for Mrs Prince. I'm assuming he was married, Inspector?'

'He was.'

'Children?'

'No.'

'I'll get on to HR and make them aware of what's happened. I expect they'll want to get in touch with Mrs Prince and offer their condolences. Of course, there will be the matter of his samples to be returned and his customers to be told. Hmm, maybe I should call Frank and have him cover till we can find a replacement.'

'Thanks, Mr Roberts. I think we'll get out of your way and let you concentrate on finding a replacement for Mr Prince.'

'Oh, yes, of course, Inspector. Was there anything else?'

'Yes, a simple question – what happens when resin goes out of date?'

'Odd question, Inspector.'

'Suppose a customer doesn't use their resin and it goes out of date, would they return it to you?'

'Yes, but not for a credit. We would charge them for returning it.'

'Why?'

'It costs money to recycle resin. Can't just take it down the waste tip and dump it, we'd have the Environment Agency down on us like a ton of bricks if we did that.'

'Thank you, Mr Roberts, you've been very helpful,' said Buchanan, standing and shaking Roberts' hand.

'And you're sure Frank's not in any trouble?'

'As I said, we only want to talk to him.'

♦

'We only want to talk to him?'

'Didn't want poor Frank to get hauled on the carpet before we had a chance to talk with him.'

'So, you think he is on the fiddle?'

'You heard what Roberts said about out of date resin, *costs money to recycle*. Our Frank probably has a nice little side-line disposing of out of date resin for customers.'

'And pocketing the cash. But who'd buy out of date resin?'

'Denman did.'

'And look where he ended up.'

'You got that address for Mrs Armstrong?'

'Yes, here, in my notebook.'

♦

'There it is,' said Street. 'The red-brick semi-detached with the tree in the front garden.'

Buchanan parked behind a Mercedes 560. He saw one of the wheels was missing and the car was propped up on a stack of house bricks. An out of date taxi licence hung on to the rear bumper with a single, rusted screw.

'Make sure you lock your door,' said Buchanan.

'Doesn't look like that kind of neighbourhood.'

He pointed to the dilapidated taxi.

Street nodded. 'See what you mean. Though it could just be someone bought it cheap and is going to restore it.'

Despite the dilapidated taxi sitting on the road outside, Mrs Armstrong's garden was neat and well-planted. The front garden consisted of rose bushes scattered about. A block paver path ran from the front gate to the front door. On either side were weeded flowerbeds planted with a riot of antirrhinums. Well-manicured boxwood bushes stood like sentinels on both sides of the path at the front door.

'You ring the bell and do the talking,' said Buchanan.

'Maybe I should be asking for a raise – that's the second time today you've left it for me to do the talking.'

'Put your request in writing and I'll sign it.'

'Only joking.'

'So was I.'

Street reached out and pressed the bell-push. It took three rings before Mrs Armstrong answered. She was taller than Street, black hair with streaks of white, tied back in a ponytail. She was wearing a pink T-shirt with a floral print, faded blue denim dungarees and open-toed sandals. In her arms was a huge marmalade-coloured cat.

'Mrs Armstrong, Detective Sergeant Street, and this is Detective Chief Inspector Buchanan. Could we come in and ask you a few questions?' said Street, showing her warrant card.

'What about? Is there something wrong?'

'No, were just making enquiries about someone you used to know.'

'Used to know?'

'Would you mind if we discussed this indoors, Mrs Armstrong?' said Street.

'Yes – yes, of course, come in.'

They followed her into the front room.

'Please, sit.' She indicated the large settee in front of the fire.

Street waited while Mrs Armstrong made herself and the cat comfortable in the wingback chair. Within minutes of settling, the cat yawned, closed its eyes, and began to purr as Mrs Armstrong stroked its head.

'That's a lovely cat,' said Street.

'Hmm, thanks.'

'What's its name?'

'I call him Marmaduke – on account of his colouring.'

'He is a lovely cat. Mrs Armstrong, we've come to ask you about your former husband, Julian Denman.'

'What about him?'

'I'm sorry to say he has died.'

'And you want me to say – what?'

'I take it your relationship wasn't a happy one?'

'That's one way of putting it.'

'How would you put it?'

Before she could answer, the door opened and a tall woman walked in.

'Dorothy, I was wondering if your guests would like something to drink?'

'Martha, this is Detective Sergeant Street and Inspector Buchanan. They've come to tell me Julian has died.'

Street noticed a smile grow across Martha's face.

'I hope it was juicy, like under a train, Sergeant?'

'No,' said Street, shaking her head, 'he was found nailed to a sheet of plywood in an industrial oven. He'd been covered in fibreglass.'

'What a waste. I'd have tied a chain round his ankles and chucked the bastard off the pier.'

'You knew Mr Denman?'

'Knew of him, and what he did to Dorothy.'

'Would you care to say what, Mrs Armstrong?' said Street.

'What is there to say that isn't already public knowledge?'

'All we know is you were married to Julian Denman, and he had been unfaithful to you.'

'Hmm, what he did would fill a book,' interrupted Martha.

'Martha, I can speak for myself. What Martha was about to tell you, Sergeant, was my ex-husband was a complete shit. The night of our wedding he paid for the services of a prostitute. He

129

was late for the ceremony and was drunk to boot. If that wasn't bad enough, he was a drug addict, spent thousands on – on – that stuff.'

'You mean cocaine?' asked Street.

'Disgusting habit.' said Martha.

'Disgusting creature,' added Dorothy.

♦

As Street drove back along the A27 to Eastbourne, Buchanan thought about all those passengers who'd been wined and dined on-board the QM2.

'Jill, I've made a decision. When this case is over I'm going to take a month's leave and take Karen on a cruise. It must be somewhere romantic, somewhere she's never been before, and somewhere she could truly be excited about.'

'How about the Med? I hear there are a lot of cruises go there. Most leave from Southampton so you wouldn't have to fly anywhere.'

'Hmm, not quite what I had in mind. Driving to the docks makes me think of the number of times I've driven her to the ferry in Newhaven. No, it needs to be somewhere exotic, somewhere that getting there would be part of the holiday.'

'A month, you said?'

'Yes, why? Do you have somewhere in mind?'

'Just thinking. One of my friend's parents flew to San Francisco, then boarded a cruise ship and sailed to Hawaii and back. That romantic enough?'

'San Francisco? That's the place Tony Bennett sings about, isn't it?'

'Thought for a minute you were going to break out into song.'

'Yes, that's it, The Golden Gate, Fisherman's Wharf. The city where the cable cars go halfway to the stars, the city where you can leave your heart.'

'You've sold me.'

'Not a word to Karen, or to Stephen. This has to be a surprise for her.'

'You'll need to tell her at some point.'

'A week before – that should be time enough.'

'How many years have you two been married?'

'Thirty-five, why?'

'When a woman goes on a holiday like the one you're planning, she needs time to plan what she will be wearing. Maybe lose a couple of pounds so she can get into that little black dress she once wore, understand?'

'Ah, hadn't thought of that. What do you suggest?'

'If Stephen was planning something like that for me, I'd like to be teased a bit first.'

'How? Or should I really be asking?'

'Don't know what you mean,' she said, grinning. 'Well, if Stephen and I were married, like you and Karen – I'd like to have him start by bringing me breakfast in bed at the weekends. Next would be flowers, delivered to where I work, sort of to show off in front of my friends.'

'Karen doesn't have a job, per se.'

'She volunteers in St Wilfred's, doesn't she?'

'Yes, but that's –'

'Not work, that what you were going to say?'

'I stand corrected.'

'Like to see you try with your seatbelt on.'

'Very funny.'

'Well, anyway, flowers to the charity shop. I'd do that a couple of times. Then when you have her wondering just how bad the mess is that you have made of something, take her out to dinner and tell her what you're planning.'

'You think that would work?

'It would with me.'

'Then that's what I'll do. But in the meantime, what do you think of our visit to Southampton?'

'Hansons was much what I expected. Their sales rep, Frank Simms, sounds like he's in for a rocket when his boss finds out about his little racket on the side.'

'And Mrs Armstrong?'

'Wondering if Martha is just a friend.'

'I think more likely her sister; their facial features are quite similar.'

Street shrugged. 'Doesn't make any difference. I got the impression Martha takes very good care of Mrs Armstrong. Either way, neither of them liked Denman.'

'You know, I've just had a thought –'

'Just one?'

'Touché. Anyway, we now have at least four women who are glad to see the back of Denman. There's Mrs Armstrong, her friend or sister Martha, and the two – or is it three? – Morelli women.

'Now that is an interesting thought. Add Mrs Prince and we have Murder Inc.'

6

'You look pleased with yourself,' said Street, placing Buchanan's coffee on his desk.

'Took your advice.'

'What was that? Don't tell me, you actually gave her breakfast in bed?'

'Yep. I'm sure she's now wondering what I'm up to.'

'Is that the first time you've given her breakfast in bed?'

'No. When we were first married, I used to take her breakfast in bed every Saturday, then head off out to watch football.'

'Good, so she's thinking you're taking up your old habits, getting ready to retire. That'll confuse her a bit. But I wouldn't send flowers right away, I'd wait a few days.'

'Not sure that's what she's thinking. More likely thinks it's got something to do with the new house.'

'That makes sense. Oh, by the way, I've tracked down the estate agency for the factory, they don't open till ten.'

'Be interesting to find out just who owns the factory. In the meantime, I'm going to see what the Environment Agency thinks about the oil drums at the factory.'

'The local number will be in the contact book – top shelf by the window.'

'Thanks.'

Buchanan looked up the number and dialled.

'Yes, this is Detective Chief Inspector Buchanan, Sussex CID. I'd like to talk to someone about some oil drums in an empty factory in Eastbourne – yes – I believe they have been abandoned – it's at the end of Edison Road. I'll meet you there in half an hour, goodbye.'

'What did they say?' asked Street.

'Didn't seem to be worried about the barrels. The guy I

talked to said they get this all the time when a company moves out. The estate agent will call saying there's abandoned waste and will the Environment Agency come and dispose of it.'

'That's not the Environment Agencies job, is it?'

'Doubt it. I think it's the estate agent trying to get the place cleaned up on the taxpayers' account. Will you call the estate agency and have someone meet me at the factory to let me in?'

'Ok, need to talk to them anyway about who owns the factory.'

◆

Buchanan drove into the factory car park and stopped beside the large white van with the letters EA on the side.

'Inspector Buchanan?' said the EA officer, Dave Kelly.'

'DCI Buchanan. Any sign of someone from the estate agency?'

'I've been here ten minutes, not seen anyone.'

'Ok, guess we'll have to wait.'

'What do these barrels look like, Inspector?'

'Blue, four to a pallet.'

'How many pallets?'

Buchanan shrugged. 'We'll know soon enough, this looks like the estate agent.'

They watched as a black Ford SUV drove into the car park and stopped bedside Buchanan's car.

The driver got out, struggling to hold on to a large manila folder under one arm and a large take-away coffee in the opposite hand. 'Inspector Buchanan?' she said, addressing them.

'I'm Inspector Buchanan, this is Dave Kelly of the Environment Agency.'

'Alice Freeman. Oh, I hope there's nothing wrong. This is my first day at the branch.'

'I'm sure it will be fine, we just need access to the building.'

'Oh, I thought – oh, never mind, hang on a minute.'

She returned to her car and placed the folder on the

passenger seat then walked back to Buchanan and Kelly. 'I've got the keys, follow me, please.'

She stopped at the front door. 'What is this police tape doing here?'

'There was an accident in the factory.'

'Oh, hope no one was hurt.'

Once the front door was opened and the alarm silenced, Buchanan led the way into the factory.

'So, this is where the body was found, Inspector?' said Kelly.

'Yes. Over there, nailed to a sheet of plywood in the rear of the oven.'

'Are these the barrels?'

'Yes, quite a lot of them. More than you'd expect?'

'I'd expect none when a company moves out. Went bust you say?'

'That's what we understand.'

Kelly walked round the stack of barrels, muttering to himself and counting as he went. 'Four to a pallet and there are five pallets. Shit, what a mess. Oh crap, these are leaking,' he said, almost stepping into a patch of oily waste. 'Watch out, Inspector, these drums are leaking. You say you had a sample tested?'

'Yes. The report described it as a mixture of transformer oil and various types of diesel engine lubricants.'

'Oh, I don't like that,' he said, shaking his head. 'If all these barrels contain a similar concoction then I'll have to get on to the office, might have to declare an emergency. Is there a drain anywhere near?'

'I don't know,' said Freeman.

'Hang on, I'll have a look around,' said Kelly.

He came back out shaking his head. 'Damn stuff's gone down the drain. This is worse than I thought.'

'You mean I can't rent out the factory?' said Freeman.

'Not until this lot is removed, and the ground tested for

contaminants.'

'What now, Mr Kelly?' said Buchanan.

'First thing to do is call my office and make a report. Also, I think it wise if we all went outside, no telling what we are breathing.'

'Excellent advice,' said Buchanan.

'We'll need the environmental services team here, pronto. No telling how far down the drains this stuff has got to.'

'I'll have to call my office and let them know what's happening, Inspector,' said Freeman.

All three of them stood outside the front door and made their respective phone calls.

'Inspector, my office wants me to return, we're short-staffed today and there are other offices to show.'

'That's ok, Alice. What do you want to do about the keys?'

'I'll take those,' said Kelly. 'This building is now under the jurisdiction of the Environment Agency, at least it is until properly cleaned up.'

'Oh,' said Freeman. 'I don't think I'm allowed to let you have the keys.'

Kelly shook his head. 'Just call your office again and tell them that the Environment Agency has taken control of the building for now.'

'Ok. Inspector, you have my number. Would you call me and let me know what's happening?'

'Will do, Alice.'

Buchanan sucked on a fruit gum and watched the seagulls wheel and dive, their peace disturbed by their presence. Kelly finally hung up from making numerous phone calls.

'Inspector, this area is now off limits to all but those who need to be here. The environment clean-up team will be here shortly.'

'Will you be in charge?'

'Indirectly. The agency doesn't actually do the clean-up, we use the services of professional contractors for that.'

'Are they local, in town?'

'Not quite in town, the contractors we use cover the south-east, and the local depot is only about a twenty-minute drive from here.'

'Good, I'll wait with you.'

Twenty minutes later the peace was disturbed by the arrival of a tanker truck, a curtain-sided articulated lorry carrying a forklift hanging from the back of the trailer, a bright yellow estate car and a fleet of transit vans.

Buchanan stood back and watched as Kelly went over to the driver of the estate. They talked for a few minutes then walked over to Buchanan.

'Inspector,' said Kelly, 'this is Jackie Hargreaves from ALVISO environmental.'

'Jackie,' said Buchanan, reaching out to shake her hand.

'Where are the barrels, Dave?' asked Hargreaves.

'The barrels we want are inside on the left, just behind the roller shutters.'

'Let's have a look at them.'

'Some of them have split,' said Kelly, as he led the way back into the factory. 'And what's worse is it looks like some of the residue has run out under the toilet walls and into the drains.'

'What's the background story, Inspector?' asked Hargreaves.

'A few days ago, we responded to a report about a dead body found inside the factory. I arrived to investigate and, along with finding the deceased, discovered the barrels. I didn't initially attach any importance to them, thought they were just materials left behind from the previous occupants.'

She nodded. 'That's usually the way. Company goes bust and the new tenants get the task and expense of cleaning up.'

'But not this type of clean-up?'

'No, that's down to experts like us.'

'And the taxpayer gets stuck with the cost.'

She nodded. 'Inspector, if you'll excuse me, I've got my team to brief.'

Buchanan followed Kelly and Hargreaves out into the car park. As Hargreaves conducted her briefing two fire trucks arrived. Buchanan walked back into the factory and the blue curtain-sided trailer. He pulled at the catches on the side of the trailer and managed to release four of them. With difficulty, he pulled the curtain away and tried to push his head up into the darkness. It took a few moments for him to realise he wasn't going to get anywhere unless he undid the whole side. His curiosity kindled, he walked round to the back doors of the trailer. Surprised there were no locks on the doors, he pulled at the handles and opened one of the doors. Inside were two rows of pallets, each with large white plastic tanks inside a steel cage. New problem, he thought, and walked back over to talk with Hargreaves.

'Dave, get them to set up either side of the roller shutters,' Hargreaves said to one of her crew. 'Don't want them to be in our way. And get the roller shutter up.'

For once in his career Buchanan felt like a spare groom at a wedding. He watched the firemen set up their hoses in case of fire. The environment contractors unloaded a forklift from the rear of the flatbed truck in readiness for putting the drums on the back. The clean-up crew donned protective clothing and set to work creating a spill cordon with what looked like sawdust to Buchanan. Another team went manhole by manhole down the street to determine the extent of the run-off in the drains.

'Excuse me, Jackie, I've just found something you might like to see.'

'Can it wait, Inspector? I've got this mess to clean up.'

He shrugged. 'Yes, I suppose so.'

Since Buchanan didn't want to get in the way, he went for a walk down the road to see what the drain team were doing.

'What's that for?' he asked as one of the drain crew were

lowering a large block of metal with wheels on the side.

'This is our drain ferret. Ah, I can see by that look on your face you think I'm joking?'

'No, I think I understand. The wheels are to propel the device down the drain, and I presume there is a camera in its nose?'

'Its real name is a drain robot, and yes, it has a camera at the front with LED's so it can see what's down there. The attached orange cable contains the power feed to the motor and the fibre-optic cable for the camera. The robot is controlled from the inside cab – if you look at that screen on the wall of the cab, you can see what the camera is looking at down the drain.'

'Has any of the oil from the factory got this far?'

He shook his head. 'No. There's so much seagull detritus down these drains, I'm surprised anything flows down there. We've checked from the end of the road back to the first drain from the factory, that's as far as the oil has leaked.'

'Lot easier to clean up then?'

'Should be. Sometimes we have to dig up the whole sewer and replace the pipes. In the case of old collapsed drains, we may have to remove all the sub-soil around it.'

'How will you get the oil out of the drain?'

'Back flush. Our truck has a pressure water hose and an extractor hose. Simply put, we flush and extract at the same time.'

'Thanks, you learn something new every day.'

'No problem.'

Buchanan walked back to the factory and stood beside Hargreaves, watching as the forklift loaded the last of the intact barrels onto the flatbed.

'What will you do with the damaged barrels?'

'Load them into a bund tank, then on to the truck.'

'Bund tank?'

'A big steel box that is liquid tight, don't want to add to the problem.'

'What about all the stuff spread on the ground?'

'After we have made sure the concrete is free of contaminates, the oil spill granules get swept up and put into sealed containers.'

'That's it?'

'That's it.'

'What will happen to the stuff in the drums?'

'We'll take it back to our plant and if it can be recycled we'll do so, otherwise it will be incinerated.'

'Jackie, as I said earlier, this is all part of a murder investigation. I would like to send two of my investigators along to your plant. After you have processed the barrel's contents, I would like my people to remove or photograph all the labels from the drums, also any other markings.'

'Didn't your SCI's take photos?'

'They did of the scene, but not the barrels. They were mainly interested in the body and what was in its immediate vicinity.'

'What about the pallets, Inspector?'

'What would they tell me?'

'Most pallets have manufacturers' markings, might give you an indication of their origin so you'd possibly be able to trace them.'

'Not sure about that, but we'll have a look, thanks.'

'The labels all look like they've been photocopied, Inspector. Wouldn't just one do?'

'Can't afford to miss anything, I think I'll have the lot.'

'Ok, I'll call you when we've made the drums safe. Now you said you have something you want me to look at?'

'Yes, that trailer inside the factory, it's full of plastic barrels.'

Hargreaves face froze. 'How many?'

'Don't know, looks like the trailer is full of them.'

'Not another one!'

'What do you mean?'

'Inspector, if this is what I think it is, you've not only got a murder enquiry to look after, you've now got a case of illegal waste dumping.'

'You mean like fly-tipping?'

She nodded. 'Except this is on a grand scale. Let's have a look.'

Buchanan followed Hargreaves across the car park to the trailer.

'Shit, another one,' she said.

'Could you explain, please?'

'Inspector, what I suspect is, on top of the waste dumping, here also are the remnants of fuel laundering.'

'Go on.'

'What happens is unscrupulous people set up bogus waste disposal companies and, for a fee, remove industrial waste. Usually forging HWCN's.'

'HWCN's?'

'Hazardous Waste Consignment Notices. The unsuspecting factory operative thinks they have fulfilled the law. But unknown to them their waste has just been loaded on to a stolen trailer and ends up being dropped off in some unsuspecting factory owner's lorry park.'

'And you think that's what's happened here?'

'Not quite, the stolen trailers are usually just dumped in an empty car park, or lay-by. I suppose this factory has been untenanted for a while?'

'A month or two at least.'

'Quite the classic case. This is the first time I've heard of a trailer being abandoned inside a factory, although it could be they were waiting to fully load it before taking it to some unsuspecting factory and abandoning it. Inspector, these people are the most despicable in the world. If it was up to me, I'd bury them in their own waste.'

'A bit of a harsh punishment for littering?'

141

'Inspector, let me tell you a story, a true one. There is an area just north of Naples in Italy — its nickname is *the triangle of death*. Several years ago, the Mafia, along with other individuals, used that area to illegally dump all sorts of toxic waste in places such as abandoned quarries. Now children are being born with all sorts of birth defects. And that isn't an isolated incident. All over that area of Italy abnormal levels of birth defects are being diagnosed. Not only was the waste dumped, but incinerated in the open with locals breathing in all those toxic fumes.'

'Glad we don't have those type of problems in the UK.'

'But we do, Inspector.'

'I've never heard about them.'

'The cases I'm referring to are civil as opposed to criminal.'

'What do you mean?'

'Ok. Corby — do you know where that is?'

'Yes, it lies between the M1 and the A1M, just north of London.'

'In 1981 British Steel closed its plant and the land was sold off for redevelopment. Unfortunately, when the site was being cleared, huge clouds of toxic dust were created and sludge was dropped onto the road by uncovered lorries. It wasn't till the late eighties that the full extent of the birth defects caused by the toxic dust being released into the environment was realised.'

'What sort of birth defects?'

'Children being born with upper limb defects.'

'But surely that's just an isolated incident?'

'I wish. In 2004, seventy-two acres of land in the Spoden Valley in Rochdale was found to be contaminated by asbestos. The council were going to approve a planning application for six hundred and fifty houses. They were about to approve the application when it was discovered the whole area was substantially contaminated with asbestos. And of course, there is the Armley asbestos disaster.'

'Where's Armley?'

'Armley is a suburb of Leeds. That area has the highest concentration of mesothelioma cases in the country. That was another asbestos factory that was closed and the land sold off for redevelopment.'

'That's the sort of thing you expect to hear on the news happening in third world countries, not here at home.'

'It's all about money, Inspector.'

'So, if I understand where you're going with this, is, you think the Mafia are now exporting their waste?'

She nodded. 'It's possible, but I think this might be different. These barrels as you call them are actually known as IBC's, that's intermediate bulk containers. There's been a spate of these being dumped in lay-bys recently.'

'Tell me more.'

'You know what red diesel is?'

'Yes, it's diesel that doesn't have road duty applied, stuff farmers and site contractors use. It's died red to stop people using it their cars.'

'Currently about half the price you'd pay at the pump. What we've been discovering is certain people buy large quantities of red diesel, then remove the die and sell the now white diesel to unsuspecting motorists at the full price. There was a case a few months ago of one of these gangs trying to sell the fuel to a small private airfield for use in jet helicopters.'

'Do they make much money out of the deal?'

'I read a report a few years ago about one gang that set up a laundering plant for a small outlay of eight hundred pounds and made a profit of fifty-two thousand in the first ten days.'

'And you think the IBC's in the trailer contain the residue of red diesel laundering?'

'Inspector, I'm sure if you have look around this factory you'll find evidence of diesel laundering.'

'What should we be looking for?'

'Large fuel storage tanks and bags of kitty litter. The kitty litter is used to filter out the die in the red diesel. Thankfully this practice is coming to an end as the diesel now has a radioactive tracer added when it's being made.'

'This trailer in the factory – you think it's one of those?'

'Looks like it.'

'This is a new one on me. What's the method employed?'

'The usual scenario is that someone steals a trailer, usually a curtain-side, or sometimes it's stolen to order when full. The contents are sold on the black market, then the trailer is loaded with waste and just abandoned.'

'Contents?'

'Mostly small consumer stuff, like mobile phones. But the most popular is tobacco products.'

'Where would they store that much illicit goods?'

'Hargreaves turned and pointed to the factory.'

'But the people who worked there would notice – wouldn't they?'

'Big enough factory. Who'd notice a few pallets of stuff wrapped in cardboard? And in the case of an empty factory –'

'The perfect solution. Do you have any idea how often trailers are stolen in the UK?'

She shook her head. 'I'd have to check with the Freight Transport Association for that.'

'Shall we see how the clean-up's going?' said Buchanan.

'I was just about to do that.'

Buchanan followed Hargreaves back over to the clean-up crew and saw that not only were the barrels gone from the floor, but the crew were completing the vacuuming up of the oil spill powder.

With the factory roller shutters being wide open, Buchanan could see right into the rear of the factory. On the left were a stack of pallets with cling-filmed cardboard boxes. Ready for anything, he walked back into the gloom to the pallets. He noticed that someone had already made an attempt to see what was inside one of the boxes. He pulled back the strands of cling-film and saw, what would once have been his delight, cartons of cigarettes.

♦

'Anything happen while I've been gone?' asked Buchanan.

'I've had an interesting conversation with the estate agent,' said Street.

'Oh, what did she have to say?'

'She said they don't actually know who owns the building.'

'Then who do they collect the rent for?'

'They pay it to a management company.'

'Get the bank details?'

'Nothing special, just a Lloyds account in Eastbourne.'

'Ok, you know the routine. Name and address of account holders, and printed copies of the last six months' transactions.'

'Already on it. Any word from Dr Mansell?'

'Not yet. Where are Stephen and Morris?'

'Early lunch, Stephen's car's ready and they've gone to collect it.'

'Must be nice to have time for lunch.'

'Do I detect all's not well?'

'You have detected correctly. Not only do we have a double murder case on our hands, we now have lorry theft, fuel laundering, smuggling, and toxic waste dumping to investigate.'

'Do we have to declare a major incident?'

Buchanan shook his head. 'No, not just yet, the environment agency is handling the waste clean-up. We will need to check into stolen curtain-side trailer cases, and notify Excise about the cartons of cigarettes in the factory.'

'So, what's happened?'

'Someone's been using the empty factory for distributing goods, including stolen tobacco products, that were contained in the trailers when they were hijacked. Also, for distribution of illicit white diesel.'

'That doesn't quite make sense. If you're going to use the factory as a distribution point, why muddy the operation by dumping toxic waste? And, we shouldn't forget, using the factory as a torture and execution chamber.'

'That's one of the things that's been bothering me.'

'Time for a conference?'

Buchanan thought for a moment. 'You're a bad example for me.'

'Me? It's you that scurries down to the pub for a drink to think.'

He shook his head. 'I'm supposed to be meeting Frank Simms this afternoon. He's on his way back from Dover.'

'Ok, Starbucks it will be.'

♦

'Your usual?' said Buchanan, as he pulled out his wallet.

'Please,' said Street. 'I'll grab the seats in the corner.'

'Ok.'

Buchanan brought their drinks and sat facing the door.

'What does he look like?' asked Street.

'I've no idea. What do you think a resin salesman look like?'

She shook her head and took a long sip of her drink. 'What time did you agree to meet up?'

Buchanan looked at his phone. 'He's fifteen minutes late, not very impressive for a sales rep.'

'It's only fifteen minutes, and you did say he was driving from Dover.'

They continued to drink their coffees. Street stared at her phone while looking at The Hydro wedding venue. Buchanan looked for holidays at sea.

'Wonder what's going on?' said Buchanan, looking up from his phone. 'That's the second fire truck in as many minutes, and that's an ambulance, followed by a squad car.'

'Shall I call control?'

Buchanan looked back at his phone. 'He's late. What? Er –

yes.'

'RTA on the A259. Witness reported a hit and run. Shall we go see?'

'I hope it's not Simms.'

'How late is he?' asked Street, as they closed the café door behind them.

'Twenty minutes. Hope nothing has happened to him.'

Street turned on the blue lights and siren and drove down the right-hand lane past the stationary cars.

'Must be a bad one,' she said. 'Two fire trucks, ambulances and patrol cars.'

She parked on the verge beside one of the patrol cars.

'DCI Buchanan and DS Street,' said Buchanan, to one of the traffic officers. 'What can you tell us?'

'Driver of the blue van said he saw two cars collide: the Audi went out of control and ended up in the bushes, the other car didn't stop.'

'Did he get an ID on the one that didn't stop?'

'Said he was distracted, too busy watching the Audi.'

'How's the driver of the Audi?'

'Not good, firemen are trying to get him out, car wrapped itself round an oak tree.'

'Where's the witness?'

'Over there in the red Ford.'

'Have the driver's name?'

'Sam Skinner. Farrier, on his way to shoe some horses.'

'Thanks, Constable, we'll go have a word with Mr Skinner.'

Buchanan and Street made their way past the rescue vehicles and over to the red Ford.

'You do the questioning, Jill. Might come better from you.

'Mr Skinner? Sergeant Street. I understand you saw what happened?'

'Mad as hell these drivers, should be in jail.'

'What did you see?'

'I was on my way to work,' Skinner said, looking at his watch and shaking his head. 'Going to be real late. I'm never late, always on time.'

'You were saying, Mr Skinner?'

'I'd just passed The Lamb.'

'The Lamb?' said Buchanan.

'Yes, The Lamb. Pub on the corner, just where the road to Ninfield branches off. I looked in my rear-view mirror and saw these two cars racing down the hill. Kept overtaking each other, like they were racing.'

'Can you remember the types of cars involved?'

'The one that crashed, that was an Audi, the other – I think was a BMW.'

'Do you remember the colour or the registration?'

'Black, last three letters were UPX'

'And you don't remember the rest of the registration?'

'No, just UPX. Remember thinking that could be the initials of United Parcels Exchange, but that doesn't quite work.'

'Did you actually see what happened, Mr Skinner? The collision specifically?'

'As I said, they were racing down the road. The BMW kept trying to overtake the Audi, but it kept getting in the way, you know, pulling out into the middle of the road to stop the BMW from overtaking.'

'How fast would you say they were going?'

'I was doing just under sixty and they flew past me – they must have been doing at least eighty.'

'Then what happened?'

'The Audi pulled in, like he'd given up and just wanted the BMW to overtake, and that's the strange bit.'

'What was?'

'The BMW hit the Audi.'

'Could you explain a bit more?'

'The Audi pulled over to the curb and the BMW turned right

into it.'

'Was there an approaching car?'

'No, the road was perfectly clear. It was like the BMW driver was trying to hit the Audi.'

'And that's all you saw?'

'Yes, the BMW hit the Audi, slowed a bit then when the Audi ran into the trees, it accelerated and shot off down the road.'

'Have you given your statement to one of the traffic officers?' asked Buchanan.

'Yes.'

'Thanks, Mr Skinner, you've been very helpful,' said Street.

'Let's go see how the firemen are getting on,' said Buchanan to Street.

'Excuse me,' he said to one of them, 'DCI Buchanan. Can you give me the latest on the driver?'

'It's not looking good. The paramedics are trying to stop the bleeding, but they say he's lost too much blood.'

'Is he conscious?'

'No, probably never knew what happened other than being run off the road.'

'Has anyone got the registration of the vehicle?'

'John will, he was first on site.'

'John?'

'Sergeant Warleggan. That's him over there wearing the high viz coat. Talking on his radio.'

Street followed Buchanan over to Sergeant Warleggan.

'Excuse me,' said Buchanan.

Warleggan looked up and held his radio away from his face. 'Can I help you?'

Buchanan shook his head and took out his warrant card. 'DCI Buchanan and DS Street.'

'Ok, what can I do for you?'

'Just wondering if you have an ID on the driver of the Audi?'

'Not yet, it's a leased car.'

'How about the BMW that was involved in the incident?'

'Reported stolen an hour ago in Bexhill. Driver went to meet someone and had his car hijacked by two thugs, as he described them.'

'And the Audi's leased?'

'Yes. Can't get the driver's ID till the firemen get him out.'

'Thanks, I'll go see how they're doing.'

Buchanan and Street walked back to the firemen.

'How's it going?' asked Buchanan.

'We've managed to get to the driver.'

'How is he?'

'Didn't make it, I'm afraid. Here's his wallet if you're looking for identification.'

Buchanan took the wallet, opened it, and looked for the driving licence.

'Is it him?' asked Street.

Buchanan nodded.

'Get a name?' asked Warleggan, who'd just joined them.

'Frank Simms, he was on his way to meet up with us.'

'Was he a witness to a crime?'

'Why?'

'Just wondering. I took the witness statement from the Ford driver. I also had a look at the Audi. The rear quarter damage looks just like when we do a tactical stop on vehicles.'

'You mean a TPAC stop?' said Street.

'No, it's what the Americans call a PIT manoeuvre. It's a technique whereby the police car forces the fleeing car to spin out and stop. It's never done at high speed as it can cause a serious accident. It's been done in the UK, but only in an extreme circumstance.'

'And you think that might be what has happened here?' said Street.

'I've investigated many road traffic accidents, I've never seen that type of damage to a vehicle. If asked for my opinion in court, I'd say Mr Simms had been forced off the road.'

Street looked at Buchanan. 'What's the matter?'

'Dr Mansell isn't going to be pleased with me. Sergeant Warleggan, this is now a crime scene. Would you let the other officers know? I'll tell the paramedics.'

7

'Another one, Buchanan?' said Mansell, shaking his head, 'I'm running out of space in the morgue because of you.'

'I don't do them in, Doctor, I simply find them.'

'That's not the way I see it.'

'So, cause of death of Mr Simms?'

'He died from multiple internal injuries, be hard pressed to say which organ failed first. Being wrapped round a tree with a car for company does that to one's body.'

Buchanan shook his head. 'Where have you got with Mr Prince?'

'Must be quiet in Glasgow since you left, Buchanan. Mr Prince's death is a case of asphyxiation: he drowned in his own blood.'

'I thought he died from the nails being hammered into his mouth?' said Street.

Mansell shook his head. 'He may have been suffering from a certain amount of paralysis below the neck, but it wasn't the nails that killed him. He just simply bled out into his lungs and suffocated.'

'I don't understand how anyone could just stand there and let someone hammer nails into the mouth' said Street.

'Nail gun, more likely,' replied Mansell. 'His mouth was badly lacerated. Just what I'd expect when someone forces a nail gun into the mouth.'

Street shook her head. 'I could see that being done in a workshop where there is compressed air, but to have dragged the victim all the way out into the woods, plus an air compressor, just doesn't make sense to me.'

'It wasn't an air-operated nail gun,' said Mansell. 'I found powder burns on the face. It was a gas-powered nail gun, and a pretty big one at that to have fired four-inch nails.'

'A first-fix gun,' said Buchanan, 'used by carpenters who work on site where there is no power available.'

Street and Mansell turned and stared at Buchanan.

He held up his phone. 'It's all on the internet. So far I've found four companies that make them.'

'And how many sell them?' said Mansell.

Buchanan grinned. 'That's a very good point, probably hundreds. And then there is also eBay and other second-hand outlets. Don't suppose there were any traces of paint flakes, or bits of torn labels?'

'You're correct if you are thinking about paint flakes from the tool itself, but there were vestiges of what the gun had come into contact with the last time it was used.'

'Like what?' said Buchanan.

'Light green paint – topcoat, I'd say from looking at it.'

'That's not going to help much, even if you could identify the manufacturer,' said Street.

'I sent samples off to the lab first thing. Told them to put a rush on, said bodies are arriving daily.'

Buchanan smiled at Mansell's humour. 'What was their reaction?'

'Said they'd do their best. I think there's a slim chance of identifying it, but worth a try.'

'Results back yet?' asked Buchanan.

Mansell held up a copy of an email. 'Thought you'd ask that. Here, take a look.'

'It never fails to amaze me,' said Buchanan, 'how they can tell so much from so little.'

'Well, what does it say?' said Street.

'Not only do they provide the colour, shade and make-up of the paint, we also know the manufacturer and the manufacturer's colour code.'

'How will that help?' asked Street.

'I imagine since this is a mix-at-the-shop paint,' said Mansell, 'the manufacturer should be able to give us a list of all the places this paint could have been sold.'

'How do you see that helping?'

'If this type of paint is only sold through approved dealers, that will reduce the number of sources. I imagine you would start with that list. Then. knowing what the colour code is, you could ask which contractors have ordered it recently –'

'And from that we could find out who used it,' said Street.

'Yes, but not necessarily who pulled the trigger on the nail gun,' said Buchanan. 'Jill, where are Stephen and Morris?'

'Morris suggested they go back and see what was going on at the Morellis' flat. You want me to get them to do the rounds of the paint shops?'

'How fresh would you say the paint was, Doctor?'

'Not any older than a few days, according to the forensic test.'

'Jill, tell them to go back four weeks.'

'Will do.'

'Well, Buchanan,' said Mansell, rising from his seat, 'I've got work to do. See you at the next body.'

Buchanan smiled. 'There won't be any, Doctor.'

'I'll believe that when it doesn't happen, Buchanan. Be seeing you.'

◆

'Where have you two been?' said Street, to Hunter and Dexter.

'We stopped in the canteen, why?'

'Oh, never mind.'

'Where's the chief, Jill?' said Hunter.

'Just gone over to Tesco's for a sandwich. What did you two find out that took you so long?'

'Turns out there are only two local companies who sell that

154

paint. The first one we tried hadn't sold any in months.'

'We were lucky at Brewers,' said Dexter. 'They sold ten litres of that particular paint to a local company five weeks ago.'

'Get a name?' said Buchanan, interrupting the conversation having just returned with his sandwich.

'Yep, and a copy of the sales invoice. The company is called Pace Decorators, they're based in Eastbourne.'

'Address?'

'Their yard is in the industrial estate on Finmere Road.'

'I'll pay them a visit,' said Buchanan, rewrapping his sandwich and placing it in his desk drawer.

'Us as well?' said Hunter.

'Anything happening at the Morellis'?'

'Not sure,' said Dexter. 'Bit difficult keeping an eye on a whole apartment building.'

'We've managed to recognise most of the residents,' said Hunter. 'We're pretty sure none of the Morellis have been out while we've been there.'

'Ok. Think you can manage a twenty-four-hour watch between the two of you?'

'Probably. Will need to get on to parking control and let them know though – we almost got towed away yesterday. The van was reported as having someone rough-sleeping in it. Tow truck driver got a surprise when I told him to piss off.'

'You didn't – did you?' said Street.

'No, not quite in those words, but we didn't want him to know we were the police.'

'I'll get on to parking control,' said Street. 'Make sure you don't have any more midnight interruptions.'

'I'll go talk to the decorators,' said Buchanan. 'Where's Finmere Road?'

'Right at the Tesco roundabout on to Seaside Road, then right again on to Northbourne Road. The first road on the right off Northbourne is Finmere,' said Street.

♦

Buchanan parked beside a well looked after red Ford-Astra in the visitor bay in front of Pace Decorators. The roller shutters were down, so he entered the side door and stood in the entrance hall. There were two doors. The one on the left, Buchanan saw through a meshed-over glass window led into the warehouse; the one in front, according to the sign, told him the office was on the first floor and to press the button on the entry phone for access.

'Yes? Can I help?' said the voice on the intercom when Buchanan pressed it for the third time.

'Detective Chief Inspector Buchanan, Sussex CID. I'd like to have a word with whoever is in charge.'

'There's no one here just now, they're all out on jobs. What's it about?'

'You're here.'

'That's not what I meant.'

'I realise that. When will someone be here?'

'Who do you want to speak to?'

'Is there a Mr Pace?'

'Yes, he's in town doing the banking.'

'I'll come in and wait for him.'

'Not sure when he'll be back.'

'How about you call him and tell him Detective Chief Inspector Buchanan wants to have a word with him about some paint your company purchased from Brewers?'

The lock buzzed. 'Come on up, I'll call him.'

'Thank you.'

Buchanan opened the door and climbed the stairs to the landing on the first floor. The door at the top had no lock so he went in.

'Can I get you something to drink while you wait?' asked the receptionist.

Buchanan eyed the six-pack of beer on top of the filing

cabinet: lager, not his taste. He shook his head. 'No thanks, I'm fine, I've got a sandwich waiting back at the office.'

'I've never met a police inspector before.'

'Hope you're not disappointed.'

'Oh, sorry, that sounded rude.'

'Nothing to be sorry about, I'm flesh and blood – like everyone else.

'If you prick us, do we not bleed?'

'If you tickle us do we not laugh? If you poison us, do we not die? And if you wrong us, shall we not revenge?'

'Why, Inspector, you surprise me.'

'I played Shylock in our school adaption of *The Merchant of Venice.*'

She looked him up and down.

'No one wanted to play the part, so I volunteered.'

'I belong to a local amdram club – we're rehearsing *The Merchant* for our next production.'

'What part are you playing?'

'I'm playing Portia.'

'I can see why. Have you called Mr Pace?'

'Left a voicemail message, he doesn't like answering his phone in public.'

'Can you tell me about this?' said Buchanan, handing her the copy of the invoice. 'Brewers said one of your men purchased this paint, I'd like to have a word with them.'

She looked at the invoice, then turned to her computer and typed details of the paint.

'That paint was a special order. It was for a job we did for a Mrs Foscatini. She was having a new summerhouse built.'

'Your company does building work as well as decorating?'

'Whatever pays the bills, says Mr Pace.'

'Where was Mrs Foscatini's summerhouse being built?'

She consulted the screen, 'Darley Road.'

'I'm new to the area – where's Darley Road?'

'I think it's off King Edward's Parade, just before you get to Dukes Drive. It's near –'

'That's all right, I know where Dukes Drive is,' he said, remembering the night he'd raced up to Beachy Head to rescue Street.

The creaking hinges of the downstairs door opening and closing announced the arrival of Mr Pace. The sound of heavy footsteps on the stairs painted a picture in Buchanan's mind of an older man, short and overweight, struggling to get his bulk up the steep stairs. He was wrong about Pace's age and agility. Pace ducked as he entered the office. He was carrying four ten-litre tubs of contractors' magnolia paint, two in each hand. Buchanan looked at the bulk that was Pace, then at the size of his hands. Big enough to hold a man by the throat, while nailing him to a tree.

Pace put the paint down beside the door, straightened up and looked down his nose at Buchanan. 'You the guy from Brewers? Marge said something about a problem with paint you'd sold us? Better not be a job we've completed.'

Buchanan reached into his jacket and took out his warrant card. 'Detective Chief Inspector Buchanan, Sussex CID. I'd like to talk to you about Mrs Foscatini's summerhouse.'

'Mrs Foscatini?' Pace said, turning to look at Marge.

'The job up in Meads. You remember, the tea and scones lady? You just banked her cheque.'

'How could I ever forget?' Pace smiled and shook his head, 'Miracle we ever got that job finished, Inspector. Every time the lads showed up she'd make them tea and homemade scones. The job took twice as long as it should have.'

'You lost money on the job?'

'No, the contract was time and materials.'

'You built the summerhouse?'

'No, that was Bourne Sheds and Garages. They lost money – Mrs Foscatini kept making changes, something about the summerhouse not facing the right direction and it being bad karma. And they'd gone in with a fixed price quote.'

'So, your company only does painting and decorating, no carpentry work?'

'Sometimes we will if there's enough of a profit in the job. If we do get construction work it is usually just hanging doors, or building timber and plasterboard partitions.'

'What about windows? We're in the process of buying a house and the estate agent says it could do with having the windows replaced.'

'We used to do timber window installations, but since the advent of UPVC double glazing no one seems to want timber anymore. Now we just stick to painting and decorating. The only times timber windows are used these days is in conservation areas. If you want PVC windows I'd go to Swain Brothers, they have a good reputation for price and quality.'

'Pity. Any problems on the job, other than too many cream teas?'

'A week ago, on Tuesday morning, Mrs Foscatini walked out with the customary tray of tea and cakes and announced she'd changed her mind about the colour of her summerhouse.'

'Does that happen often?'

Pace shrugged. 'Sometimes, not very often.'

'Did it cost you money to repaint?'

'No. My guy told her how much and she just said to go ahead.'

'So, you weren't out of pocket with the job?'

'No.'

'What about Bournes? You intimated they lost money?'

'You'd have to ask them. All I know is they'd completed fitting out the interior and had gone out Saturday evening to celebrate one of the lads' birthday.'

'Thank you for your help, Mr Pace,' said Buchanan, as he passed over his business card.

'Anything else, Inspector?'

'Do you know a Julian Denman?'

Pace looked at Buchanan. 'Are you asking about the guy who was found dead in a factory a week ago?'

'Yes, how did you hear about it?'

'Read it in the *Herald*.'

'Did you know him?'

'Met him at Rotary meetings a couple of times. He asked us to do some work in his offices, stiffed us. We're still waiting to get paid, don't suppose that will happen now that he's gone.'

'Did he owe your company much?'

Pace turned to Marge. 'What was the damage from Denman?'

She opened a filing cabinet drawer and removed a manila folder, bounded in red. She opened it and shuffled through some pages. 'Seven thousand, four hundred and seventy-five pounds.'

'Not the end of the world, Mr Pace. A successful company your size should be able to absorb that much.'

Pace looked back at Buchanan. 'Inspector, no one cheats me out of anything.'

◆

A lead, thought Buchanan, as he walked down the corridor to the office. He couldn't shake the image of the size of Pace's hands. Big enough to hold a man by the throat, jam a nail gun into his mouth and nail him to a tree.

Jill was sitting at her desk, talking on the phone. She nodded to him and returned to her conversation. He sat down at his desk and turned on his computer.

'What are you looking for?' asked Street, hanging up from her phone call.

'There was an incident weekend before last, something about a tool robbery. I need to find the details.'

'Shall I?' she asked. 'I know my way round records quite well.

Do you have the details?'

'No, all the incident board said was there had been a break-in and a quantity of tools stolen.'

'Last weekend?'

'Weekend before.'

'Ok. Should be easy to find. Ah, here it is. A John Sampson reported his workshop being broken into. Incident reported Monday morning at eight forty-three. The report says he locked and barred the doors before going home on Friday, came back Monday morning and found the thieves had pulled the side window out of its frame.'

'What did the thieves get?'

'Reports says Mrs Samson's grandfather's carving chisels, set of Halfords spanners and a half-inch socket set. That what you're looking for?'

Buchanan shook his head. 'No, I'm looking for a nail gun. Anything else?'

'A report of a van break-in reported this morning. Owner says he left his van parked in front of the company office a week ago while on holiday, and the tools were missing this morning when he came to work.'

'That sounds promising. Go on.'

'He says he was sure he'd locked his van, yet when he arrived this morning he found the side door unlocked.'

'Unlocked, not broken?'

'Just says it was unlocked.'

'Where did this happen?'

'Company car park in front of Bourne Sheds and Garages.'

'Very interesting. What's the van owner's name?'

'Daniel Hardwick.'

'Wonder if someone had a spare key?'

'You think someone borrowed the tools and didn't return them?'

'It happens. I'm still waiting for my neighbour to return my lawnmower, remember?'

'You did mention it.'

'Is there a list of missing tools?'

'Like a nail-gun by chance?'

Buchanan smiled. 'There is, isn't there?'

'Yep. A Paslode IM350 framing nailer. Whew, he puts the replacement cost at five hundred and seventy pounds.'

While Street continued with the list of missing items, Buchanan googled the nail gun part number. 'Says here on this website they'll fire nails up to ninety millimetres.'

'That's what Dr Mansell says was used to kill Prince.'

'Now all we have to do is find the nail gun.'

'eBay?'

Buchanan shook his head. 'Unlikely. Probably chucked in a ditch somewhere.'

'What else was reported missing from the van?'

'Makita cordless drill, Impact driver and three batteries. Bosch hand planer and a Henry vacuum.'

'No hand tools?'

'No. Just what's on the list.'

'What does that make you think about?'

Street thought for a minute. 'If the tools were old, I'd reason he's out to get them replaced on insurance. Maybe they weren't all stolen, just the nail gun and he's going to sell the old cordless tools and get the insurance company to replace them all?'

'What's a Henry vacuum?'

'You've never seen a Henry?'

'No, should I?'

'A Henry is a small, usually red, pull-around vacuum cleaner. Thousands of them are used daily in hotels and the like.'

'Hmm, do they have little eyes stuck on the front?'

'That's the one.'

'Can't see someone flogging one of them down their local pub. What's the matter? What have I said?'

'The image of a big burly builder, shirt off, whip in hand, flogging a Henry vacuum, sounds quite funny.'

'C'mon, enough of the jokes, we need to go talk to Mr Hardwick. Got an address for Bourne Sheds and Garages?'

'Hang on, let me have a look – here it is. Oh, they're also on the Finmere Road estate, right next door to Pace Decorators.'

'Let's go, you drive.'

◆

'Slow down.'

'What?'

'Slow down, don't pull into the Pace Decorators' car park. Park in the next unit, I want to watch this,' said Buchanan, as he wound down the passenger-side window.

'Watch what?' asked Street, turning into the car park next to Bourne Sheds and Garages.

'I want to see what Pace is up to.'

Street glanced over to see what had attracted Buchanan's attention. Pace, with his back to Buchanan's car, was deeply involved in an argument with a young man in white decorators' overalls.

'You had no right to borrow my tools, they were my own personal tools, nothing to do with the company,' the younger man was saying.

'Then you shouldn't leave your van on company property when you go on holiday.'

'You don't complain when I get you out of a jam! My van and tools aren't a problem then.'

'I only borrowed them for the weekend, the carpenter needed them to finish a job he was doing in my house. They're back in your van, aren't they?'

'Covered in paint, yeah. How the hell did you manage that?'

'I tried to clean them for you, didn't I? It'll wipe off, see, I already did a bit for you.' Pace pointed to one of the drills. 'Stop bitching about it.'

'You borrowing them cost me two hundred quid.'

'I heard about that, tried to pretend they'd been stolen so you could claim on the company insurance and get new ones.'

'That's bullshit, who told you that?'

'Nobody told me. I know a scam when I see one. You'd better keep your mouth shut about me borrowing your tools, or else.'

'Or else what?'

'It's a criminal offence to make a claim for lost items when they were never lost in the first place. Remember that, and where you were this time last year.'

'That's right, bring up my past. I told you that wasn't my fault, I'd been set up. I never broke into the off-licence and stole all that booze.'

'It was your van.'

'Yeah, and who did you lend it to while I was away on holiday?'

'I told you, I didn't lend it to anyone.'

'Well, it certainly wasn't me who drove it that night.'

'That's your story, Danny. I believe you, pity the jury didn't.'

'Fuck you.'

'Leave if you don't like working here. See who'd hire you, an ex-con.'

'I've heard enough, Jill,' said Buchan. 'Let's go have a word with Danny and see just what state his tools are in.'

Buchanan and Street got out of the car and walked over the where Pace was having the argument.

'Good afternoon, Mr Pace.'

Pace turned to see who'd spoken. 'What do you want? I told you everything earlier.'

'It's your young friend Danny I'd like to have a word with.'

'You bastard, Pace. You shopped me to the cops.'

'Relax, Danny', said Buchanan. 'We're not here about any insurance scam.'

'You're not?'

'No, but we would like to talk to you about your missing tools that have mysteriously shown up.'

'They weren't here when I opened the van earlier this morning.'

'That why you reported them stolen?'

'Yeah.'

'They here now?'

'Yeah, they're all covered in paint.'

'But they weren't here when you arrived?'

'No. Pace had them, he was trying to clean them. Now they're ruined.'

'That's all right. I'm sure Mr Pace won't mind you charging his company for your time cleaning the paint off them.'

Danny sneered at Pace, who turned to walk off.

'Ah, Mr Pace, please don't go anywhere till we've had a talk with you,' said Buchanan.

Danny slid back the side door on his van and went to climb in to retrieve his tools.'

'Please don't get in, Danny. I'd like to have them checked by our CSI team first.'

'You going to arrest him for borrowing my tools, Inspector? Can I watch?'

'No, Danny. I'm interested mostly in your nail gun. Without touching anything, can you see if it is still in your van?'

'Did he borrow that as well?'

'Shall we find out? Please have a look.'

Danny leaned into his van. 'It's not here. The spare battery and charger are here by the door, but not the gun.'

'Could it be lying somewhere in the back of the van?' asked Street.

Danny shook his head. 'If it was here I'd see it – it's bright orange.'

'Why am I not surprised?' said Buchanan.

'Are the drills and spare batteries there?' asked Street.

'Yes, they're here. It's just the nail gun that's missing. Cost me almost six hundred quid.'

'And you're sure it was there last time you used your van?'

'Used it a week ago Friday, just before we went on holiday.'

'Where did you use it?' asked Buchanan.

'Mrs Foscatini's house.'

'Up in Meads?'

'Yeah.'

'You were doing carpentry? Thought you were a painter?'

'I'm self-employed. Do most things, prefer to do carpentry though.'

'Do any work for Bourne Sheds?'

'Not a lot.'

'Why's that?'

'They take for ever to pay my invoices, and I've got a wife and kids to support.'

'How many children?' asked Street.

'Two. Young Danny is four, and Grace is two.'

'Does your wife work?'

Danny's face went blank, his shoulders slumped as he looked down at his boots. He took a deep breath and lifted his head. 'My wife had an accident last year. She was thrown from a horse while exercising it. She broke her back.'

'I'm so sorry, Danny,' said Street.

He smiled. 'Thanks. Doctor says she should eventually make a complete recovery.'

'About your cordless tools?'

'That bastard Pace. I was going to sell them, now I can't with all that paint splattered over them.'

'Money tight?'

'No, it's not that. Screwfix have a special on this week, almost half off on a Makita eighteen-volt cordless drill and driver set – includes a spare battery. I had to have the money by today. It's the last day of the sale. The two hundred I was going to get for the old tools was going towards the cost of the new ones – I had no intention of claiming on insurance.'

'You sure?' said Buchanan.

'Of course I am. You can't get insurance for tools kept in a work van.'

'Thanks, Danny. Please don't disturb anything in your van till the CSI's have had a look.'

'How long will that be?'

Buchanan looked at Street. 'I've just called them, they should be here within the next half hour.'

'In that case, I'm going over to Bournes' to chase up my last two invoices.'

'Good luck. Maybe they've been keeping your nail-gun safe in their office?'

'That'd be a cold day in hell, Inspector. It's probably long gone by now.'

'Well, let me know all the same,' said Buchanan, as he and Street headed for the stairs up to Pace's office.

◆

'Mr Pace,' said Buchanan, as he entered Pace's office, 'did you borrow Danny's tools?'

'You know I did.'

'His nail gun as well?'

'I didn't actually borrow his tools.'

'What did you actually do?'

'It was Nigel who borrowed them, he's putting in a new kitchen for me.'

'And where might I find this Nigel?'

'He works for Bournes.'

'And how did he get access to Danny's tools?'

'I gave him the keys.'

'How do you have Danny's keys?'

'The lads that work for us sometimes leave their vans here.

We ask for a spare set of keys in case we have to move them.

'And you gave Danny's keys to this Nigel?'

'Well, not exactly.'

'How about you start from the beginning, Mr Pace? What exactly did you do?'

'As I just told you, I'm getting a new kitchen. Nigel's doing the work.'

'And the tools?'

'I was coming to that. Saturday afternoon Nigel called to say he couldn't finish the job he was working on because he'd burnt out the motor on his drill.'

'Why didn't he go buy a replacement?'

'He said Screwfix was out of stock, they've got a special sale on. I said to go borrow Danny's, the van was in the yard and the keys were on the hook in the office.'

'Do you know what tools he took?'

Pace shrugged. 'Who knows? You need to ask Nigel.'

'Do you know where Nigel is just now?'

'Probably at work. Try Bournes, they're next door to us.'

'Thank you, Mr Pace, I'll do just that.'

◆

The entrance to Bourne's was similar to that of Pace's. A notice on the door said the office was on the first floor. Buchanan pulled the door open and saw, unlike Pace's, the door through to the ground-floor workshop was missing. A fine layer of dust covered every surface except for the footprints on the steps leading up to the office. The smell of cedar, mixed with oak and linseed oil permeated the atmosphere.

Buchanan looked into the workshop. Pride of place in the middle, reaching up to the workshop ceiling, was a huge, partially complete, oak staircase. Its moulded handrail lay across three saw-horses. Buchanan walked into the workshop and wandered across to the staircase, being careful not to touch anything. He stopped in front of it and saw, lying on the third step, a bright orange Paslode nail-gun. Beside it was an open box of nails. Buchanan leaned over and looked at the size of the nails: twenty millimetre finishing pins. Buchanan sighed – close but no cigar. He wandered on round the workshop and saw at the back a figure bent over a pile of long planks of wood that were resting on two saw-horses.

'Hello.'

The figure hunched over the wood pile stood and looked at Buchanan. 'Can I help?'

'DCI Buchanan, Sussex CID.'

'Harry. I'm the shop foreman.'

'You're not the boss?'

'The boss isn't in, I'm the only one here.'

'Is there a Mr Bourne?'

He shook his head. 'The old man died four years ago, there's only Mrs Bourne now.'

'Who runs the business?'

'The nephew, Eugene, or at least he thinks he does.'

'And where is Eugene?'

Harry smiled and looked at the workshop clock. 'At five-fifteen, probably getting ready to go down the pub.'

'This early?'

'He likes to party. I've never seen him in here much before ten and most nights he's gone by four.'

'Who actually runs the business then?'

'Me and Mrs Bourne.'

'She works with you?'

'No, not quite what I mean. I do all the technical things, such as quoting, plus overseeing what the sub-contractors are doing on site.'

'And Eugene, where does he fit in to the equation?'

'He spends the profits, or at least he used to. It took three years, but Mrs Bourne has finally managed to wrestle control of the company back from him and now holds the purse strings

169

tight.'

'You don't approve of him?'

'I don't approve of anybody who uses my tools without my permission.'

'Did he do that often?'

'At first it didn't bother me too much, he never did much around the workshop anyway. Spent most of his days on his mobile phone. But the day when I found my power tools lying in the car park in the rain with no one around, that was the last straw.'

'What did you do?'

'I told him that if he ever touched my tools again, I'd castrate him with a rusty Stanley blade.'

'How did he take that?'

'It was weird, his face turned white and he fainted.'

'Did he buy his own after that?'

'No, the cheeky bugger would go next door and borrow theirs.'

'Couldn't you just get rid of him?'

'What choice did I have? He owned part of the company.'

'Which part?'

'He used to own a majority share, now he only owns a minor percentage.'

'Why did he sell his controlling share?'

Harry shook his head. 'You'd need to ask Mrs Bourne. All I know is he no longer runs things around here.'

'Do you have an address for him?'

'You need to talk with Mrs Bourne.'

'How do I get in touch with Mrs Bourne?'

'She's only here on the last Thursday in the month. She does the bookkeeping, pays the bills and wages. She has a house in Meads. The house name is Finnart. It's on Baslow Road.'

'Thanks, I'll go have a word with her. What are you working on?' Buchanan pointed at the timber.

'Making a rowboat, it's an old design by Herreschoff for his yacht *Ticonderoga*.'

'How long will it take to make?'

'The perennial question, how long's a piece of string? I hope to have it complete by retirement.'

'And when's that?'

'Two years from now.'

'Good luck with it, and thanks.'

'You're welcome.'

◆

Buchanan wondered if living in Meads might be preferable to Westham when he saw Mrs Bourne's house. He parked his car in the driveway in front of the house and got out. To his right he could see across to the Downs and Beachy Head golf course. Behind he had a view across the bay, all the way to Hastings. He thought about the price of the house, then policeman's wages and shook his head.

He rang the bell and waited. His hand reached for his inside jacket pocket before he remembered. Old habits die hard.

He was watching a group of sailboats beat back and forth as they made their way towards the harbour when the door was opened by a tall, muscular, well-tanned man in his forties.

'Good evening, sorry to disturb you at this time of the day. Detective Chief Inspector Buchanan. Could I have a word with Mrs Bourne, please?'

'Is she expecting you?'

Buchanan shook his head. 'Not unless Harry called to say I'd be visiting.'

'Come in, Inspector. My name is Jason, I look after Mrs Bourne.'

He swung the door back and stood aside as Buchanan entered and waited for the door to be closed.

'Follow me, Inspector.'

As they walked down the hallway, Buchanan wondered what

171

Jason meant by *taking care of Mrs Bourne*. The sound of piano music could be heard from somewhere in the house. It got louder as they got to the end of the hallway. 'Mrs Bourne is practising. She won't be long, and – please don't interrupt her when you go in.'

The hallway ended at a set of double doors. Jason opened the right-hand door and ushered Buchanan through. As Buchanan walked past, Jason whispered, 'Remember, not a sound and wait till she's finished playing.'

The room was laid out with three rows of ten, high-backed chairs, all facing a small raised stage upon which stood a Broadwood grand piano. Seated at the piano was, Buchanan assumed, Mrs Bourne.

He walked quietly across the polished wooden floor and sat in one of the seats on the front row to the right of the piano. Buchanan closed his eyes and was back in his grandmother's front room, the room where she gave piano lessons. He sat, with eyes closed, as Mrs Bourne played.

'Hello, you wanted to speak to me?'

'Oh, sorry, I was – I was...' He shook his head. 'Your playing, it brought back so many memories of my grandmother. She taught piano and sometimes gave performances in our local church.'

'Ah, Bach does that.'

'What were you playing?'

'His English suite in A minor. But you didn't come here to listen to me play piano, did you?'

'Inspector Buchanan, Mrs Bourne. I'm here to ask you a few questions about your company.'

'I'm not surprised, what's Eugene been up to this time?'

'Did Harry call you?'

'He did call, Ma'am,' interrupted Jason. 'You were playing and I didn't want to disturb you.'

'Thank you, Jason. Inspector, would you like some

refreshments?'

'That would be nice.'

'Jason, would you make us something cold, and – and I suppose non-alcoholic, Inspector?'

'Orange squash, if there is any?'

'Jason – I'll have an elderflower Pimms. We'll take them in the conservatory.'

'Yes, Ma'am.'

Mrs Bourne got up from her piano and beckoned Buchanan to follow her through into the conservatory.

'Well, Inspector, tell me,' she said, sitting down on a huge settee, 'what's that rascal Eugene been up to? Has he been snatching old ladies' handbags?'

'No, not that I'm aware of,' said Buchanan, sitting in an equally overstuffed armchair opposite. 'I'm investigating three deaths in the Eastbourne area –'

'Eugene, a killer?' She shook her head. 'Inspector, Eugene may be many things – but a killer?' She shook her head again. 'I don't think so.'

'Do I understand that there is no love lost between you and Eugene?'

'He tried to swindle me out of my inheritance, Inspector.'

'How was he going to do that?'

Her reply was interrupted by the return of Jason and their drinks, three of them. Buchanan was puzzled for a moment till he realised that Jason was more than just someone who looked after Mrs Bourne's house. He served Mrs Bourne and Buchanan their drinks, then placed the tray on a side table, took the third drink and sat down beside Mrs Bourne.

'Inspector, I see you are puzzled. Let me introduce you to Jason, properly. About fifteen years ago, my husband developed multiple sclerosis complicated with vascular dementia. At first, I was able to look after him …' she shook her head.

'Inspector,' said Jason, 'Mr Bourne was a big man, six feet

173

four and when the dementia worsened he also became angry and confused.'

'So, I called my husband's doctor and said I needed help. The doctor referred me to a nursing agency and the result was – Jason,' said Mrs Bourne, looking at Jason and patting him on his knee. 'I loved my husband very much, Inspector, but when his illness progressed, well, I had to come to the realisation the man I married and lived with was now just an empty hulk, ravaged by an illness that would eventually destroy him. Jason stayed on after my husband died – that was four years ago. I was an emotional mess, Inspector, I needed someone to look after the house – and me.'

'And Eugene, where does he come into the picture?'

'He was my husband's business partner, albeit a junior one. We had no children and Eugene sort of got adopted as a nephew. They used to get along well, then when my husband's illness became apparent, Eugene went to work on him. In those days, the company was a lot larger than it is today. We were a major player in the housing industry. One year our company built eighteen hundred houses, now we're reduced to replacing windows, garage doors and building sheds.'

'This house?'

'I know what you are thinking, how does a shed-building company afford me such a luxurious lifestyle?'

'It's the way I'm trained to think, Mrs Bourne.'

'During the company's heyday of house building, my husband managed to invest quite a large amount of the annual profits. It is that investment which affords me such a lifestyle as you now see.'

'In what way did Eugene go to work on your husband?'

'He made himself indispensable, wormed his way into my husband's confidence. For instance, when my husband started having issues driving, Eugene was always there, no matter what time of day, or how far it was. I don't care to drive and since

Eugene was so accommodating I didn't see any problem or realise what he was up to. Later, as the dementia worsened, Eugene started advising my husband on what to do, business-wise. The final straw was when he got my husband to transfer control of the company to himself and his wife.'

'What did you do?'

'I didn't find out till after the funeral, when the lawyer read the will. As I said, it took three years, and quite a large legal bill to have the transfer of ownership overturned.'

'How did Eugene take it?'

'He was mad with anger, not only had he lost his egregious salary, he also lost access to the company investments. Unfortunately, the court decision only overturned the transfer, it didn't get rid of him. The decision returned the company to its former composition with Eugene retaining thirty-two percent of the shares. While I still had fifty-five percent, Eugene's wife held the remaining twenty-three.'

'So, he was still involved with the company?'

'Thirty-two percent's worth.'

'So, they can outvote you and effectively still run the company?'

Mrs Bourne smiled. 'Mildred, that's Eugene's wife, caught him in a compromising situation with a male co-worker and uses that to keep him under control. So now, anytime I need to keep Eugene in line, I just mention Mildred. Besides, Eugene doesn't know that Mildred sold me some of her shares last year and, knowing his despotic lifestyle, she's taken out a very large life-insurance policy on him.'

'Mrs Bourne, do you know a Mrs Foscatini?'

'Yes, we play Bridge together. Why would you want to know that?'

'And her daughter and husband, Mr and Mrs Morelli?'

'Yes, of course I do.'

'And Eugene, does he have any friends?'

'Not many that I'm aware of, unless you include his friend, Nigel, he's one of the carpenters who work for the company.'

'Do you have a photo of Eugene I could have, Mrs Bourne?'

'I'll get on for you, Inspector,' said Jason.

♦

The golden domes on the pier looked good, much better than the drab colour they used to be mused Buchanan, as he drove slowly along the sea-front pondering the complicated relationships between Mrs Foscatini, the Morellis, Paces, and now Mrs Bourne.

Mrs Foscatini was, he thought, the focal point of what was going on, but just what was going on? He had two murders, one suspicious death by driving, a missing painter, fuel laundering and the dumping of toxic waste to consider. Time for a conference with the team.

♦

'Can I have your attention?' said Buchanan, interrupting the intense activity in the office. 'I want to go over where we are in the investigation. Stephen, you said something interesting happened the night before last. What was it?'

'Yes. Jill and I were in the transit watching the Morellis' flat. At two thirty-five in the morning Mr Morelli came out and went for a walk.'

'What did you do?'

'We let him get a hundred yards down the road, then got out and followed him.'

'He was probably getting stir-crazy and felt it safe to go out for some fresh air.'

Stephen shook his head. 'Don't think so. Want to guess where he walked to?'

Buchanan shook his head 'Go on, I like a mystery.'

'He turned left at the end of Blackwater Road and headed off along Meads Road. He walked past the roundabout and then on to Milnthorpe Road.'

'Where is this narrative leading?'

'Darley Road, and Mrs Foscatini's summerhouse.'

'Did he stay long?'

'About an hour, then he retraced his steps to Blackwater Road and his apartment.'

'He's a fit man for his age, but I can't imagine walking that distance in the middle of the night.'

'We did.'

'Enough of that. Now – the name Foscatini. There can't be many people with that name living in Eastbourne.'

'There aren't,' said Street. 'I checked with county records. Only one person with that name registered: a Mrs Foscatini in Darley Road.'

'What next, Chief?'

'Stephen. First thing tomorrow, I would like you and Jill to go see Mrs Foscatini. Say you are investigating a report on an attempted break-in nearby. Make out that you are there to reassure the local residents. Tell her the police are putting on additional night-time patrols and she shouldn't be concerned.'

'Ok.'

'Jill, see if you can get her talking, maybe she'll offer you tea and scones. If she does, try and find out about her family.'

'You'll like that, Stephen. You drive. See you all tomorrow,' said Street.

'What do you want me to do tomorrow?' said Dexter, as Street and Hunter left.

'Get on to ECRIS, see if they have anything on the Morellis and the Foscatini family. Also check the Interpol Red Notices, maybe one of them is listed.'

'Ecris?'

'European Criminal Records System. See if the names show up. If they're in there, it will probably show up in Italy, sometime in the twenties or thirties.'

'Never been on that before.'

'Ask at the reception desk, someone there should know how to access the Ecris.'

'Are you going home now, Chief?'

'No. I'll be here in the office, I have loads of paperwork to catch up on.'

♦

Buchanan looked away from his computer screen, thinking one of his team had returned for something. Instead, and to Buchanan's dismay, it was the ACC and the crime commissioner.

'Buchanan, finally tracked you down.'

'Been busy.'

'That's what I hear, and am very concerned about. Before you turned up, Eastbourne was a quiet place to live, never appeared on the list of top 100 crime locations, now – now I'm getting calls from the Home Secretary wanting to know what's going on.'

'She worried about her job?'

'Buchanan, just because there's the possibility of a leadership change in the government, there's no reason to make snide remarks like that.'

'Politics and policing don't mix, that's all I'm saying.'

'Buchanan, Mr Duncan is an elected representative of the government, he's our boss,' said the ACC.

'And, Detective Inspector Buchanan, my job, as police and crime commissioner – of which you seem to be unaware – is to be the voice of the people and to hold the police to account for all their activities, and that includes you.'

'I am well aware of what you do, Mr Duncan.'

'What do you mean by keeping the Morellis under house arrest?'

'I'm not. They're perfectly at will to leave any time they want.'

'What do you mean by that?'

'Exactly as I say, they're free to come and go as they please. Any time they want.'

'You need to explain that one, Buchanan.'

'They're on the run from someone, we're not sure who yet. It's they who have decided to go to earth. All we are doing is keeping an eye on them, sort of providing them with police protection.'

'Just where are we on the investigation, Buchanan? Two murders are two too many?'

'The number is actually three. We believe that the three deaths are linked, by someone yet to be identified.'

'Are you trying to hide something from us? Your answers seem to be a bit vague for someone who is supposed to be *in charge* of the investigation.'

'It's early days yet.'

'Are you all right? You look a bit tired, Buchanan. Have you thought about the ACC's suggestion of retirement?'

'I'm fine, it's always this way when an investigation begins, so many threads to hold on to.'

'Detective Street – she could take over if you're needing a break.'

Buchanan shook his head. 'She's not ready.'

'She's sat her Inspector Exam, hasn't she?'

Buchanan looked at the ACC. 'I was aware she wanted to advance, didn't realise she had actually sat the exam.'

'I didn't say that, Buchanan,' said the crime commissioner. 'I was assuming someone bright, ambitious and intelligent like her would have. Although if she is getting married, being a mother and staying home to raise children might be more to her liking.'

'You have children, Mr Duncan?'

'What on earth has that got to do with what we are discussing?'

'My point, exactly. Jill's family life has nothing to do with her job.'

'Buchanan, I want you to make a statement to the press. I want you to reassure the public that these maniacs are about to be caught and brought to justice. I want to see progress, I want these people off the street and into jail where they belong.'

'I was waiting for the results of some tests before I talked to the press.'

'Buchanan, I said I want *you* to make a statement. Do I make myself completely clear?'

'What do you suggest I say?'

'Buchanan, do I need to wipe your arse as well?'

'No, Mr Duncan, I can do that fine myself. I'll get on to it right away.'

'Make sure you do, or you'll be back in Glasgow frying Mars bars for a living.'

'They have batter on them, quite tasty.'

'Buchanan, catch this killer. I don't want the Home Secretary calling me again wanting to know why we have a maniac running loose in East Sussex. Do I make myself completely clear?'

Buchanan sat without moving as he listened to their footsteps go down the hall and out of earshot. When he could no longer hear them, he got up and went over to the window to watch them leave.

He wasn't surprised to see the ACC wave goodbye to the crime commissioner and head back into the building. He returned to his chair and waited her arrival.

'I'm sorry about that, Buchanan. The man's an absolute ass.'

Buchanan leaned back in his chair and smiled at the ACC as she sat in the chair opposite.

'Stop that, Buchanan. I'm supposed to be your boss.'

'He is a bit of a –'

'Buchanan, enough. Where are we in this investigation? You said there are now three deaths –are they all related?'

'It's starting to look that way. The latest was supposed to

look like a traffic accident. The deceased was known to one of the other victims.'

'Buchanan, I really do need you to bring this to a conclusion. I can't protect you much longer.'

8

'Good morning, Mrs Foscatini. I'm Detective Sergeant Street and this,' she said, turning to Hunter, 'is Constable Hunter.'

'What's wrong? Nigel, it's Nigel, isn't it? I told him not to go.'

Street shook her head, 'Mrs Foscatini. I'm sure Nigel is all right. This is just a courtesy call. We're informing residents in the neighbourhood about the email campaign called *In The Know – Surrey and Sussex*. It's an email notification system to inform the residents about criminal activity in their area.'

'You are? I've never heard of it.'

'We have a leaflet that explains how it works,' said Street, holding the leaflet out to Mrs Foscatini. 'Would you like a copy?'

'My eyes, I need my glasses. Wait a minute – no, come in. I don't like keeping the front door open, lets in the flies.'

Street and Hunter followed Mrs Foscatini down the hallway and out into the conservatory at the rear of the house.

'Please sit, I'll be right back.'

'Nice house, Jill. Be nice if we could afford one like this one day.'

'And who'd clean it? Can you imagine how many rooms this house has?'

'I'm sure you'd do a wonderful job of keeping house.'

'Me? Marriage is a partnership, remember?'

'Of course I do, I'm just joking. We'll have servants to do the cleaning.'

'And a butler, someone to pour your wine at dinner?'

'Now who's joking?'

'I can't wait. Let's elope?'

'Elope? You want to alienate my mother before we even get

started?'

'It's all this waiting, I want to be married now, not in a few weeks' time – sorry, I'm being ungrateful. Your mother has been wonderful helping with all the arrangements.'

'Don't forget Mrs Buchanan, she's been busy as well.'

Their conversation was interrupted by the return of Mrs Foscatini.

'That's better,' Mrs Foscatini said, replacing her glasses. 'The optician wants me to wear varifocals, I did try them for a few weeks, but they made me queasy. Tea will be ready in a minute. I've just made a batch of scones for the WI tea. I'm sure they wouldn't miss a few. Now what is it you wanted me to look at?'

'This is the brochure I mentioned. It gives you all the details of the scheme. All you have to do is go on-line to the website and put in your email address.'

'That's all?'

'Yes. Then when something has happened in your area, we send you an email with the details.'

'What sort of details?'

'Details such as are in this brochure. You can keep it. I printed several copies before I left the office.'

'Says here that the police caught three suspects within the hour following a burglary in Halland. I am impressed.'

'We're not always that fortunate. But, as you can see, the newsletter will keep you informed when something in your area has happened. You can contact us about anything you see in the newsletter or something you are concerned about. Simply click the *contact us* online text in the email, or dial 101 on your phone.'

'Thank you, dear. I'll think about it.'

'Mrs Foscatini, when you opened the door and we said we were the police, you gave us the impression you were worried about a Nigel. Is there anything we can help with?'

'He's my grandson. He's been working on my summerhouse. He lives with me, but I haven't heard from him since a week ago

Friday.'

'Have you reported him as missing, Mrs Foscatini?'

'No, should I have?'

'Yes, if you are worried and he doesn't stay away as a rule.'

'He's such a lovely young man, but –'

'But, Mrs Foscatini?'

'He hasn't been himself lately.'

'In what way?'

'He comes in late, sometimes stays out all night, slams doors, even shouts at my dear little Gracie.'

'Gracie?'

'My pet Papillon.'

'Papillon? What is a Papillon, Mrs Foscatini?'

'It's a breed of dog, related to the spaniel. The name comes from the look of the dog's face and ears. It resembles a butterfly, hence the name Papillon. You quite often see them included in paintings by the old masters.'

'Oh, he sounds adorable, is he here?'

'No, not at the moment, he's having his pedicure.'

'Pity, I would have liked to see him.'

'I'm sorry, if I'd known you were coming I would have changed the appointment.'

'Maybe another time. Is there anything else you can tell us about Nigel?'

'He's been drinking too much. I don't agree with that, told him so.'

'How about identification marks, tattoos perhaps?'

She shook her head. 'No, I don't think so. Oh, silly me, how could I forget? He has a tattoo of a spider on his shoulder.'

'How tall was he?'

'Just over two metres, but quite thin for his size, and he has long hair down to his shoulders.'

'Colour of his hair?'

'Dark brown, or black. I'm not too sure, he doesn't take care of it, unlike your hair, Sergeant.'

'Thanks.'

'When exactly did you last see him?' said Hunter.

'Last Friday morning, just before he went off to work.'

'I thought you said he was working on your summerhouse?'

'He was, but he had to go to his workplace first.'

'And do you know where that is?'

'The company name is Place something or other. I don't know where it is.'

'Could it be Pace Decorators?' said Street.

Mrs Foscatini nodded as she pulled dead petals off from the flower arrangement on the side table. 'That sounds like the name. My daughter's former husband owns the company.'

'So, your grandson works with his father, Mr Pace?'

'Detestable man, glad my daughter has nothing to do with him anymore.'

Street looked over at Hunter and raised her eyebrows. 'Your daughter remarried?' she asked.

'Yes, she married a lovely man from Argentina.'

'Is that where she now lives?'

'Yes.'

'Why doesn't Nigel live with them in Argentina? Sounds such an exotic place for a young man to grow up in.'

Mrs Foscatini shook her head. 'Unfortunately, Nigel got into a lot of trouble with the police when he was a young boy – that created problems in getting him a visa.'

'Surely his past record could have been explained to the Argentinian authorities? After all, he would have been going with his family.'

'He didn't want to go. I think he was scared about having to learn a new language and the different culture was too much for him.'

'So, he stayed behind with his father?'

'Yes – unfortunately for him.'

'What sort of trouble did he get into as a lad?' asked Hunter. 'Most child offences are spent before they become an adult.'

'It was his father's fault.'

'What was, Mrs Foscatini?'

'His father – oh dear – and I thought I was over this. His father was reputed to be a champion bare-knuckle fighter, boasted he never lost a fight. That was the only thing my late husband had any respect for him about. Used to say something about Pace having science when he fought. I never understood what he was talking about.'

'It's a boxing term, Mrs Foscatini,' said Hunter.

'He also used to pick up stray dogs then teach them to fight.'

'That's illegal,' said Street.

'I know it is, dear. But that didn't stop him.'

'Was he ever caught?' asked Hunter.

'If he was, I'm unaware of it.'

'How did you know he was doing it?'

'He used to boast about it. I think he was trying to impress my husband.'

'Why? Was your husband a violent man?'

'With a name like Francesco? Sergeant, my husband was named after St Francis, the patron saint of animals. He loved animals and hated those who abused them.'

'Do you get to see your daughter often?' asked Street.

'When my husband was alive we used to fly south to see them every second year, occasionally they would visit us. Now I'm getting too old to fly that far on my own.'

'What does your son-in-law do?'

'They have a cattle ranch.'

'Your husband is no longer living?' said Street.

'No – he passed away just over five years ago.'

'How did Nigel react to the passing of his grandfather?'

Mrs Foscatini's face relaxed as she searched her memory, then she pursed her lips. 'That was when he changed. He and my husband never quite got along, there was always a acknowledged truce between them. I think Nigel was caught between obedience to his father and the gentleness of my husband. But, when Francesco passed away, it was as if – how is it said – when my husband died, Nigel went over to the dark side.'

'In what way, Mrs Foscatini?' asked Street.

'As I said, he drank a lot more, stayed out late at night. I couldn't go to sleep till he came in. Sergeant, I'm eighty years old. I like consistency in my life, regular hours for everything.'

'Was he violent towards you?'

'No, I think the memory of my husband kept his anger towards me at bay.'

'And you have nothing to do with his father?'

'No, nothing.'

'Mrs Foscatini, I'm a bit confused. You say you have nothing to do with him, yet his company has been working on your new summerhouse.'

'That was for Nigel's sake. He said things were very quiet where he worked and that the carpentry company next door was going through a difficult patch as well. So, I ordered a summerhouse from them. I stipulated that Nigel had to be in charge of the build, sort of a project manager. I thought the work might tide both companies over for a few weeks, thus protecting Nigel's job, and maybe – just maybe – help him to see there is more to life than just drinking and whatever other nefarious activities his father gets him involved in.'

'You have quite a complex family.'

'Sergeant, let me tell you about my family – more tea?'

'Yes, please,' said Street, spreading strawberry jam on the other half of her scone.

'The Morellis go far back in time. My husband was only able to trace them back as far as his grandfather, Luca. He was born in 1890, in a small village in Sicily. Unfortunately, a great deal of our family records were lost during the war.'

'World War Two?'

'Yes, dear, that was World War Two.'

'What happened next?'

'All was well till 1922 when the Fascists took over the running of the country.'

'That was when Mussolini was elected,' said Hunter.

'A black day for Italy,' said Mrs Foscatini. 'But worse was to come under the Nazis.'

'Can't imagine living like that,' said Street.

'My husband saw the writing on the wall, and, after a particular bad year in business, he'd had enough. Late November in 1958, at about two o'clock in the morning, he woke the whole family and drove us down to the docks in Naples. The next thing we knew we were bundled on to a ship bound for England.'

'The whole family, Mrs Foscatini?' said Street.

'My husband, myself, and our son and daughter.'

'You have no other children?'

'Another daughter. She was born in England a year after we arrived. She now lives in Argentina.

'Sounds exciting,' said Street, 'dashing through the town in the dead of night, thinking about a sea voyage and a new home, a new start in life.'

'We're getting married in a few weeks, Mrs Foscatini,' said Hunter. 'Jill is quite excited, as you can hear.'

'How lovely for you both. Where are you getting married?'

'The Hydro Hotel.'

'Oh, how nice. I have tea there every Thursday afternoon.'

'You were telling us about your family, Mrs Foscatini.'

'Are you really sure you want to hear about them? There's not much of interest to tell.'

'Oh, but it is interesting. It's not every day one gets to hear such an exciting story as yours.'

'If you're sure.'

'Please.'

'Now, where was I?'

'You were telling us about how the after effects of the war made your husband emigrate.'

'He told me he didn't like the way that life had changed with the Mafia.'

'Like what, Mrs Foscatini?'

'The one thing that bothered him the most as a businessman was he had to pay for protection. That and the fact that it was getting difficult to run a business under the control of the unions, who themselves were controlled by the Mafia.'

'I can't imagine that happening here in England,' said Hunter.

'There was also the Rienzi incident.'

'What was that?' asked Street.

'Benito Rienzi was a young director in the family business – another Mafia trick.'

'What kind of trick was that?'

'They'd find a respectable company, one that's very profitable, then get one of their own people placed onto the board of directors.'

'How would they do that?' said Hunter.

'The way it's usually done is to find the weakest link in the chain, a director that has something embarrassing or criminal to hide. Then the Mafia put on the pressure. That way they have someone on the inside and can influence what the company does. All this as well as knowing all about the finances of the company.'

'Is that how Benito Rienzi became a director?'

'Yes.'

'An open door for money laundering,' said Street. 'Were there any stories in particular you remember?'

'This story about Benito Rienzi, one I was told by my

mother, was – oh dear, this is going to sound dreadful...'

'Benito Rienzi, Mrs Foscatini?' said Street.

'Rienzi was a very naughty boy and upset the family –his Mafia family, you understand?'

'What did he do?'

'He castrated a man, and made his lover watch as he bled to death. She later went mad and ended her days in an insane asylum.'

'What happened to him?'

'Nothing. Rienzi was a Capo, he was an untouchable. He even had a nickname.'

'What was that?' said Street.

'They called him *Il Castrator.*'

'Did he stay on with the company?'

'Once a worm is in the apple, you can never get it out without destroying the apple. That's what my father-in-law is reputed to have said.'

'That's a dreadful story, Mrs Foscatini, and Rienzi got away with it?'

'Yes dear, he got away with it. I think that was the real reason my husband left Sicily and started again in England.'

'What became of Rienzi, Mrs Foscatini?' said Hunter.

'From what my mother said in a letter, he ended up crippling the company with debt and then was gunned down leaving his office.'

'Can you tell us anything about CSM?'

'You need to talk to my son about that when he gets back from his holiday. I know very little about what went on with CSM. Except there was something he mentioned about someone called Denman and some sort of business deal he'd been working on.'

'And you don't know anything about the deal?'

'No, as I said, you'd need to talk to my son.'

'And your family has been in the Eastbourne area since?'

'Yes, dear. It was as I said, the family arrived in Southampton and my husband took the first train from the station and, after a couple of changes, we ended up in Eastbourne.'

'And you don't know anything else about the deal Denman was working on?' asked Street.

'No, sorry. I should do, but these days life has a direction all of its own.'

'So, Nigel came to live with you?'

'My son has two grown daughters. I think they were done having children in the house.'

'Mrs Foscatini, do you know a family by the name of Morelli?'

'Yes.'

'Are they related to you?'

'That's my son's name.'

'Excuse me a moment, Mrs Foscatini. You say your husband's name is Morelli and your son's name is Morelli, yet you are a Foscatini. Can you explain?'

'When we arrived in England, as I've already explained, my husband wanted a new start. So he took my family name, Foscatini. My son, suffering an attack of nostalgia, reverted back to Morelli.'

'And they live in Eastbourne?'

'Yes, they have a flat on Blackwater Road.'

'Do you know if they are at home?'

'No, I told you, they've gone away – on holiday.'

'Do you know where they've gone?'

'I think they were going to visit their daughter.'

'In Italy?'

'Yes, that's where she lives.'

'When will they be back?'

'I – I'm not sure.'

'When did you last talk with your son?'

'Two weeks ago, we had lunch in town.'

'Where was that? Stephen and I are always looking for new places to eat.'

'I don't remember, he picked me up in his car and drove us. My knees, they don't permit me to walk very far. I have osteoarthritis. I've been waiting four months for an operation for a new knee.'

'And you haven't seen your son since?'

'No, Sergeant.'

'And you think they've gone to see their daughter in Italy?'

'Sergeant, what have all these questions got to do with my grandson?'

'Could he have gone with them, Mrs Foscatini?'

'I can't answer that. I'm sorry, I just don't know.'

'Are they close – your grandson and your son, Mrs Foscatini?'

'Not really, Nigel is very English. My son, on the other hand, is more Italian than English, despite being born and brought up in this country.'

'Can we have your son's address, Mrs Foscatini?'

'It's on Blackwater Road, I don't know the number. You can't miss it, they live on the fifth floor, It's the only block of flats on the road.'

'Thank you, Mrs Foscatini, we'll pay them a visit. If they're not home, maybe their neighbour will know when they are returning.'

◆

'Don't think I will ever look at a scone the same way again,' said Hunter, as they drove down Grand Parade.

'You had enough of them, I counted you eating three.'

'So? I'm a growing boy.'

'Can you afford another suit before the wedding?'

'Don't worry, I'll run an extra couple of miles tonight, that'll burn off at least two of them.'

'So, the interview with Mrs Foscatini, what did you think of it?'

'Never had one quite like it before. She was definitely lying on some answers, evasive on others and this – this is what bugs me. She was trying to say that she thought her son's company, CSM, was in trouble because of a deal Denman was working on.'

'If that was the case, why was there nothing recorded at Companies House?'

'I think we need to have a chat with someone in the Serious Fraud Office,' said Street.

'Also, Inland Revenue, remember the old saying?'

'What? Oh, of course. When in doubt, follow the money trail.'

◆

Ah, there you two are. How did the visit with Mrs Foscatini go?' said Buchanan.

'Very well in some ways, others, we're not sure.'

'Explain.'

'She gave us a potted history of the family, both family and business,' said Hunter.

'There's a but in there somewhere,' said Buchanan.

'The but is, she was evasive with some of her answers, out and out lied about others.'

'Right, let's start with the evasions, what were they?'

'First, when we arrived she thought we were there about her grandson, Nigel.'

'Why, what's he been up to?'

'He was supposed to be project managing the construction of her summerhouse, sort of a character-building exercise.'

'And was he?'

'She hasn't seen him since a week ago Friday.'

'Probably hung over from partying,' said Hunter.

'Interesting. Are we talking about the same Nigel that works for Pace Decorators?'

'At first she made out she didn't know Pace, then she said she did,' said Street.

'Yes. Also, Pace is his father,' said Hunter. 'Another interesting fact, Pace steals dogs and trains them to fight.'

'Anything known about him?'

'Last arrest was three years ago, according to the PNC,' said Street.

'What happened, was he convicted?'

'Nine months suspended, and one hundred and fifty hours community service.'

'Anything since?'

'Nothing on the record, though the *Herald* had an interesting news item at the beginning of the month. It was about a man walking his dog at Beachy Head; he was punched in the face by two robbers who tried to steal his dog.'

'You think that could have been Pace?'

'I checked the description of the two attackers: one was described as tall and muscular, the other, dark and wiry.'

'Pace and his son?'

'Pace maybe. What does his son look like?'

'We have a rough description. Tall and thin with a tattoo of a spider on his shoulder.'

'What else did Mrs Foscatini have to say?'

'She said Pace used to be married to her daughter. She's now remarried and moved with her husband to Argentina where they own a cattle ranch.'

'And Nigel stayed behind?'

'Yes, doesn't make sense, does it?'

'And they say that women are contrary,' said Hunter.

'Stephen!'

'Just teasing.'

'And the lies?'

'She said she hadn't seen her son for two weeks. Yet Stephen and I followed him to her house just a few days ago.'

'You mentioned something regarding her concerns about CSM and an outside investor?'

'Yes, when I checked with Companies House, regarding CSM and its directors, there was nothing about any associations with other companies.'

'I think a call to the SFO is due,' said Buchanan.

'That's what I suggested,' said Street, smiling at Hunter.

'Ok, get on it, I'm going out.'

'Will you be back today?'

'Not sure. There's a message that Mrs Foscatini called. You two must have really spooked her. I think I'll go have a word with her.'

'Would you like me to come with you?'

'No, thanks.'

'Any idea how late you'll be?'

Buchanan looked up at the office clock. 'It's late in the afternoon, doubt if there'll be any scones, after that I'm meeting Karen at Prestige Kitchens.'

'That mean you've got the house?' said Hunter.

'Karen called while you two were with Mrs Foscatini. We sign the papers tomorrow.'

'And the house in Glasgow?'

'As long as I stay employed, we can afford the mortgage and continue to rent out the Glasgow house.'

'Good, I'm glad,' said Street.

9

As Buchanan turned on to Seafront Road he glanced in his rear-view mirror and saw the black BMW that had been behind him on Lottbridge Drove was still behind him. Not directly behind, but always at least three cars between. He smiled and pressed the speed-dial on his phone and waited for an answer.

'Jack, you going to be late?'

'Not there yet. Jill, can you run a licence plate for me?'

'Sure, what is it?'

'Echo, Alpha, sixty-three, Echo, November, Uniform.'

'You have a lead?'

'No. The car has been following me since I pulled out on to Lottbridge. Followed me all the way up to Gardners roundabout, then all the way back down to the Sovereign Centre. It's still behind me now.'

'Are you sure it's following you? You know what Lottbridge is like.'

'I know when I'm being followed.'

'Hang on then, be right back.'

Buchanan reached the pier, still being followed.

'Is it a black, series seven BMW?' asked Street.

'Yes, but the windows are tinted. I can't see who's driving.'

'The car's registered to Carswell, they're a private hire company. They specialise in runs to the airports, docks, and urgent parcels.'

'Wonder if it's the same company Denman used for his Friday top-ups?'

'It's possible, want me to enquire further?'

'Yes, see if the company really exists, and if so who runs it. Pound to a penny it will be a front for something other than a taxi service.'

'Will do, call you as soon as I have anything.'

He stopped in front of Mrs Foscatini's driveway. Curiosity got the better of him so he sat and waited to see what the BMW would do. It slowed as it passed him, a shadowy figure in the passenger seat looked his way, then the car drove on. He watched it slow, then do a three-point turn and drive back down towards where he had stopped. It slowed then stopped about forty yards away from him; no-one got out.

Buchanan got out of his car, locked it and walked up the drive to Mrs Foscatini's front door. He rang the bell and waited. The door was opened by Mrs Foscatini.

'Good evening, Mrs Foscatini. Detective Chief Inspector Buchanan.'

'Inspector – I didn't expect to see anyone from your office so soon, is something wrong?'

'No, Mrs Foscatini. Someone in the office said you'd called and left a message you wanted to talk to me.'

'Oh dear, I think someone is pulling your leg, Inspector. I didn't leave any message. Do you have any news about Nigel?'

Buchanan shook his head. 'I'm sorry, Mrs Foscatini.'

'Oh dear, what am I going to do?'

'Can I come in?'

'Oh yes, certainly.'

'You did report him missing?' said Buchanan, following Mrs Foscatini into the morning room.

'Yes, I reported him missing, just as your sergeant told me to.'

'And we had nothing on file?'

'Sorry?'

'When you reported Nigel as missing, did the person taking the report say if there were any cases of unidentified people on file that matched Nigel's description?'

'They didn't say.'

'They didn't? Hmm. Please excuse me for a moment.'

Buchanan took out his phone and called Street; she answered on the fifth ring.

'Jill – no, not that, can you get on to missing persons and check on young Nigel? Hang on. Mrs Foscatini, can you give me a description of Nigel?'

'Yes, he's quite tall, about your height, Inspector, quite thin, makes him look taller than he is.'

'What about hair, tattoos, anything that would help us identify him?'

'I already told your sergeant - didn't she report him missing?'

'I don't think so, Mrs Foscatini. Did you get that, Jill? Good. Call me as soon as you find anything, even if it's negative.'

'While we wait for your sergeant, would you like a cup of tea, Inspector?'

'Yes, please.'

Cup in hand Buchanan stood in the bay window and surveyed the view out over Pevensey Bay then he looked back to the road outside the house. The BMW was still parked across the road.

'You told my sergeant,' Buchanan said, turning to Mrs Foscatini seated beside the fireplace in her chair, 'that your family business was controlled by the Mafia?'

'In Italy, yes.'

'And your grandfather couldn't get protection from the police?'

'Inspector, the reach of the Mafia has been described as that of an octopus: its tentacles reach out into many different areas of the business world, even to the local police station.'

'Who's this?' said Buchanan, while holding a yellowed photograph of a man with hair slicked back and sporting a well-tended moustache.

'My father-in-law. It was he who owned a transportation company. At first, he was very successful, then things began to happen. Drivers would find their tyres slashed, engines that had been running previously now wouldn't start. The worst case was lorries were hijacked and would be found weeks later at the bottom of a quarry with the contents gone.'

'How did he manage to survive with all that going on?'

'He gave in and paid an insurance premium for lorry breakdowns, lost contents and of course fire.'

'Sounds like modern car insurance.'

'Yes, but these payments weren't to insurance companies. Inspector, your insurance company doesn't break or steal your car to get you to sign up with them, you have a choice. With the Mafia you have no choice but to pay up.'

'Mrs Foscatini, your husband came to this country with his family. What happened to the company? Was it sold?'

'At the time, my husband's father was still the chairman, but it was Rienzi who actually ran the company as a cover for his criminal activities. Rienzi made my husband's father an offer he couldn't refuse.'

'What was that?'

'The health and well-being of his son and family.'

'He actually threatened to kill them?'

'Not in those words. He apparently said the English air would be better for the health of the family. He even had the audacity to pay for the ship tickets to get us to England.'

'What happened to Rienzi?'

'He was shot while leaving the office.'

'When was that?'

'About ten years ago.'

'Did he have any children?'

'Yes, a son.'

'Do you know his name?'

'Guido.'

'Did he take over the company after his father's death?'

'No, he disappeared, no-one knows where he went.'

'Is the company still going today?'

'Yes, but I hear it's having problems. I had a letter from my cousin a few weeks ago and she said the police had raided the office and taken all the computers away with them.'

'Now that is a problem.'

'The government's anti-corruption campaign is hitting it, and others like it, very hard.'

'You say the company is still in business – what does it do?'

'It's still a transportation company, so my son tells me.'

'So, he has an interest in the company?'

'He owns shares in it. He lives with the hope that one day he can buy the controlling share and extract revenge on Rienzi for his father.'

'Can you tell me the company's name?'

'How can I forget it? It's called Morelli Trasporto Internazionale.'

'Thank you, Mrs Foscatini,' said Buchanan, standing to go. 'If there is anything else you can add, please call me.'

'Certainly, Inspector.'

'And please don't worry about your grandson, I'm sure he'll turn up.'

'I'll show you to the door.'

Mrs Foscatini stood at the door and watched Buchanan walk down the driveway to his car. He wasn't a happy man. From about fifteen feet away, he could clearly see there was something wrong. The front passenger-side tyre was flat. He stopped at the side of the car and wondered how a well-serviced car could suffer from a flat tyre, especially since it was only driven on the local roads. He shook his head. He'd parked close to the kerb and realised even if he had the inclination to change the tyre, there was no way he could get a jack under the body. He took out his phone and dialled Street. 'Jill, who do we use for breakdowns?'

'Not sure, never needed to have a car recovered. I suppose you need to call control. Need a lift home?'

Buchanan looked to his left, the BMW was still parked across the road about fifty yards away.

'No thanks, I'll wait for recovery. Also I think there's someone waiting to talk to me.'

'The BMW?'

'Yep. Was there anything known about it?'

'No. It appears to be what it is. Be careful.'

'I will.'

Buchanan hung up from Street and called the control centre to report the flat tyre. As he waited for the tow truck, the BMW pulled away from the kerb and drove slowly towards him. It came to a stop directly opposite him. The driver's window lowered.

'Inspector Buchanan, sorry to see your predicament. Mr Palmari sent us to extend his invitation for you to visit him. We can give you a lift if there's a problem with your car.'

'So, Mr Palmari wishes to have a chat, does he?'

'So he said.'

'You do know what abduction is? The taking of someone without their expressed permission?'

'Look, all we were told was to offer you a lift and, if you got in, we were to take you to see Mr Palmari. Then when he's had his chat with you, we're to bring you back here. Nothing about abduction.'

Buchanan got in and fastened his seatbelt.

The car went down Darley Road, turned right onto Beachy Head Road, then left onto Denton.

'Do you guys drive for a company, or are you freelance?'

'No company, we're independent.'

'Like Uber.'

'Not quite, we work for ourselves, we just do special private work.'

'You share this car?'

'Yes, I do days, Harry usually does nights and the airport

runs.'

'Day off today?'

Harry shook his head and laughed. No such thing as a day off when you work for yourself.'

'You guys deliver packages?'

'Sometimes.'

'Ever deliver to CSM?'

'Them and other businesses.'

'What did you deliver?'

'Quite inquisitive, our fare, eh Harry?'

'He's a policeman, Dave, it's his job to be inquisitive.'

'Well, what about it? What did you deliver?'

'No idea, we were warned not to be curious.'

'By whom?'

'The chap we collected the package from.'

'Have a name?'

'No, we never asked, figured it wasn't any of our business.'

'How about an address where you picked up the packages?'

Dave, the one driving, shook his head. 'Different place each time, but always a pub.'

'Who took delivery of these mysterious packages?'

'Whoever we were told to deliver them to.'

'What about CSM? Who did you deliver to there?'

'Denman, he always took the delivery.'

'How did you know who he was?'

'We were told to ask for him by name, but I didn't need to.'

'You knew Denman?'

'I used to do some work for his company, nothing technical. Just helped out round the workshop when things needed shifting.'

'How big were these packages you delivered?'

'Couldn't really call them packages. They were usually small bubble-wrap envelopes, sort of size when you order a CD from Amazon.'

'Heavy?'

'No.'

Halfway down Denton the driver turned off the road into a private residence. The well-worn driveway turned sharply to the left behind a large sycamore tree and ended at a tall box hedge.

'I take it I'm supposed to get out here?'

There was an audible click as the rear passenger door unlocked. 'Thanks for the ride. I suppose you'll be joining me?'

'We're not welcome in the front door; staff entrance is round the side.'

Staff entrance is round the side, mused Buchanan as he climbed the steps to an imposing varnished oak door. He reached for the enormous, polished brass knocker, but before he could lay his hand on it, the door swung open inwards.

'Good afternoon, sir, you are expected.'

The butler, or bodyguard? wondered Buchanan. Probably a bit of both.

'Would you follow me, please? Mr Palmari will join you in a minute.'

Buchanan followed the butler across the entrance hall towards an oak-panelled corridor, past an enormous polished oak staircase that led up at least two flights.

As far as butlers went, this one was the biggest Buchanan had ever come across. Lurch from the Addams family would be a good description. From the back, he looked like a prize fighter, his smart butler's jacket struggling to contain the wide and muscular shoulders. His hands were the size of dinner plates. Another candidate for tree nailing, thought Buchanan.

As they made their way along the corridor, lights came on as they approached, then went out as they passed. Buchanan counted two CCTV cameras, one at each end of the hallway. At the end of the corridor was a small ante-room with two chairs.

'Wait here,' said the butler, pointing to the chairs.

The butler knocked on the door, entered the room and shut

the door behind him. Buchanan stood still and looked back down the now darkened, thickly-carpeted hall. The oak panelling stopped a foot from the ceiling, with the ornate plasterwork of the cornice topping it off. There were no pictures adorning the panelling, just the brass candle holders, each fitted with electric imitation candles that had illuminated their way down the hallway. He looked at the chairs then back to the ceiling. It wouldn't make any difference which seat he sat in – they both were under the constant gaze of the CCTV camera.

After a few minutes, the door opened and Buchanan was ushered into the room.

'If you'll be seated, sir. Mr Palmari is temporarily indisposed, but will be with you shortly.'

Buchanan surveyed the room. Behind him was the door he'd just come in. Set in the far wall directly opposite was another well-polished oak door which the butler had just gone through. On his immediate right, double French doors led out into a glass conservatory. Two large oil paintings of horses hung on the wall to his left, while the wall opposite sported a zebra skin shield with two crossed wooden spears in front. Pride of place in the room, in front of the paintings, was an enormous polished oak desk. A black leather swivelling office chair sat behind the desk. To the left of the desk was a complementary oak four-drawer filing cabinet. Against the wall on his immediate left was an oak bookcase.

Books make a man; Buchanan's grandfather had once told him as they wandered through the Barrows on a Saturday morning while looking for a bike for the young Buchanan. Curiosity got the better of him and Buchanan walked over to inspect the Palmari library.

The books were laid out in random order. Just like someone had taken them out, four or five at a time to dust the shelves, then put them back without regards to alphabetic order or subject matter. *You can't give out what you haven't taken in, remember that and you'll never be lost for words*, his grandfather had added. Buchanan wondered what words Palmari gave out? It was obvious it wouldn't be what he read. The middle three rows weren't in fact books, but book spines carefully fixed to two doors, the lock of one was craftily concealed as part of the book cover design.

Buchanan glanced down at the desk; the top centre drawer was partially open. Should he, or shouldn't he? It would only take a few seconds for someone as experienced as him to have a quick look through the drawer's contents. He listened for the tell-tale sounds of anyone approaching, then decided to go and sit down. He'd remembered a trick his old CID sergeant used when interviewing suspects.

The trick was to have the office set up with details of the crimes, such as witness statements, investigation reports, complete with copies of lifted fingerprints. These would be on display pinned to the walls, before the miscreants were herded in by an anonymous PC. At that point, they were told to sit down and not touch anything. Of course, unknown to them, they were being observed through a one-way mirror by the investigating officers.

Buchanan smiled and retraced his steps to the chair. As he sat down to wait the arrival of Palmari he recognised another trick: someone had shortened the legs on the chair. He tried to cross his legs but gave up. He didn't have to wait long for Palmari, a mumbling of voices rose to a shout, then silence announced the arrival of Palmari and the butler.

He hadn't grown an inch since they'd last met at Greyspear's wedding, though he did look shorter than when they'd last met. He still had dark thinning hair brushed straight back that resembled a 1960s Brylcreem commercial.

He closed the door behind him and smiled as Buchanan stood.

'Please sit, Inspector, good to catch up with you again,' said Palmari, as he settled into his chair and looked down on Buchanan.

'Giovanni, whiskey for our guest – is that correct, Inspector?'

Buchanan shook his head. 'No thank you, not while on duty.'

'Ah, but who would tell? You wouldn't, would you, Giovanni?'

Giovanni feigned a hurt expression and shook his head.

'See, Inspector, Giovanni won't say a word. Now what is it to be? We have a nice selection of Scotches. Which one do you fancy? Giovanni, show the inspector what we keep for very special guests.'

Buchanan turned his head to see what Giovanni was doing and saw that he'd produced a key and had opened the two doors on the book shelves to reveal two shelves of spirits. From where he was seated Buchanan recognised three of his favourite whiskeys along with an American Bourbon he enjoyed from time to time.

'Giovanni, my Scotch, and pour the inspector one as well.'

Buchanan shook his head. 'I'll just have water, thanks.'

'So be it. Giovanni, a glass of water for my friend the inspector.'

Buchanan accepted the offered glass of water, took a sip and thought, *round one to m*e.

Palmari took a long slow sip of his drink and smiled while keeping his eyes on Buchanan. He put his glass down and said, 'Lovely malt, you Scots certainly know how to make it.'

'Mr Palmari, I'm sure you didn't ask me here to talk about whiskey.'

'Toni, Inspector, all my friends call me Toni.'

'Mr Palmari, I repeat myself, you didn't ask me here to talk about whiskey, did you?'

'Ah, Inspector, you need to relax, get way from work more. I know what would make Jack a happy boy, a holiday. How about you take the lovely Mrs Buchanan on a holiday? I have a friend who could do you a wonderful package, flights, hotel, food, and all the drinks you want at a very special price, one tailored just for you and your dear lady wife, Karen. That is her name, isn't it?'

He's certainly persistent, thought Buchanan, wondering what he would try next.

'Inspector, I apologise. I see I have misread you. I understand you are investigating some very, very nasty goings-on in the town. Now I, due to my business operations, have the ability to find things out, I'm sure you know what I mean. I have avenues I can explore of which someone in your position can't avail yourself. Maybe I could be of assistance?'

'Mr Palmari, are you offering to aid the police in their enquiries? If so, I can call the office and they'll be only too happy to send out a car to bring you in.'

'Such quaint language you policemen use, Inspector.'

'Consistency, Mr Palmari. Left foot in front of right, right foot in front of left, just keep plodding and we get our man in the end.'

'Jack – it is Jack – your first name?'

Buchanan nodded.

'Jack, I have to say I have met many policemen in my career, but few – very few – like you.'

'I'll take that as a compliment. Now, what is it you wanted to chat about? If I don't get home soon my dinner will be in the dog.'

'Oh, didn't know you had a dog! Must get my facts correct before we meet again. The reason I wanted to have this friendly chat is, I think I can help you by taking some of the load off your back.'

'Thought you were into transport?'

Palmari nodded. 'Si, that's just one of my ventures.'

'So, why ask me? I've got nothing to do with transport, or

private security.'

'I like to have people work for me who know how to take charge of a situation, think on their feet, you know what I mean?'

'No, I'm sorry, I don't know what you mean.'

'You have a reputation, Jack.'

'What reputation are you referring to?'

'I'm talking about Porter's bar in Glasgow, Jack. You chased two miscreants under a police car, end of story, two paedophiles off the streets of Glasgow. Then what was it, a few months ago, a case of poetic justice the *Herald* called it? The poor chap you were supposed to bring in on a multiple murder charge accidently fell in the harbour and was drowned. And he just happened to be the husband of your friend Sir Nathan Greyspear's new bride. Interesting coincidence wouldn't you say?'

'That's exactly what it was, an accident.'

Palmari nodded. 'Yes, I'm sure it was, and when they hold the enquiry as to why so many criminals die when you're investigating a crime, I'm sure they will rule in your favour.'

'And, why wouldn't they?'

'I hear there were witnesses who would say differently.'

'What are you inferring?'

Palmari shrugged. 'All I am saying is, if it was known there were a few civic-minded people who were prepared to say they saw you push – what was his name? Ah yes, Rodney Richardson – then your reputation would be mud. You might even end up in the slammer with some of those you helped put there.'

'Mr Palmari, I'm sure when, and if, there is an enquiry into the matters you have just outlined, I will be exonerated.'

'Jack, relax. I'm just having a little fun at your expense. I'm sure you would be exonerated. I'm just trying to make you see how important a man with your expertise would be to the smooth functioning of the business venture I'm organising with my business partners.'

'And where would I fit into your plans?'

'As I said, I have been talking with a few business acquaintances and we feel the police are stretched to the limit. Too much time spent filling out forms, ten pages just to put on a pair of handcuffs, I hear,' he said, shaking his head. 'All those wasted hours at the weekends, and nights arresting and locking up those who let themselves become a nuisance to the public.'

'We don't discriminate, we lock up all offenders. It's what we're paid to do.'

'Tell me something, Inspector. When was the last time a policeman wrote out a parking ticket, arrested someone for trespassing on private property, or how about something really simple like littering?'

'We don't, that's a civil matter.'

'Exactly, Jack. Jobs once done by policemen are now quite successfully done by civilians.'

'Where is this going?'

'Jack, my group is planning to present a plan to the crime commissioner. One, when fully implemented, that will save the police budgets millions. We foresee the release of many more officers out into the community, solving crimes they currently don't have time to work on.'

'And my part?'

'You don't have to do anything, except maybe have a word in the commissioner's ear, say we've talked and you give the plan your blessing.'

At last, thought Buchanan, we get to the nub of the meeting. 'Mr Palmari, if you think the commissioner will take any notice of what I have to say, you've chosen the wrong messenger. He wants me out of the way, preferably to retire.'

'Jack, I'll bet he said something about you being too expensive, sergeants could do the same job for less. Am I right, eh?'

'I have to admit, you do have a point there. But I do need to go, dinner is waiting.'

'Of course, Jack. Head home to your dinner and say hello to Karen for me. Your ride is waiting outside for you.'

'Where will they take me?'

'Back to your car – home – the office,' he said gesturing with his hands, 'anywhere you want, Inspector. All you have to do is ask.'

◆

Buchanan watched the BMW disappear down Darley Road. He looked at his car; beside it was a large yellow ATS van. His tyre was fixed. The miracles of modern technology, he mused.

'Your car?' said the mechanic.

'Yes. What was wrong with the tyre?'

'Nothing, the valve and cap were lying on the kerb beside the tyre. Looks like someone was having a laugh at your expense.'

'Thanks.'

Buchanan was about to climb into his car when he was stopped by a voice he recognised.

'Ah, Mrs Foscatini, just heading off home.

'Do you have any news about Nigel?'

'I'm sorry, Mrs Foscatini,' he said.

'But you gave his description to your sergeant, can't you call her?'

'Ok, just a minute. Hi Jill, it's Jack – yes, just now, someone had deliberately let the air out. It was as I suspected, someone wanted to talk to me – I'll tell you all about it tomorrow. You're still at work? There is – he's what? An American? Listen, Jill, did you get anywhere with finding Mrs Foscatini's grandson, Nigel?'

'What's she saying, Inspector?'

'In a minute, Mrs Foscatini. Thanks, Jill. What? No, he can stew in the cells till the morning –   you can head home for the day. I'll see you in the morning.'

'She has news, doesn't she? Oh dear, I hope it's good news.'

'That was my sergeant and, yes, she has news of Nigel. It's good and a bit bad. Nigel was found on a building site under a pile of rubble. He was unconscious when he was pulled out and has been in a coma since. It was your description of the tattoo that helped us track him down.'

'Where is he? Can I go see him?'

'He's currently in the trauma unit in the Conquest Hospital in Hastings. According to what my sergeant has found out, Nigel's condition has stabilised and he is going to be transferred to Eastbourne in a couple of days.'

'Why didn't someone call me?'

'One of the other issues is he's severely concussed. He doesn't know who he is, and has no memories of what happened to him. The doctor has ordered complete isolation for him.'

'What should I do? I don't drive.'

'I suppose you could call a taxi, or your son, and ask him to drive you? Oh, but they're away aren't they? I'm not sure, Mrs Foscatini. I'm sure you'll work something out. I need to go now, goodbye.'

10

'Right, Jill, where is our uninvited visitor?' said Buchanan, as he met Street at the booking-in desk.

'He's in cell three. Want to have a look at him first?'

'Was he carrying anything?'

'Like a gun, or knife? No. Strange thing, all he had with him was a briefcase.'

'That all?'

'Yes.'

'Where is it?'

'The desk sergeant has it.'

'Constable, where's the desk sergeant?' said Buchanan.

'In the evidence room, sir. Want me to get him for you?'

'Yes please, and while you're at it ask the sergeant to bring the American prisoner's briefcase with him, will you?'

'Be right back.'

'Things are getting interesting, Jill. Wonder what surprises are waiting for us in the briefcase?'

'You wanted to see the prisoner's effects, Inspector?'

'That's right. I hear all he had on him was a briefcase?'

'Yes, want to have a look inside?'

'Please.'

The desk sergeant put the prisoner's briefcase on the desk and opened it.

'Fortunate it wasn't locked, eh Sergeant?' said Street.

'Ah, but it was. We also have his car keys and a separate bunch, presumably his house keys.'

Buchanan and Street rummaged carefully through the briefcase's contents.

'Strange contents for going breaking and entering,' said Street.

'Strange indeed,' said Buchanan.

'Look here, a portable DNA sampling kit. Now why would anybody carry one of these with them?'

'Our CSI's do.'

'And look here,' said Street, 'someone's DNA test results.'

'He's looking for someone. That's why he's got the printout of the previous test with him. Constable, can we see cell three?' said Buchanan.

'Coming right up.'

The three of them looked in on cell three on the desk monitor.

'Give you a name?'

'No.'

'Has he said anything at all?'

'Nope.'

'What's he been doing?'

'Nothing, just sits and stares at the wall,' said the desk sergeant, looking over the shoulders of Street and Buchanan.

'But not like your average criminal,' said Buchanan. 'Look at him, look at the way he's sitting, ramrod straight, staring straight ahead. He's been trained for these types of situations. My bet is he's ex-military, probably now CIA.'

'You think so?' said Street.

'Let's go find out.'

The constable led them through to the holding cells and opened the cell door. The prisoner maintained his stare at the far wall.

'Good morning.'

The prisoner turned to see who'd addressed him. 'Why am I here? I've done nothing wrong.'

'My name is Detective Chief Inspector Buchanan; would you mind telling me yours?'

'You the man in charge here?'

'For the moment – your name?'

'Joseph Esposito'

'You wish to tell us what you were doing at the scene of a murder, Mr Esposito?'

'I was looking for something.'

'At ten-thirty at night?'

'I was in a hurry.'

'Let's start at the beginning. What were you looking for in the building?'

'Am I under arrest?'

'Not yet, but unless you can convince me your ten-thirty visit was legitimate, you soon will be.'

'I'm not talking here.'

'Mr Esposito, I decide how and where I interrogate a prisoner in this station.'

'Inspector, could we talk in private, please?'

'Constable, do we have an interview room available?'

'Yes, room two.'

'You first, Mr Esposito,' said Buchanan, as they entered interview room two.

'No recordings, please,' said Esposito.

'Sorry, sir, it's the rules, every interview has to be recorded. Home office procedures,' said the constable.

'Constable, has Mr Esposito been charged with anything?'

'No, sir.'

'In that case, I think we'll have our chat in my office.'

'That's not regular procedure, sir.'

'That's all right, Constable, I'll be responsible for Mr Esposito.'

◆

'Well, Mr Esposito, what do you have to say about your breaking and entering?' said Buchanan, closing the door to his office.

'I am trying to trace a businessman of Italian origin. He arrived in the USA sometime early in the 1970s, and is now thought to be somewhere in the UK.'

'Bit of a needle in a haystack search?'

'Yeah. Do you have any idea of how many immigrants entered the United States during the 1970s?'

'No.'

'Thousands, Inspector, thousands.'

'Yes, I'm sure that's correct. But you're only interested in one of those thousands – do you have a name?'

'Guido Rienzi.'

'Rienzi – 'Jill, did you tell Stephen where we have gone?' said Buchanan.

'Sorry – oh, er, no. Should I call him?'

'In a minute, Jill. Now Mr Esposito, why didn't you go through the regular channels?'

'It's a private business affair.'

'Which business?'

'Our head office had word that Rienzi was trying to make a deal with a guy called Denman. I was trying to find out if there were any records that would help me find Rienzi, that's all.'

'Why does your office want to talk to Mr Rienzi?'

'That's confidential.'

'You work for the IRS?' said Street.

Esposito shook his head.

'Then who do you work for?'

'I'm a private investigator.'

'Who are you really working for?' said Buchanan.

'Who I work for is not so important. All I want to do is find Rienzi and report back.'

'You're not very good at being a private investigator if you get caught breaking and entering by a couple of beat coppers,' said Buchanan.'

'Ah, yes. Your British policemen are not quite what I

expected.'

'Yes,' said Street, 'we talk first, then shoot, but only if necessary.'

'Jill,' said Buchanan.

'Sorry.'

'Mr Esposito, can we get back to what you're doing in the UK?'

'As I said, I'm tracing the whereabouts of Guido Rienzi, born in 1951, in Taormina, Sicily. His family moved to Turin when he was five. When he arrived in the USA in 1971, he was listed as having a wife and two children.'

'Have you talked to his wife? Maybe she knows where he is.'

'We're still looking for her, social security has no record of her, or her children.'

'The children – they must be grown adults by now.'

'No trace of any of them, it's as if they just disappeared into the kaleidoscope of the American underworld.'

'The whole family?'

'We only have information on the father.'

'If you're not working for the IRS, how do you come to know so much about Mr Rienzi?'

'I have contacts in high places.'

'And you're saying Rienzi's wife and children aren't listed on his tax return as dependants?'

'Nothing. All we have is his first year's tax return, no mention of any family members.'

'Sounds like they never arrived and someone in your American immigration department screwed up.'

'Maybe. So, do you think you can help me, Inspector?'

'Do you have anything else?'

'His mother's maiden name was Morelli.'

'Father – have his name?'

Esposito shook his head. 'There were so many immigrants coming in to the country that only basic information was collected. I've seen the immigration log, the name is a bit of a scribble, could be Bonito, or several other names that start with B.'

'What's he done to deserve this hue and cry?'

'In the States, he's wanted by the police for racketeering, money laundering, tax evasion, and probably a few murders. He also controlled gambling, drugs, prostitution, and enforcement. You name it, he was involved. Guido Rienzi became involved in anything illegal that could produce an income. There's a very large reward posted for his arrest and conviction.'

'So, you're a bounty hunter, not a private investigator?'

'I'm a licensed bail bondsman if you don't mind; bounty hunters went out with the wild west. I've got a living to make, Sergeant.'

'So why do you think he's in the UK?' said Street.

'We think he might have family here.'

'Here in Eastbourne?'

'Yeah. I'm following a lead. One of Rienzi's American partners recently died and when his apartment was cleared, a letter from Rienzi was found with an address in Eastbourne.'

'Which address?' said Buchanan, leaning forward.

Esposito shook his head. 'Relax, Inspector. The building's gone, it's now part of what the locals call the Arndale Centre.'

'That's tough for you.'

'Isn't it?'

'When did he go missing?'

'About fifteen years ago.'

'Know the reason why?'

'The word on the street was he'd encroached on another boss's territory. A meeting between the bosses was arranged in a neutral bar to resolve their differences. Unfortunately, the meeting descended into a shooting war, the building where the meeting was held caught fire and lots of people died.'

'Was his body found?' said Street.

Esposito shook his head. 'The fire burned so hot, there weren't any bodies to identify. Police forensics spent two and a half months combing through the remains. There were twenty people at the meeting, the CSI's could only identify the remains of eighteen. Two were never accounted for, Rienzi and his first lieutenant.'

'How would they have identified Rienzi?'

'His DNA was on file. He was in a street fight and left a large sample of his blood on a hospital towel.'

'So, now all you have to do is test every male in the UK and you have him?' said Street.

'If only it was that simple.'

'Before I let you go, Mr Esposito, can you tell me how you got in to the factory and managed to reset the alarm so efficiently?'

'I called the alarm company and said I was you and needed access.'

'And they let you in?'

'Yeah, suckers.'

'How did you know my name? We've never met before.'

'I read newspapers, Inspector.'

♦

Buchanan said goodbye to Esposito and walked slowly back to his office. The missed-call light was flashing on his phone. He picked it up and looked at the display; it was Palmari's number. Buchanan smiled, the pieces were starting to fall into place. He pressed the play-message button.

'Palmari called, and left a message,' Buchanan said to Street, as she entered the office after reuniting Esposito with his hire car.

'Oh, and what did Mr Palmari have to say?'

'Asked if I'd had time to think about his offer and would I pay him another visit.'

'Nice of him to call,' said Street.

Buchanan smiled. 'He's getting desperate.'

'Is that good?'

'For us it is, he's likely to make a mistake when desperate.'

'Why are we interested in Mr Palmari?'

'I don't really know, but since he seems to be very interested in us, I think I should at least go along with his ruse.'

'You think he's mixed up in the murders?'

'There's too many Italians in the mix for him not to be.'

'Oh, Mr Esposito left us a present.'

'What was that?'

'He was in so much of a hurry to say goodbye he left his briefcase on the back seat of my car.'

'I suppose we should return it to him.'

'How will we do that? All we have is his name.'

'Let me have a look, his address should be in there somewhere.'

Street passed the briefcase to Buchanan as her phone rang.

Buchanan sat down at his desk and read through the flimsy file, then smiled.

Street hung up from her call and saw a look of triumph on Buchanan's face.

'What's got you so excited?'

'Rienzi's DNA results.'

'That won't do us much good without Rienzi.'

'You're right, but at least we could identify him if we had to.'

''Be a bit difficult when we don't know where he is.'

Buchanan nodded. 'I think we'll take a copy of these results, just in case – and while we're at it, I'll photocopy all the other documents as well, especially his passport.'

'Does he have a phone in there?'

Buchanan lifted all the contents of the briefcase out and laid them on his desk. A passport in the name of Michael Esposito, a car-hire agreement, the DNA test results with a faded photo of a young man in a Ferrari sports car smiling at the camera, a folder containing yellowed newspaper clippings, but no phone.

'This is interesting,' said Buchanan unfolding the newspaper clipping.

'What have you found?'

'It's from the New York Times.

> 'Brooklyn man Guido Rienzi, accused of the recent murder of gang boss, Salvatore Biaggio.
>
> In his absence, he was hit Wednesday with a twenty-four-count indictment, authorities said. The indictment returned by a Queens grand jury charges Guido Rienzi, with eighteen counts of first-degree murder, along with raps for second-degree murder, racketeering, prostitution, sale of untaxed liquor, extortion, and gambling. Rienzi faces up to life in prison without the possibility of parole if convicted. He is currently on the run having failed to show up for a bail hearing. The FBI has posted a substantial reward for his capture.'

'Quite a good photo of him, pity it's not a recent one. No phone though Was he searched?'

Street looked at the charge sheet. 'Nothing recorded.'

'How long will it take to photocopy the contents?'

'Just a couple of minutes, there's not that many documents.'

'Good.'

'Why?'

'Esposito is downstairs asking if we've got his briefcase.'

After copying the contents of Esposito's briefcase, and saying goodbye for the second time, Buchanan and Street walked back up to the office.

'Where's Stephen and Morris?' said Buchanan.

'At the hospital. Nigel's just been transferred to the DGH.'

'Call them and tell them they're needed for a meeting, it's time we started tying up some of the loose ends.'

'Where do you want them to meet us?'

'Starbucks is closed for the night,' Buchanan said, looking at his phone. 'I know, let's try The Heron in Westham, they also do food, so we can get dinner. It's usually quiet at this time of the evening.'

'Shouldn't you call Karen? She'll probably want to know how late you'll be, probably want to keep your dinner hot for you,' said Street, looking at her watch. 'Though, it's still early for dinner.'

'Ah – yes, good point. I'll call her. Can you get on to Stephen and Morris, and tell them to get over there, say, at about five-thirty to six?'

'Where will you be in the meantime?'

'I'm going to pay a visit to Mr Palmari.'

'Need me to come along?'

'That, I think, would be an excellent idea. He's an arrogant snob, be good to put him off his stride.'

◆

'Where does he live?' said Street, as they buckled up.

'He has a rather splendid house up on Denton Road.'

'Never been up there before.'

'Before we do that, I need you to stop by my house.'

◆

'You were certainly correct when you said his house was rather splendid,' said Street.

The front door, as before, was opened by Giovanni.

'Yes? Can I help?'

'Detective Chief Inspector Buchanan and Detective Sergeant Street, to see Mr Palmari.'

'Please wait, I'll see if he's in. Wait there,' said Giovanni, as he closed the door.

'See if he's in?' said Street.

'I'm sure a man as important as Mr Palmari has to be very careful who he sees,' said Buchanan, gently nodding up at the CCTV camera tucked up under the eaves of the porch.

Two minutes later the front door opened. 'If you'll follow

me, I'll take you to Mr Palmari.'

Street followed Buchanan who followed Giovanni down the oak-panelled hallway.

'Please wait here, Mr Palmari is in conference, he will call for you when he is ready.'

'Wonder what business Mr Palmari is in?' said Street, nodding at the two CCTV cameras.

'I'm sure it's many,' said Buchanan.

'He must be very successful at whatever he does,' said Street, 'this house must have cost over a million.'

'Probably more.'

'And when I think of what Stephen and I will be living in when we get married. I can't see us, even in a lifetime, affording anything this glamorous.'

The door opened, and Giovanni came out. 'Mr Palmari will see you now, follow me.'

Once again, the office was empty. This time there were two chairs in front of the desk. Buchanan indicated to Street to sit in one of them.

'Would you like an office like this one, Jack?' said Street, wiggling in her chair trying to figure out why she was looking up at everything.

Buchanan looked at her and smiled. 'Could you see the ACC condoning the expense?'

'But didn't you say Mr Palmari offered you a job? I'm sure he'd want his senior managers to have such an office as this. Maybe not in this house, but in an office suitable to your standing in his organisation.'

Buchanan looked at Street, smiled and wiggled his eyebrows; she was playing the game admirably.

Buchanan glanced around the room, the bookcase was closed and so was the desk drawer.

Moments later the inner door opened and Palmari swept in to the room and sat in his chair. No suit this time. He was in white shorts and a tailored short-sleeved shirt. He had a bulky white towel wrapped round his neck.

Street started to stand, then looked at Buchanan, and relaxed back into her chair.

Palmari rolled his shoulders and cocked his head to one side. 'Giovanni, that last rally – I've pinched that damn nerve again.'

Giovanni stepped behind Palmari and commenced to massage his neck and shoulders.

Street was mesmerised by the sight of Giovanni's huge hands as they squeezed and pummelled Palmari's scrawny neck and shoulders.

'Ah, blessed relief, thanks, Giovanni. Jack, I see you've brought your assistant with you today, how nice.'

'It's Detective Sergeant Street, Mr Palmari.'

'Call me Toni, Jill. It is Jill, isn't it?'

'Yes – Toni.'

'That's better. Now Jack, the last time you were here we discussed a little business matter. Have you had time to think things over?'

'Yes, but there's the issue of my pension. My superiors want me to go early, but they won't even make me an offer that would make it financially feasible.'

'Ah, yes. Bureaucracy at its worst. Of course, if you did decide to come work for me, there wouldn't be such restrictions on retirement. In fact, come to work for me and you'd never want to retire. Your skills and experience would always be appreciated, you would forever be part of the family.'

'I could drink to that type of offer,' said Street.

'You'd also like to work for me, Jill? My, what a day. Giovanni, you're needed,' said Palmari into his desk phone.'

The inner door opened, and Giovanni entered the room.

'Drinks all round, Giovanni. We're going to toast the addition of Jack and Jill – Jack and Jill, how odd. Never mind, Jack and Jill have decided to join us, isn't that grand?'

Giovanni stared at them, expressionless.

'What would you like, Jack?'

'Last time you offered me a whiskey.'

'Yes, a most suitable drink on this occasion. Jill, I suppose you're driving?'

Street nodded. 'I'll have lemonade, if you have any.'

Drinks in hand, Palmari offered a toast.

'Well, Jack, Jill, here's to a never-ending friendship.'

'Cheers,' said Buchanan, downing his drink in one go.

Palmari took a large sip of his.

'Now that was very nice,' said Buchanan, holding up his empty glass.

'Giovanni, Jack's glass is empty.'

Buchanan grinned and went to pass his glass to Giovanni.

Palmari downed his drink and said, 'Me too, Giovanni.

Buchanan withdrew his glass and reached for Palmari's. In doing so he dropped his own glass on the floor, breaking it. 'Oops, he said, 'clumsy me.' He passed Palmari's glass to Giovanni and tried to pick up the pieces of his own glass.

'Never mind, Jack. Giovanni can clean it up later.'

'Giovanni, we'll take our drinks on the veranda. Follow me Jack, and Jill,' Palmari said, breaking out into laughter again.

'This is a spectacular view, Mr Palmari,' said Street.

'Toni, call me Toni, Jill, we're all on first name terms.'

'We, Toni?' said Buchanan.'

'Oh, don't worry about names at the moment, Jack. You'll get to meet everyone eventually.'

'What exactly would you want me to do, Toni?'

'Very much what you do now, Jack. I see you keeping an eye on my affairs worldwide, you could keep Jill as your secretary if that works for you.'

◆

'Keep me as your secretary! What a creep that guy is. A bit of a wasted journey, Jack,' said Street, as she drove them to The

Heron. 'We didn't get much out of him, other than he wants you to keep an eye on his affairs.'

'Oh, but I did get this,' said Buchanan, holding up a small whiskey glass.

'Won't he miss it and get suspicious?'

'I doubt it. When I was last there I saw he had whiskey glasses similar to the ones we have at home.'

'I don't see.'

'You saw me drop and break my glass?'

'Yes.'

'What you didn't see was, I dropped the glass I brought with me and made sure it broke when I did. Then during the commotion, I simply swapped his glass, the one he was drinking from, for mine.'

'You can't use that for evidence, can you?'

'Probably not, but it does help in the investigation. Can you send it off to forensics in the morning?

◆

Street drove into The Heron car park and parked next to Hunter's recently repaired car.

Buchanan looked at it and scowled. 'Why's he driving that when he's still on duty?'

Street remained silent as they entered The Heron.

'Hi Stephen, where's Morris?' said Street.

He nodded towards the toilet door.

'Thanks. Eaten yet?'

'No, we've been waiting for you.'

'Good. Stephen, grab that table in the corner.'

'I'll get a menu,' said Dexter who'd just returned from the toilet

◆

Food eaten, three pairs of eyes stared at Buchanan, waiting for him to begin.

'Right everyone, down to business. The story so far. We get a call that a body's been found in a derelict factory. The victim has not just been killed, he'd been made an example of to someone and cruelly dispatched. Then we find out that the factory, while it is unoccupied, is being used as a diesel distillery, stolen goods distribution warehouse and a centre for the distribution of toxic waste. Jill, over to you,' said Buchanan, taking a long swig from his beer.

'We deduce who the previous tenants were, a company called Crown System Mouldings, owned by a family called Morelli. They specialised in fibreglass mouldings for the marine, automotive and marine markets. Next, we find out that the victim was one of the employees of that company, a struck-off bankrupt director. After investigating his doings, we are led to a company rep, a Mr Clive Prince. This Mr Prince represents a plastics company and is not averse to a little cash business on the side selling out of date resin.'

'Another version of the *let us do your driveway, because we've got some left over tar*,' said Stephen.

'Exactly,' said Street. 'Unknown at that time, the same evening that Denman met his end, Mrs Foscatini's grandson, Nigel, is being dumped, presumed dead, under a pile of bricks, on the Arndale shopping mall extension. Then, two days after Jack has a word with Mr Prince, he is found nailed to a tree in a way that the nail-gun manufacturers never thought of their guns being used.'

'Then,' said Buchanan, 'as Jill and I are waiting at Starbucks for one of Mr Prince's colleagues to show up to answer some questions, he unfortunately ends up wrapped around a tree with his car for company.'

'I've just thought of something,' said Dexter

'What's that?' said Street, turning to Buchanan and grinning.

'Nigel. Am I correct he's only just been identified?'

'Yes,' said Street.

'And only the hospital and his grandmother knows he's

alive?'

'Go on,' said Buchanan.

'Don't you see? He's in as much danger now as he was the evening he was dumped on the building site.'

'You think we should arrange a twenty-four-hour guard for him?'

'Yes, I certainly do. He's the only living witness to what's been going on.'

Buchanan downed his pint and said, 'Since it's your idea, Morris, you can have the first shift. Stephen, you have the other twelve. Work out between you who does which hours till I can get a full-time replacement shift organised. It shouldn't take long, can't have two of my best investigators sitting at a bedside twiddling their fingers.'

'Thanks, Chief,' said Morris.

'What's the latest on Nigel?'

'We stopped in at the hospital an hour ago and the doctor is now being more positive about his condition.'

'Details?'

'They have taken him off the ventilator and he is now breathing on his own. The CT scan was negative and they've set his broken legs and left arm, the ribs will heal on their own.'

'I'm surprised he lasted, that was quite a beating he took. Has he regained consciousness yet, said anything?'

'No, not a word. Apparently when his eyes are open, he just stares at the ceiling.'

'What a crazy world,' said Street.

'Anyway,' said Buchanan, 'back to the case. As a result of us talking with the Morelli family they feel scared enough to go into hiding.'

'Stephen and I talked with them today,' said Dexter.

'Ah, I was coming to that, but, since you've brought it up, what did the Morellis have to say for themselves?'

'It took a bit of talking through the door to convince them

we weren't going away,' said Hunter.

'We were fortunate,' said Dexter, 'the Tesco van was in front of us doing deliveries to the flats so we waited for the delivery guy to knock on the door. The door opened, but as soon as Mr Morelli saw us he slammed the door shut; the delivery chap didn't quite know what to do.'

'We showed the driver our warrant cards,' said Hunter, 'and convinced him to just leave the groceries on the floor.'

'What got Mr Morelli to open the door?' said Buchanan.

'I threatened to open his bottle of Rioja and have a picnic on the landing,' said Hunter.

'That's showing imagination,' said Street.

'So, they opened the door and invited you in?' said Buchanan.

'Morris and I carried their groceries in and helped put them away. They are emotional wrecks, something or someone has really put the fear of God into them.'

'I doubt God has anything to do with it, Stephen,' said Buchanan. 'What did they have to say for themselves?'

'Not much,' said Hunter. 'We tried to get them to open up about Denman, but they were too scared about something they wouldn't tell us.'

'Did you offer them police protection?'

'Yes, but they wouldn't budge, said they'd stick it out in the flat till you caught the killers.'

'Hmm, nice to be trusted, but don't they realise that without them and others mixed up in this mess, we won't be able to catch the killers?'

'Jack, a few days ago you said that you thought there was some sort of master criminal behind all these murders. Do you still think that?' queried Street.

Buchanan took a long slow sip of his beer. 'Yes, I do.'

'What about this Palmari character? He sounds like a real sleezeball.'

'I'm not sure if he's just some opportunist, or someone we need to keep an eye on. He tried to proposition me…'

'What?' said Dexter.

Buchanan shook his head. 'Not that way, Morris. He said he was working on providing a security contract that would provisionally remove the need for us, the police, to carry out the mundane tasks of street patrols and their like.'

'That's crazy,' said Hunter. 'That would amount to a second-class police presence on the streets, and probably there would all sorts of opportunities for corruption to creep in.'

'Do you think it was a legitimate suggestion?' said Street.

'I doubt it. I first met him at Sir Nathan's wedding, didn't like him then and, after my recent meeting with him, I now like him even less. He even had the balls to threaten me with some cock and bull story that there were witnesses who would testify in court that I deliberately pushed Rodney Richardson to his death.'

'But that's nonsense,' said Hunter. 'We were all there, we saw what happened.'

'And the ruckus in Porter's toilet, supposedly he's got someone in Glasgow who says I pushed the nonces under the police car.'

'So, why are we looking for this Rienzi chap?' asked Morris.

'We're not. That Yank, Esposito, is.'

Hunter shook his head and swallowed the last of his beer. 'I don't understand why we're suddenly overrun by Italians.'

'Stephen, Morris,' said Buchanan, 'I think it's time one of you headed off to the DGH and Nigel. In the meantime, I'll see what I can do to arrange for a full-time watch for him.'

'I'll take the first watch,' said Dexter.

'I'll give you a lift, be back for you shortly, Jill,' said Hunter, kissing her on the cheek.

'Ok.'

'Jill, another drink? Don't worry, Karen is going to pick me up.'

'Pinot Grigio., please.'

Buchanan returned with their drinks.

'Thanks.'

'You're welcome. What did you find out about the CCTV cameras on Edison Street?'

'Nothing, there aren't any.'

'Not one?'

She shook her head.

'Hmm, well, that's one avenue closed. Jill, first thing tomorrow, I think we'll go have a word with whoever found Nigel on the building site.'

11

'You're late, where have you been?'

'Two slashed tyres. I had it towed to Jim's, he'll fix it tomorrow.'

'Hmm, Jim's going to be able to retire on what you've spent on that car to keep it running.'

'I said I'm going to sell it. Besides, slashed tyres are not the car's fault.'

'And when are you going to sell it?'

'Before we're married, I told you that.'

'Stephen, the wedding is only a few weeks away.'

'What's the matter? It's not just the car, is it?'

'Natalie's been offered a job.'

'Good for Natalie. What is it?'

'Senior project manager for Renault.'

'Will she have to commute? There's no Renault offices around here.'

'What, Eastbourne to Paris and back every day? I suppose it's possible. No, she's moving out, has already rented an apartment just outside Paris. She says her commute will only be fifteen minutes on her bicycle.'

'That mean you'll be living in that big empty flat on your own?'

'And there lies the problem. I can't afford the rent on my own.'

'Will you find someone to share with you – eh?'

'Don't tempt me. We've already been down that path. When we're married, then you can move in.'

'You're so old fashioned – and that's one reason I love you

so much.'

'Come here, you big softy.'

They walked to the bus stop and waited for the number 56.

'What will you do?' said Stephen, as the bus passed through Stonecross.

'I mentioned it to Karen. Guess what she said?'

'I don't need to guess, bet she said go and live with them?'

Street nodded. 'I move in Saturday. Want to give me a hand?'

'I'll rent a van, how much stuff do you have?'

'Not much.'

They left the bus at the Langney shopping centre and waited for the 1A.

'You want to come out with me this evening?'

'A date? You're asking me out on a date? Why, Mr Hunter, what would my daddy say?'

Hunter smiled at the remark. 'I'm sure Jack wouldn't mind in the least.'

'Does it bother you that I have no parents – no grandparents for our children?'

'There's my mum and dad, and what about Jack and Karen? They're as close to parents as you can get. Don't forget they had no children of their own, and you are the closest they'll ever get to having children.'

'What a wonderful, lovely, crazy world we live in.'

'I agree.'

'So, Mr Hunter, where are you planning on taking this waif and stray out to?'

'I'm on duty in the town centre this evening.'

'Why? You're seconded to CID, not street patrols.'

'There's a big engagement party at Jukes this evening and I've been asked to help out. The word on the street is there's going to be trouble. The young lady who's celebrating her engagement has got a very unhappy ex-boyfriend who has sworn to break up the party.'

'So, you volunteered to go out on patrol, why?'

'Don't get me wrong, working for CID is rewarding, and fun. I simply miss the buzz on the street at night. I just thought it would be fun to go out with the gang, just one more time.'

'Will you be in uniform? Not sure mine still fits.'

'Just wear your normal work clothes and your stab-vest over the top.'

'Ok.'

'Things won't kick off till gone midnight, so we should have plenty of time to have dinner first.'

'Where shall we eat?'

'Hmm, I know. How about we go to the Two Bulls?'

'Where's that?'

'It's a gourmet steak restaurant on Church Street.'

Street shook her head.

'It's in the Tally-Ho pub.'

'Didn't realise there was a restaurant in the pub.'

'Some of the best steaks in town.'

'You've sold me. What time?'

'Seven-thirty give you enough time to get ready?'

'As long as we can get off work on time today.'

'What are you doing first?'

'I have a list as long as my arm. First, I've got to check on Nigel's criminal background, then see if I can track down the former directors of CSM. You, what are you doing?'

'The chief wants me to get in touch with HMRC and find out what they know about CSM.'

'Thought he was going to do that?'

'He got hung up with the ACC.'

♦

'Morning, Chief.'

'Morning Morris, seen Jill and Stephen?'

'Stephen had car trouble, they're taking the bus.'

'Anything from HMRC?'

'Yes, but –'

'You know I don't like buts.'

'The person I talked to asked if you would call them, said to ask for an Andy Meggs. The number is on your desk.'

'Thanks.'

Buchanan dialled the number and waited. 'Yes, this is DCI Buchanan, Sussex CID. Can I have a word with Andy Meggs, please? Ok, I can do that.'

'He's not in?' said Stephen.

'He's on another call. I'm going over to see him at the tax office.'

'Hang on, what address did they give you?'

'Number 2, St Anne's Road.'

'Thought so. The tax office closed two years ago. This address he gave you is the Jobcentre.'

'How ironic is that?'

'What?'

'Oh, nothing, just a conversation I had with the ACC about the generous pension schemes that are available to senior policemen.'

'Will you take it?'

Buchanan looked directly at Dexter. 'I will if Prince Charles gives up his right to the throne.'

'So, the answer's no.'

'Got it in one. I should be back by lunch time.'

'Ok, I'll tell Jill when she gets in.'

'Oh, what are you working on now?'

'Just had a phone call from the alarm company that looks after the building where we found Denman. Wanted to know if you'll need to get back in the building. Said if you do they can fix you up with a door code.'

'Any other details?'

'No. They just wanted to be helpful. Want me to call them and let them know it wasn't you who called?'

'No, I'll talk to them later. I want you and Stephen to go bother the Morellis. It's about time we interrupted their holiday. Ring their doorbell and let them know we're watching them. Call me if anything develops.'

♦

Buchanan turned off St Leonards Road, into the St Anne's car park and parked in the only available area beside a builder's skip. He pressed the entry door bell and waited.

'Yes, can I help?'

'Detective Chief Inspector Buchanan to see Andy Meggs, HMRC.'

'One moment.'

The door-lock buzzed and Buchanan walked into the building and climbed the stairs to the first floor. Meggs was waiting for him at the top.

'You'll have to excuse meeting here, Inspector. Since the government has decided to move tax operations on-line they've closed all our local offices. I was fortunate to find this office at such short notice. Can I get you something to drink?' said Meggs, as he ushered Buchanan into the tiny windowless office.

'I could do with a coffee.'

'Americano, cappuccino, or how about a latte?'

'You have those here?'

'No. One of the young lads downstairs goes out for coffee every morning and gets me one when he's out. This is a non-smoking building and he has a quick one while out getting the coffee.'

'In that case, I'll have an Americano.'

'Be right back.'

Buchanan looked at the large pile of files on the desk and wondered just what had been going on at CSM.

Meggs returned threeminutes later and said, 'Coffee will be with us shortly.'

'Good.'

'Now, Inspector, CSM, what I have to tell you is strictly confidential and cannot be disclosed to anyone without the express permission of the HMRC. Do you understand?'

'It's that bad, eh?'

'Worse.'

'Just how much worse?' said Buchanan, as he sipped from his just-delivered coffee.

'I'll start with what we've found out so far. CSM came onto our radar screen a few years ago. On initial inspection, it looked like a case of sloppy bookkeeping, someone had forgotten to file the company interim reports on time. We sent out the usual reminder about how they must be on time and how much the fine could be for late reporting.'

'Did they respond?'

'We received an email from someone purporting to be the company accountant. This person said there had been a problem with the building roof during a rain storm and the records had been damaged.'

'A sort of *the dog ate my homework* excuse?'

'That's a good one, Inspector. At HMRC we try to help, especially with start-up companies. Our approach is, if we get the start-ups running right at the beginning, we won't have trouble with them later on down the road.'

'That makes sense. You provide a personal service?'

'Not quite. We at the HMRC are extremely busy all through the year and unfortunately sometimes things go wrong, companies slip through the net.'

'Is this what happened to CSM?'

Meggs grimaced. 'It's my job to find out why and how things went wrong.'

'And have you?'

'Yes, and it's not good. Whoever managed the subterfuge did a very good job of it. In the trade, it's called the cuckoo in the nest manoeuvre'

'Can you explain what you mean?'

'The way it works is, someone sets out to defraud the exchequer. They scout out a successful business, say one that has a turnover in the millions. Next step is they find out all about the existing directors, their strengths and very importantly their weaknesses and vices. Using the knowledge gained, usually by blackmail, they go to work on the victim, then get one of their own people on to the board of directors. One sad case I once heard about concerned a married man, he had a dalliance with his secretary, just once, but when they told him they were going to tell his family, he took an overdose of his medication and died.'

'But how does that get them anywhere?'

'Once on the board, and with the help of the compromised director, they set about grabbing control of the company. The act of usurping directors may have to be repeated till full control of the company is completed.'

'Still don't see how this leads to making an illegal gain.'

'You will. Once the company is running under the new regime, the next trick is to create a new company, or purchase one from the receivers. The advantage of that is the company usually still has physical assets, employees and customers. A board of directors is appointed, usually with their cronies of the gang. These directors are paid a small salary, especially since it is a start-up company. I see you shaking your head – wait, the best is yet to come. Money is transferred from the parent company to cover the start-up costs of the new venture.'

'So, the parent company gets their tax deferred for investing in the new company?'

'That's only part of it. Where the deception comes in is when the parent company stops paying HMRC and transfers all the company cash to the new company.'

'How do they do that, write a cheque?'

'Not quite. They start by creating a business plan, cash flow projection and how the funds are to be raised for the venture and a projected return outline. Next, they invite wealthy investors to come along to hear the proposal.'

'How long can they get away with that?'

'I've heard of cases where the company concerned managed to avoid paying for almost four years. We shut them down in the end, we were lucky to get pennies in the pound.'

'Can't you just get the money back from the new company?'

'By the time we find out what's happened, the money has all been spent on consultant's fees.'

'How much did they get from CSM?'

'My rough calculations show the exchequer is out of pocket to the tune of one and a half million pounds.'

'That much?'

'That's the traceable amounts. Who knows how much was under the table dealing?'

♦

'You're early,' said Street. 'Come in, I'm nearly ready. You can wait in the lounge, Natalie's watching TV.'

'I'm hungry, you ready?'

'In a minute, just need to do my hair,' said Street.

'Your hair's fine.'

'Typical man. I'll just be a minute.'

'Hi, Natalie,' said Hunter, as he pushed the door open to the lounge.

'Hi, Stephen. Where are you taking Jill?'

'Going to the Two Bulls.'

'Carnivore.'

'Just because you're a vegetarian, don't go judging others.'

'I don't, just trying to wind you up.'

'So, you're off to Paris?'

'Yep, can't wait.'

'When do you go?'

'Next week.'

'Have somewhere to stay sorted?'

'*Oui.*'

'Come on, Stephen, you're not the only one who's hungry,' said Street, from the hallway.

'Ok. Bye, Natalie, see you – oh, see you at the wedding, if not before.'

'I'm sure you will, there's the rehearsal to come yet.'

'Ok, see you.'

♦

'Thanks for dinner, Stephen. The steak was everything you said it would be.'

'My pleasure.'

'Where are we to meet your team?'

'I said we'd see them in town. I thought if it was dry, we could walk down.'

'I'm all for that, walking out with my beau.'

'Where did that come from?'

Street shook her head. 'Not sure, probably one of those black and white movies I watched when it's cold and raining outside.'

'Well, it's certainly not cold outside this evening. I can't remember the last time it was twenty degrees at nine-thirty in the evening. Wonder if it will be this hot at this time in the evening on our honeymoon?'

'Oh – you intrigue me, where are you whisking me off to on your magic carpet?'

'Not telling, it's a surprise, remember?'

Street poked Hunter in the ribs. 'You tease. Just you wait till I get you on your own.'

'I'm looking forward to that.'

♦

'There they are,' said Hunter, pointing to a marked police-van parked on the pavement outside Debenhams. 'Hi guys,' he said, 'Much happening?'

The driver shook his head. 'We've ID'd the troublemakers, they're all in the Scarlet Pig getting pissed. So far they're behaving themselves.'

'Is the ringleader there?'

'The jilted lover? He's the guy with the tattoo of a parrot sticking up from his collar on the left side of his neck.'

'Should be easy to follow.'

'What you going to do?'

'Thought I'd go in for a drink with Jill, shouldn't be too conspicuous.'

'I'd watch my step if I were you two. Don't turn your back on them, they're a nasty bunch, they've all done time.'

'What for?'

'GBH. Three of them been in for knife crimes, they're on our knife-crime watch list.'

'Charming,' said Street.

'Don't worry,' said Hunter 'nothing's going to happen to us.'

'I'll go in first,' said Hunter, 'count to twenty, then follow me in. Make it look like I've been waiting for you.'

'Oh, I like this. Being in CID is fun.'

The driver shook his head. 'I wouldn't be so relaxed about it. Those scum seem to have a nose for the police, regardless of how they're dressed.'

'Stephen?'

Hunter shook his head. 'Don't worry, what could go wrong? I'm with you, and there's a van load of fit young cops outside that would just love to have a barny with those cretins in the pub.'

'Ok,' said Street, rubbing her hands together, 'wouldn't mind getting stuck in myself.'

'Oh no you don't, remember the last time you got involved?'

'Ah, you have a point there. Don't fancy another night in the cells, once is enough. I was so embarrassed when Jack came to get me out.'

'Glad that's settled. Now, count to twenty and follow me in.'

Street smiled, waved at the team in the police van, then went into the Scarlet Pig.

'Hi, Jill, glad you could make it. Want a drink?'

'Hi Stephen, yes please. White wine, could you make it a Pino Grigio, please? Where are you sitting?'

Hunter pointed to an empty table by the door.

'Wild looking bunch,' said Street, as Hunter put their drinks on the table and sat down beside her.

'The one with the parrot tattoo looks, well, he looks quite out of place with the others.'

'You're right. They are an odd collection. Two of them, including parrot-man, could have come right off a building site; the other two, they look quite normal.'

'Probably the knife-crime ones.'

'Why do you say that?'

'The builders look just like they probably are, it's the other three who bother me.'

'The short one with the black, curly hair, gives me the creeps. He keeps staring at me, I'm sure he thinks I'm police.'

'Nah, you're just imagining things. He's just struck with your beauty.'

'Flattery will get you anywhere, my dear.'

'Don't worry, I'm here to protect you.'

Street looked at her watch. 'It's about time we headed outside, it's almost midnight and our parrot friend has just gone out with his cohorts.'

'Fine, I could do with some fresh air.'

They left the Scarlet Pig and walked down to Jukes. There was a long line of party-goers waiting to get in, including the troublemakers.

Street followed Hunter down to the entrance to talk with the door staff.

'Evening. All quiet?'

The tall doorman replied as the line of revellers moved slowly past, 'Don't ask that, it's unlucky.'

'You know what I mean.'

The doorman shrugged. 'We've got the troublemakers pegged. The first sign of any aggro, they'll be out the door on their ear.'

'Glad to hear that, though it might be better if you let us deal with it. A couple of them have GBH with knives – what's that smell?' said Street. 'Smells like something's burning.'

'Your hair, it's smoking.'

'What?'

'Quick, turn round, let me see.'

'See what?'

'It's all right, you're not on fire,' said the doorman. 'Someone's blown cigarette smoke into your hair.'

'That's not cigarette smoke,' said Hunter.

'Something's wrong, I can't turn my head.'

'Hang on, let me have a closer look.'

'What is it, can you tell?'

'It's some sort of sticky liquid, could be jam, or honey. Did you see who did it?'

'No, I was talking with one of those kids arguing with one of the door staff.'

'Ah, I'm afraid it's something worse than jam, or honey. Someone's sprayed superglue into your hair. We need to get you to A&E right away.' said Hunter.

'Superglue? Hurry, feels like my neck is on fire.'

◆

'Jill, what happened to you?'

Street tried to turn her head and answer Karen. 'Some arsehole sprayed superglue in my hair and it's glued itself to my stab-vest.'

'You, poor baby, how can anyone be so cruel? Have you been seen yet?' asked Karen.

'The triage nurse has seen me, says it's too late to do anything. Unfortunately, they are running late and, since I'm not an emergency, I have to wait my turn.'

'How long, did they say?'

'The information screen on the wall says there's a three-hour wait for non-emergency treatment.'

'It'll be breakfast by the time they get to you. You say there's not much they can do for you?'

Street shrugged. 'They're going to cut the hair away, that's about all they can do.'

'Surgeons they may be, hairdressers I think not. You're coming home with us, we'll sort out your hair.'

'We?'

'Stephen's mum and I. Between us we'll soon get you sorted.'

'Margo's here?'

'Just parking her car. I called her as soon as Stephen called.'

'Jill, how are you?'

'I'm fine, Margo, now that you two are here.'

'What does it look like, Karen?' said Margo.

'I think we should take Jill home and see what we can do to save her hair.'

'It's that bad?'

'Don't worry, Jill. The glue has only set on the surface and at the ends. We won't have to cut all your hair off.'

'I'd rather go to my place,' said Street. 'I'll fix it myself.'

'No, no, that won't do,' said Margo. 'Karen's right, your hair needs sorting out.'

'You come home with me, Jill,' said Karen. 'We'll fix your hair; besides it will be good to get to know you better. In fact, since you are coming to stay with us shortly, why not stay with us tonight?'

'I'll try not to hog the bathroom.'

'You have your own bathroom on the landing. We have an en-suite.'

'Where's Jack, Karen?' said Street.

'He's was still at the office when I called.'

'How do you put up with it, Karen? All those years, never knowing when – or if – your husband will be home. Having to look at the news reports and wondering if he will be involved.'

'Prayer, Margo. It's the only way I get through. And besides, as Jack would say, *who's going to lock up the bad guys if I don't?* He said he's waiting for a phone call from the Italian Embassy, then he'll be right home.'

Margo pushed her hair away from her face, her gold bracelets jangling. Street looked up at her. 'Are you sure you can do something with my hair?'

'Of course, we can,' said Karen, looking at Margo. 'And if we are going to, we need to get on with it.'

'I hope you can, the wedding's only a few weeks away.'

12

Buchanan's phone rang. 'Buchanan. He is? Good, I'll be right down.'

'Good evening. I'm Inspector Catalano from the Italian Intelligence Agency.'

'DCI Buchanan. Thank you for taking to time to come talk to me.'

Catalano shook his head. 'It is of no problem, Inspector. It is my life's work to rid the world of these vermin.'

'Can we offer you some refreshment?' said Buchanan, looking at the office wall-clock. 'It's going to be a long day for you coming all the way down to Eastbourne.'

'Yes please, coffee, American style if you please. But it's not too long a day, my plane leaves from Gatwick at ten-forty, I go home to my family and two weeks' vacation. I have been here for four weeks on business with my embassy.'

'Anything to do with this case?'

'No, I am seconded here in London at the Embassy on another matter completely.'

Buchanan smiled. 'Good, then we won't be stepping on each other's toes.'

'Shall I get the coffees?' asked the desk sergeant.

'Inspector, it's dinner time, shall we go out to eat?'

Catalano nodded. 'A great idea. I didn't fancy any more of your English sandwiches, how you eat them I cannot understand.'

'Me neither, I have a lovely place in mind, it's right on the beach and serves good food. Then after dinner I'll drive you to the station. There is a direct service to Gatwick airport from Eastbourne.'

♦

Buchanan parked beside the Beach Deck. They walked up the steps to the promenade and surveyed the view out across the bay.

'You live in such a beautiful location, Inspector Buchanan.'

'Yes, though it did take me a while to settle in, I would now struggle to go back to live in Glasgow.'

'Really? I have family in Glasgow. They say it is a city of culture.'

'I suppose it is, with the university and museums. Which part of Glasgow do they live in?'

'Kelvinside.'

Buchanan nodded, he knew the area well. He'd once solved a case of extortion, when a gang had tried to get a businessman to pay to not have his premises burned to the ground.

'Shall we go in?'

'*Grazie*, and please call me Pietro, or Peter if you prefer the English.'

'Peter, it shall be. I'm Jack.'

They climbed the steps up on to the deck.

'Would you prefer to eat in, or out here on the deck?' said Buchanan.

Catalano took in a deep breath then exhaled slowly. 'Why not out here? The air is so bracing, and we can see the little sailboats racing each other along the seafront.'

'Fine with me. Shall we sit here?'

'Si.'

Buchanan nodded to one of the waiters. 'Could we see the dinner menu, please?'

'Yes, sir.'

'Peter, I understand from talking to your office in the Embassy in London, you can help us with details on the Rienzi family?'

'Si, I've been able to trace the Rienzi family history back as far as 1890.'

'That's thorough.'

'Can I get you something to drink?' said the waiter.

'Peter?'

'I'll have a glass of white wine, please.'

'And you, sir?'

'I'll have whatever Long Man you have on tap.'

'Will that be a pint?'

Buchanan nodded.

'I'll be right back with your drinks.'

'From church records that weren't destroyed in the war, we find Agostino Rienzi was born in 1893. He was married in the church where he was christened. He died in 1944, as did his son, Aldo.'

'An accident?'

'There's not much known about Aldo's early days but he and his father both were involved in the Italian underground during the Second World War. Unfortunately for them, they were both arrested by the Gestapo and shot as spies working for the British government.'

Buchanan shook his head. 'The war's been over for seventy years, but we still are affected by its aftermath.'

'Excuse me, sir, your drinks. Are you ready to order?'

'Peter?'

'I'll start with the calamari, then follow with moules marinière.'

'And, sir?'

Buchanan looked back at the menu. 'I'll start with the haddock chowder. What's the special of the day?'

'Pan-fried sea bass, all locally caught.'

'That sounds good to me.'

'Thanks

'So, to continue. Aldo's birth records say he was born in 1911 in Palermo, Sicily. He was married and had a son, Benito.

In 1949 Benito, at twenty-three, went to work as a driver for a local family trucking company called Morelli Transporto Internazionale.'

'Does it still exist?'

'Si. The story goes, he became friendly with a young girl who worked in the office. He would get her to fake his time sheets and say he was working, when he was in fact in the backroom of the local bar, gambling and drinking. Records show he got her pregnant and, under threat of losing his job, he married the girl.'

'Sounds like the Morellis are a moral family.'

'Maybe they are,' Catalano said, shrugging. 'The story now shifts from newspaper records to police records. Due to his gambling debts, Benito became an associate for the Mafia.'

'Like he was not already a member?' said Buchanan.

'It's one of several terms the Mafia use to denote rank. It describes someone who is just involved with the Mafia, though not actually a member. Basically, an associate can be anyone, a criminal, a mayor, shopkeeper, even a policeman.'

'I heard a bit about that during training,' said Buchanan.

'He was assigned as a debt collector for the local family at the same time he did his delivery rounds for Morelli.'

'Were the Morellis ever suspected of being involved with the Mafia.'

'Nothing on record.'

'Your starters, gentlemen.'

'Thanks, could we have another round of drinks, please?'

'Certainly.'

'Glad to hear that about the Morellis, I sort of like them.'

'Bento soon gained a reputation for being a violent and ambitious young man and was promoted to collecting debts owed by awkward customers. All he had to do was show up at a place of business and the owner would be off down to the bank for cash.'

'A nasty bit of work.'

'It's worse than you can imagine, Jack. Being an ambitious young man, Benito wanted more, but the only way he could advance was to become a made man and what they call a soldier.'

'What's that?'

'A made man is someone who swears an oath that the Mafia comes before their birth family, and God. A soldier is a made man who goes out to do the bidding of the boss, it's sort of bottom rung in the hierarchy.'

'Is there some sort of ceremony involved in becoming a member?'

'Yes, but that varies depending on which family you are joining. A few months later his opportunity arose. He was sent out, under the supervision of a *capo* – that's someone who heads a team of soldiers – to collect from a bar owner who had refused to pay his debts. This was supposed to be a final warning to pay-up. The bar owner refused point blank to pay, so Benito beat him to death with his fists, right in front of the other soldiers. Based on that show of loyalty, and past exploits, he was invited to become a *capo* and put in charge of his own band of soldiers.

'Over the next couple of years, he continued to gain notoriety amongst the other family members. As part of joining a Mafia family you are required to bring in your share of the takings to the boss. So, Benito worked his way into the Morelli family business, like a cancer invading a body. It wasn't hard for him to organise missing deliveries, lorry crashes, even having trucks hijacked and their contents sold on the black market. He acted as an aggrieved director and said for the good of the company they should arrange for protection, an insurance policy against fire, theft and damage.'

'How could Morelli let him continue to work for them and rob them at the same time?'

'It was either that, or go bust, or worse.'

'You mean they could have been killed if they didn't pay up?'

Catalano nodded. 'He was given a contract to kill a soldier who had stepped out of line one time too many. He had dishonoured the clan by having an affair with another man's wife. Benito broke into the house late in the evening, dragged the man out of bed and castrated him, then made the woman watch while the man bled to death.'

'What an evil man.'

'That's the way it is: an order is given, you obey, or suffer a similar fate.'

'What happened after?'

'There was a problem. He'd killed the wrong man. In his haste to obey he had broken in to the wrong house and killed the mayor's nephew, who was visiting the town with his wife.'

'What happened to him for that?'

'He had to watch as his wife was gang-raped. She subsequently committed suicide.'

'What about him, what happened to him?'

'He was an untouchable, nothing happened to him. When the story of his wife being raped and subsequent suicide got out, he was seen as the poor, unfortunate, husband. But that didn't stop the mayor's family wanting revenge.'

'Sounds like a Hollywood movie.'

'Where do you think they get their ideas from?' said Catalano.

'What happened next?'

'He played to the town's sympathy. The Morellis took pity on him, especially Angelica, their daughter. Before long wedding bells ring, and Benito is now part of the Morelli clan.'

'Did they have any children?'

'One son, Guido, and he was worse than his father, though his criminal career was cut short when the press got wind of his father's crime-led life. As a result of the publicity, Guido's father was shot dead as he came out of his office.'

'What did Guido do?'

'He must have felt for his safety, because a few days after the assassination of his father, he left Sicily and eventually settled in the USA.'

'Do you know where he settled in the USA?'

'He'd left our soil, and that's where we left it. I might suggest you contact the American Embassy if you are interested in finding out what happened to him.'

'Thanks for that information, Peter.'

'And thank you for such a wonderful dinner.'

'You're most welcome. Shall I drive you to the station for your train?'

'I'd be most grateful. I hope what I have told you this evening has been useful to you. Here's my card, call me if I can be of further assistance.'

♦

Buchanan parked in front of the house and went in the front door.

'I'm home,' he called.

'We're in the conservatory,' shouted Karen.

We, wondered Buchanan, as he entered the conservatory.

'Hello, Jack,' said Margo. 'Come to see what's happened to Jill?'

'Why, what's happened to her?'

'Oh, it's not that bad,' said Karen.

'Someone sprayed superglue into her hair,' said Stephen, who had just come in from the garden.

'Where is she?'

"Relax, she's upstairs taking a shower, she'll be down in a minute.'

'How did it happen?' asked Buchanan.

'We're not sure. While mum and Karen were trying to sort out Jill's hair, I went back into town and had a look at the CCTV footage.'

'Show anything?'

'Not much. We think it was someone in the bunch who we saw in the pub earlier. Three of them were locals, bit loud and boisterous, the other two were strangers, probably just in town to cause trouble. I got some stills from CCTV, just in case we see them again.'

'Can I have a look?' said Buchanan.

'Here,' said Hunter, passing the photos.

'I recognise two of them,' said Buchanan, 'these two here. Their names are Dave and Harry,' he pointed as he went to pass the photos back to Hunter. 'They work for Palmari. They were also the two that used to deliver Denman's Friday treats.'

'Keep them, I've got copies. These two here, Jill says they work for a private hire company called Carswell.'

They were disturbed by female voices in the hallway.

'Jill, how are you?' said Buchanan, as she came into the room wrapped in a huge bath towel, her hair in a smaller towel, turban style.

'I'll feel better when I've had a night's sleep. Karen's made up my bed, I've just come down to say goodnight.'

'Oh, ok then,' said Hunter. 'Oh, Jack recognises two of the group that we saw in the pub and outside Jukes.'

'Is that right?'

'Two of them drove me to see Palmari, I suspect they work for him. I'll track them down in the morning, they have a lot of questions to answer.'

There was an awkward moment as Hunter, in front of his mother and the Buchanans, cuddled Street and kissed her goodnight.'

'I'll see you in the morning, Stephen. Don't be late, we're moving my stuff tomorrow morning and then I've got a dress fitting appointment.'

Hunter looked at his watch. 'Two o'clock, better be off then. See you in the morning.'

13

Buchanan was up and out of bed before anyone else, he was on a mission. Not only was he going to make Karen her breakfast, he was going to make breakfast for Street as well.

'Oh,' said Karen, 'breakfast in bed! What have I done to deserve this?'

Buchanan smiled. 'You haven't had to do anything.'

'Is Jill up yet?' said Karen, as she plumped up her pillows and spread out the blankets on her lap.

'Hope not, her breakfast tray is sitting on the kitchen counter.'

'Jack, you're a lovely man. I'm so glad I married you.'

Buchanan tiptoed back down the stairs to the kitchen and collected Street's breakfast tray. He knocked gently on her bedroom door.

'What – who is it?'

'Room service, I have your breakfast.'

◆

Buchanan said goodbye to Karen and climbed into his car. Street was already in the passenger seat.'

'Morning, Jill.'

'Morning.'

'How did you sleep?'

'Fine. Only woke once when someone knocked at my door with a breakfast tray.'

'I wonder who that could have been?'

'Bit odd, Stephen and I moving into a house in the marina, and you and Karen moving out.'

'I'm sure we'll all get used to the new arrangements.'

◆

'I've been ordered by the ACC, and the crime commissioner, to make a police statement to the newspaper,' said Buchanan, as they entered the office.

Street looked at the wastepaper basket beside Buchanan's desk. 'Want some help?'

'Please, public grovelling is not my choice of occupation.'

'What sort of information do they want you to give out?' said Street, turning on her computer.

'Oh, some sort of bumph about how we, the police, are getting close to solving the recent unfortunate deaths in the Eastbourne area.'

'Got it. Give me a minute and I'll work something out for you'.

'While you're doing that, I'll get the coffees. Your usual?'

'No, could I have a latte, please?'

'Your wish is my command.'

♦

'Your latte,' said Buchanan, placing the cup on Street's desk. 'How are you doing with the statement?'

'You mean, your statement?'

'Ah, yes, of course, how could I think otherwise?'

'Want to hear it?'

Buchanan nodded as he sipped on his coffee.

'The bodies of two middle-aged men, one found recently in an abandoned factory in Hampden Park, and the second found in the grounds of Pevensey Castle, are the signs of infighting within criminal gangs, says the officer investigating the two deaths. Detective Chief Inspector Buchanan went on to say members of the public should not be concerned for their own safety. DCI Buchanan asked the public contact the police, either by email at 101@sussex.pnn.police.uk, or online at sussex.police.uk/appeal response or phone 101, quoting serial number dcb1946, if they have anything to report.'

'That's good, I would never have thought of saying it that way.'

'I deliberately left out the road death of Simms, anything referring to Nigel, and of course anything about the toxic waste dumping.'

Buchanan nodded. 'That's good. As far as the public is concerned, Simms' death was just another road death on the notorious A27.'

'A259, actually. The A27 ends at the roundabout by Starbucks.'

'You learn something new every day.'

'Shall I send this in to the *Herald*?'

'Yes. Then we need to get busy.'

'Where first?'

'Who's watching Nigel?'

'Stephen.'

'Any change in his condition?'

'Stephen said he'd call if there were any developments.'

'Good, let's get going.'

'Where to first?'

'Your car, I need to think. As far as Nigel is concerned, I'm not going to replace Stephen and Morris.'

'Why not?'

'I would prefer the hospital staff to think that they are concerned relatives, not a police guard.'

'You think if word gets out that Nigel is alive, something terrible might happen to him?'

'Exactly. The newspaper report only mentioned that a rough sleeper had been found under rubble on the building site. The perpetrators will know who he is, but will probably assume that we are none the wiser and wait it out and see if he survives.'

'And if he does?'

'Hopefully by then we'll have nabbed the culprits. But just in case I want Stephen and Morris to maintain their vigil at the bedside.'

They climbed into Street's car and were about to leave when the ACC pulled up beside them. She motioned to Buchanan to wind down his window.

'Where are you off to, Buchanan?'

'Catch criminals, where else?'

'Hang on a minute, I want to have a quick word with you – alone.'

Buchanan shrugged, undid his seatbelt and got out of the car.

'Buchanan, I'm – I'm sorry about the other day. What I said wasn't very professional.'

'I don't know, made me chuckle,' he said, shrugging. 'I've had worse said to me in the past.'

'Anyway, I shouldn't have said it. The commissioner, well, he's –'

'Being difficult, wanting instant results?'

The ACC nodded. 'Exactly. He's worried about his future career, fancies himself as home secretary one day.'

'And these three murders and one attempted murder could get in the way?'

'Three murders? I thought there were only two, and what's this about an attempted murder?'

'I was coming to see you later this week and bring you up-to-date on what's been going on.'

The ACC thought for a minute, then shook her head. 'No, that simply won't do. I want to hear it all – now. Let's go to your office.'

'Ok,' said Buchanan, nodding to Street and heading back into the building.

'No, Buchanan. I meant your other office. The commissioner's in the building and I don't want to have to spend the morning listening to him go on about how the police need shaking up and improving.'

'You mean Starbucks?'

'Of course, where else?'

Buchanan climbed back into Street's car, and to their surprise the ACC got in the back.

♦

'I'm buying, what do you two usually drink?'

'Could I have a coffee Frappuccino, please Ma'am?' said Street.

'Buchanan?'

'Just black coffee, an Americano.'

'The corner seats,' said the ACC, pointing to the seats by the condiment table. 'The blonde said she'd bring the coffees over,' she said, sitting down.

'That's Jade, Ma'am,' said Street.

'You drink here that often you know them by first name?'

Buchanan grinned.

'Right, Buchanan. I had a look online at the *Herald*, excellent statement, should keep him off my back for a few days. Where have you got to in the investigation, any suspects yet?'

'Thank you, Ma'am, but it was Jill who actually wrote that piece for the *Herald*.

'Well done, Jill.'

'Thanks, Ma'am.'

'I'll start with who we don't think are suspects,' continued Buchanan. 'The Morellis living on Blackwater Road are just bit players in the drama, but I'm pretty sure they know little of the details of what has gone on. We're letting then continue with their self-imposed house arrest. They were the first stop this morning, I still have a couple of questions to get sorted out. Mr Morelli's mother, Mrs Foscatini,' he said,   'I think she knows more than she's telling. Not so much about the present crimes, but she also hasn't told us everything she knows about the family history.'

'You think there's a Mafia element? I say that due to the preponderance of Italian names in this case?'

'We have no direct evidence, but I'm coming to that conclusion.'

'What else?'

'If we are going down the Mafia road, last night, a couple of our beat police caught someone in the CSM factory. His name, at least that's what his ID said, is Esposito. During interrogation, he admitted he was a bail bondsman.'

'A bail bondsman!'

'They still have them in the States,' said Street. 'Lots of people jump bail, or are on the FBI's most wanted list. It's big business over there, they even have television shows based on the day-to-day goings on of the modern bail bondsmen and women. They used to be called bounty hunters.'

'Who, or what, was Esposito looking for in the factory? Surely we've removed all pieces of evidence from there?'

'He said he was looking for a Guido Rienzi. Apparently, he's on the FBI's most wanted list and carries a large bounty.'

'How much, do you know?'

'At least half a million dollars,' said Street.

'How did he trace Rienzi to the factory?'

'A letter found in a house search in New York,' said Buchanan.

'So how did he get in the factory?'

'Fire door at the back, it's still not been fixed.'

'Surely the alarm would have gone off?'

'The cheeky sod called the alarm company and said he was me doing a bit of investigating. Had them send someone out to reset it. Luckily for us the two cops on patrol were in the vicinity and arrested him.'

'What did he have to say for himself?'

'I interrogated him, but since there wasn't any sign of a forced entry, I let him go.'

'You just let him go? Did you check his credentials?'

'Didn't need to, we took copies of the contents of his

briefcase, including the test results of a DNA sample of the Rienzi he's looking for.'

'What good will that be in your current investigations?'

Buchanan shook his head. 'I'm not sure, but my gut says there's a connection somewhere in what Esposito was up to.'

'What else should I be aware of?'

'We have a young man under police protection in the DGH.'

'Explain.'

'He is Mrs Foscatini's grandson. He was pulled from under the rubble of a collapsed wall on the Arndale shopping mall building site. The *Herald* report said he'd been a rough sleeper who'd just been unfortunate to select that particular wall to shelter beside'

'What has he told you?'

'Nothing yet, he has been in a coma for a couple of weeks, is now partially conscious but doesn't know who he is. I have two police officers in plain clothes guarding him round the clock.'

'Other than him being Mrs Foscatini's grandson, what other connections has he got with this affair?'

'His father was once married to Mrs Foscatini's daughter. He runs a decorating firm besides being another player in this drama.'

'Where is she now?'

'She's happily remarried and living in Argentina.'

'Who's the other mystery player?'

'Not so much an individual. It's a joinery firm next door to Pace Decorators. There's a connection somewhere other than Pace being Nigel's father, but I haven't figured out what it is yet.'

'Anyone else in the family involved?

'One of the Morelli daughters. There's two of them, twins, both married. One lives in Italy, the other in France. We think that one of the daughters lured Denman to his death.'

'Is there more to this epic?'

'Yes, I was invited to meet up with another Italian. His name is Palmari. He's someone who I took an instant dislike to. He tried to sell a security contract to Sir Nathan Greyspear, then invited me to a meeting where he set out his ideas for saving the police a substantial amount of the police budget. He even had the cheek to offer Jill and me jobs working for him.'

'Will you accept?'

Buchanan shook his head, 'It is my intention to put him out of business as soon as possible.'

'What was his idea?'

'He didn't explain in detail, just said he was able to replace the beat policemen, especially on the evenings at the weekend.'

'That sounds interesting, maybe I should have a word with him. Where does he live?'

'He said to me to say that we'd had a chat and to mention to you and the commissioner that the plan had my blessing.'

'And does it?'

'Definitely not. Just imagine the scenario: a fight breaks out in Jukes, his men pile in and, with no controls, can you imagine the outcome? We'd be back in the dark ages.'

'It's also an open door for drug distribution,' said Street.

'Thanks for that input. Anything else I should know about, Buchanan?'

He shook his head. 'No, nothing comes to mind.'

'How close are you to resolving the case, percentage-wise?'

'I'd say we are about sixty percent there.'

'That's better than I'd thought. Where are you off to after dropping me back at Hammonds Drive?'

'First, I want to talk to the first responders who found Nigel Pace, then it is on to the Morellis.'

◆

Street parked on the right-hand side of the fire station car park out of the way of a fire crew cleaning one of the fire engines.

'Excuse me,' said Buchanan, 'DCI Buchanan, and DS Street,

Sussex CID. We're looking for anyone who was on duty a couple of weeks ago when a rough sleeper was pulled from under the rubble of a collapsed wall on the Arndale shopping centre building project.'

'Who was on watch?' said one of the firemen to the one with the hose.

'Not sure, probably Harry Jordan. He's in the kitchen preparing lunch. Hang on, I'll take you to him, Inspector.'

Buchanan and Street followed the fireman into the fire station and on through to the kitchen.

'Harry, this is DCI Buchanan and DS Street. They want to talk to anyone who was on duty the night the rough sleeper was pulled from the rubble on the Arndale site.'

'I was there, Inspector. What do you want to know?'

'First impressions?'

'Site security called us and said there was a body buried under some rubble.'

'He described it as rubble, not a collapsed wall?'

'The wall was still standing, at least the bottom half was.'

'Was it the top half that had fallen on top of the sleeper?'

'From what I remember, none of the wall had fallen on him. The rubble looked like it had been placed on him to make it look like part of the wall had fallen on him.

'What about his injuries? Maybe he'd fallen off the wall and the rubble fell on top?'

'The wall was four-foot high, Inspector.'

'So, could it be possible he was beaten up and covered with the rubble to make it look like an accident?'

'That's what I thought.'

'Thanks, Harry. Oh, did you make out a report?'

'Yes, want a copy?'

'Please.'

◆

'Try Flat 1 first, maybe they've moved back home,' said

Buchanan.

Street shook her head. 'Flat 2 it is then.' She pressed the bell push and waited.

'Try Flat 3. Maybe Mrs Dickson is home.'

Street pressed the doorbell and stepped back.

'Ah, Mrs Dickson. It's Sergeant Street and Inspector Buchanan.'

'Are you looking for, you know who?'

Buchanan smiled and shook his head at the remark.

'Yes, do you know if they are home?'

'I heard noises earlier, shall I buzz you in?'

'Please.'

'This lift reminds me of one I rode in when I was a child,' said Street, as the lift creaked its way to the fifth floor.

'Where was that?'

'Can't remember. It must have been when I was really young, my parents were with me.'

'I have a memory like that. This one was in a hotel in Glasgow, just big enough for me and my parents, my dad had to go back down for the suitcase.'

Mrs Dickson was waiting for them on the fifth floor.

'I'm sure they're in, Inspector. I just heard Mr Morelli, he was complaining about something not being where it should be.'

'Right,' said Buchanan, pressing the doorbell and hammering on the door, 'time to put the cat amongst the pigeons. Mr Morelli, it's the police, open up!'

There was silence for a few minutes, then the sound of chains being taken off the door and the deadbolt being withdrawn. It was a very tired-looking Mr Morelli who stood in the open doorway, his wife three steps behind him.

'What can I do for you, Inspector?'

'Can we come in, please?'

'Yes, of course.'

Buchanan and Street followed the Morellis through to their

sitting room.

'Can I get you something to drink, Inspector?' said Mrs Morelli.

Buchanan looked at Street, who nodded. 'A cup of tea would nice, thanks, Mrs Morelli.'

Mr Morelli got up and walked over to the sideboard and poured himself what looked to Buchanan like a large whiskey.

'Can I help?' said Street, standing up and following Mrs Morelli into the kitchen. They returned a few minutes later with a tea tray and a box of biscuits.

Buchanan waited for the tea to be poured and offered round the room before he started.

'Mr and Mrs Morelli, as you are well aware, we have been watching your apartment for several days now. Mostly to see who visits, but also to make sure that nothing happened to either of you.'

'We realise that now, Inspector. Thank you.'

'Mrs Morelli, when we were here before, I asked you when you'd last seen Julian Denman. You said you had no idea where he was. Yet a few days prior, you'd arranged with one of your daughters, Antonia, to come over to Eastbourne for the sole purpose of exacting revenge on Julian Denman. She met him in the Polygon bar with the express intent on getting him drunk, then lured him out of the bar and into a waiting white van. From there he was driven to the former CSM factory where he was executed in a most cruel fashion.'

Mrs Morelli extracted a scrunched-up handkerchief from the sleeve of her cardigan and blew her nose. 'It was Paula, Antonia's sister, who agreed to the plan.'

'What was the plan, Mrs Morelli?'

'One of the people Denman had cheated suggested we teach him a lesson he wouldn't forget. Antonia had been so traumatised when Denman attacked her, she said she couldn't even be in the same town as him without having an emotional breakdown.'

'So, her twin sister said she'd help?'

'Yes. She came over on the train Thursday evening and stayed here in this flat. That way no one would know she was here with us.'

'Sorry, I don't understand why she couldn't just stay hidden in your own flat?'

'Mrs Dreyfus, nosey bitch. Has keys to most of the apartments in the block. Our dishwasher was broken and we needed it repaired. The only day the repairman could come was Friday.'

'And you were both out, and you were concerned that Mrs Dreyfus would go snooping round your flat and find your daughter?'

Mr Morelli cuddled up to his wife on the sofa and gave her a hug; she wiped the tears away with the now ever-present handkerchief.

'Mr Morelli, who suggested that Denman should be taught a lesson?' said Buchanan.

'I don't remember his name.'

'You don't remember his name?' said Buchanan, looking at Mr Morelli's face. It had changed from a concerned husband to that of a cowering dog about to be beaten. 'Jill, do you have the mugshots with you?'

'Yes, they're in my pocket.'

'Would you show them to Mr and Mrs Morelli? Maybe they can identify their unknown advisor.'

Street passed the photos one at a time for the Morellis to study.

When they were finished looking at the photos, Buchanan was smiling. 'Can you tell us which of those photos is the man whose name you don't remember?'

Mr Morelli looked at his wife; she nodded.

'It was the fourth one, Inspector.'

'You recognise some of the others?'

Mr Morelli nodded again. 'They're mostly family.'

'You are in police protective custody, Mr Morelli. Tell us the name of the man who arranged for Julian Denman to be punished.'

'He called himself Toni Palmari.'

'Where did you meet'

'We met sometime last year – what was the occasion, dear?'

'It was in March last year, Inspector. CSM was hoping to formalise a contract with Greyspear Yachts for off-site manufacturing of sub-assemblies for their yachts. That's where we first met Palmari. He said he was there as a financier, and a friend of Julian's. I seem to remember it was he who suggested we teach Julian a lesson.'

'Why? Was he aware of the altercation between Antonia and Denman?'

She shook her head. 'It was something more than that. I think Palmari had invested a lot of other people's money and Julian had lost it.'

'Lost it, or misappropriated it?'

'Palmari said Julian had embezzled a great deal of money and had hidden it in a foreign bank account, and the only way to get it back was to get Julian to give him the bank details and authorise the transfer of the money back to the UK. He said Julian might be a bit reluctant to do it, so he, Palmari, needed to be alone with Julian and convince him to do the right thing by the investors.'

'And was he successful?'

She shrugged. 'I don't know. With Julian dead, and Palmari not answering his phone, what does it matter now? Everything has gone: the business, our freedom, and the family honour. Will we have to go to jail, Inspector?'

'That's not for me to decide, Mrs Morelli. Did Paula go in the van with Denman to the factory?'

'No, of course not. She was only supposed to get him to drink and then make an excuse to go outside for a cigarette. When Denman followed her outside, she was to be gone.'

'Where did she go?'

'Here, of course.'

'And Denman?'

'He was supposed to be told that Antonia would be waiting for him at her apartment and to get in the waiting van.'

'Don't you think he would have thought it odd to be getting in a van?'

'It was supposed to be dressed to look like a taxi, it was to have stickers on the doors, or something like that. Palmari convinced us that Denman had to be taught a lesson.'

'Why was that?'

'Because Denman had bankrupted the company and brought dishonour on the family by trying to rape Antonia.'

'Did he tell you what he had planned for Denman?'

'He said that they were only going teach him a lesson.'

'What kind of lesson?'

'He didn't say.'

'Who was it that suggested Paula should become involved?'

'It was Palmari. I think during the early days of his friendship with Denman, he heard about Denman's antics. It was he who suggested that Antonia's twin sister, Paula, might be able to get Denman drunk and pliable if Antonia wouldn't go along with the plot.'

'How was it arranged, Mrs Morelli?'

'I called Paula and explained. I said Antonia couldn't stand to be anywhere near Denman and that the family honour was at stake. I assured her that Denman was only going to be taught a lesson. A false assurance that turned out to be.'

'And she agreed?'

'Yes, she and Antonia are really close. It was arranged that she would come over on the Friday morning, lure Denman out of the club, then go home again.'

'What about the Rohipnal?'

'Sorry, what's that?'

'It's sometimes called GBH. It's a tranquiliser drug.'

'I have no idea, I don't remember. Most likely it was Palmari's idea.'

'So, Paula contacts Denman, pretending to be Antonia, and suggests they meet up for a drink and to let bygones be bygones?

'Yes.'

'When they meet, Denman is too drunk to realise he is being duped. Someone slips Rohipnal in his drink, and when he is sufficiently pliable she suggests they go outside where they can be alone together?'

'Yes.'

'Whose van did they use to take Denman to the factory?'

Mrs Morelli shook her head. 'I don't know, I didn't want to know. I was just happy that Denman was going to pay for what he tried to do to Antonia, and for destroying the company.'

'Thank you, Mrs Morelli.'

'What are you going to do now, Inspector?' asked Mr Morelli.

'Mr Morelli, when did you last see your mother?'

'My mother? Why would you want to know that?'

'Simple question, Mr Morelli.'

'Er... recently. I don't quite remember.'

'Let me remind you. It was two weeks ago, at three in the morning.'

'How could you possibly know that?'

'I followed you,' said Street.

'What did you discuss when you went to see your mother, Mr Morelli?' said Buchanan.

'She wanted to see me, that's all.'

'At three in the morning?'

'She couldn't sleep, it's a family thing. We Morellis need little sleep.'

'What did you talk about?'

'Mostly what could have been, before Denman crippled the business, and the slight possibility that Palmari might be able to regain the money that Julian embezzled.'

'Can you explain?'

'You've talked with my mother, you know the family history. Our family business in Italy was destroyed by a criminal element. When I took over Perfection Mouldings, I diversified us into manufacturing fibreglass components for the marine and automotive industries. As the business grew, we started to take on the finishing of other companies' products.'

'Sorry, can you explain?'

'In the fibreglass moulding business there is the initial moulding of the parts, then, secondarily, there is the finishing of these parts. We would take the rough moulding and trim the edges, drill whatever holes were needed, fit additional parts and decorations.'

'Couldn't the people who made the mouldings do that for themselves?'

'Most customers didn't want to be bothered with sourcing parts and fixings. Most of our customers were in the UK, and the mouldings came from Eastern Europe. Since the products were finished in the UK, they could then be re-exported to Europe, and sold back in the UK as UK products.'

'At a premium price?'

'Exactly.'

'What went wrong?'

'Denman.'

'How?'

'His salary to start with, it was grandfathered in when we took over his company. The next, and most crippling item, was we'd inherited the debts of his company. At first, we thought we could service the debt, but the final straw was the bill from HMRC for unpaid taxes. In the end, it was too much and we had to close the door and say goodbye to what could have been a very successful business.

'Who are you hiding from in this flat? Who's got you so scared that you'd go to so much trouble? Can't be Denman, he's dead.'

'No one, Inspector.'

'Mr Morelli, does the name Esposito mean anything to you? Or you, Mrs Morelli?'

Buchanan watched for a reaction in their faces.

'No, Inspector, should it?' said Mr Morelli.

'How about the name Rienzi?'

'It was a man by that name who ruined our family business in Italy.'

'You haven't seen or heard from him these last few months?'

'Inspector, that Rienzi died several years ago. He was shot.'

'And you don't know anyone by the name of Esposito?'

The Morellis shook their heads.

◆

'Where to next?' said Street, as they descended in the lift.

'I want to have another word with Mrs Foscatini.'

'Wonder if Stephen and I will ever be able to afford such a lovely house – it's got such a beautiful view over the bay,' said Street, as they parked at the top of the drive-in front of Mrs Foscatini's house.

Mrs Foscatini opened the door before they had time to ring the bell.

'Inspector, how is Nigel? When can I go to see him?'

'I'm sorry, Mrs Foscatini, not just yet. He's still in intensive care and he hasn't recovered his memory.'

'Oh, what if something happens to him? Suppose those who hurt him come back?'

'Who are those people, Mrs Foscatini?'

'Oh, I don't know. Why did the paper say he was sleeping rough on a building site? He lived here most of the time – he has his own bedroom. Go and see it if you don't believe me.'

'Thank you Mrs Foscatini, that would be helpful. Would you show us the way?'

They followed Mrs Foscatini down a plush carpeted hallway to the rear of the house.

'He lived with you all the time?'

'I think he also had a flat in town that he shared with a friend. I think it was where he used to go with his young woman. This is his bedroom,' she said, opening a door on the right.

'You said he would come in late – did he use the front door?'

'No, Inspector. There's a back door in the kitchen that leads out onto the driveway.'

'I see he liked football,' said Buchanan, looking at the posters of various players in the throes of scoring a winning goal. Then he realised they were all from the Argentine national team.'

'He was football mad.'

'Did he have a favourite player?'

'Sorry, Inspector, I know nothing about football.'

'Would you mind?' said Street, as she put her hands on the top drawer of the bedside table.'

'No, please. Go ahead if it will help find who did such a dreadful thing to Nigel.'

'Do you know anything about Nigel's friends?' said Buchanan, as Street went methodically through the drawers and cupboards.

'I never met any of them.'

'What about girlfriends?'

'There was one who would call him.'

'Do you remember her name?'

'I think it was Rebekah – she called herself Becky.'

'Would you have her telephone number, or know where she

lives?'

'No. Nigel never confided in me about her.'

'Mrs Foscatini, when we last talked, you said you hadn't seen your son for several weeks –'

'I'm sorry, Inspector. I didn't tell you the truth. He came to see me two weeks ago.'

'What time?'

'He phoned me at two o'clock in the morning.'

'He phoned you? What did he say?'

'He said he needed to see me, urgently.'

'Was he in the habit of calling at two in the morning?'

'No.'

'What happened next?'

'He came over.'

'In his car?'

'My son doesn't drive, he has no licence.'

'A taxi?'

'No – he walked.'

'What time did he get here?'

'It was three o'clock. I made him a cup of tea and we talked.'

'What about? You realise we will find out everything in the end.'

'We talked mostly about the business and what could be done to resurrect it.'

'Can it? I thought it was too late for that.'

'The assets have all been sold off, the building is up for sale, or at least the lease is. I doubt if we'll ever see any of the money Denman embezzled.'

'You own the building?'

'Till the receivers manage to sell it. Most of our customers have found other suppliers. I suppose it is too late.'

'Is that what you told your son?'

'Yes.'

'Can you confirm what your son's business did?'

'They made parts for boats and cars.'

'Thank you, Mrs Foscatini. As soon as we hear about any change in Nigel's condition, we'll let you know, but please, for his sake, don't tell anyone that you know he's alive.'

'I won't say a word to anyone, and thank you, Inspector.'

'For what, Mrs Foscatini?'

'For being so understanding.'

'It's my job to understand, Mrs Foscatini.'

She stood by the front door and waved as Buchanan and Street drove off down the road.

'Where to next?' said Street, as they turned on to Royal Parade.

'Let's go see Mrs Bourne. You haven't met her yet, have you?'

'No, what's she like?'

'Quiet, personable, and an exquisite pianist.'

♦

Buchanan rang the bell, and as before the door was opened by Jason.

'Good afternoon, Jason. Could we have a quick word with Mrs Bourne?'

A look of consternation came across his face. 'Is there something wrong, Inspector?'

'No, everything is fine, just a quick word, if you please?'

'Please come in, I'll see if Mrs Bourne has time to see you.'

'Bit posh,' said Street, as Jason left to see Mrs Bourne.

He returned a few minutes later. 'Inspector, Sergeant, if you'll follow me, Mrs Bourne is in the conservatory.'

She stood as Buchanan and Street entered.

'Inspector, so nice to see you again.'

'And you, Mrs Bourne. This is my partner, Sergeant Street.'

Mrs Bourne smiled. 'Your names, Buchanan and Street. Isn't that the main shopping street in Glasgow?'

Buchanan nodded.

'Can we offer you something to drink?'

'Tea would be very nice, Mrs Bourne,' said Street.

'Inspector?' said Mrs Bourne.

'I'll have tea as well, thanks.'

'Jason,' said Mrs Bourne. 'I think we'll have the Wedgwood tea set.'

'As you wish.'

'Mrs Bourne, the last time my Sergeant talked with you, you mentioned you have a nephew, Eugene.'

'Oh, he isn't my nephew, Inspector, he is my late husband's nephew – well, not quite a nephew.'

'What do you mean by that?'

'Eugene's parents died when he was only sixteen.'

'What happened?'

'They were passengers on the *Herald of Free Enterprise* when it overturned in the English Channel.'

'They died?' said Street.

'Unfortunately, yes.'

'Did Eugene have any relatives he could go to?'

'None – sadly for Eugene. His father and my husband had been friends since university days and, since Eugene had no other family to go to, we agreed to look after him till he came of age.'

'So, you were his guardians?'

'Yes, for the next three years. He was in his first year at university when the tragedy struck. Fortunately for Eugene his father had purchased him a flat to live in during his time there.'

'Wouldn't that make going to university a trifle expensive?'

'Not if you consider how the prices of houses have risen during the last few years. By the time Eugene had finished university, the increase in value of the flat, when sold, covered a large amount of his university expenses.'

'Smart dad.'

'He was.'

'How about your husband's parents? Are they still alive?'

'No. My husband never knew his father. He was one of those that the press like to refer to as an absent father. His mother died when he was very young, so in effect he was an orphan.'

'Do you know his mother's name?'

'I only ever heard him refer to her as Maria.'

Further conversation was curtailed when Jason returned with the tea trolley, complete with the Wedgwood tea set and a plate of biscuits.

As Jason did the honours, Buchanan said, 'Mrs Bourne, Sergeant Street has some photographs with her. I wonder if you would have a look at them and tell us if you recognise anybody?'

Jason sat down beside Mrs Bourne and between them they went through the photographs.

'I'm sorry, Inspector. The only one I really recognise is Eugene. I don't recognise any of the others, though the second one, this one, does look a little familiar. Not sure where I've seen him.'

Buchanan smiled. 'That young man, Mrs Bourne, is Nigel Pace. He's the son of Andrew Pace of Pace Decorators. Their company is almost next door to your company.'

'Of course, he is such a handsome young man,' she said. Then, turning to Jason, added, 'But not as handsome as you, my dear.'

'And you don't recognise anyone else, Mrs Bourne?'

'No, I'm sorry, Inspector.'

'Mrs Bourne, you said your husband passed away a few years ago. Did you keep anything of his as a memento?'

'Why would you ask that, Inspector?'

'When we, as detectives, investigate a crime, a lot of our time is spent on eliminating things that once thought to be evidence, are now no longer evidence. Let me give you an example: a crime scene investigator finds a glove at the crime scene. It is bagged and sent off for analysis. After testing it is found not to be a glove belonging to the victim or the perpetrator, so it is then eliminated.'

'But what has my husband got to do with what you are working on today? He's been dead for several years.'

'Mrs Bourne, as part of our very widespread investigation, we have collected many DNA samples. If you could provide us with something unique to your husband –'

'Ah, I see. If his DNA had shown up in your investigation, you could eliminate it from your enquiry.'

'Couldn't have said it better myself, Mrs Bourne.'

'Jason, what do we have that the inspector could use?'

'Inspector, Mr Bourne used to smoke a pipe – would one of those do?'

'You would get it back as soon as the investigation has concluded, Mrs Bourne,' said Buchanan.

'I'll get you one, Inspector. I think there's one in the desk drawer in the office.'

◆

'I think they enjoy the game of lady of the house and servant,' said Street, as she drove them along Seaside Road to Pace Decorators.

Buchanan sat in the passenger seat, a huge grin on his face, while holding Mr Bourne's pipe in an evidence bag.

◆

Street drove up to the front of Pace Decorators' workshop, and parked between a white van and a dark blue Mondeo estate.

'That's Danny's van, and the Mondeo is probably Pace's. Let's hope he's still in,' said Buchanan.

The bottom door to the office was blocked open with an empty ten-litre paint tub full of sand and littered with discarded cigarette ends. Street followed Buchanan up the stairs and into the office. There were voices coming from the back office. Pace was seated at his desk berating someone. At the sound of footsteps, he turned to see who had arrived and squinted into the sun. 'We're closed, come back tomorrow.'

'Won't keep you long.'

'I said we're closed, come back tomorrow.'

'Mr Pace, it's Inspector Buchanan and Sergeant Street.'

'I'm busy, make an appointment with Marge in the morning.'

Buchanan continued across the floor and into Pace's office.

'Ah, Danny, find your nail gun yet?'

Danny looked up from his chair to see who was talking to him.

'No, and this bastard won't reimburse me for the loss.'

'I told you, Danny,' said Pace, 'tools left in your van over the weekend are not the company's responsibility. You need to take them home with you.'

'Danny,' said Buchanan, 'would you mind waiting outside for a moment? There's something we need to discuss with Mr Pace, in private.'

'Screw all of you. I'm going home, the kids need taking care of, and the missis isn't well again, all because of you, *Pace*.'

Danny slammed the door and went down the stairs three at a time. Minutes later there was the sound of his van spinning the wheels as he drove out of the car park.

'Bit of a hothead, that Danny,' said Pace. 'He'll be fine in the morning after a meal and a good night's sleep.'

Street moved to the right-hand side of Pace's desk. Buchanan sat down in the now vacant seat in front of Pace.

'Mr Pace, how are you? Keeping busy?'

'You didn't come here to enquire about my business,' said Pace, while flexing his fingers as if he was about to give a piano recital.

'Your health OK?'

Pace looked at his watch, then back to Buchanan. 'It's time for me to go home.'

'What is home, Mr Pace?'

'What do you mean, what is home? It's where I live.'

'You live alone?'

'You know I do. Why are you asking these stupid questions?'

'You hammer nails, I ask questions.'

'I could hammer you, but it would be a waste of time,' Pace said, standing up, his fists clenched tight.

'Gone for a dog walk on Beachy Head lately, Mr Pace?'

'I don't have a dog.'

'Oh, that's right, I forgot. The court banned you from possessing a dog – community service, is that what you did?'

'That was a long time ago.'

'Yes, three and a half years to be precise.'

'It was a long time ago, enough said.'

'Mr Pace, where is your son, Nigel?'

The blood drained from Pace's face, his hands started to tremble. 'What do you – I don't know, he's away on holiday. Yes, that's it, he said he'd be going away for a few weeks.'

'So, you say he's away on holiday? Where did he go?'

'I – I don't remember.'

'Somewhere he could rest maybe? Lie about without being disturbed?'

Pace collapsed into his chair and shook his head slowly.

'Mr Pace, Nigel was found under a pile of rubble on the Arndale building extension project. But you knew he would be found, didn't you?'

Pace nodded.

'Was it you who beat him up, then carried him to the site and buried him – hoping to make it looked like the wall had fallen on him?' said Buchanan, passing a copy of the photo taken by the fireman.

Pace sat with his head bowed, hands in his lap, staring down at the photo on the desk in front of him.

'I'm waiting for your explanation, Mr Pace.'

The only sound in the office was that of Pace's tears dripping onto the photo.

'Mr Pace, I'm waiting.'

Pace looked up, his eyes full of tears. 'He was my son, my only family.'

'What happened, Mr Pace?'

'I – I was too late, it's all my fault.'

'What were you too late for, Mr Pace?'

'Nigel. I've always been too late, that's what she used to say.'

'She?'

'His mother.'

Buchanan looked at the time on his phone. 'Mr Pace, how about we go somewhere where we can talk?'

'Wha – what?' said Pace, looking back down at the photo of his son, buried under the building rubble, the shoulder and top of the left arm with the tattoo of the spider sticking out.

'You said it's time to close for the day. I'm suggesting we go somewhere quiet and you can tell us what's been going on.'

Pace shook his head. 'I don't want to go anywhere.'

'Fine, we'll talk here. Jill, can you rustle us up a couple of coffees?'

'There's beer in the fridge,' said Pace, pointing to the small desk fridge behind the secretary's chair.

Street took out two beers, opened them and handed one each to Pace and Buchanan. Buchanan waited for Pace to take a long drink from his bottle.

'Mr Pace, you were telling us about Nigel's mother.'

'You know, she really was beautiful. At first – at first everything was wonderful. You know, it was her father helped me to get started in business. The first few years were great, the business expanded, the workload grew. It was like the days got shorter. I'd have a few drinks at the end of the day to relax, the few turned to many and I disappeared down the neck of a whiskey bottle – the genie trick in reverse. Home life got bad. Finally, she said she'd had enough and divorced me. She now lives somewhere in South America, Argentina I think. I heard she got remarried to a cattle rancher.'

'And Nigel, how old was he when you and his mother divorced?'

Pace shook his head and took the beer offered by Street. 'Five, or maybe six, don't remember exactly.'

'You raised him alone?'

'His grandmother helped. He was the only grandson she had.'

'He worked for you?'

'Yes. When he was little, we'd go round the building sites together. I made him his own little tool kit, just a few small brushes and a toy bucket, we were mates.'

'What about Nigel's schooling?'

'That wasn't an issue. I'd work when he was at school, and when he got out I'd pick him up and go back to work. It worked well till his teenage years.'

'What went wrong with your relationship?'

'Like father, like son. He started drinking. At first it was just a father and son beer on a Saturday afternoon when work was over. I should have seen the warning signs, I should have –'

'Does he have any friends?'

'Eugene, he works at Bournes.'

'How are they related?'

'I don't know,' said Pace, downing the remains of his second beer.

Buchanan passed him his untried bottle and took Pace's empty and carefully put it in his jacket pocket.

'Do you know where Eugene lives?'

Pace shook his head.

'What happened on the Friday night? You said you were too late?'

'We were supposed to meet for a drink. We'd had a major row two nights before and this was a make-up and be friends again drink.'

'Where did you have the row?'

'Outside the Duke of Devonshire, everyone knew about it. The door staff had to separate us.'

'Why did you have to meet? Didn't you say you worked together?'

'He no longer works for me. He goes subbing now, makes a lot more money than I could pay him.'

'So, what happened?'

'He called earlier in the day and said could we meet up for a beer.'

'Where was that?'

'The Duke of Devonshire, it's on Terminus Road. I was late and by the time I got there he'd gone.'

'What time did you get there?'

'Ten-fifteen.'

'What did you do?'

'I called his mobile.'

'Did he answer?'

Pace nodded.

'What did he say?

'He was crying, he said he needed me.'

'Where was he?'

'He said he was at the back of the Arndale centre.'

'Did you ask him what was wrong?'

Pace shook his head. 'My boy needed me and I was too damn late.'

'What did you do?'

'What did I do? I got in my truck and drove round to the back of the Arndale centre.'

'Was he there?'

'No. I parked in the railway car park, you know the one. It says pick-up only, I laughed, I was driving a pick-up. I walked across the street to look for Nigel, but he was nowhere. Then I noticed the contractors' entrance gate was unlocked. I thought maybe Nigel was somewhere on the construction site, maybe he'd fallen and couldn't get help. I pushed the gate open and started looking.'

'Did you find him?' said Buchanan.

Pace shook his head. 'I was too late, he was gone, or that's what I thought.'

'What changed your mind?'

'The report in the *Herald* about the body of a rough sleeper being found under a pile of rubble. I knew it wasn't any rough sleeper.'

'How do you know it was Nigel?'

'I just knew. He'd said that was where he was when he called, you see?'

'And when you looked for him and couldn't find him, you assumed he'd gone?'

Pace nodded. 'I need another beer.'

'Jill,' said Buchanan.

'If only I had looked harder I might have been in time. I just gave up – the story of my life.'

'Can you think of anyone who might have wanted him dead, Mr Pace?'

'No.'

'Why didn't you come to us? Why didn't you report him missing?'

'We'd had bust-ups in the past. He'd go running to his grandmother.'

'Did you call his grandmother?'

'We don't see eye-to-eye.'

'So, you thought he'd come back when he was ready to?'

Pace nodded. 'Now I'll never be able to make it up to him, say I'm sorry for being such a rotten father.'

'Will you be all right, Mr Pace?'

He looked up at Buchanan. 'Yes, I'll get through somehow. Marge will be here to pick me up soon.'

'Marge?'

'You met her earlier, she's my secretary. One of the few people who really understand me.'

'I'm pleased for you both.'

'Thanks.'

'Mr Pace, Sergeant Street has a couple of other photos, would you have a look at them and tell us if you recognise any of them?'

'Yeah, let's have them.'

Street took out the photos and handed them to Pace. He shuffled through them, 'These here,' he said, passing the remainder back to Street, 'this is Nigel, that's the rat Denman, and the third one is Eugene, he works for Bourne's next door.'

'And you don't recognise any of the others? This one for instance?' said Buchanan.

'Why do you want me to keep looking at the photos? I've already pointed out who I know.'

'Just have another look at them, please, Mr Pace.'

'I've seen that one before.'

'Know his name?' said Buchanan.

'Don't remember a name, had an American accent.'

'What did he want?'

'Came around here a couple of weeks ago. Said he was looking for someone. Said he worked for a company that reunited missing heirs with their inheritance.'

'And you don't recall his name.'

Pace took out his handkerchief and blew his nose. 'No, Inspector, I don't.'

'One more question before we go.'

'What?'

'You said you have no family. Are your parents still alive?'

'Don't remember much about my father. My mother said he died when I was just a child, and she passed away eleven years ago.'

'What was her name?'

'Maria. Don't know her maiden name.'

Buchanan stood and walked round the desk and put his hand on Pace's shoulder. He gave it a gentle squeeze. 'Please don't worry, Mr Pace, I'm sure everything will work out in the end.'

'Will it bring back my son?'

Buchanan shrugged.

♦

'You're becoming a bit of a magpie,' said Street. 'I saw you pocket Pace's empty beer bottle.'

'Just working on an idea.'

'Why didn't you tell Pace that Nigel was still alive?'

'The fewer people who know Nigel is alive, the better. Especially for Nigel's sake. Whoever beat him wanted him dead.'

'Pity you told Mrs Foscatini.'

'Can't be helped. I just hope that the fact she doesn't drive and that I said Nigel was in intensive care will keep her away for now.'

'Did you get the bit about both Bourne and Pace's mothers have the same first name?'

'Yep.'

'Coincidence?'

'No such thing as coincidence in my book.'

'Do you think this case is drug related?'

'Unfortunately, these days drugs are everywhere. From street addicts to doctors oversubscribing.'

'Members of the jury, you are hereby instructed to disregard that last answer. Inspector, when the examining magistrate, Sir Guthrie Featherstone, QC, MP, asks you a direct question, the court expects a direct answer. Sir Guthrie, please ask your question again.'

'Have you gone off Chandler and are now reading Mortimer?'

'Been watching the old *Rumpole of the Bailey* DVD's. You ever watch them?'

'Yes, but that was a long time ago. One of my current favourites is Maigret.'

'With Rowan Atkinson?'

Buchanan shook his head. 'No, they are very good – Atkinson has done a good job – but my favourite is the series acted by Michael Gambon.'

'So, if I understand you correctly, drugs are involved in this case, but are not the motivating factor?'

Buchanan nodded.'

'So, what is the motivating factor in this case?'

'Money, and control. If you have the money, you can control what goes on in your sphere of influence. If you have the control, then the money is yours for the taking.'

'That's a bit philosophical for seven forty-five in the evening.'

'My mind's running at a thousand miles an hour. I need somewhere to think things out. There are too many loose ends.'

'Starbucks?'

'No, not this time.'

'Where then?'

'You know what?'

'No, I don't know what.'

'Remember the night we brainstormed our first case?'

'We've already done a tikka masala dinner on this case.'

'So, we have. How about fish and chips? The Swan should still be open.'

'Not my favourite dinner, but OK,' said Street as she drove past Lottbridge Drove and onwards to Westham and The Swan.

◆

Street grabbed two paper plates and a couple of plastic forks from what passed for a canteen and walked back along the corridor to their office. Buchanan already had his supper unwrapped and was carefully picking at the batter on his fish; a bottle of St Omer sat half empty where his coffee cup usually sat.

'I've got you a plate and plastic fork, couldn't find any ketchup.'

'Doesn't matter. Beer's on your desk.'

Buchanan belched, scrunched up the wrapper and pitched it into the wastepaper basket. Street got up from her desk and removed the wrapper from the basket. 'I'll take these down to the canteen, the office will smell of vinegar otherwise.'

'Bring us a coffee when you come back, please.'

'I'm surprised they get away with calling this muck coffee,' said Street, on her return as she passed the paper cup to Buchanan.

'Thanks.'

'Where do you suggest we start?'

'The Duke of Devonshire.'

That's it, I've given up my evening to ferry you around the pubs of Eastbourne?'

'No, lass. We'll pay a visit to the Duke of Devonshire and have a look at their security tapes for Friday the sixteenth, the night Nigel was supposed to meet his dad.'

'Well, what are we waiting for? I'd like an early night, if possible.'

♦

'Is the manager in?' Buchanan asked the bartender.

'Who wants to know?'

Buchanan took out his warrant card. 'Tell him it's Detective Chief Inspector Buchanan, Sussex CID.'

'It's a her.'

'Who's a her?'

'The manager, she's a her.'

'Ok. Well go tell *her*, I want to have a word with *her*, now.'

The bartender returned. 'She'll be right out, she said to offer you a drink while you wait.'

Buchanan shook his head. 'Not while on duty, lad. Thanks.'

While they waited, they scanned the ceiling of the pub for CCTV cameras.

'Whoever installed those,' said Buchanan, pointing to the two cameras in the far corners of the room, 'knew what they were doing. Let's hope the tapes are still available.'

'Inspector Buchanan, Lesley How. I'm the night manager, how can I help?'

'We're hoping you still have copies of the security tapes from Friday evening the sixteenth of this month.'

'Oh, we should have. We don't use tapes, it's all stored on a hard-drive. I think the system is set to keep the recordings for thirty days, then it auto-overwrites.'

'You're quite precise on that.'

'My Davy, he sells and installs the systems, he did the pub. The monitor is in my office, come on through.'

Street followed Buchanan and the manager through to her office. It smelled of lavender and the walls were covered in a flower-patterned wallpaper.

'I'm not sure how to use computers, Inspector. Give me an iPhone and I'm in my element, computers leave me cold.'

'I can help,' said Street.

'Be my guest,' said the manager, standing up so Street could sit down in front of the screen.

It took Street a couple of minutes to work the recording back to the evening of the sixteenth. As on previous occasions, Buchanan realised it would take quite some time to scan through the recording.

'Lesley, would you mind if we take a copy of the recording back to the office?'

She shook her head. 'No problem, there should be a blank disk somewhere.'

'It will take more than one disk, is that all right?' said Street, as she opened a DVD jewel case.

'Go ahead, Davy has loads of them.'

Armed with a full recording of the evening of the sixteenth, Buchanan and Street exited the Duke of Devonshire.

'While we're in this end of the town,' said Buchanan, 'I think we'll make a quick visit to the Polygon and see if your photographs can jog Carlos or Oskar's memories.'

As they walked down Terminus Road, he asked Street, 'Ever shop at the market?'

'That's only on Wednesdays, I think. Sometimes I shop at Debenhams or, if I'm in the mood, try New Look. How about you?'

'I don't usually go into town to shop – Karen buys my clothes. If we go into Eastbourne, while she shops, I head to Smiths for a paper, then Starbucks for coffee.'

'Why am I not surprised at that?'

'How about you and Stephen? Do you two go shopping together?'

'Couldn't really call it shopping, we sort of just hang out together.'

They wandered down Mark Lane and up to the Polygon entrance. Oskar was on duty.

'Oskar, Inspector Buchanan and DS Street. Can we have a quick word with you?'

'Sure, what do you want?'

'Do you recognise any of these people?' said Street, showing Oskar the photos.

Oskar looked at each photo once, then shuffled back through till he came to one he appeared to recognise. 'This one, I saw him two weeks ago – on the Friday night you were asking about.'

'How did you recognise him?'

'Just did. In this job, you get quite good at remembering faces.'

'What was he doing?' said Buchanan.

'He was the driver.'

'What was he driving?'

'A van, a white – sort of a typical builder's van, just like I already said.'

'Thank you, Oskar. Is Carlos on with you this evening?'

'Yeah, he'll be back in a minute.'

'Did you recognise any of the other photos?'

'Yes, one of them, but he wasn't with the others.'

'Oh, which one?'

'Let me see them again?'

Street handed the photos back to Oskar.

He shuffled through them again then stopped. 'This one. He was talking to the driver earlier, like they were planning something.'

Street looked at Buchanan. 'Wonder why Giovanni was talking with Eugene?'

'You could ask Carlos when he gets back, he had an argument with the Italian.'

'What about?'

'Ask him yourself, here he is. Carlos, the police want to know about your argument with the Italian guy a couple of weeks ago.'

'What, on the sixteenth?'

'Yes, if you don't mind,' said Buchanan.

'I told the van driver he couldn't park his van outside the door of the club. It was against the fire regulations.'

'What did he say?'

'Nothing, he just shrugged and got back in to drive it away. That's when the Italian guy got involved.'

'What happened?'

'He tried it on, told me to get lost and mind my own business if I knew what was good for me.'

'What did you do?'

'Nothing. We're not allowed to hit people any more, bad for the image I've been told.'

'Really, Carlos?' said Street.

'No, just joshing with you. It's our code of conduct. We use force if there is no other way to resolve a solution. Most times these days we just listen, then talk quietly but forcefully.'

'So, how did it end up?'

'Your people came out of the club and got in the van, just like I told you earlier.'

'What happened to the Italian?'

'He moved to the side as they drove off, then got into a dark blue BMW and left.

14

Street pressed the play button and started viewing the night's events of the sixteenth in the Duke of Devonshire. It wasn't difficult to find Nigel. Davy had installed the latest HD CCTV recording equipment.

'He's proud of his tattoo,' said Street. 'Wonder if he gets cold wearing that T-shirt?'

'Have a look at the rogues' gallery and see if we can ID who he's talking to. Looks like it could be Eugene.'

Street consulted her stack of photos. 'It *is* Eugene.'

As they scrolled through the evening's events, they noticed that Nigel kept looking at his phone.

'He was waiting for his dad, probably wondering where he's got to,' said Buchanan.

They continued to watch and saw Eugene answer his phone, talk for a few minutes then hang up. Next Eugene said something to Nigel. They downed their drinks and left.

'Wonder where they were going?' said Street.

'What time was that?' asked Buchanan, as he picked up his desk phone.

'Ten twenty-three. Looked like they turned right out of the door.'

'Yeah, hi. This is DCI Buchanan, Sussex CID. Can I have someone check the CCTV recording in the Terminus Road location on Friday evening the sixteenth, please – hold a minute. Jill, can you send CCTV a copy of Nigel and Eugene's photos?'

'Will do.'

'They're on their way. The one with the tattoo of the spider on his shoulder, can you have a look and see if you have video of him and where he goes, and also if the other one goes with him. You will? Good, you can call me back at this number. It's a murder enquiry. Thanks.'

'Nice to have people who want to help,' said Street.

'They'll call back if they have anything.'

Within a few minutes, Buchanan's phone rang.

'Buchanan. You have? They did? Can you send us a couple of stills of them together – yes – that's the correct email, thanks.'

'What do they have?'

'Pictures of Nigel and Eugene talking to a third party, just at the end of the road across from the Arndale building site. We should have copies through any minute.'

Buchanan turned on his computer and waited for the incoming email. It duly arrived and was opened.

'I didn't expect that,' said Buchanan. 'Isn't that Esposito talking to Eugene?'

'It certainly looks like him.'

'When did Esposito arrive in the UK? Have a look at the photocopy of his passport.'

Street opened the filing cabinet and removed the Esposito file. 'He's a busy boy, a bit of a globe trotter. Ah here it is, last entry into the UK was on the 18th of June, this year.'

Buchanan got back on the phone. 'Yes, it's DCI Buchanan again – yes, we did, they were exactly what we wanted, thanks. Can you have a look for the third individual – yes, the tall one – no, don't necessarily need it right now – when you can find the time will be fine – from the 18th, he didn't arrive in the UK till that day. Yes, it's part of that investigation.'

'What was that?'

'I've asked them to see if Esposito shows up on any other recordings.'

'Where are you going with that line of thinking?'

'I'm not sure at the moment. Did Esposito rent a car, is there a rental agreement in the file?'

Street shuffled through file again. 'Yes, he rented from Enterprise.'

'What did he rent?'

'A series 5 BMW.'

'Registration number?'

'AF 17 UPX.'

'What was the registration for the car that ran Simms off the road?'

Street looked through the file. 'We only have a partial on that: last three digits, UPX.'

'Get on to traffic and see if the car has been reported as stolen.'

Street checked the stolen car records on the NPR. 'Reported stolen on Friday the 25th at ten-fifteen in the morning in Bexhill. One hour before Simms was run off the road. Car was found abandoned an hour later in a layby on the marsh road at Rickney.'

'Who reported it?'

'A farmer. The car was blocking the gate to one of his fields.'

'What happened to the car?'

'It was collected by Hobbs Recovery to Chandlers in Hailsham for repair.'

'Damn, that car was a murder weapon. It's too late to do anything about it now. I suppose by now it will have prints and dust all over it, and any damaged bodywork will have been repaired. I suppose we could give them a call and see if they took photos prior to the repair.'

'They should be open, I'll call them now.'

'Be right back, going down the hall.'

Street hung up from calling Chandlers, a huge grin on her face, as Buchanan walked back into the room.

'What did you find out?'

'They haven't touched the car yet. They're waiting for the rental company adjuster to came and have a look at the damage.'

'Right, get on to forensics to get over to Chandlers and impound it. I don't want it touched till forensics have had time to go over it.'

'Should we go look at it?'

'Absolutely, you drive, I want to think. Oh,' he said, rubbing his hands together, 'we're getting there, lass.'

'You haven't called me that in a long time.'

'What?'

'Never mind, let's go.'

As they drove, Buchanan called control.

'Where are we going, Jill?'

'Hailsham, Chandlers are just off the A22.'

'Control, I need any marked police car in the vicinity to go over to Chandlers and make sure no one touches the BMW, licence number: Alpha, Foxtrot, seventeen, Uniform, Papa, X-ray. It was recovered three days ago by Hobbs.'

♦

There were three marked police cars and a white van in the Chandler car park and someone Buchanan didn't want to see: Ricky Tar, the crime reporter for the *Herald*.

'Inspector Buchanan,' said Tar, as Buchanan walked across the car park.

'Not now, Tar, I'm busy.'

'You're always busy!' shouted Tar, as Buchanan walked through the police cordon.

'Where's the manager?' Buchanan asked the smart-suited salesman.

'He's in the workshop with one of your colleagues.'

Buchanan walked through the showroom to the workshop. There was an individual wearing white overalls, bent down in front of the BMW's front bumper. She turned as she heard Buchanan approach.

'Inspector Buchanan, we've been all over the outside of the car. Looks like either a very clumsy attempt at overtaking, or a deliberate attempt of ramming. Possibly an attempt to run someone off the road.'

'What have you to tell me about the inside?'

'We'll take the car back to our garage and go through it there, less likely to be cross-contaminated by what's here in this garage.'

'Ok, let me know what you find out. Oh, what about the impact area?'

'Plenty of paint chips, should be easy to identify the make and model. I suppose you have a candidate?'

'A black Audi, currently residing in the police compound.'

'The accident on the A259?'

'The very same.'

'Then that means this wasn't an accident, the Audi was forced off the road by this BMW?'

'Circumstances point to that conclusion.'

'Should be done here in a minute, Inspector. I'll send the results through as soon as I confirm my diagnosis.'

'Thanks, er –'

'It's Stephany, Inspector.'

'Thanks, Stephany. Right, Jill, back to the office.'

♦

'Anything from CCTV?' said Buchanan

'No, nothing yet, want me to give them a call?'

'Please.'

'Are you going back out?'

'Yes, got some papers to sign, shouldn't be too long. Oh, if you hear from CCTV, tell them I'll call them back as soon as I return.'

♦

'CCTV called, suggested we look at the recordings. When we're ready they'll stream them to us.'

'What are we waiting for? Let's get on with it.'

Street called the CCTV control room. 'Yes, it's DS Street.

Inspector Buchanan has returned, we're ready to see the recordings – yes, I'll put us on speaker. Go ahead.'

'Inspector Buchanan – Harry Ramsey.'

'Hi, Harry. What have you found for us?'

'We have been quite fortunate, since it was early in the evening our cameras were all in their resting orientation.'

'What does that mean?'

'Just what it says, resting. We usually leave them pointing straight down the road, and in the case of the cameras you're interested in, they were pointing straight down Terminus Road.'

'Take me through what we are going to see, please.'

'The first camera that picks up your guys is from the camera at the junction of Terminus and Langney Roads. It just catches a glimpse of the two of them coming out of the Duke of Devonshire. I looked to see if we had a reverse angle from the camera on Lismore Road, but unfortunately that was looking along Pevensey Road at the time. But the camera at Bolton and Terminus Road picks them up. As you can see, the two individuals are deep in conversation. No sign of anything untoward.'

'Harry, can you freeze the video for a second?'

'Sure, there. What is it you've seen?'

'See the individual about ten yards behind our two? I'm sure he's following them. Harry, can you take us back to the scene just outside the Duke of Devonshire and freeze the video?'

'Certainly, hang on a minute. There.'

'Does he look familiar to you, Jack?' said Street.

'Harry, is there any way you can enlarge the image?'

'Sure, hold on a minute, there, how's that?'

'Bit of an odd angle to make out any facial features. Can we go back to the scene on Terminus Road now?'

'I'm sure it's the same person,' said Street, 'and I'm sure he's following them. Look, just then. Eugene turned round, the follower sidesteps into the shop doorway.'

Nigel and Eugene continued their walk along through the pedestrianised area of Terminus Road.

'You're in luck here,' said Harry, 'the operator on duty must have thought there was something untoward going on. He zooms in right here, and you can now see their faces clearly. Also, the face of the person who you thought was following them, Jill.'

'That's Esposito. What's he doing following them at ten-fifteen at night?'

'We now change to the camera at the junction of Cornfield and Terminus,' said Harry. 'It picks them up as they walk past Boots the chemist. The one you call Eugene is obviously getting edgy, see, right there he turns round again, and, once more the one you call Esposito ducks into a doorway, this time it's Smiths. I'd say Eugene knows they are being followed. But why doesn't he say anything to Nigel? Doesn't make a lot of sense. Makes me think this is a set-up.'

'How far can we track them, Harry?' asked Buchanan.

'The camera at Grove Road tracks them all the way past Starbucks and McDonalds. They cross the road at that point due to the pavement being closed for the building demolition work for the new Arndale centre. As you can see, their tail is still following them.'

'Harry, was anything done about this?'

'No, Jack. Since there wasn't any noise, or violence, the operator on duty put it down to normal late evening activities.'

'How much more did he track?'

'They stopped at the London and County and waited for the lights to change, which in itself is odd.'

'Why's that, Harry?'

'There's very little traffic at that time of the evening, most people seem to just walk without waiting for the light.'

'Thanks.'

'I think,' said Street, 'he's waiting for Esposito to catch up with them. See, as soon as Esposito reaches the crossing. Eugene grabs Nigel's arm and the three of them cross the road.'

'Unfortunately, we lose them here,' said Harry. 'The station building gets in the way.'

'Pity, would have been good to see where they went.'

'But you can,' said Harry.

'What do you mean?'

'Our camera operator kept the camera recording the intersection. The one you are calling Esposito reappears thirty minutes later from across the road and disappears up Gildredge Road.'

'Any other cameras we could look at, Harry?'

'There's one on top of the station. It's directed at the Arndale building site, not sure if it records during the night.'

'Thanks, we'll get on to the contractor and ask.'

'You could try the station, maybe one of their cameras has picked up something.'

'Thanks, for the help, Harry,' said Buchanan. 'Can you lock those videos? We'll need them as evidence for trial, I hope.'

'Certainly, bye for now.'

'Wonder where Eugene and Esposito went? One minute Eugene's talking to Nigel, then Esposito shows up, and thirty minutes later there's only Esposito.'

'Do you think we should be looking for another body in the rubble at the Arndale?' said Street.

'Not sure, Esposito doesn't look like the type of guy that would do his own digging.'

'Maybe for reasons yet unknown to us they beat up Nigel and, thinking they had killed him, decided to try and make it look like an accident by burying him under the rubble? Perhaps Esposito made Eugene dig a grave and put Nigel in it. But Eugene got cold feet and did a runner and is now hiding somewhere in Eastbourne waiting for Esposito to go back to the USA?'

'Pity it's been two weeks since Nigel was found, any evidence will now be long gone.'

'Might still be worthwhile going to talk with the site manager,' said Street.

Buchanan looked at the office clock. 'They're still there, I'll give the manager a call.'

'I have the number.'

Buchanan hung up from the call.

'Get somewhere?'

'Just talked to the assistant site manager. He says we can come over now, he can introduce us to the night security team.'

'He's either very early or doing a double shift.'

'Ok, let's make sure no turn gets un-stoned.'

'What?'

'Nothing, just a bit from a song, something from my younger days.'

Street drove into the Arndale car park and stopped on the first level by the lift. They descended to the ground floor and walked round to the site office. The site agent was waiting by the door for them.

'Inspector Buchanan?' he said, holding out two white hard-hats.

Buchanan nodded. 'This is Detective Sergeant Street.'

'Bill Johnson, assistant site manager. Please come through, you'll need to sign in first, and get your site pass.' he said, pointing to a logbook on the desk by the door.'

Buchanan and Street, complete with their site passes pinned to their jackets, followed Johnson into the office.

'Wasn't this the old HMV shop?' said Street.

Johnson shook his head. 'Sorry, can't answer that. The space was empty when we took it over for our site office.'

The office was just that – an empty, white walled and ceilinged space. Various architects' drawings and artists' impressions of the completed centre hung from the walls.

Desks, complete with large screen monitors sat, pride of place, in the middle.

'Inspector, how can I help?' said Johnson, closing and locking the door behind them.

'Are you aware that two weeks ago the body of a rough sleeper was found under some rubble on the site?'

''How could I not be? First thing the next morning we had a visit from the Health and Safety Executive. Did you know they don't require a search warrant to enter a building?'

'Neither do the police if they are in pursuit of a suspected felon, Mr Johnson.'

'What a world we live in. I'm afraid you won't be able to see where the body was recovered, that's now gone off to be part of a road foundation in Kent. But as I told you, Inspector, you can have a word with the night security chap who discovered the body.'

'Bit early for him to be starting a night shift?'

'He's in early. The day guy's gone to the hospital to be with his wife, she's gone into labour.'

Johnson led them through to the back of the office and out onto the building site. He looked at Buchanan's face.

'It is relatively safe at this time of the day, Inspector, it's lunch time. The equipment is shut down, it's also a lot quieter.'

They walked over to a small cream-coloured portacabin; the door was open and the sound of a radio could be heard.

Johnson climbed onto the step directly in front of the door. 'Ivor, you in there?'

'Yeah, what do you want?'

'The police are here to ask you about the body you found,' said Johnson, leading Buchanan and Street into the portacabin.

'A bit late for that,' said Ivor, standing up from the table and closing the newspaper he was reading.

'Ivor,' said Buchanan, 'can you tell us what you saw the evening you discovered the body?'

'Yeah, I was doing my rounds, thought I'd heard some noises coming from one of the old buildings on Terminus Road. I climbed in through the back door and saw the body. Well, I saw the arm – tattoo of a dirty great spider on the shoulder.'

'What did you do?'

'At first, I thought it might have been one of the lads who had had an accident, but then quickly I thought not.'

'Why would you think that?'

'Everyone has to sign in and out of the site. I always look at the logbook when I come on duty. Everyone had signed off and left the site for the day'

'What did you do next?'

'Went over and felt the body – it was warm. I cleared away some of the rubble and saw he was still breathing. As soon as I realised he wasn't dead, I called 999.'

'Did you try and remove any more of the rubble?'

'Not on your life – I've seen too many instances where an unfortunate man has been trapped under a fallen wall, only to get buried by the rest of it when rescuers try to dig him out.'

'How high was the wall beside where you found the body?'

'That was the part that didn't make sense. It was only about six feet.'

'Did you notice anything else before the rescue team arrived?' said Buchanan looking at Johnson's face.

Ivor looked down at the ground, as if trying to recall something.

'What was it, Ivor? What did you see?'

'There was a short length of scaffold pole lying on the ground.'

'Anything else? Money, jewellery, perhaps?'

'There was a mobile phone,' he shrugged. 'It didn't work though, screen was smashed and the battery was flat.'

'What did you do with the phone?'

'It's here, in the drawer,' he said, pulling out the desk drawer and handing the phone to Buchanan.

'Why didn't you turn the phone in?'

'Thought it was just rubbish. I asked some of the lads when they came to work the next morning if any of them had lost a phone, but they all said no.'

'What were you going to do with it?'

Ivor shrugged again. 'Don't know, thought there might have been some music on the sim card, but the phone's in such a mess I didn't bother with it.'

'Was there anything else?'

'No. That was it, just the scaffold pole and the phone.'

'Why did you notice the scaffold pole? There must be hundreds of bits of that on a site like this?'

'You don't know the site safety motto, Inspector, do you?'

'No, please enlighten me.'

'*A tidy site is a safe site.* Isn't that right, Bill?'

'Ivor is quite correct, Inspector. Everyone working on this site is encouraged to keep the site tidy. Apart for being painful for those getting hurt, injuries cost time and money.'

'So, this piece of scaffold pole shouldn't have been where Ivor found it?'

'Definitely not and, besides, scaffold poles are expensive and are not just left lying around.'

'Where would this have come from, do you think?'

'Probably by the main gate,' said Ivor. 'There's a rack of them there, all different lengths.'

'Has anyone else touched this piece of scaffold pole?'

'Not likely, I've been the only guard on duty at night these past two weeks. My oppo, Mike's wife is expecting a baby. I'm covering for him for a couple of weeks.'

'Ivor, we'll have one of our CSI's come and take your fingerprints. And a DNA sample. Don't worry, we just want to eliminate yours from those on the scaffold pole.'

'You think they used that to do the poor lad in?'

'Possibly.'

'Oh, did he survive?'

'Thanks to your quick thinking, he's still breathing, Ivor. But unfortunately, he has no memory of what happened to him.'

'Is that all, Inspector?' said Johnson, looking at his watch.

'Yes thanks, for now.'

'Be nice to hear how the lad gets on, Inspector.'

'I'll make a point of letting you know, Ivor.'

♦

'What time did you get in this morning?' said Street, looking at the clock.

'Couldn't sleep, thought I'd catch up with the paperwork. I've put in a request for a SCI to go see Ivor for a copy of his prints and I've just sent the phone off for detailed analysis.'

'Did they say how long that would take?'

'The usual, *we'll get to it right away, but you must realise we are extremely busy at the moment.* I managed to get them to commit to sending through an initial finding by the end of the day. I stopped in to see Stephen on the way in. He said there was no change on Nigel. They did another CT scan last night and the doctor in charge said Nigel's brain showed no physical damage, so at least he's sleeping well. Whatever is causing memory loss is not organic. He must have been really traumatised.'

'I'm not surprised when you think of that scaffold pole and then the results of Doctor Mansell's report.'

'Has Nigel's condition worsened?'

'No, said Buchanan. 'I asked the doctor to have a look at the wounds on Nigel's body, just to give me an idea as to the extent of the beating Nigel sustained.'

'Still wondering where Eugene has got to. If he'd been killed and buried on the Arndale site his body would have been found by now.'

'Or buried under tons of concrete more likely.'

'We haven't been to see where Nigel's love nest is yet. Maybe we could find out something that would help pull this investigation together.'

'Do we have an address?'

'No. Shall I call Mr Pace? He should know where Nigel hangs out with his lady love.'

'Good idea, he should be in a more receptive mood by now.'

'Street looked through her files for Pace's phone number.'

'What did he say?' said Buchanan, as Street hung up from calling Pace.

'It's a flat on Pevensey Road. He has a key, said he'd meet us there.'

♦

'Why is there never anywhere to park in this town?' said Buchanan, as he squeezed in between an old Astra and a Mondeo estate.

'Top floor flat?' he said Buchanan, leading the way up a narrow stairway. 'Number seven, Pace said. How can people live like this? It smells like – ah shit!' He shoulder-charged the door, which disintegrated in a shower of splinters and a broken door frame. 'Cover your nose,' he said, heading for the back of the flat.

'How long do you think he's been there?' said Street, trying not to vomit as Buchanan pulled a sheet over the prostrate form of Eugene.

'I'll leave that to the doctor. Let's get out of here, can't have Pace walking in on this mess.'

♦

'Well, Buchanan, you are tempering your body finds, this one is quite different, no blood at least,' said Dr Mansell, as he exited the bedroom.

'Was it suicide?'

'Looks that way. There's a note beside the bed. Give me a couple of minutes and I'll have the body out of your way, if that's ok with you?'

'That's fine, Doctor, I've seen all I need. Jill, I think I'll have the CSI's go through this flat. Eugene may have decided to end it all, but I don't think it's finished at all. We still have a killer to catch,' said Buchanan.

'Could this have been a set-up? Someone made it look like a suicide?' said Street.

Buchanan shook his head. 'I've seen enough of them in my career to know that this was a suicide.'

'I'll call control and see if there's a team available,' said Street.

While Street called control, Buchanan walked back into the bedroom. He returned three minutes later, a grin on his face and a bright orange nail gun hanging from a coat-hanger hook in his hand.

'Where was it?' mouthed Street.

'Under the bed.'

Street hung up from her call. 'CSI's will be here in ten minutes. So, it was under the bed. Do you think Nigel put it there?'

'I doubt it, more likely Eugene stuffed it there to incriminate Nigel. You wait outside for the CSI's.'

'Thanks, the smell in here is getting to me.'

'What's going on?' said a weary-looking Pace, as he reached the landing and walked into the flat through the broken door.

'Ah, Mr Pace. Would you mind waiting on the landing? We've found Nigel's friend, Eugene,' said Buchanan.

'How is he? Where is he?'

'I'm afraid he's dead. The doctor is just about to remove the body to the morgue, we're waiting for the crime scene investigators.'

'That's me done, Buchanan. I'll call you with the results,' said Dr Mansell, as he exited the rear bedroom.

'Thanks, Doctor.'

'What a waste, two young men cut down in the prime of their lives. How did it happen?' said Pace.

'There's a note,' said Street.

'What a waste.'

'You said he and Nigel were good friends, Mr Pace?' said Street.

'Yes.'

'Did they live together?'

'What? No – they weren't that kind of good friends.'

'Are you sure, Mr Pace?' said Buchanan, coming out of the bedroom.

'I've just said, not that way. Eugene might have had a crush on Nigel, but it wasn't reciprocated. As far as Nigel was concerned they were just good friends.'

'Is that the note?' said Street.

Buchanan nodded.

'What does it say? Does he mention Nigel?' said Pace.

'I'll read it,' said Buchanan.

> *To who it may concern. I don't have any choice in the matter. After what he did to Nigel I can't live with myself for not trying to stop it. It's all my fault, I shouldn't have done it. I'm so scared and I want out but oh I don't know how to undo what has been done. Eugene.*

'After *who* did what to Nigel?' said Pace.

Street looked at Buchanan, who nodded. 'Mr Pace, we haven't been quite honest with you. Your son Nigel is alive, he's in police protective custody at the hospital.'

'What – what did you say?'

'Mr Pace, Nigel has been in a coma for two weeks –'

'But you – you told me he was dead!'

Buchanan shook his head. 'Mr Pace, Nigel is still in danger. Whoever tried to kill him may try again if they find out he's alive.'

'Why would they want to do that?'

'At this moment, we don't know. We are hoping that Nigel will regain consciousness and be able to tell us.'

'I want to see him, now.'

'Mr Pace, you going to see Nigel at hospital will indicate to whoever attacked him that he is still alive. Nigel is getting the best care in the world and is guarded twenty-four hours a day. Really, it is best this way.'

'You're sure?'

'Yes. I'm sure.'

'Mr Pace, I think you know more than you have told us.'

'Like what?'

'This time I think we will go find somewhere quiet to talk. Where's the nearest pub, Mr Pace?'

Pace thought for a moment, 'The Marine is just down the road, and you're buying.'

Buchanan pulled what was left of the flat door closed and locked it. 'Constable, make sure no one gets in except the CSI's.'

'Yes, sir.'

Buchanan quickly descended the stairs after Street and Pace and out into the Eastbourne sunshine.

'The Sunshine Coast, Mr Pace,' said Buchanan, as they walked along the pavement towards the Marine pub.

'What is?'

'East Sussex. That's what the tourist office calls it.'

♦

Buchanan put Pace's pint on the table.

'Thanks,' said Pace.

'Mr Pace, what do you remember about your childhood?' said Street.

'Not much.'

'Your mother's name was Maria?'

'Yes.'

'When did she die?'

Pace put down his beer and stared at Street. 'Why on earth would you want to know about my mother?'

'Because,' said Buchanan, 'whether you realise it or not, your family is mixed up in what has been going on these last three weeks.'

Pace shrugged and downed his beer.

'I'll get the next round,' said Buchanan.

'What do you remember about your father, Mr Pace?'

'He died when I was about five or six. That's what my mother told me. One thing I do remember, Dad used to play cards with a friend from Italy.'

'Do you remember the friend's name?'

'How could I? I was just a child.'

'What do you remember about his friend?'

'Ah – one thing I do remember,' said Pace, smiling for the first time. 'One night, it was raining and they were going out somewhere. I don't remember what it was about, but Dad's friend borrowed one of his old coats and a hat. I remember thinking they could have been brothers.'

'What happened to the friend?'

'My mother said he and Dad were working on a building site demolishing an old building. There was an accident and my dad's friend died.'

'Did he have any family?'

'I don't think so. I suppose Dad was his family. Mum said Dad and his friend emigrated from Italy together sometime in the late fifties'.'

'How did your father take the loss of his friend?'

Pace shrugged. 'I don't know. I have no memories of my dad after that.'

'He left you and your mother?' said Street.

Pace nodded.

'Mr Pace, if your father came from Italy, why don't you have an Italian surname?'

'My parents weren't married. I was given my mother's maiden name, Pace.'

'Do you know what your father's name was?'

'No. After my father disappeared my mother tried to find out, but was unsuccessful.'

'Do you have any brothers or sisters?'

'No.'

'Mr Pace. Something for you to think about. We have good reason to believe that Mr Bourne and you are related.'

Pace shook his head, then looked up. 'You're saying something about me being related to Bourne?'

'Yes.'

'What? That's nonsense. Just because our businesses are next door to each other doesn't mean we're related.'

Street looked at Buchanan.

'Mr Pace, in the process of our investigations we have discovered, through DNA testing, that you are, sorry *were*, related to Frank Bourne, possibly you were brothers.'

Pace shook his head. 'Well I never! And all these years we'd go out for a drink and never knew. But – wait a minute, if he was my brother, how come I have no recollection of him?'

'Maybe he was adopted out,' said Buchanan. 'It's possible your mother couldn't cope with two of you.'

'You also have a sister-in-law, Mr Pace: Mrs Bourne,' said Street

'Mrs Bourne, my sister-in-law? And you say Nigel is alive?'

'Yes. But the doctor has said it will be a long recovery for him.'

'All right, Inspector. I'll be patient. But you'd better not mess with me again, you understand?'

'Yes, Mr Pace, we understand.'

Pace smiled and shook his head. 'And to think that this time last week I thought I was alone in the world, now I have a family! Inspector, Sergeant, if you'll excuse me, I have a business to run.'

They watched Pace walk out of the pub, shoulders back, head held high.

'There goes a changed man,' said Street.

'There goes a family man,' said Buchanan. 'But we've got work to do, back to the flat.'

◆

'Everything ok, Constable?'

'Yes, sir. No one's been in.'

'Mind if we wait on the landing for the SCI team?' said Street.

'Not at all, I'll leave the door shut, at least what's left of it.'

'So, it looks like it was Eugene who borrowed the nail gun,' said Street, 'but who did he pass it on to? And who gave it back to him to hide under Nigel's bed?'

'Whoever it was must have known of its existence, and where and how they could get their hands on it.'

'There's Danny who owns it, Nigel who borrowed it from Danny's van, and Pace who told Nigel to use Danny's tools,' said Street.

'So, it looks like the point of control shifts from Nigel to whoever used it to kill Prince?'

'And that's why that person tried to kill Nigel?'

'The question is, was Nigel directly involved in the killing of Prince, or was he just an innocent bystander? Just remembered something,' said Buchanan.

'What?'

'Couple of weeks ago, I had a chat with the foreman at Bourne's. He told me Eugene was in the habit of borrowing people's tools.'

'So, you think he may have borrowed Nigel's nail gun?'

Buchanan shook his head. 'We need to consider how Prince got to the castle grounds in the first place. If Prince had driven to the castle, where was his car? Did you check to see if it was still at his home?'

'No, sorry.'

'Never mind, we'll do that later when we're through here.'

'You think the person who killed Denman used the same method to get rid of Prince?'

'It was a white van dressed to look like a taxi that ferried Denman to the factory. It would make sense if they used the same van for Prince. Jill, ever go to London by train?'

'Yes, many times, why?'

'Do you know the part where you come out of the tunnel, just before you get to Gatwick?'

'Not sure what you mean.'

'As the train comes out of the tunnel, the tracks go from two tracks to four. All tracks end up at Victoria but, after Gatwick, one pair goes via Redhill, the other curves out into the country. It's not till they get to East Croydon that they come back together again.'

'Ok, I've got that, but I don't see what you're getting at.'

'We've taken the scenic route in this investigation. We need to go through Redhill.'

'That's one of your more ambiguous explanations. Help me, what is it you are trying to say?'

'Somewhere in our endeavours we've done it again. We've missed something, and ended up in Waterloo instead of Victoria.'

'I've been there, took the train down to Portsmouth for Navy Day.'

'As soon as we get back to the office, Jill, I want you to get Dr Mansell to send a copy of Eugene's fingerprints off to forensics. I want to know if there are any matches with what the CSI's found when they went through Danny's van.'

'I'm following you now. You want to be sure it was Eugene, not Nigel, who borrowed Danny's van? He drove it to pick up and deliver Denman to the factory then, later, Prince to the castle?'

'That would provide transport for the nail gun to and from the scene of the crime.'

'But why not just leave the nail gun in the van?'

'Eugene's the one to answer that question. He must have known something about something, or – someone.'

'Someone? Who?'

'Remember what Esposito said?'

'He said a lot, but actually very little if I remember.'

'He's looking for someone by the name of Rienzi.'

'You think Nigel knows who Rienzi is but wouldn't talk? That's why he was lured to the building site and confronted by Esposito? But we don't even know if Esposito was on the building site.'

'Where are those SCI's?' said Buchanan. 'We don't have all day to wait.'

Ten minutes later the sound of footsteps had Buchanan staring down the staircase.

'Where have you been?'

'Inspector Buchanan?'

'Yes.'

'Sorry we're late, had to make a detour via Beachy Head.'

'Ah, sorry to hear that.'

'What do we have?'

'Suicide in the bedroom, the doctor has already removed the body. Should be routine. The deceased was not the tenant.'

'You going to wait?'

'No, let me know if anything turns up. We're headed back to the office.'

'Will do.'

'First, Mrs Prince, and her husband's car?' said Street.

'Yes, please.'

'You know you can take the Bakerloo line to Embankment, then the District or Circle line to Victoria?' said Street.

'Then let's do that. First the Bakerloo line to Mrs Prince, then the Circle line back to the office and a phone call to forensics.'

'How about Mornington Crescent?'

'I give in,' said Buchanan.

♦

Street parked in front of Mrs Prince's house. In the driveway was the late Mr Prince's car.

'Should we go in?' said Street.

'Might as well since we are here.'

Street knocked on the door. It was opened by Mrs Prince, attired in a bright orange leotard and blue tights. Her hair was tied up in a bright yellow silk scarf. The sound of dance music emanated from the back of the house.

'Good afternoon, Mrs Prince. Just a courtesy call to see if you are all right?'

'Never felt better in my life. Didn't realise what being married was doing to me. I'm free, Sergeant, free to do what the hell I want, when I want. You do Zumba?'

'Not for a while.'

'Mrs Prince,' said Buchanan, 'we just wanted to know when Mr Prince's car was returned.'

'Returned? I had to go collect the bloody thing from the pound, been there for two weeks, cost me a fortune. Want to buy it? I'll sell it to you cheap.'

'No thanks, Mrs Prince.'

'Is that all, Sergeant? I'm cooling down too fast.'

'Yes, thank you, Mrs Prince.'

'Wow, what a transformation,' said Street, as they left. 'I would have never recognised her.'

'Still sure you want to get married?' said Buchanan, as they drove back to the office via Starbucks.

'You bet. But no way will I end up like Mrs Prince.'

♦

'Want me to call forensics?' said Street.

'Yes please. I'll be back in a minute.

'I've put them on speaker,' said Street, as Buchanan returned.

'Buchanan here. Who am I talking with?'

'Sajid Javid, Inspector. How can we help?'

'We're working on the case of the body found in the factory two weeks ago.'

'Oh, the case of the laminated man.'

'Is that what you call it?'

'Some of the lab technicians like to put a personal touch to what they do –no offence intended to the deceased.'

'Maybe we should do that, Sajid. Can we go through your results chronologically?'

'Beginning with what?'

'Can we start with the cigarette samples?'

'One of the samples marked as CSM1, a Benson and Hedges cigarette, had one match with the sample marked PBGAR1.'

'So, Prince was at the factory the night Denman was killed,' said Street.

'Looks that way. Next?'

'Next was item marked CSM 1, an Italian cigar, a Toscani Garibaldi, the ring-label was still on the discarded butt. We got a DNA match with the EBP 1, a whiskey glass.'

'Now that's very interesting. How about the handle on the fibreglass spray gun?'

'We didn't find anything, must have worn gloves.'

'Front door handles?'

'Inconclusive, too many hands had touched them.'

'All the doors to the factory?'

'All inconclusive except the rear door. There was a perfect match with the mobile phone.'

'That's not what I expected,' said Buchanan.

'Ah, the date on that sample was last week, two weeks after

the initial samples were taken.'

'That makes sense now,' said Buchanan. 'Those DNA samples came from our American all-round nice guy, Esposito.'

'The DNA from the briar pipe has a family match to the DNA sample on the beer bottle.'

'What sort of match?'

'I'd say the two samples come from two siblings.'

'So, Pace and Bourne were brothers. I'd wondered about that when we found out that their mothers had the same first name,' said Street.

'Anything else?'

'We got two sets of DNA from the scaffold pole.'

'Did they match anybody?'

'One matched the blood sample from the injured lad.'

'And the other?'

'The crumpled mobile phone.'

'No one else's?'

'No. But you didn't let me conclude with the first results.'

'Go on.'

'The two samples that show direct family connection also have a family connection with the sample taken from the whiskey glass.'

'You're sure about that?'

'Absolutely.'

'What sort of relationship? Can you tell?'

'You said the first two are brothers, I'd say the third sample could indicate it being from their father.'

'So Palmari is Bourne and Pace's father.'

'Wait, there's one more.'

'More?' said Buchanan.

'The copy of the test you gave me.'

'Yes, that was from a test done in the USA by our bail bondsman, Mr Esposito.'

'An exact match for the sample from the whiskey glass.'

'Palmari is Rienzi,' said Street. 'And Palmari is Pace's father!'

'Wonder if Esposito has made the connection yet?' said Buchanan. 'I think we need to find him, and quick.'

♦

Buchanan parked between a familiar Mercedes and Street's.

'The crime commissioner is in the building, Inspector,' said the desk sergeant. 'He says he wants to talk with you.'

'Thanks for that. I just remembered I've got a witness to interview. If he asks, tell him I should only be gone for an hour.'

Buchanan was almost at the door when he was intercepted by the crime commissioner.

'Ah, there you are Buchanan. Your office – now!'

Buchanan followed the crime commissioner up the stairs and along the corridor to his office.

'Oh, Jack, we've – heard.'

'Not now, Street,' said the commissioner. 'Inspector Buchanan and I have some things to sort out.'

'I've just remembered I need to have a word with Hanbury,' said Street, as she disappeared from the office.

'What is this rubbish, Buchanan? Pace walking the streets of Eastbourne! Who knows who he is going to kill next?'

Buchanan shook his head. 'Mr Pace may be many things, Sir, but a murderer, I think not.'

'That's not what we think.'

'We, Sir?'

'The Home Secretary and I that's who.'

'Do you want me to call her and tell her about Pace? Is that what you are implying?'

'No, I'm certainly not. I want you to arrest Pace, just – just look at the size of his hands, they're strangler's hands, Buchanan. Just the thought of him holding poor Mr Prince against the tree while he pulled the trigger. I don't care if his prints weren't on the piece of scaffold pole, he was there, he murdered them.'

'I think you are getting a little confused, Sir.'

'What – just what are you inferring, Buchanan?'

'Nothing, really. I'm just saying, with you being so busy being the crime commissioner, that the killing of Mr Prince and the severe beating of Mr Pace's son have become a single crime in your mind. Yes, Mr Pace was at the Arndale construction site the night his son was beaten and left for dead, but I don't think he had anything to do with the death of Mr Prince – they didn't even know each other.'

'And I suppose you are going to say that Pace didn't know Denman?'

'Oh, he certainly knew Mr Denman, and yes Denman owed him several thousand pounds for work Denman asked Pace to do, but never paid for. I still don't think Pace killed Denman or anyone else for that matter.'

'He has form, Buchanan.'

'Yes, for dog baiting, not murdering people.'

'Buchanan, stop wasting department funds on all these DNA tests. Do some real police work instead,' said the commissioner, as he stormed out of the office.

Street reappeared. 'Has he gone?'

'Depends on how you want to interpret the term *gone*.'

'I'm glad I don't have to deal directly with him.'

'If you go up the ladder of responsibility you'll end up running into types like him, it's a case of The Peter Principle.'

'What's that? Or do I really want to know?'

'Simply put, it states that all managers eventually rise to their own level of incompetence.'

'And you think that's what's happened to the crime commissioner?'

'No. He passed that level at primary school.'

'Thanks, I'll watch for that on the way up. For now, the results are back for the mobile phone found on the building site,' said Street.

'What are they?'

'No much good. The phone was a tourist phone, pay as you go type. You can purchase them at airports and just about any motorway service station.'

'How about the call records?'

'Only two incoming calls recorded.'

'Who from?'

'Both from Eugene's mobile.'

'And the outgoing calls?'

'Three to Eugene. One to a number in the USA which we think is Esposito's office. One to a known drug dealer, and one to an escort service.'

'Something isn't right. I can't see Esposito heading out on such a mission as he's on, yet rely on only using a pay as you go type mobile phone. He must have another for day-to-day use.'

'That makes sense.'

'I have an idea.'

'What's that?'

'Call the American number. Tell them we have a lead on the absconder they are looking for, but we are unable to contact their agent. Say we don't have his number.'

Street looked up the file for Esposito. 'It's a New York number, they should be open.'

'You'd probably get an answer out of hours anyway. Those type of businesses are usually twenty-four hour organisations,' said Buchanan, as Street dialled.

'Yes, hello. This is Detective Sergeant Jill Street, Sussex CID in England – no, it isn't raining just now – no, it doesn't rain every day either – yes, I've been to New York, Christmas shopping, thank you. I'm trying to contact one of your agents who is currently on assignment in England – yes, that's his name, Joseph Esposito – we need to have you contact him and tell him to get in touch with Detective Chief Inspector Buchanan, Sussex CID – yes he'll have the number – please tell

Mr Esposito we have information that will help him trace the person he is looking for. No, we have no interest in him ourselves – nor the reward. Thanks, bye.'

'Did you get the name of the company?'

'Brasher Bail Bonds, NY. It matches what we have in the file. Of course, the company Esposito works for could be a front for the Mafia.'

'That had crossed my mind,' said Buchanan, gazing out the window. 'You know, Jill, this case is like doing a jigsaw. We have all the pieces, they are all on the board and connected to each other, except we have one last piece and it doesn't fit the space left.'

'So, what you are saying is we have one in the wrong place, find that then the last one will drop into place where it should be?'

'Jill, as I see it, we have two main protagonists in this case. The first is Esposito. He says he is looking for Rienzi, supposedly to collect a huge reward for turning him in. Then we have Palmari, who we know to be Rienzi. Palmari appears to be a front man for an international criminal gang who dump toxic waste, smuggle illicit drugs and off-load stolen goods from hijacked trailers.'

'I'm following you, go on.'

'It could be we are apportioning the wrong crimes to the wrong criminal.'

'Interesting, what are you thinking?'

'Let's start with Denman. Did Esposito kill Denman?' Buchanan shook his head. 'I don't think so. He wasn't in the country till a days after Denman was discovered. We are quite sure that Eugene borrowed Danny's van, and drove it to the Polygon. Morelli's daughter, Paula, had enticed Denman to meet her there. Denman shows up thinking he is going to meet Antonia and is drugged. He follows Paula out of the Polygon and into what he thought was a waiting taxi. The next thing he knows is he's back at the CSM factory and unable to do anything to help himself and ends up being a temporary dartboard before being encased in fibreglass and resin.'

'Which we know was supplied by Prince,' said Street. 'And Prince was buddy-buddy with Simms. Between them they ran a nice side business getting rid of surplus and out of date resin for cash.'

'Remember what Danny said? He was home looking after the wife, who was recovering from back surgery, and feeding the kids. All this time his van sat outside Pace Decorators, who are next door to Bourne Sheds and Garages.'

'Pace is having his kitchen remodelled by Nigel,' said Street. 'Unfortunately, Nigel has a problem with his cordless drill. He calls Pace who tells him to use Danny's tools. Van locked? No problem, the keys are on the hook in the office.'

'So, Nigel never borrowed the van, only Danny's tools.'

'Exactly.'

'Wonder how the paint got on to Danny's drills? Can't imagine Nigel using the drills if they had paint on them.'

'He didn't. Remember what was in the CSI report about the drills?'

'No prints, so the paint was spilled on them after Nigel returned the drills.'

'It is quite likely that when Denman was dragged into, or out of, the van, the paint was spilled then.'

'But wait a minute – if Nigel didn't drive the van and Eugene did, how did Eugene get the keys?'

'I imagine everyone knew about the keys, including Eugene. It would have been a simple job for him to – ah, wait a minute. The keys were in Pace Decorators' office, how did Eugene get in? It had to be late in the afternoon because Nigel had to return Danny's drills first.'

'A question for Mr Pace, I think. And let's not forget the late Mr Prince,' said Buchanan, 'he also had a late-night taxi ride in the van. Eugene must have had access to Pace's office. Can you have a look at Dr Mansell's report on Denman?'

'What am I looking for?'

'We were so wrapped up in Denman's gruesome death, we neglected to look at how he was dressed.'

'Thought Dr Mansell discarded the clothes in removing the fibreglass?'

'There should be some preliminary photographs of the body.'

Street looked through the file on Denman's autopsy.

'Anything?'

'Yes, photo of his left lower trouser leg, patches of white paint.'

Buchanan picked up his desk phone and called Mansell's office number. He let it ring then hung up. *I'll try his mobile*, he thought. Five rings later the ringing was replaced by the booming voice of Dr Mansell.

'Mansell here, who's this?'

'Doctor, it's Buchanan.'

'Not another body, Buchanan! You've exceeded your quota for the month.'

'No, Doctor, no more bodies this month, we hope. I have a question about your autopsy on Denman.'

'It's all in my report.'

'I have a question about the white paint on Denman's trouser leg. Were you able to identify it?'

'I'm in the morgue just now. I'll call you when I get back to my desk.'

'Thanks, we'll wait for your call. Jill, have a look at the CSI report on Danny's van. I would like to know what they thought of the paint.'

Street started to type when Buchanan's phone rang. He pushed the speaker button.

'You there, Buchanan?'

'You're on the speaker-phone, Doctor. What do you have?'

'The analysis says it is a trade paint, manufactured by Crown Paints, a subsidiary of Hempel. It is made exclusively for Brewers Paints and is sold under their own label.'

'That's the same paint found in Danny's van,' said Street.

'I've completed the autopsy on your latest victim, Buchanan.'

'The suicide on Seaside Road?'

'That's the one. I'm still betting on it being suicide, Buchanan. An overdose of heroin. By looking at the needle tracks on his body, I'd say he was a habitual user.'

'A weak link in his armour. Anything else, Doctor?'

'I've sent a sample of his DNA and prints to forensics. I told them this is a rush job and to get the results to you as soon as.'

'What did they say?'

'That's not repeatable over the phone.'

'That bad, eh?'

'They are overworked, understaffed and short on funds.'

'Who isn't, Doctor?

'You working late, Buchanan?'

'Yes, I need to get this case wrapped up soon. I've got a holiday booked and Jill's getting married.'

'Where are you going on your honeymoon, Jill?'

'Don't know, Doctor. Stephen said it's a surprise.'

'Updated your passport?'

'Yes, did it last month. Strange, but exciting, to see my new name, Mrs Jillian Hunter.'

'You can call me anytime up to eleven, Buchanan. I'm clearing the backlog, getting ready for your next victim.'

'Very funny, Doctor. Have a good evening.'

'You too, Buchanan.'

Street looked at the clock. 'Shall I order dinner?'

Buchanan nodded and reached for his wallet.

'Chicken tikka?'

Buchanan grinned. 'That will be just perfect.'

'Dinner will be here in twenty minutes,' said Street, as she hung up the phone. 'So, we've established that Eugene somehow has access to Danny's van keys and drove the van on both evenings when Denman and Prince were murdered?'

He nodded. 'Jill, I'm going over to Tesco's, I fancy a beer, be back in time for dinner.'

♦

'Dinner just arrived, said Street. 'I've got plates and forks, yours is on your desk.'

Buchanan opened two beers and placed one on Street's desk.

'I've been thinking,' said Street, between mouthfuls of tikka masala.

'Go on.'

'Esposito might be many things, but I don't see him as being the one who controlled Eugene's supply of drugs. That kind of control comes from many months of conditioning.'

'You think Palmari was his supplier?'

'Not directly, but certainly part of the supply chain. What are your thoughts on Palmari?' said Street, as she collected their plates.

'You want a hand to wash those?'

'No, thanks. It's only two plates, I'll be right back.

She returned two minutes later..

'You asked me what I thought about Palmari.'

'Yes, is he the mysterious, evil person who I would never guess really is?'

'Let's find out. We first hear of him at Sir Nathan's wedding where he puts it about that he's proposing to replace the beat policemen with his private security firm. Next, I get an offer I can't refuse, to meet with him at his house. There I was introduced to Giovanni, a definite shoe-in for the *strangler's hands* prize.

'We talk with Mrs Morelli who tells us she, or at least her family, used to own Crown Systems Mouldings of which Denman caused the company to crash under a pile of unpaid debts, including a substantial amount owed to the HMRC.

'I get a call to the CSM factory where I find Mr Denman incapacitated by being nailed to a sheet of plywood, had his forehead used as a dartboard then was completely encased in a layer of fibreglass. Upon further investigation, we discover the factory –'

'Owned by the Morellis,' said Street.

'As I was saying, the factory owned by the Morelli family was being used to launder red diesel, which was then sold to unsuspecting drivers. It was also used as a distribution point for the resale of goods, mostly cigarettes and electronics, stolen from trailers which in themselves had been hijacked.'

'Those seem to be two different types of crimes,' said Street.

'What do you mean?'

'Hijacking a trailer that's full of cigarettes or electronic items such as mobile phones, is quite a different operation from the reselling of laundered red diesel. I think you were right when you said you thought Denman's death was a warning to someone. The original crime was that of drug distribution, the dumping of toxic waste and selling of the cargos from hijacked trailers. When word got out about Denman's side-line, he was made an example of.'

'That makes sense,' said Street. 'And I suppose Denman, in a desperate attempt to maintain his lifestyle, saw the empty factory as a blessing – although why he would think it would remain empty for long shows him up for the woolly-brained individual he was. It would have been relatively easy for him to buy in the red diesel, set up a laundering plant and sell the cleaned diesel to some selected few white van drivers, who were only too happy to buy diesel at well under the pump price.'

'Palmari gets to hear of it and wants in on the action. Denman objects and ends up dead. But how did Palmari get to be part of the equation? His type always wants to keep a respectable veneer over all that they do,' said Street.

'I think that's a question for the Morellis, or maybe we should be talking with Mrs Foscatini. After all, she's the matriarch of the whole family, even Pace and his son, Nigel.'

'First thing tomorrow?' said Street, looking at the clock.

Buchanan shook his head. 'At the moment we are one step ahead of whoever is running the crime spree. We'll go pay Mrs Foscatini a visit now, see what mischief we can get up to.'

'I'll lose the empty beer bottles,' said Street, dropping them in the white takeaway plastic bag.

'Thanks, lass. Oh, how I'm going to enjoy this.'

They were halfway down the stairs when Street's mobile rang.

'Hi Stephen, sorry can't talk just now, just heading off to see Mrs Foscatini. He has? Has he said anything? No –'

'What is it?' said Buchanan.

'Hang on a minute, Stephen, the chief wants to know what's happening, thanks I'll tell him.'

'Tell me what?'

'It's Nigel, he's regained his memory, wants to talk to his dad.'

'Pace can wait, Mrs Foscatini can wait. Let's get to the DGH, and in a hurry.'

♦

The room where Nigel was being looked after was at the end of a dimly-lit, windowless, corridor. A single chair sat outside the only door. As Buchanan and Street got closer the sound of excited voices could be heard from the room.

Far from there being just a comatose patient and a watcher, the tiny room contained the patient, Hunter, two nurses and a doctor.

'Who are you?' asked the doctor as Buchanan walked in.

'Detective Chief Inspector Buchanan, Doctor.'

'Detective Sergeant Street,' said Street.

'James Maung, Inspector, I'm the duty neurologist.'

'Good to meet you. Could we have a word outside?' said Buchanan, indicating the door.

'If you wish,' said Maung.

'How is your patient, Doctor Maung?' asked Buchanan, looking down the empty corridor.

'He appears to be fine. The last CTI scan showed no physical damage and normal brainwave activity. In my opinion, he was severely traumatised by his beating. Have you caught whoever did it to him?'

'Not yet, but I am expecting to interview the person responsible within the next forty-eight hours.'

'Good, that sort of person needs to be locked up.'

'Oh, he will be, Doctor. You can take my word on that to the bank and deposit it.'

Maung looked at Buchanan. 'Are you all right, Inspector?'

'Yes, never felt better, why?'

'Would you mind if I take your pulse?'

'Why would you want to do that?'

'You seem quite agitated, and you're breathing quite hard.'

'I've just eaten a curry dinner and run up two flights of steps, Doctor.'

'Sleeping well?'

'When I get to bed.'

'Can I suggest you have a word with your GP?'

'It's your patient I need to have a word with, Doctor. Lives depend on it. Can I talk to him?'

'Oh yes, he's fine. Do him the world of good to get it off his chest.'

'Get what off his chest?'

'Whatever he's been trying to avoid thinking about.'

'Thanks Doctor, and I will have a word with my GP.' *After I've finished this case*, he thought.

Buchanan waited for the nurses to leave and follow the doctor down the corridor before he walked into the room.

Nigel was sitting up in bed eating a hospital dinner.

'Hello, Nigel. I'm Inspector Buchanan. How are you feeling? The doctor says you are making a good recovery.'

'Tired.'

Buchanan picked up a chair from the corner of the room and placed it beside the bed.

'Can you tell me what happened to you? Do you remember?'

'I could do with a beer, all they give you here is water.

Buchanan smiled and pulled out a small beer from his jacket pocket. 'Thought you might like one.'

'Shall I open it?' said Hunter.

Buchanan handed Hunter the bottle.

'Back in a minute,' said Hunter, heading out of the room. He returned with the beer bottle minus its cap.

Nigel took the bottle and drained it in one long, slow, motion. 'I needed that,' he said, lowering his arm and letting the bottle roll away across the bedspread.

'Nigel,' said Buchanan, 'can you tell us what you remember about the evening you were attacked?'

'I feel so sorry for Eugene.'

'Why?'

'He's so mixed up. Look, don't blame him, it wasn't his fault.'

'What wasn't his fault, Nigel?'

'Borrowing Danny's van.'

'Who borrowed Danny's van, Nigel?'

'He did. He said since Danny was home looking after his missus and the kids he wouldn't notice.'

'How did he borrow the van?'

'I got the keys for him.'

'When did you get the keys?'

'He called me Friday afternoon and said he had a friend with a leather settee to move and could he borrow the firm's van? I told him no way would my dad allow him to borrow the firm's van, and why didn't he borrow Bourne's?'

'What did he say to that?'

'He said that wouldn't work, it had to be a van, his friend was worried that the settee would get wet if it rained.'

'Did he give up?'

'No, that was when he suggested Danny's van, said it was just sitting there, wasn't needed for anything.'

'Is it normal to borrow Danny's van?'

'He never seemed to object, especially since we always made sure the tank was full when we brought it back. He's a decent chap, Danny, pity about his missus breaking her back.'

'So, tell me what happened that Friday afternoon.'

'My dad had asked me to do some work in his kitchen at home, my drill burnt out and I called him to say I had to finish for the day because my drill was no good.'

'What did he say?'

'He said to go down to the shop and borrow Danny's drill. That was when I thought of Eugene's request. I called him and said I needed some of the tools from Danny's van but he could borrow the van when I brought it back.'

'So, you took the van as well as the tools?'

'Yes. Danny is a bit of a tool nut, has just about every tool needed to fit kitchens. I thought it made sense to take the van with the tools in case I needed something else.'

'Does Danny have a nail gun?'

'Yeah, bit of a beast. Not much use in kitchen fitting.'

'So, did you use it for anything?'

'No, just left it laying in the back.'

'What time did you get back to the yard on Friday afternoon?'

'About six.'

'What arrangement had you made with Eugene?'

'I was to call him when I got to the yard and he would come down and collect the keys.'

'You called, then waited for him?'

'Yes.'

'How did he get to the yard?'

'His friend drove him.'

'Do you remember what kind of car his friend drove?'

Nigel shook his head, then winced. 'I think it was a dark blue BMW. Not one of the small ones like the series three. This was a series seven, the size used for limousines.'

Buchanan looked at Street.

'Did you get a look at his friend?' said Buchanan.

'Couldn't miss him. He was a mountain of a man. My dad is six foot-two, this guy must have been a good three inches taller.'

'Was he the driver?'

'No someone else was behind the wheel.'

'What about a name? Did Eugene mention his name?'

'I don't remember.'

'What arrangements were made for the return of the van and the keys?'

'He was to park the van back where he got it from and push the keys through the letterbox. I was to pick them up on Monday morning and put them back on the hook.'

'Were the keys there when you came to work?'

'I was late. I assumed someone else had picked them up and returned them to the hook in the office.'

'Did you look inside the van?'

'No.'

'What happened during the week?'

'Nothing.'

'Did you talk to Eugene?'

'Yes, we usually meet up for a beer after work.'

'Every night?'

'No, usually it will be once or twice during the week, usually either a Monday or Thursday.'

'The week after he borrowed Danny's van, did you meet up

for a beer?'

'Yes, we met that Monday.'

'How was he?'

'Agitated, I think he was worried about something.'

'Did he ever ask for money from you?'

'No, he knew better than to ask for money. He knew I didn't agree with him doing drugs.'

'What did you talk about?'

'Not much. Mostly about the Seagulls, and how they were going to do this season in the Premiere league.'

'Anything else?'

'His friend needed help again.'

'Did he need to borrow Danny's van again?'

'Yes, he asked me to get the keys for him.'

'Same arrangement as before for returning the keys?'

'Not quite. We arranged I would pick up the keys after work on Tuesday and take them to his flat –'

'The flat you share on Seaside Road?'

'How did you find that out?'

'I'm a policeman, Nigel. I'm paid to find things out. Was he there when you arrived?'

'Yes.'

'How was he?'

'He was sleeping.'

'Soundly?'

'Why are you asking that?'

'Was he sleeping because he was tired or was it something else?'

'You know, don't you? Have you arrested him?

'No, Nigel, we haven't arrested Eugene. Had he taken something to make him sleep?'

'I told you, he is a heroin user. I'm trying to get him to stop, but he just seems to be getting worse, and, before you ask, no, I don't know where he gets it. He has terrible trouble going to sleep at night. Strange thing is he falls asleep at odd times during the day. I used to think it was narcolepsy until I found out about his heroin habit.'

'Did he wake up when you came into the flat?'

'I had to shake him, but yes, he did eventually wake up.'

'What did you do?'

'I gave him the van keys and as before, we arranged for him to drop the keys through the letter box when he returned the van later that night.'

'That was Tuesday night?'

'Yes.'

'Were they there Wednesday morning?'

'Yes. I picked them up and took them up to the office and hung then on the rack.'

'So, the van sat there till the following Monday when Danny came to work and discovered his drills were covered with paint?'

'I suppose so, I wasn't there. I was in hospital, remember?'

'What happened on the Thursday evening?'

'Nothing happened.'

'You and your father were fighting outside the Duke of Devonshire. Had to be separated by the door staff.'

'That was nothing.'

'What was nothing?'

'He wanted me to stay clear of Eugene. Said he was a bad influence.'

'That all?'

'Yes, that was all.'

'How about Friday, where were you working?'

'I had a job in Bexhill.'

'What were you doing?'

'Painting a couple of rooms in an apartment.'

'Did you meet anyone, other than your customer?'

'No. I got there about nine-thirty, started work, and finished about four.'

'And you drove straight back home?'

'Yes.'

'You went out in the evening?'

'Yes.'

'Did you meet anyone you knew?'

'Yes.'

'Eugene?'

'Yes.'

'How was he? Happy, sad, worried?'

'He was very agitated. I'd never seen him like that before.'

'Did you ask him what was the matter?'

'Yes. At first, he just told me to mind my own business. That worried me, he's never been rude to me like that before. I let it go, thinking that he'd had a bad fix and would get better as the evening went on. About ten-thirty he said we needed to go. I said *we*? He repeated it and said he'd arranged to meet a friend arriving on the Brighton train at eleven o'clock.'

'What did you do?'

'I thought it was odd, but that was Eugene. I assumed he'd run out of his stuff and had blanked out to what was going on. I figured the person he was meeting was going to sell him some dope, and there probably wasn't anyone arriving on the eleven o'clock train from Brighton. I thought it best to humour him, at least the walk to the station would get us a taxi home.'

'Did you make it to the station? Was there anyone waiting?'

'We got as far as the crossing. That was when Eugene said he need to pee. I said it was no problem, we were at the station. He shook his head and said the station toilets were always locked in the evening.'

'What did he do?'

'He staggered off to the Arndale building site. I almost left him to get on with it, but when he almost got run over by a taxi I went after him. He found an opening in the fence, I think it was the contractor's entrance, and I followed him in.'

'What happened next?' said Buchanan.

'We'd gone about twenty yards, there was a partially dismantled building with an opening where a door used to be, I followed Eugene inside. That was when it happened.'

'What happened?' said Street.

'Somebody hit me on the head, the next thing I remember is I was tied up.'

'Were you lying down, or standing up, when you came to?' said Buchanan.

'I was laying on my face in the dirt, my hands were handcuffed behind my back.'

'Go on.'

'I was dragged to my feet then shackled to something above me on the wall, that's when it started.'

'What started?' said Street.

'The questions.'

'Who was asking the questions, was it Eugene?' said Street.

'No, it was someone I didn't recognise.'

'Could you describe him?' said Buchanan.

'He was taller than you, and he had an American accent. Reminded me of one of the characters in the television programme, the Sopranos.'

'Could you recognise him if you saw him again?'

'I'm not sure, it was quite dark, we were in a deep shadow.'

'Jill, would you show Nigel some of the photos, please?'

Street put her collection of photos on the bed in front of Nigel.

He picked them up, one at a time, and looked at them. 'I know some of them, good shot of my dad. The only one who comes close is this one,' he said, pointing to the passport photo of Esposito.

Street looked at Buchanan and was about to say something when Buchanan put his hand up and stopped her.

'Made you think of a Mafia gangster, Nigel?'

'Yes.'

'What sort of questions did he ask?'

'Started by asking my name, then went onto where I lived, who I lived with and the names of my family members.'

'Did you tell him?'

'No, it wasn't any of his business.'

'What did he do?'

'He just kept asking me my name, where I lived, that sort of thing.'

'What did you tell him?'

'I told him to go get stuffed.'

'What did he do when you said that?'

'He hit me in the ribs with something, I think it was a piece of scaffold pole. The doctor said that blow broke three of my ribs.'

'Did you then tell him what he wanted to know?'

'How could I? I couldn't breathe. Every time I tried to breathe the pain made me faint. That didn't stop him though. He hit me on the leg with the same pole, that pain was worse than the pain in my ribs. Every time my good leg got tired I would sink down. That in turn put all my weight on my manacled hands. When I tried to push up, my ribs began to hurt worse. Eugene tried to get him to stop, even offered to tell him what he knew about my family.'

'Did that satisfy him?'

'No. He wanted me to tell him who my father was. At that point I couldn't think straight, I kept passing out. I may have said my dad's name, because he then went on to ask who my grandfather was. Was he still alive and if so where did he live?'

'What did you say?'

'I couldn't say anything. I never knew who my grandfather was or even if he was still alive.'

'Did he believe you?'

'No. That's when he broke my other leg. I blacked out at that point. I don't remember anything after that till I woke up here in hospital.'

'That was two weeks ago, Nigel.'

'Why am I under arrest? Why am I being guarded by two policemen?'

'You're not under arrest, Nigel. You are in protective custody. These two policemen are making sure that whoever did this to you doesn't come back to finish what they started.'

'You mean I was left for dead?'

'Dead and buried. The night security guard found you buried under a layer of building debris. Whoever did this to you was probably hoping you'd end up being road-fill after going for a trip through the concrete crusher.'

'Thanks, Inspector. You've given me something to think about.'

'The doctor says you should be able to leave here in a couple of days.'

'What will I do, Inspector? I can't spend the rest of my life hiding from whoever wants to kill me.'

'Don't worry, Nigel. By the time you are ready to come out of hospital the person who did this to you should be behind bars.'

'You think so?'

'I'm sure of it. You will in the meantime continue to have twenty-four-hour protection. Stephen and Morris will be here.'

♦

'You realise I'm getting married soon?' Street said to Buchanan as they walked across the car park to the car.

'Won't be an issue.'

'You think we're that close?'

'We just need to be patient and let the pieces fall into place.'

'Should I wear a hard hat?'

Buchanan smiled. 'I like working with you, we do well as a team.'

'Thanks. So, where should we look for the first of the last pieces of this jigsaw we're working on?'

'I'd say we need to bring in Esposito. He has a lot to answer for.'

'Do you think my phone call will do the trick?'

'Let's see what happens tomorrow, it's been a long day.'

15

'Inspector, you have a visitor,' said the desk sergeant, as Buchanan entered the police station.

'Where are they?'

'He's in the waiting room.'

'Someone I know?'

'An American, he said you wanted to talk to him.'

'Give me a couple of minutes then escort him up to my office.'

'Is he a suspect, or a witness?'

'Both, but let's not let on. Make an excuse, say to him that I've returned but will be busy for a few minutes. Offer him a coffee, make him feel at home. He might as well get used to the feeling.'

'Pity we don't have enough to arrest him for the attempted murder of Nigel,' said Street, as the climbed the stairs to Buchanan's office.

'He doesn't have enough rope yet. Things just don't quite add up. As far as I can figure this out, Palmari is responsible for the deaths of Denman and Prince and, I thought, Simms.'

'What doesn't add up?'

'As we know, it was Esposito's car that ran Simms off the road. If Esposito knew about the connections between Simms, Prince and Denman, why hasn't he made the connection to Palmari, unless – got it!'

'Got what?'

'It's the other way around. Palmari has realised that Esposito is getting too close. I'll bet if we could ask Eugene, he'd say it was Palmari who put him up to the job of running Simms off the road with Esposito's car.'

'To frame him?'

'Exactly. Palmari would have reasonably thought that we would be connecting Simms' death to that of Denman and Prince, and if we were able to convict Esposito for the death of Simms, we'd stop looking for who killed Denman and Prince.'

'Would we? Would we be that lax?'

'How long have we been working together?'

'I'll take that as a no.'

There was a knock at the door and the desk sergeant came in, followed by Esposito.

'Ah, Mr Esposito,' said Buchanan standing and offering his hand. 'So pleased we get to meet again. Coffee?'

'No thanks, I've tried your coffee.'

'Yes, so have I. Jill? Would you mind going to Starbucks and getting us some proper coffee? Would that do, Mr Esposito?'

Esposito nodded. 'Could I have an Americano, no milk or sugar, please?'

'Jack, your usual?'

Buchanan nodded.

'Be right back,' said Street.

'The desk sergeant mentioned we were very busy, Mr Esposito?'

Esposito nodded. 'Said something about a suicide and an attempted murder?'

'Yes, poor lad got beaten up and left for dead on a building site, unfortunately he wasn't able to identify his attackers.'

'That's a pity.'

'Happens all the time. Guys go out for a quiet pint, drink one too many then the testosterone takes over and they think they can take on the world.'

'So, he couldn't identify his attacker?'

'Afraid not. At least he will make a full recovery.'

'Good for him.'

'If you'll excuse me, Mr Esposito. While we wait for our

coffees, I need to make an urgent phone call,' said Buchanan, picking up his phone and dialling Dr Mansell's number.

'Doctor, it's Buchanan, just calling to see if you have a result on the autopsy of the suicide on Seaside Road – just a minute, let me get a pen, I'll put you on the speaker. Right, Doctor, what were your findings? Was it suicide?' said Buchanan, opening a manila folder on his desk.

'No, Buchanan, it wasn't suicide. Oh, it was meant to look that way, the syringe and needle hanging out of the arm. Given his dependence on heroin and the frequency of his taking it I'd say his last shot, albeit a large one, wouldn't have killed him.'

'So, what did?'

'He was smothered, probably by a pillow.'

'I thought that only happened in the movies.'

'The pillow didn't kill him, his weak heart did that. With the combination of the heroin, weak heart and stress, all it took was a pillow, or similar, over the face and his poor heart couldn't take any more. It simply stopped beating.'

'Was there a pillow nearby?'

'Yes, hadn't been washed for months, not much good for a DNA test.'

While Mansell was talking, Buchanan wrote down his comments and squinted up at Esposito's face. Buchanan smiled; Esposito was thinking.'

'Thanks for that, Doctor. I'll get back to you.'

'Bye Buchanan, don't kill anyone today, I could do with an early night.'

Buchanan hung up the phone and looked at Esposito. 'Just tying up the ends of a small matter.'

'You kill guys. I thought you British cops didn't carry guns?'

Buchanan smiled. 'We don't need guns, Mr Esposito.'

'Coffees,' announced Street, as she walked into the office. She put Esposito's down on the desk in front of him, passed Buchanan his, then sat down on the chair slightly behind and off to the right of Esposito.

Esposito glanced over his shoulder at Street, 'Thanks for the coffee, Sergeant,' then back at Buchanan. 'Inspector, my office in New York informs me you know the whereabouts of Mr Rienzi?'

'First things first, Mr Esposito. Where were you on the 30th of June at about eleven in the morning?'

Esposito thought for a moment. 'Not sure what that has to do with you, Inspector?'

'Please answer my question, Mr Esposito.'

The 30th you say? I was in your town of Bexhill.'

'How did you get there?'

'I drove my damn car, but you already know that, don't you?'

'What were you doing in Bexhill?'

'I've already told you – I'm trying to locate Guido Rienzi. I was given a lead, told that someone in Bexhill knew where he was. I arranged to meet my informant in the car park of the De La Warr.'

'Did they tell you?'

'Please, let me finish. I got out of my car and someone jumped me. During the scuffle, my car keys were taken and the car driven off. I didn't see that one coming.'

'You were set-up all right.'

'Look, I've come here at my own volition based on a message you gave to my New York office. You are supposed to be answering my questions. Now, tell me, where is Rienzi?'

'Mr Esposito. On the 27th of June, did you report your car stolen, the one you hired at Heathrow Airport on the 18th of June, a 2017 BMW series seven sedan?' said Buchanan, reading from the file on his desk.

'How do you know all that?'

Buchanan looked up, smiled and said, 'It was a nice car, wasn't it, Jill?'

'Oh, yes. Chandlers say it will cost quite a bit to put right –

it's touch and go whether it gets written off.'

Esposito turned to look at Street. 'You've seen it?'

'A few days ago. I agree it was a lovely car.'

Buchanan resumed reading from the file, 'Nothing in the boot, that's the trunk to you, Mr Esposito. Did you have your briefcase with you when your car was stolen?'

Esposito thought for a moment and Buchanan noticed his eyes; they were wandering, wondering if he'd said something that he shouldn't have. 'Yes, I did.'

'Mobile phone?'

'Yes.'

'What about the one you purchased in the airport? Why do you need two mobile phones, Mr Esposito?'

'Er – my phone battery was flat, the charging station on the plane wasn't working. Besides, I was going to use the Brit phone for local calls. The office doesn't like it when we field operatives run up a big telephone bill.'

'Could I see your phone, the Brit one?'

Esposito shook his head. 'It was in the car when it was stolen.'

'What did your office say when you told them about what happened to your car?'

'Not much. It happens from time to time in the States, just an everyday hazard when driving a nice car and doing the kind of work we do.'

'How are you getting about, without your shiny series seven BMW, Mr Esposito? Must be difficult for an American to get around without four wheels and a V8?'

'Very funny, Mr Inspector. And since you ask, we Americans are more used to using taxis than you are.'

'Excuse me, Mr Esposito, my little joke at your expense, I apologise. The reason we are investigating the theft of your car is that it was used in the deliberate running-off the road of another car. Unfortunately, the driver suffered serious injuries which he didn't recover from.'

Esposito let out his breath and leaned back into his chair. 'So, you thought I'd been involved in a hit and run accident then reported my car stolen, that it?'

'Precisely, Mr Esposito.'

'Inspector, there was no way I could have been involved in that accident, I was making a report to one of your policemen in a car park wondering who'd stolen my car when it happened.'

'When what happened, Mr Esposito?'

'Inspector, enough. We both know I wasn't involved in any accident, my car was stolen, end of story. Now, what do you know about my quarry, Guido Rienzi?'

'Mr Esposito, do you have any identification?'

'What? Of course I do – why would you ask that?'

'Do you have your passport with you?'

'Yes, it's in my briefcase.'

'Could I see it, please?'

Esposito reached down for his briefcase, opened it and handed his passport to Buchanan.

'Thank you, Mr Esposito, I'll hold on to this pending verification of your identity.'

'You can't do that! That's – that's American property.'

'Mr Esposito, I can and I will. Be thankful I haven't arrested you for the hit and run death on the A259.'

'That's nonsense. I told you my car was stolen.'

'You can have your passport back when I have checked its veracity with the US Embassy.'

'You can do that?'

Buchanan smiled. 'Yes, Mr Esposito, I can.'

'How long will it take?'

'A couple of days, that's all. Leave me your phone number where you can be contacted and I'll personally let you know when you can come and collect it. Now, you were asking what we know about Mr Rienzi.'

'Finally, we're getting to the meat in the sandwich.'

'We think he came to the UK in 1969 along with his wife and children. Our research says he was working on a building site and there was an accident. He wasn't killed, but apparently suffered some sort of traumatic shock. Shortly after he abandoned his wife and children and disappeared. We did manage to find a reference to someone of that name being a passenger on the *Queen Mary* sailing to New York on the 17th of June, 1972.'

'Inspector, I already know all that. When did he come back to the UK, and under what name? That's what I want to know.'

'I'm sorry, Mr Esposito, I've told you all I know. We're currently investigating four murders and one attempted murder. We do not have the time or resources to aid you in your search for someone who, for all we know, could be long dead. Now if you'll excuse us, we have work to do. Sergeant Street will show you down to the door.'

Street returned ten minutes later. 'I think he's a worried man.'

'Worried about losing the reward? Or maybe getting arrested for something he didn't do? Jill, I'm packing it in for today. Karen wants to go see the kitchen designer.'

'Ok, see you at dinner.'

16

Buchanan looked at the bedside clock for the fifth time that morning: three fifty-five.

'What's the matter, Jack?' asked Karen.

'Can't sleep, too many ideas running around in my mind. I'm going in to work, no point in keeping you awake.'

♦

Buchanan took a long sip of his fresh coffee, swivelled in his chair, put his feet up on the desk and watched as the sun came up above the factory roofs across Lottbridge Drove.

The threat of a forced early retirement didn't appeal one bit. On top of that was the upcoming wedding of Jill and Stephen, and he still had to do something about booking the surprise holiday for him and Karen.

The thought of flying for nine to ten hours didn't appeal to him, but if not San Francisco where else? He certainly didn't fancy the Maldives, Stephen's surprise honeymoon for him and Jill. That left somewhere closer to home – but where?

He wanted it to be special, short travel time, somewhere exclusive. A small hotel... no, how about several exclusive hotels in several European cities? Yes, that was it, they'd go on a grand tour of the Mediterranean towns, just like his grandparents had done in 1931. An hour of searching the internet made him realise he'd need a much larger budget than he presently had, especially since they had just bought a new house. He still wanted the benefit of a luxury hotel plus the travel to several cities. That was when he saw the advert for river cruising. The best of all worlds, luxury on the move.

By nine-thirty he'd booked a veranda cabin on the upper

deck of a luxury river boat from Amsterdam. Ten days of being spoiled. Now, with that settled, he could get back to work on the problem of who killed Denman, Prince, Simms and Eugene.

Normally at this point in an investigation, he would be setting the trap to catch the villain, he'd be following the tramlines to the depot, but of course tramlines go in two directions. Was that what his subconscious was telling him? Was he going in the wrong direction?

They knew who, when and how, but not the why, or by whom. Who was the master criminal, who was orchestrating the crime wave? The attack on Street, and the slashing of the tyres on Hunter's car were doubly worrying.

Initially, Buchanan had Pace as the prime suspect in the killing of Denman, and possibly that of Prince to cover up Denman's death. But where did that leave the death of Simms? And Eugene – who had killed him and tried to make it look like a suicide?

Esposito, where did he fit in to the equation? Buchanan boarded the tram going in the other direction and waited to see where his imagination would take him. First stop was Esposito, the bail bondsman. Just how big a reward was there for capturing Rienzi? Buchanan called Brasher Bailbonds in New York and discovered that there was, indeed, a half-million dollar reward for the apprehension of Guido Rienzi, dead or alive.

He next googled Brasher Bailbonds and found several unhappy people had posted reviews of the company. The most telling was from a Tony Spinelli: he'd used Brasher Bailbonds to get his brother out of jail pending trial, only to find out that the cash he'd posted as bail had mysteriously disappeared and his brother was now doing ten to twenty for failing to turn up for trial. Out of curiosity Buchanan googled the name Tony Spinelli and discovered he'd been a FBI informant in a trial against the Gambino clan. So much for Brasher Bailbonds he thought, sounded like a front for the Mafia. So, did that mean Esposito was working for the Mafia, and was the reward the ultimate goal? Or would proof of death be sufficient? Was that why Esposito had a DNA sampling kit in his briefcase?

Next stop on the tramline was Simms' death: had Esposito been driving his BMW when Simms had been run off the road? No, he had an alibi for that, so who had hijacked his car? Buchanan brought up the file on his computer and looked at Espositio's statement. According to what he said, he'd been lured to Bexhill on the hunt for Rienzi. He'd got out of his car in the De La Warr Pavilion car park and was immediately set on by three men who'd knocked him to the ground. Then one of them had driven off in his car. But who knew he'd be in Bexhill, who had lured him there? And more importantly who knew Simms would be driving along the A259 that very morning? As far as he could make out, only he, Jill, and Dave Roberts at Hansen's knew of their meeting at Starbucks on the A259.

Buchanan looked at the clock: eight forty-five. He called Hansen's and asked the switchboard if Roberts was at work this morning. The switchboard put him through.

'Good morning, Mr Roberts, DCI Buchanan, we talked a couple of days ago about Frank Simms. Could you tell me if anyone else knew he would be meeting me at Starbucks?'

'Only your office.'

'What do you mean?'

'No long after you left I had a call from someone in your office. They said they had an urgent message for you and they couldn't get through on your phone.'

'What did they say?'

'Just asked if you'd left and had you managed to talk with Frank.'

'What did you tell them?'

'I confirmed your meeting at Starbucks – was that all right?'

'Yes, that's fine. Thanks, Mr Roberts. Oh, did the person who called have an American accent?'

'No. Sounded more Italian then American.'

'Thanks.'

So that's how they'd found out where Frank Simms was going to be on the Thursday thought Buchanan, as he hung up from the phone call.

The tram rumbled on. Esposito must have been getting to close to his quarry and instead of doing a runner, Palmari had tried to frame him for the death of Simms. Had Esposito figured out that Palmari was in fact Rienzi? Because it was quite obvious that Palmari knew Esposito was on his trail. *Not likely,* thought Buchanan.

The tram shuddered to a halt at Eugene, poor confused Eugene. Never really knew his parents, raised by a friend of the family. His adopted father, never really accepting him, rather wanting to be known as Eugene's uncle. Was that why Eugene never settled, was that the reason for his drinking and drug addiction? But his drinking and drugs hadn't killed him. The pillow on the face had been all that was required to stop his frail heart. Pillow on the face made Buchanan think. What would he do if someone tried that on him? He'd grab the hands that held the pillow, he'd claw at them. Buchanan picked up his phone and called Dr Mansell.

'Bit early for you, Buchanan. What can I do for you?'

'The young lad, the supposed suicide. Did you check his hands, nails especially?'

'Took you long enough. Yes, I did. Unfortunately, he had a habit of biting his nails, but I was able to get samples of scraped flesh from whoever killed him. Waiting for forensics to come back to me.'

'Good, I think I will have the matching hands in custody soon. Bye.'

The tram rumbled on and ground to a halt at Giovanni. It was time to bring him in. A search of his clothes should, in all likelihood, find traces of fibreglass strands. From Giovanni it was a short tram ride to Palmari and the end of the line.

♦

'You were out the door early this morning,' said Street, placing a fresh coffee on Buchanan's desk. 'When did you find out he'd bought the other phone at the airport?'

'I didn't, it was a moment of inspiration, that's all.'

'Want me to track down the sale?'

'Shouldn't be too difficult. We know which flight he came in on, and the subsequent terminal, start there. If you do find a record of the sale, there should be a phone serial number we can match with the one found on the building site.'

'I wonder if he has realised his phone was found underneath Nigel when the firemen dug him out from under the rubble?'

'I doubt it. He probably assumes the phone is lost and if found would never be connected to him.'

'Did you notice his quick reactions about the car key question?'

'Nice to make him squirm, he must have felt such a prat to have fallen for that trick.'

'The half a million dollars reward has clouded his reasoning.'

'I hope I've put him off the need to go back and finish what he started with Nigel.'

'I think he's thoroughly rattled. Can you legally hold his passport?'

'I don't see why not, and besides, he can't go far without it.'

'The town version of house arrest.'

'Precisely,' said Buchanan, looking at the clock. 'We need to go back and see Mrs Foscatini.'

'Why?'

'She's still hiding something from us.'

♦

'Good morning, Mrs Foscatini.'

'Inspector, it's late.'

'It certainly is late. In fact, it's later than you think. Can I

347

come in? I won't keep you very long.'

Buchanan followed her down the hallway and into the conservatory.

'Can I get you something to drink?'

'No thank you. Mrs Foscatini, would you have a look at this photo and tell me if you recognise the person? Make sure you look very hard at it, please,' said Buchanan.

She looked up from the photo, 'I'd hoped I'd never see that man again, Inspector.

'Can you tell me his name?'

'It's Guido Rienzi.'

'When was the last time you saw him?'

'I'm not sure, but not long enough to eradicate the memory of what he did to the family. Is he dead?'

'No, he's very much alive.'

'Pity.'

'What can you tell us about him?'

'His father ruined the family business in Italy. I heard when Italy got too hot for Guido, he moved with his wife and children to England. Two years after they arrived, he disappeared. No one has heard from him since.'

'Do you know where his wife and children are?'

'His wife died at least twenty years ago. I'm not sure what happened to the children.'

'Are you sure about that?'

'Yes, of course I am.'

'Don't you think it's time to for the gloves to come off, Mrs Foscatini?'

'What do you mean?'

'You know very well what happened to the children. Your daughter was married to one of them, Andrew Pace.'

'Inspector, the past is best left where it lies. I live for today and what may come tomorrow, yesterday is a foreign country that I chose not to visit.'

'Unfortunately, the past has come visiting you.'

'What do you mean?'

'Guido Rienzi is very much alive. He's now calling himself Toni Palmari and he lives less than a mile from you. This is a current photograph of him.' Buchanan handed her another photo.

'I wouldn't recognise him, he's changed quite a bit. Why are you telling me this?' she said, handing the photos back to Buchanan.

'He may have had plastic surgery to change his features. I'm telling you because I want you to be on your guard. We think he is very dangerous.'

'Nigel?'

'No, we don't think he knows anything about Nigel. Why he's living here in Eastbourne we have yet to find out.'

'You have no idea?'

'It may have something to do with the demise of CSM.'

'That sounds about right, like father like son. How is Nigel?'

'He's awake and talking. His memory has returned, and the doctor says he should make a full recovery.'

'If Rienzi didn't hurt Nigel, do you know who did?'

'We have a very good idea who did. We're still collecting the evidence needed to arrest the individual. Till we have, I suggest you be wary when you are out and about.'

'I will, Inspector. When can I see Nigel?'

'I was going to ask you if he could convalesce here. I believe when you see him, you will see a very much changed young man.'

'That would be lovely, I'll get his room ready for him. Do you have any idea when he will be discharged?'

'No, but we will let you know as soon as we find out.'

♦

'Where next?' said Street, as she did up her seatbelt.

'Palmari, or at least his servant, Giovanni. We'll try a new tack on Palmari.'

'What's your idea?'

'We don't actually have any evidence to convict him, what we need is proof that he was there on the two occasions, first with Denman and the second with Prince. I'm pretty sure it was Eugene who was responsible for Simms' death. Nigel was beaten by Esposito.'

'Ok, so, what do you propose?'

'We're going fishing and Giovanni is going to be the bait.'

'How will we do that?'

'It is my intention to arrest Giovanni on suspicion of killing Simms. When his lawyer gets on the case, as he will, we'll hit them with accessory to murder of Denman and Prince. That should enable us to generate a search warrant for Palmari's house, at which there should be forensic evidence of them being involved in the deaths of Denman and Prince.'

'What sort of forensic evidence?' said Street.

'I was remembering back to the time I went to the Greyspear factory in Scotland. I saw the extreme ends the company went to for health and safety when working with fibreglass and resin. I am sure that, when we have Palmari and Giovanni's clothes tested, we will find traces of resin, strands of glass from the CSM factory, pollen and who knows what from the woods behind Pevensey Castle.'

◆

The shadows were lengthening when Buchanan knocked on Palmari's front door. As before it was answered by Giovanni.

'Good evening, Giovanni, is the boss in?' said Buchanan.

'Mr Palmari has retired for the evening. Would you please call back tomorrow and make an appointment?'

'Never mind, Giovanni. It's you we've come to talk to. I want you to accompany us to the police station, where you will be questioned about the murder of a Frank Simms.'

'Who? Never heard of him.'

'Giovanni, you have a choice. You can come with us voluntarily, or we can simply arrest you. What is your choice?'

'I'll have to inform Mr Palmari first.'

'We'll wait inside – shall we just come in?' said Buchanan, pushing past Giovanni.

◆

'Can we have your full name, please?' said Buchanan.

'Giovanni Rosso. The boss said not to answer any of your questions till my lawyer gets here.'

'Giovanni, you haven't been arrested, you have no need for a lawyer.'

Giovanni looked at Buchanan and smiled.

'Right, since you have decided not to answer any of my questions, I am going to keep you here till you do.'

Giovanni scowled and slouched down in his chair.

'Mr Rosso, if you will accompany us, we shall take you downstairs to the booking-in clerk and arrange for your room for the night. This way,' said Buchanan, opening the office door.

'This is bullshit, you can't keep me here.'

'You should have given thought to that while you had the opportunity,' said Buchanan.

◆

'That should put the cat amongst the pigeons,' said Street, as they walked back up to their office. 'Wonder how long it will take the lawyer to show up.'

'He needs to be quick about it, we're done for the day.'

They were about to open the door when the desk sergeant caught up with them.

'Inspector, Mr Rosso's lawyer is here – he's in reception.'

'Damn. Ok, show him in to an empty interview room. Which one is available?'

'One, sir.'

'Fine. Show him into room one, then bring Mr Rosso up from his cell.'

'What are we going to do, Jack?' asked Street.

'I was hoping to make him stew overnight. No matter, we'll do battle now. First, I want the Palmari file – would you run upstairs and get it? Take your time, I want Rosso to sweat a bit more.'

♦

Buchanan entered interview room number one, ignored the stare from Givanni and the outstretched hand of his lawyer, and sat down.

'Inspector –' began the lawyer.

Buchanan put up his hand. 'In a minute, I'm waiting for the file.'

Five minutes later Street entered. 'The file, Chief.'

'Thanks, Sergeant,' said Buchanan, opening the file and commencing to read, page by page.

Street sat in the spare seat on Buchanan's right.

'Inspector, I must protest.'

Buchanan looked up from reading the file. 'Yes, Mr – er – didn't quite catch your name?'

'It's Alistair Hardwick. Inspector, I wish to point out that my client is innocent of any charges you may have deemed necessary to imagine.'

'Mr Hardwick, I don't need to imagine four bodies in the morgue. I have seen them and it is my belief that your client, Mr Giovanni Rosso, is responsible for at least one of them.'

'You have evidence to support this wild theory of yours, Inspector?'

Buchanan's answer was prevented by the arrival of the desk sergeant. 'Sorry to interrupt, sir, but you're wanted at the desk.'

'Who is it?'

'The crime commissioner, sir, and the assistant chief constable.'

Buchanan grimaced and looked at Hardwick, who licked his lips and grinned at Buchanan.

'Thank you, Sergeant, I'll be right there. Please excuse me, Mr Hardwick. Sergeant Street, would you look after Mr Hardwick and Mr Rosso?'

Buchanan followed the desk sergeant out of the interview room.

'They're in the reception area, sir.'

'Thanks, Sergeant.'

Buchanan took in a deep breath, pulled back his shoulders and waked through into the reception area.

'Buchanan, you have Mr Palmari's manservant in custody? Have you charged him yet?' said the crime commissioner.

'He's here helping us with our enquiries, Sir.'

'Have you charged him?'

'No.'

'Are you intending to?'

'Eventually.'

'Just what does that mean?'

'Eventually I intend to charge him with the murder of Frank Simms, Eugene Bourne and possibly as an accessory along with Toni Palmari to the murders of Julian Denman and Clive Prince.'

'You have evidence for all of those charges?'

'Not for all of it at this moment, I'm still waiting for forensic reports,' said Buchanan, looking at the ACC. She was standing just behind the crime commissioner and trying to keep a straight face.

'Buchanan. Until you have definite evidence of Mr Rosso's involvement, I want him released, do you understand? It's about time you realised you are not in Glasgow any more. This is Sussex, where the great and good of society come to relax. They don't need people like you accusing them of murder.'

Buchanan was about to object, then realised this could work in his favour. 'An excellent idea, Sir. Whatever Mr Palmari wants. I will release Mr Rosso immediately. Be right back.'

He returned to the interview room. 'Ah, Mr Rosso. You are free to go. Goodbye.'

'Finally, you see sense,' said Hardwick.

'Oh, before you go, Mr Rosso. Please be sure to tell your boss that there is a certain American in Eastbourne looking for a Guido Rienzi.'

Giovanni stopped and looked at Buchanan.

'That's right, Giovanni. Guido Rienzi. Apparently, there is a half-million dollars reward for his apprehension and return to the USA. Did you know he's wanted for murder, extortion, drugs and a few other crimes against society?'

17

'Morning, Chief.'

'Good morning, Jill.'

'I've got confirmation on Esposito's phone. It was purchased at the phone booth in terminal five arrivals.'

'Any sign of his lawyer yet?'

'Nope, but you have a message on your phone from you-know-who.'

'Really, did you listen to it?'

'Just the start, I hadn't had my coffee at that time.'

'In that case I won't put it on the speaker.'

'No, go ahead, I'd like to hear what he has to say.'

Buchanan pressed the speaker button and dialled in for his phone message.

'Inspector Buchanan, you had my man in your cells. If you wanted to talk to him all you had to do was ask. I would have been most pleased to drive him down to see you. You had no right to do what you did without asking me first. If you have anything to say, come say it to me, face to face.'

'Shall we?' said Buchanan to Street.

'Why not?'

♦

'Getting quite used to visiting Mr Palmari,' said Buchanan, as Street turned off the engine and undid her seat belt.

'Let's not make it a habit, please.'

'Don't worry, the noose is tightening round the neck of Mr Palmari. I would be very disappointed if by your wedding day he's not banged up inside.'

The front door opened as they climbed the steps. Giovanni glared at them. 'The boss said to come right through, he's not very happy with you, Mr Buchanan.'

Buchanan smiled. 'Feeling the cold, Giovanni? Gloves suit you.'

This time there was no pretence of any developing business relationship.

Buchanan and Street took their seats and waited for Palmari to compose himself.

'You really disappoint me, Buchanan. I thought we were playing on the same team, but your actions make it very obvious that we are not.'

'Is that what you wanted to tell us, Mr Palmari? I thought maybe you might want to discuss the arrival of an American bail bondsman, a Mr Esposito? Perhaps you've heard of him? He was driving a very nice BMW, now sadly waiting for extensive, and no doubt expensive, repair. I should have the forensic report of the accident on my desk very soon.'

'Never heard of him.'

'I think you have. It is my intention to prove, beyond a shadow of doubt, that you instigated the theft of his car in Bexhill, and had your man, Giovanni, follow a Frank Simms and run his car off the road and into a tree killing him outright. Now what do you say to that?'

'Who the hell is Frank Simms?'

'A friend and co-conspirator of Clive Prince, who you nailed to a tree.'

'And who was Clive Prince?'

'He was cheated by Julian Denman, who you nailed to a sheet of plywood and then smothered with fibreglass and resin.'

'Do you hear that, Giovanni? I'm a mass murderer, aren't you scared to work for me?'

Buchanan caught a fleeting look of concern in Giovanni's face, before he burst out laughing.

'What are you wanted for in the USA, Mr Palmari?'

'No idea what you are talking about.'

'A fire – perhaps in a warehouse – in New York City. There was a meeting arranged between families to sort out some misunderstandings. The building caught fire and twenty people died, some bodies were never recovered. Twenty went in, no one came out alive. When the bodies were counted, there were only eighteen. Now I wonder what happened to the two who disappeared? Was that you and Giovanni, Mr Rienzi?'

'You are talking fairy tales. I've never been to New York.'

'No? What about the fight you had in the bar, where your forearm was slashed pretty badly? Someone wrapped a towel round the wound to stem the bleeding. You went to hospital to get the wound taken care of. You left without the towel. Some enterprising PI had your DNA analysed and held on to the results. That enterprising PI has a name, shall I tell you what it is? No, I'll tell you anyway. His name is Esposito. Has he been sent by someone to bring you back?'

'You writing a screen play, Buchanan? Fancy yourself as a new Coppola?'

'Someone else has analysed your DNA.'

'Who? What the hell are you getting at, Buchanan?'

'I had your DNA tested and the results of that match exactly the test results from the blood found on the towel that had been wrapped round your arm. So, you see, there is no point in denying your identity.'

'That is just your hearsay, Buchanan. You could never use it in a court of law.'

'I wouldn't have to. All I have to do is tell Mr Esposito where you are. He will apply for a warrant to have you extradited and he will be half a million dollars better off, while you spend the rest of your years rotting in a maximum-security prison. Maybe you'll get lucky and only have to share with four or five others, now won't that be cosy?'

'I will never go to prison, in the USA or anywhere else Now, if you've finished, I have important matters to attend to.

Goodbye. But before you go, remember I have eyes and ears everywhere, Buchanan.'

'I'm counting on that, Mr Rienzi.'

◆

'You're managing to get a lot of people very angry with you,' said Street, as she drove them along the seafront past the pier.

Buchanan smiled. 'I'm not done yet,' he said, as he looked through the folder he'd brought with him.

'Do we have enough evidence to charge anyone yet?'

'Close. We still need the forensics on Esposito's car, the samples of flesh taken from Eugene's fingernails and from Eugene's flat.'

'Why don't we just arrest Esposito for beating up Nigel?'

'I need him on the loose. You heard Palmari, he said he has eyes and ears everywhere. I want Palmari to be worried that Esposito will find him and drag him back to the USA.'

'But that leaves Nigel in danger.'

'Don't worry about Nigel, I have a plan to take care of that issue.'

'Esposito? How?'

He nodded. 'Yes, I have a nice surprise in store for him.'

'You're not going to tell him where Rienzi lives, are you?'

'No. But I will hint a bit at it. When we get back to the office, will you call Esposito and tell him I have some information for him about the person he's looking for?'

'That means he'll want his passport – will you give it to him?'

'Oh, he'll get it all right.'

'Somehow I don't think I'm on the same page as you.'

'No, I don't suppose you are. Jill, instead of going straight to the office, I would like to have a quick word with Pace.'

◆

For once the car park in front of Pace Decorators was empty of all but one car.

'That's Pace's car. Good, no one else around.'

Street followed Buchanan up the stairs to Pace Decorators' office. Pace looked up to see who had just entered.

'Good afternoon, Mr Pace,' said Buchanan. 'How are you?'

Pace stood and looked at Buchanan and Street. He exhaled slowly and let his shoulders drop. 'I'm fine. Especially since I've got my boy back.'

'Good, I'm glad.'

'Is that why you've come to see me?' said Pace, sitting back down at his desk.

'Yes,' said Buchanan, sitting down opposite Pace and putting his folder on the edge of the desk. 'You've been to see Nigel?'

'Just got back. I'm going to collect him from the hospital tomorrow morning and take him up to his grandmother's.'

'You're on speaking terms with her?'

'Strange how tragedies can bring families together. It's early days yet, but I see us eventually being able to sit in the same room without ending up in a shouting match.'

'I'm glad to hear that.'

'Inspector, are you anywhere nearer to catching whoever beat up Nigel?'

'We have identified a suspect, but we have very little evidence. Nigel said it was very dark and he'd been drinking. If Eugene had been still with us, he might have been able to tell us more.'

'Who is it? Let me at the bastard, I'll make him confess!'

'I'm sorry, Mr Pace, that would not be ethical. After all, I could be wrong in my assumption as to who is guilty.'

'At least let me know that he isn't going to get away with it, please.'

'I can assure you, Mr Pace, he will not get away with it,' said Buchanan, standing. As he did so he accidentally knocked his folder off the desk and on to the floor. Several sheets of paper slid across the floor.

'I'll get it,' said Street.

'No, that's all right, lass. I knocked it off, I'll pick it up.'

♦

'You're still not telling me what's going on,' said Street, as they parked in the police compound.

Buchanan grinned. 'It will all become clear soon.'

His phone rang. 'Buchanan. He is? Good. Would you escort him up to my office, please?'

'Esposito?' said Street.

'Yep.'

'Are you going to tell him about Rienzi?'

'Not quite.'

There was a knock at the door and it opened. 'Mr Esposito to see you, Sir.'

'Show him in, please. Good morning, Mr Esposito. How are you today?'

'Can I have my passport back, please?' he said, putting his hand out, palm up.

'Certainly, Mr Esposito. It's all in order.'

'Your sergeant said something about you having information on the whereabouts of Rienzi?'

'Not quite, but I have found a relative of his who might be able to tell you something. We're still waiting on DNA results, but this person is related to your Mr Rienzi. You could ask him if he knows anything about Rienzi's whereabouts.'

'Certainly, can I have his contact details?'

Buchanan wrote down the address of Pace Decorators on a plain piece of paper and handed it to Esposito.

Street looked at Buchanan, a smile slowly growing on her face.

'Where is this place, Finmere Road? Do you know?' asked Esposito.

'I can tell you,' said Street. 'You go back down to the Tesco roundabout, turn right onto Seaside Road, then a right onto Finmere Road.

They watched through the window as an excited Esposito climbed into his car and drove off.

'Why did you give Esposito directions to Pace Decorators? Surely he knows that Pace is Nigel's father?'

'Yes, he does know that. But what he doesn't know is that Pace now knows who beat up Nigel.'

'How does he know that? I didn't hear you tell him.'

'Remember I dropped my folder on the floor?'

'You didn't, did you?'

'I accidentally lost the sheet of paper from my report where I laid out my evidence for Esposito being the one who beat up Nigel.'

'We're very naughty, aren't we?' said Street. 'But aren't you a bit worried that Pace might kill Esposito?'

'Do you remember what Mrs Foscatini told us about Pace?'

'Which bit?'

'Pace used to be a champion bare-knuckle fighter, never lost a fight. He'll know just how much to take Esposito apart.'

'Good, he deserves it.'

'I think we'll have an early night, Jill. I'll drive.'

18

'Good morning, much happen last night?' Buchanan asked the desk sergeant, as he and Street walked past the reception desk.

'No, quiet night. Except for one thing.'

'What was that?'

'We had a report of a fight at a unit on Finmere Road. Turned out someone had a bit too much to drink and fell down a flight of steps. The victim is currently under observation in the DGH.'

'Do you have a name?'

'Yes, it was that Yank who's been hanging around here, name of Esposito.'

'How is he?'

'He'll survive, he's just got a few broken bones.'

'Thanks, Sergeant,' said Buchanan.

'Should we go see him?' said Street.

'Yes, definitely. It's about time I felt his collar.'

'Sir,' said the sergeant, 'you have a message from a Giovanni Rosso.'

'Oh, what is it?'

'He asked could you come to see him, please.'

'He actually said, please?'

'Yes, sir. His actual words.'

'Let's go, Jill. Let's hear what Mr Rosso wants to tell us.'

◆

Buchanan stopped the car in front of the steps that lead up to Palmari's front door.

'Looks deserted, no lights on inside,' said Street. 'Could this be his way of getting back at us, having us here when he's gone out?'

'One way to find out,' said Buchanan, undoing his seatbelt and opening the car door.

Street followed him up the steps.

'It's open,' said Buchanan. 'No need to knock and be invited in.' He gently pushed at the door and stepped in to the entrance hall. It took him a few minutes to find the light switch.

'This is creepy,' said Street. 'The house feels empty. Do you think they've done a runner?'

'Mr Rosso,' Buchanan shouted down the empty hall. 'It's an open door, Jill. We're invited, no warrant required.

Street followed Buchanan as he made his way along the hall to the door at the end. At least the hallway lights still worked on automatic. The door to Palmari's office was ajar. Buchanan gently pushed at it. It opened slowly. Street followed Buchanan into the room. It was in all but complete darkness, illuminated by the daylight shining through the French doors from the conservatory. Buchanan walked across to the far wall and turned on the lights. He turned to say something to Street and saw Palmari. He was sitting at his desk, apparently sleeping, his head resting on his chest.

'I don't like this, Jill,' said Buchanan as he carefully approached the sleeping form of Palmari, touching him on the neck with his fingertips.

'Jill, will you call control? We need an ambulance and SCI team here.'

'Will do,' said Street.

'I wonder where Giovanni is hiding?' said Buchanan.

'He's in the conservatory,' said Street, opening the door. 'He's lying on the settee.'

'How is he?'

'Breathing, but it doesn't look good, he's bleeding profusely from a knife wound to his side.'

Buchanan left Palmari and followed Street into the conservatory.

'Giovanni, can you hear me?' he said, kneeling down beside Rosso.

Giovanni opened his eyes and turned his head to see who was talking.

'Inspector, you're too late.'

'What happened?'

'We were having an argument.'

'What about?'

'I told him it was over. It was time to cut and run.'

'Why did you think that?'

'You're asking me? I thought you were in charge of the investigation?'

'Go on.'

'I was trying to convince him it was no good, but he wouldn't listen. He said with Esposito heading back to the USA and you and your partner out of the way, there would be nothing stopping him from completing his plans.'

'Us out of the way? Was he contemplating killing us both?'

Giovanni grimaced and nodded gently. 'He was going to arrange an accident for you both. I tried to make him see sense, but it only made him angrier. I grabbed him by the shoulders and tried to talk sense into him, and that's when he stuck me with the knife. I must have squeezed a bit too hard because he just went limp.'

'Why didn't you call for an ambulance?'

'He was dead – what difference would a few minutes make? I called you, then the ambulance, it's on its way.'

'When did you call for the ambulance?'

'A few minutes ago.'

'A few minutes? You called the police station twenty minutes ago – why wait so long to call the ambulance?'

'I was in shock.'

'You were in shock? I find that hard to accept. Could it be you were getting rid of embarrassing paperwork, computer records, that sort of thing?'

Giovanni grimaced as he tried to move.

'What was the last thing you and he were talking about?'

'He said he'd never go back to jail. It would be worse than death.'

'Is that what he said?'

'You really scared him, with all that talk about jail.'

'Did you take Esposito's car and run Simms off the road?'

'No, I don't drive.'

'You don't drive?'

'I don't have an English licence.'

'So, who does the driving?'

'Dave and Harry. It was them who brought you here the first time.'

'Who ran Simms off the road?'

'Don't know, you'd have to ask them. Look, I need a drink. Whiskey's in the cupboard in the office.'

'Shouldn't you wait for the paramedics?' said Street, as she held a folded towel to Giovanni's side.

'I'll be dead before they get here.'

'While we wait for the doctor and the ambulance –'

'I don't need a doctor, I've already told you it's too late for me.'

'The doctor is not for you, Giovanni. It's the police surgeon, he'll be the one that determines the cause of death of Mr Palmari. The paramedics will be here first, they'll tend to you.'

'Oh.'

'Giovanni, what can you tell me about the evening Julian Denman died?'

'It was Toni's suggestion that Prince go with Paula to pick up Denman from the club.'

'Did Paula go with them to the factory?'

'No, as soon as Denman got in the van she walked back to her parents' flat.'

'Who drove the van?'

'Eugene.'

'Did he work for Palmari?'

'When he needed a fix. He'd do almost anything for Toni if it meant getting what he needed.'

'Heroin?'

'Yeah, poor kid, he had it really bad.'

'Who nailed Denman to the plywood and covered him with the fibreglass?'

'Harry and Dave put him on the plywood. It was Toni who sprayed him with the fibreglass.'

'What about Prince?'

'He said he felt sick and headed outside.'

'How did he die?'

'I tied him to the tree. I thought Toni was just going to give him a good beating. But he'd found the nail gun in the back of the van and just went crazy when he saw it and nailed Prince.'

'Eugene drive again?'

He nodded.

'What happened the day Eugene died?'

'He called Toni and said he needed his usual, and some spending money.'

'Was it usual for him to get money as well as his drugs?'

'Not as far as I know.'

'What was different about this time?'

'Eugene said he'd found the nail gun and threatened to go to the police if Toni didn't pay to get the gun back.'

'How much did he want?'

'Two thousand.'

'What did Palmari say about that?'

'Toni laughed when he heard, said the kid was selling himself too cheaply.'

'What did he do?'

'He called Harry and got him to drive him over to Eugene's

flat. Toni told me he went up there and gave Eugene his dope. Then when the kid was lying on his back in cloud cuckoo land, Toni smothered him with a pillow. He looked for the nail gun but was disturbed by the sounds of footsteps on the stairs, so he beat it out of there.'

'I found the nail gun hidden under the bed,' said Buchanan.

'It doesn't matter, Inspector. I'll never go to court, I'm a dead man walking.'

'Here's your whiskey, Mr Rosso,' said Street.

'It's too late for whiskey, Jill. He's gone.'

19

'He's here,' said the desk sergeant, on the phone.

'Who's here? And while we're at it, where is he – whoever he is?' said Buchanan.

'Nigel Pace. He's downstairs in reception with his father. They want to talk to you.'

'DS Street will be right down to escort them up.' Buchanan smiled and waited while Jill went down to reception to escort Nigel and his father up to Buchanan's office.

'Nigel, how are you?' said Buchanan.

'I've been better.'

'Pace?'

'Couldn't be better, now that I've got my son back.'

'The doctor tells me you should make a complete recovery, Nigel.'

'Yeah, they told me the same.'

'Pity about Esposito,' said Pace.

'What about Mr Esposito, Mr Pace?'

'He came to see me yesterday. He said he was looking for someone, pity he fell down the stairs when he was leaving. I think he's in the same ward that they had Nigel in.'

'Did he fall very hard?' said Buchanan.

Pace smiled and rubbed the knuckles of his right hand with the left. 'All the way from the top. He won't be climbing those stairs again in a hurry.'

'You want something to drink – tea, coffee, water, Nigel?' said Street.

'I'll have the water. I've drunk the station's coffee before.'

'Fine. Jill, a cup of the station's finest for young Nigel.'

'Mr Pace, can I get you something from the vending machine?'

Pace shook his head.

'Nigel, you realise you are not under arrest and are here of your own volition?'

'Yes. I just wanted to get things clear in my mind before I go.'

'Where are you going?'

'Argentina'

'What did you think when you heard that, Mr Pace?'

'I smiled and wished him luck.'

'I'm going to change my name to Rodriguez, Inspector. I have decided to go to join my mother and make a fresh start.'

'You're all right with that, Mr Pace?'

He nodded. 'I've had a long chat with my former wife last night and explained what's been happening here in Eastbourne. We at least are now talking without shouting at each other.'

'So, Dad will be able to visit me in Argentina. Isn't that great, Inspector?'

'If you say so.'

'Inspector, I have something to confess, but I don't want it to get in the way of me going to start my new life in Argentina.'

'What is it, Nigel?'

'See, if I tell you, you'll arrest me and I'll have a criminal record and won't be able to go.'

'You wish to confess to something you've done that would get you a criminal record?'

'It was Eugene's note that made me think.'

'I'm not sure what you are trying to say.'

'Eugene was forced to frame me for the death of Mr Prince, you know, the nail-gun. I suppose Eugene couldn't live with that thought. I can't live with my thought that something I did got someone a prison sentence.'

'Nigel, as long as you haven't murdered someone, or robbed the Bank of England, I'm sure we can sort it out.

'It's about Danny. He didn't rob the off-licence. It was

Eugene.'

'I'm not familiar with that case, Nigel,' said Buchanan.

'Just over a year ago an off-licence was robbed. Danny's van was used to carry of the stuff. I borrowed it for Eugene and his mates. It had nothing to do with Danny. I just wanted to set the record straight.'

'Thanks, Nigel. I'll let the appropriate authorities know, maybe we can get Danny's conviction quashed.'

'I have more information about your family, Mr Pace.'

'You do?'

'As part of our investigations, we have discovered that your father, a Guido Rienzi, died as a result of an accident on a building site. He and another builder had been taking down a wall which had been damaged during the war. The wall collapsed with them under it. Your father didn't survive. I'm sorry to bring you sad news on a day like this.'

'It was a long time ago, Inspector. But thanks for letting us know.'

◆

Buchanan sat in the chair beside Esposito's hospital bed.

'Hello, Mr Esposito, how are you feeling?'

'I've felt better.'

'Sorry to hear about your accident.'

'Yeah, I'm sure you are.'

'Oh, just to let you know. You don't have to look for Mr Rienzi anymore, I know exactly where he is.'

'You do, where is he?'

'He's in the morgue, Mr Esposito.'

'What happened?'

'There was an accident, sort of like yours. Mr Rienzi was having a neck massage and the masseur was a bit too energetic and accidentally broke Mr Rienzi's neck.'

'Yeah, you sure about that?'

'Oh yeah, I sure am. I suppose you think you'll now be flying home?'

'Next Wednesday.'

'I hope you can get a refund on your about to be unused return portion. Michael Esposito, I'm arresting you for the grievous bodily assault on Nigel Pace. You do not have to say anything. But, it may harm your defence if you do not mention when questioned something which you later rely on in court. Anything you do say may be given in evidence.'

20

'You're going to be late for work if you don't get up and dress.'

Buchanan sniffed. 'Don't feel like going in to work.'

'What – you who's

never missed a day's work in his life?'

Buchanan sat up and slowly shook his head. 'They don't need me anymore. I'm just an old toss-pot whose day has come and gone.'

'What did you have to drink before you came to bed?'

'Nothing, maybe I should have.'

'You sound like a bear with a sore head. What's the matter with you?'

'Nothing's the matter, just didn't sleep well.'

'You really don't want to go in to work? Is it the crime commissioner that's bothering you?'

'Who the hell is he to tell me what to do? Did you know he's never even walked the beat? I said to him last week, to come out with us, see just to see what goes on at night in the streets.'

'And what was his reply?'

'*Can't, I have a conference to go to.* That's all those buggers do. Talk, talk, talk, wouldn't know a criminal if they bit them on the backside.'

'Jack, come on downstairs, your breakfast is going to get cold.'

'I don't feel hungry.'

'Jack! You may be angry with your boss, but remember who you're talking to. I'm Karen, your wife. Don't take it out on me.'

'I'm sorry, you're right. It's just. That jerk –'

'Jack!'

'Sorry, that – so and so. I tell you, Karen, the day's coming when the whole police administration will disappear up its own –'

'Jack, I said, your breakfast is going to get cold!'

'All right, let me get out of bed and shave. I'll be right down.'

'I'll go butter your toast, hopefully your eggs haven't boiled solid.'

♦

'Marmalade?'

'On the table in front of you.'

'Oh, thanks, didn't see it.'

'What time did you come to bed?'

'Don't know.'

'Oh, Jack, come on, we've been married thirty-five years. I know it's not the crime commissioner – what's really bothering you?'

'I've decided to resign, pack it all in. I'm going to accept Nathan's offer to run his security firm.'

'You're what?'

'I've had enough, they've won. I can't take the pressure anymore.'

'You're really serious about resigning?'

Buchanan nodded as he took a mouthful of toast.

'What do you mean, you can't take the pressure anymore? That doesn't sound like you?'

'Listen,' he said, taking a folded-up piece of A4 paper from his shirt pocket.

'To whom it may concern: I, Jack Buchanan, hereby resign forthwith. I have had a wonderful career during these last thirty-four years of being a policeman. I cannot imagine a more rewarding job. Some might say I'm an old fart who can't see the wood for the trees, an aged thespian who doesn't know when to bow out, and others, who say they mean well, tell me I should just retire and take up a hobby. What sort of hobby could ever replace the thrill of the chase of hunting down those who seek to subvert our system of justice, our way of life in this glorious country? I've never sought the limelight. I realise that policing has changed since I started as a police cadet. I see now how technology has become the de facto method employed in modern policing. Yet, with all these shiny tools at the disposal of today's police men and police women, I still feel there is room for traditional methods. The eye to eye, toe to toe methods employed when I began my career. The feeling of a criminal's collar when you make an arrest. The satisfaction when you hear the jury say *guilty* and the relief when the judge sends the defendant down for a lengthy sentence commensurate with the crime. That's my hobby, that's what I've dedicated my life to –'

'Jack, you're never going to submit that as your resignation letter, are you?'

Buchanan shook his head. 'No. I was just getting it off my chest, this is what I'm going to say:

> To whom it may concern,
> I, Detective Inspector Jack Buchanan, hereby tender my resignation. My last day of service will be one month from the date of this letter and will include any holiday time remaining.
> Yours sincerely, Detective Inspector Jack Buchanan.

'Will that be before Jill's wedding?'

'Yes, before. I don't want it to get in the way of Jill and Stephen's big day.'

'Glad to hear that, and I hope you are going to start winding down, especially since you and your team have finished the case.'

'Don't worry, the resignation letter will be on the ACC's desk by noon today. I'm going to deliver it myself.'

◆

Buchanan did up his seatbelt, looked inside his jacket to make sure his resignation letter was still there, tucked safely in the inside pocket. The sun was shining, a new day and a new beginning. They had the mortgage signed, keys delivered and the new kitchen would be installed while they were away on their holiday. Wasn't life great? Though he still had to tell Karen about the holiday, it certainly was going to be a surprise.

Once more, and for the last time, thought Buchanan. He headed for the A27, Lewes and police headquarters.

How was he going to tell Karen about the holiday? He'd forgotten Street's advice to give Karen sufficient time to prepare. He didn't even know if he had suitable clothes for a holiday. Well, they'd work something out – he was done, plenty of time now. He turned on the radio and tuned into Radio 3.

Good morning, I'm Rob Cowan, with you until Composer of the Week at midday. First this morning, a piece to get your foot tapping: J S Bach's Prelude in C minor, BWV 847.

He'd been following a tractor from Selmeston, finally it turned off at the Charleston exit Buchanan put his foot down hard and accelerated up the hill. He almost ran head-on into a car coming the other way on the wrong side of the road over the brow of the hill. Instinctively, Buchanan swerved to the left, into undergrowth and an eighty-year-old oak tree.

◆

'Where am I?' said Buchanan, regaining consciousness.

'You're in the Accident and Emergency Department of Eastbourne hospital,' said the nurse.

'What happened?'

'Apparently your car ran off the road and hit a tree.'

'What about the other car?'

'I don't know about that. The traffic police said there wasn't any other car involved.'

'My wife?'

'She's waiting outside till the doctor looks at you.'

The curtain drew back and the doctor entered.

'Inspector Buchanan, we've got to stop meeting like this.'

'Doctor Maung.'

'Good, there doesn't appear to be much wrong with your memory.'

'Am I all right?'

'You don't have any broken bones. All you have are a few cuts from broken glass and there will be bruising in various places. Your body will tell you where you hurt in good time. You have people waiting to see how you are.'

'My wife?'

'And your daughter.'

'My daughter?'

'Well, I assumed that's what she is.'

'That's Jill, my partner.'

Maung looked at Buchanan and slowly shook his head.

'Detective Street, she's my work partner.'

'Mr Buchanan, the last time we talked I suggested you talk to your GP. Should I assume you still haven't done so?'

'Guilty as charged, Doctor.'

'Well, since you've been here you've had a full check-up and I'm pleased to say you are in perfect health for man of your age, except for one thing.'

'What's that?'

'You're showing signs of stress, you really do need a rest.'

Buchanan smiled at the doctor. 'Got that sorted. We're booked to go on a ten-day cruise of the European canals.'

'That's a good place to begin from. I'll let your wife know you are ready to go home.'

A few minutes later the door opened and Karen, followed by Street, entered.

'Jack! How, what –?'

'I'm fine, honestly I'm fine. The doctor says there's nothing wrong other than a few cuts and bruises.'

'Do you remember what happened?'

'All I remember is a car coming over the brow of the hill, and the driver's face. The next thing I know is I'm waking up here in the hospital. I'm just another A27 statistic.'

'The doctor says you can come home.'

'He also said I needed to rest.'

'That'll be the day.'

'It will be in exactly twelve days' time.'

'What will?'

'I've been planning a surprise. I've booked a ten-day holiday on the European canals. We leave on the Tuesday after Jill's and Stephen's wedding.'

'But we can't, I've nothing to wear.'

Buchanan looked at Street. She gave him a *I told you so* look.

'Jill?' said Buchanan. 'What about the car that ran me off the road?'

She shook her head. 'Nothing. Unless you can remember the car's registration or positively identify the other driver, there's not much we can do. There were no witnesses.'

◆

'Jack, hurry and dress! Why are you still in bed? Get up – it's Jill's big day,' said Karen.

'Oh, my head.'

'What's the matter with you? Did you and Stephen celebrate a bit too much last night?'

'My head, feels like there's a bunch of riveters banging around in there.'

'That'll teach you. You're not a young man any more, Jack. You should leave the drinking to the young ones.'

'I'm to be thrown out with the rubbish then, that it?'

'If you decide to go out and drink like a fish, then you'll get no sympathy from me. Now are you going to get out of bed and get ready, or do I call Nathan and say you're too hung over to give Jill away?'

'Oh, I'll be fine. Let me get showered and I'll be right down.'

'Just how much did you have to drink last night?'

'Don't remember much. I only had a pint or two, then went on to whiskey.'

'Jack Francis Buchanan,' said Karen, shaking her head, 'you should know, especially at your age, never to mix drinks. Now, out of bed and go have a shower, you smell like a stale brewery.'

Buchannan rolled slowly and carefully out of bed and shuffled over to the bathroom and the shower.

♦

Hello, and good morning. This is BBC Sussex Breakfast with Olli Stephens. The time is six o'clock, it's Saturday the fifth of August and here to read the news this morning is Fred Walker – Fred.'

Thanks, Olli. A wildfire in Vilardevos in Spain threatens to …

'Jack, you can't wear that for breakfast! What'll you do if you spill food on your suit? Take it off before you sit down.'

In other news, there is still no end in sight for the …

'But –'

'Oh, of course, Jill – you don't want her to see you in your underwear,' said Karen, shaking her head. 'At least take your jacket off and put this towel over your lap.'

Buchanan took off his jacket and hung it up on the hook on the back of the kitchen door, then wrapped the towel round his waist, she smiled.

'What's the matter now?'

'You look like a short order cook with the towel round your waist and your trousers sticking out the bottom.'

Brighton and Hove Albion say …

'Morning all,' said Street, as she bounded into the kitchen. 'You're not wearing that, Jack, are you?'

'No, I'm not. I thought I should cover my trousers while

378

eating my breakfast, wouldn't want to spill food on them.'

Street looked at Karen.

Karen smiled and gently shook her head.

And this just in. A startling announcement this morning from the Police and Crime Commissioner's office. Gary Duncan has announced he will be stepping down from his post as police and crime commissioner to take up a position as private secretary to ...

Buchanan, his dignity intact, sat down for his breakfast.

'Did Stephen get home all right?'

Buchanan nodded while downing a mouthful of toast and black coffee. 'His dad took him home.'

'What time?'

'Quite early.'

'Jack, you know quite well what time it was,' said Karen. 'Jill, it was three-thirty when Jack came home – I presume it was the same for Stephen. Jack?'

'If you say so – could you get me a couple of aspirins, please?'

'I should make you get your own. Be right back.'

'You sure Stephen got home safely?'

Buchanan looked up from his newspaper and smiled. 'Of course, he did, we shared a taxi back and he and his dad were dropped first.'

Street's face relaxed.

'Here's your aspirin, Jack.'

'Thanks,' he said, giving Karen's hand a squeeze.

'You're welcome. Now, Jill, what time is your make-up person due?'

'Jenny said she'd be here by nine o'clock.'

'Is the photographer coming as well?' said Buchanan.

'Yes, but he's not due to be here till nine-thirty.'

◆

'Jack, you ready? The cars are here.' said Karen, from the bottom of the stairs.

'Be right down.'

Karen opened the front door and went out to the cars sitting in the driveway.

'The bride will be right out,' she said to the driver of the wedding car.

'Morning, Karen,' said Hanbury, the driver of the second car. 'You look very smart.'

'Thanks, got to look our best for Jill and Stephen. You ready to go?'

'Yes, but first let me help Jill into the car.'

Buchanan held the wedding car door open for Street to climb in. Karen helped with carefully working Street's dress into the back of it.

Karen bent down and kissed Street on the cheek.

Street nodded and sniffed, she had a tear in the corner of her eye threatening to run down her cheek. Karen took a tissue out of her pocket and carefully dabbed at the errant tear on Street's face.

'Bye, Jill. See you at the hotel,' said Karen walking over to Hanbury's car.

Buchanan shut the front door of the house, made sure it was locked and went round to the other side of the wedding car. He got in and sat beside Street.

The car with Buchanan and the bride drove off and headed along the A259 into town and the Hydro Hotel for Street's wedding to Hunter.

As they passed the pier Buchanan looked across at Street and thought about the first time they'd driven together. It was when he'd just arrived from Glasgow. She'd picked him up at the station in Lewes and driven him, along the A27 to Eastbourne. She'd had long hair then, but with her hair now cut short Buchanan decided she was still just as beautiful. He looked away, blinked, took out his handkerchief and wiped his eyes.

The wedding car pulled up in front of the elegant entrance to the Hydro Hotel. Karen was waiting with Natalie, one of Street's bridesmaids. Between them they helped Street out of the wedding car, up the steps and into the hotel reception.

The three couples waiting at the reception desk turned to stare. 'Isn't she so beautiful?' said one of the women.

'This way, Jill,' said Karen, as she led the way into one of the small reception rooms.

'Everyone is here,' said Natalie.

'In that case we'll leave you two,' said Karen, to Buchanan and Street.

Karen and Natalie left the room and closed the door behind them.

'Ready?' asked Buchanan, looking down into Street's face.

Street nodded and gently put her hands onto Buchanan's arms. She stood on her tiptoes and kissed him on the cheek. 'Love you, Dad.'

'Stop that, you'll make me cry,' said Buchanan, grinning and reaching for his handkerchief.

There was a knock on the door.

'Come in,' said Buchanan.

The events manager came into the room.

'Everything ok, Mr Buchanan?'

'Absolutely,' said Street.

Buchanan nodded.

'Good. The guests are all seated, if you'd care to follow me.

Street put her arm in Buchanan's as they walked towards the door to the ceremony. They paused momentarily at the entrance and waited for the *Bridal March* music to be played.

The End